RESERVATION

HIGH

JUDITH D. SURBER

Surber Books

Hoopa, California

Cover illustration: Curtis Kane
Book design and consulting: Robert Marcus Graphics
Printed in Canada

ISBN 978-0-692-75918-9

Dedication

This book is dedicated to everyone who has lost his or her way in the maze of addiction. May you find your way out and live the life that you were created to live with hope, joy and happiness.

A special thank you to my mom, husband, children and friends who encouraged me and supported me while I wrote this book.

Chapter One

She turned her head for one last look as she drove out of the Valley. A blanket of fog covered the valley floor and the mountains popped their heads up around the edges. It was a brisk October morning, but at least it was clear and Amanda knew the sun would break through the clouds in a few hours. By afternoon it would be hot and then cool off again by evening. She could see smoke coming out of the stovepipes of many of the houses up and down the river. She had almost started a fire herself this morning, just to knock the chill off but the woodpile was low so had decided against it. Soon enough they would have to have a fire 24/7.

A beautiful place surrounded by mountains, the Hoopa Valley Indian Reservation in far Northern California was her home. The Valley had long been home for her ancestors before her and the Trinity River running through the reservation was paramount to the people and their way of life. A two-lane highway running through the Valley was basically the only way in and out of the small town. Although well maintained by the state, the highway to the highway and beyond was winding and unforgiving.

She had mixed feelings about the Valley. On the one hand it was her home and she felt safe there, with a big family whom she was close to. This was the place where she was born and raised and when she died she would be laid to rest there with all of her family that went on before her. She really had never lived anywhere else; not for any period of time anyhow.

But on the other hand she hated the Valley too. She felt trapped there at times and just wanted to run as far from there as possible. It had started to represent grief, loss and pain; unbearable unending pain. And then there was shame. Shame of the life she was living and what she had become. There was no escaping that; everyone knew everyone else's business, including hers.

The older man driving her looked over and smiled, "You okay, hon?"

"I guess so, Uncle," she replied. She looked at him and gave him a faint, not really convincing smile. She loved her Uncle Ben. The long black braid hanging down his back was getting the slightest tinge of gray and his toothless grin was infectious. He was from the hard school of knocks and had lived hard and fast. She still remembered him as a handsome young man who had always been there for her. He was settled down now, older and calmer but had done enough in his life that he never judged her or anyone else for that matter.

"You'll make it this time. I know you will. It took me three tries too and look at me now. A regular citizen Kane," Ben said with a chuckle.

As they passed through Willow Creek she reflected on the last few years of her life. At twenty-four years old she was already wise to the world and somewhat jaded. She had been living on the dark side for quite a while now and wondered at times how she had survived and often wished she hadn't. She had gone through the rehab stint twice before; once at the age of nineteen and once at the age of twenty-two. It always felt so good once she was clean and she always swore that she would never use again. When she was clean her priorities were straight. Her kids came first and because of guilt for neglecting them during her drug periods she would sink herself whole-heartedly into the mommy role.

She still didn't understand how she could go back to the drug life. The cravings were strong, that was a given, but there was something else that always drew her back. Once she returned home everything would be good for a while but then a cloud would come over her, a feeling of hopelessness, despair and the only thing that took the pain away was a fix. Once that needle went into her arm, everything seemed right again, even if she knew that it was only temporary. It was a euphoria that she couldn't describe and it made the unbearable, bearable.

As they drove along the mountain roads for the next forty-five minutes her thoughts were on her children; Michael, her son who was six and Melanie, her baby girl who was almost four. She was lucky, she thought, that they were safe with her mom who had been raising them off and on since they were born. At times she felt guilty. She knew her mother was older now and sometimes seemed tired and worn out after working all day and taking care of her two grandchildren. But her mother had reassured her that she could handle it and "didn't want anyone else raising her grandbabies."

Besides, when she was high, she really wasn't able to care for her children the way that they needed her to. It was hard to get her hustle on and take care of them too. Things that should come as natural instinct, like feeding and bathing them, just didn't. And there was no consistency when dealing with her children. When high, everything was over the top; she played, had energy and the patience of a saint. When coming down and hurting, she was impatient and grouchy, often snapping at them for no reason.

She wished that their father would take more interest in them but he had his own issues and from what she had heard wasn't doing well right now either. His sister had told her that he was in county jail right now doing 120 days for theft. Knowing him as well as she did, she would bet that it was drug related. He had never really been a thief when they were together but when push comes to shove and desperation sets in you do what you have to do— and she understood that better than anyone.

About fifteen minutes from the rehab they pulled into a gas station with a food mart. "Do you want anything to eat or drink?" Ben asked his niece.

"Just a Pepsi. I'm going to the bathroom. It might take me a few minutes." Amanda gave him a look and he knew exactly what that meant. This was her last chance to get high before she checked in to the rehab. Although his addiction had always been to alcohol, he knew the concept. Whether it's one last drink or one last fix, an addict had to feel that they got that one last high before committing to a sober life.

She went into the bathroom, locked the door and pulled out her supplies. Her hands were shaking as she put a lighter to the bottom of her spoon. She was nervous; nervous about rehab and whether she would make it this time. Good intentions were no match for comedowns and she knew she was in for a rough time. Tying off her arm she took a deep breath and stuck the needle in. That instant warm feeling that came over her was indescribable. For that one moment everything felt right. She threw her "kit" into the trashcan. Obviously she couldn't take it with her. She washed her face and hands and went back outside.

She knew she would be good until evening and wouldn't start hurting really bad until the following morning. Then there would be hell to pay.

"Do you have everything you need? Enough cigarettes and supplies?" her uncle asked.

"I'm good" Amanda answered. "Mom made sure that I had enough to last until her next pay day."

Ben pulled out his wallet and handed her a twenty. "Just in case you need something," Ben said.

"Thanks, Uncle. Will you check on Mom and the kids when you get back?" she asked. "I'm worried about her.

"Of course, you know I will" he answered. He knew what she meant. He was worried about his sister too. He wasn't really sure why, couldn't put his finger on it but she looked depressed and pretty beat down by life right now. Although she was only forty-eight, she looked much older.

They pulled in to the rehab parking lot and she took a deep breath. "Here goes nothing," Amanda thought.

The woman who came out to greet them was familiar to her. She was in rehab herself the first time that Amanda had checked in, almost five years ago. Now she worked here. "Amanda, how good to see you" she said, walking up and giving her a hug. "Unload your stuff and we'll go in and start your paperwork."

"Rayna, I didn't know you worked here." Amanda exclaimed, hugging her back. In many ways it was a relief to see someone she knew.

Amanda was on the verge of tears as she gave her uncle one last hug. Every ounce of her wanted to get back into his truck and leave. Self-doubts washed over her and she felt a fleeting moment of panic. He knew the look and so did Rayna. She wouldn't be the first to have a change of heart at the last minute and leave. It happened quite often.

Ben got into his truck and started backing up to leave. He knew that his niece would do better once he was gone and her option to leave with him was gone. Not into this new school of technology he didn't have a cell phone. Didn't have one and didn't want one, for that matter. Once he pulled out there would be no turning back; at least not for today.

Rayna quickly helped carry her things into the office and seated her in a chair. "Once we get your intake done I'll take you to your room. You won't have to go to meetings today since it's your first day but tomorrow we'll expect you to attend."

The intake took almost an hour, and mostly asked about her current drug addiction; what she was using, how much and when her last use was. Her drug of choice was Oxycontin but with the prices for an 80 now going up to sixty dollars a pill it had become out of her reach. Needing at least two a day to be comfortable but preferring three or more a day, $180.00 a day was out of her range. Although she didn't like heroin as much, it was cheaper and lately becoming easier to get.

Out in the main living room, after she finished, Amanda saw a familiar face: her cousin Barbara. Barbara was a third cousin on her dad's side who had been raised on the Coast. They hadn't really grown up together but had been together at a family reunion and several funerals and then had reconnected on drug buys out in Eureka. Barbara was more into methamphetamine than opiates and had the look of a "tweeker." Amanda could tell by looking at her that she hadn't been in rehab too long. The hollow face, sideways jaw and sores on her skin were a dead give-away.

"Hey girl," Barbara said. "I'm so glad you're here. I was wondering when someone I knew would check in."

"How long have you been here?" Amanda asked.

"I got here last week. This is my sixth day. Really didn't have a choice. It was either jail or rehab so here I am," Barbara answered. "How about you?"

"I'm here on my own. Well, with pressure from my family, but you know, it was time. Things were getting crazy." Amanda explained.

"Yeah, I know how that goes." Barbara smiled. Boy did she know.

There were ten other women in the rehab right now. There was one other Indian woman, from Covelo. She was in her fifties and had a long alcohol history. One too many "drunk in public" arrests. She too didn't have a choice and had decided rehab would be easier than jail. Five of the women were addicted to heroin or other opiates, three were meth addicts and two were alcoholics.

Rayna showed Amanda to her room which she would be sharing with Barbara and one other woman; Leona who was a heroin addict.

The rooms looked pretty much the same since her last stint here with the exception of a coat of new paint and possibly some new dressers. She put her stuff on the empty bed and started unpacking, arranging it into one of the empty dressers. After unpacking she went out into the living room and watched television for a while. A few of the women were making lunch, and working in the adjoining kitchen. She wasn't really hungry but decided to eat anyhow. By tomorrow she would be too sick and probably would be throwing up for days.

Amanda ate her tuna sandwich and made small talk with the other women at the table. She knew that they would be going to group soon and would be gone for several hours. Since she was excused for the day she was going to take a nap and maybe write a letter to her kids. She finished her lunch and went to her room, turned the light off and lay down. Sleep came easier than expected and she drifted into a deep sleep. It seemed like only a few minutes when she awoke with a startle. She felt disoriented and didn't know if it was morning or night. She looked at the clock and saw that she had been asleep for almost three hours. Hearing the voices of people talking in the main room and pots and pans clattering, Amanda felt her anxiety starting to set in. At home she would have already been getting her hustle on and would have her next fix lined up. Her mind raced around trying to find some legitimate excuse to leave but nothing came to her. It was too soon to go home without disappointing her family and herself. Thinking of her mother and children she knew she had to try and get through the first week but right now it was becoming increasingly doubtful.

Chapter Two

Ben turned into his sister's driveway and could see her peeking out the window as he pulled up.

Her anxious look told him that she was nervous and had probably been looking out the window for the last hour; scared that maybe her daughter had come back. He got out of his truck and she met him at the door.

"It's okay," Ben said, answering her unasked question. "She stayed. She definitely had second thoughts at the last minute but in the end she stayed. That's a good sign." Putting his arm around her shoulders they walked into the house.

The minute the door opened he was rushed by two small children. "Uncle, you're back. Do you have any treats for us?" the older of the two asked.

"Well, let me see. Have you been good and listened to your grandma today?" Ben asked.

"Yeah, we have. Huh, grandma?" the little boy, Michael, answered.

Ben pulled two suckers out of his pocket and handed one first to the boy and then held his arms out to the girl. "Come here baby and give Uncle a hug." Shyer than her brother, the little girl came over and held her arms out. Ben lifted her up, gave her a big hug and handed her a sucker. She was small for her age but a beautiful little girl. She reminded him so much of her mother in her looks but her temperament was much quieter than her mother at that age. She was always watching everyone around her and seemed much wiser than her age. He put her down and she scrambled off with her brother into the living room, to the television.

"You can watch TV till dinner," Beverly told her grandchildren. She poured her brother a cup of coffee as she motioned for him to sit down at the kitchen table. She sat down across from him and studied his face intently. She loved her brother so much. They were the last of 5 siblings. Only 12 months apart, they grew up especially close.

"Do you think she will stay, Ben? I know she says she will but her problems seem worse than the last two times she went to rehab. I'm so scared that if it doesn't work this time we will lose her forever," Beverly asked, her speech showing just how nervous she was.

"Well, Bev, we can only hope and pray that she stays and gets with the program. Once she gets through the first few weeks things will get better for her. The hardest part will be coming home." Ben said, confidently. This he knew firsthand.

Nodding her head in agreement, Beverly knew exactly what he meant. They had both seen it more often than not. People went away to rehab and stayed clean for months, sometimes years and then came home and within weeks start using again. The Valley was a hard place to stay clean. The drugs were readily available and so-called friends made it seem all right. Even if the intent was just to use once, it never happened that way. Within days full-blown addiction would be running its course. And users always picked up where they left off before going to rehab.

"Stay for dinner. I made some stew with that deer meat you gave me and I promised the kids that I would make some fry bread to go with it," Beverly told her brother.

"Well Sis, I can't pass that up but I think I'm going to go set a net first. Can I take Michael with me?" Ben asked hesitantly, knowing how paranoid his sister could be about the kids around the river. The fall run was good this year and Ben had been catching 6-8 Chinook salmon every night. He only planned to fish a few more nights because stripping and hanging the fish was a big job, especially for one person.

"Sure, but Ben please watch him close in the boat. Make him wear a life jacket. You know how nervous I get about the kids, especially around the river." Beverly said anxiously.

"Of course I will. I'll watch him like a hawk. Nothing to get nervous about. How's your blood pressure by the way? Have you been checking it?" Ben asked with concern. He knew that his sister's blood pressure had been dangerously high for the last few months and it was no wonder. The stress she had been under, dealing with her daughter and her addiction was more than most people could bear.

"You know, the CHR's from the clinic came by and took it on Friday and it was pretty good. I think the relief of Amanda finally agreeing to go to rehab really helped. At least for the time being I know that she is safe." And it was true, Bev thought. Once they had pulled out this morning she had felt her whole body calming down little by little but when Ben came back alone the last of her tense nerves finally vanished.

"Come on, Michael. Get your boots on. You are going to go with Uncle and set net tonight. Then we are going to come back and have a good dinner and go to bed early if you want to go check net with me in the morning," Ben explained to his small nephew who was jumping up and down, not able to contain his excitement.

Michael jumped up and ran to get his boots beside the woodstove. "Yah, I get to go set net," he yelled, proudly looking around even though the only person to notice was his little sister who wasn't very impressed.

After the two had left and Melanie contented herself to sit in front of the TV watching her Princess movie, Bev started mixing her flour and patting her dough into fry bread. Her mind went over all of the events of the last twelve months and she marveled at how they had survived the year. She had been through a lot in her life. Nothing had ever come easy but this was the worst of the worst. Every day was like living a nightmare and she never knew what was next. She had lost a lot in the last year; the least of it jewelry, sentimental items. Anything of value had been stolen or hocked, usually for a twenty-dollar sack. The pieces she still had were those that she had given to her brother to put in his safe.

But what she had lost most in the last year was her peace of mind. Every day was a battle, with her daughter begging at first and then moving on to threats, usually threats to kill herself if her mother didn't give her money. Bev wished she could have said no and at first she sometimes did but after a while she was so worn down that she would give until there was nothing left to give. Besides, if she didn't give her daughter money it wouldn't end until she did. Hours and hours it would go on. When the money ran out it still didn't stop. The demands were endless; borrow it from someone, get a loan, sell something. And usually she did.

Beverly had watched "Intervention," the television show with professionals doing interventions on addicts and while it made her sad for those families it wasn't something she could really relate to. The thought of kicking your child out and cutting them out of your life was beyond what she could comprehend. She had already lost one child tragically and from that point on, she guarded her kids and if that was enabling, then so be it. Her life was her daughters and grandchildren now and the thought of losing them was more than she could bear.

Two weeks ago her worst fear had almost been realized. Hearing a loud thump in her daughter's bedroom she ran into the room and found her daughter slumped over, half on the bed and half on the floor. Sometimes it played over and over in her mind. She hadn't really slept well since that night and although they had been lucky that time, she now lived in constant fear of it happening again. Even a loud noise or a siren in the distance would put her into a state of panic. During the day, with people around, it was easier to put that image in the back of her mind. It was the nights that seemed endless with the whole event replaying over and over in her mind. She heard her brother pulling up and went back to finishing dinner.

Dinner was good and after putting the kids to bed, for the first time in months Bev slept really hard. If she dreamt she couldn't remember what her dreams were about. She woke up at six thirty, her usual time, panicked at first. Most mornings her first thought was to run in and check on her daughter and make sure she was there, alive and breathing. Sometimes, on a bad night, she would get up several times a night to check on her daughter. At times it felt like she had a newborn baby instead of a grown woman with children of her own. Taking a deep breath she got up and went out to put coffee on. "Please God," she prayed, "please let this be a good day and give my daughter the strength to make it."

Chapter Three

Amanda woke up at 6 and, as expected, was already coming down and feigning for a fix. Every bone in her body hurt; she had a bad headache and felt nauseous as hell. On top of that her nerves were shot and she was having bad restless legs. She knew that it was going to get worse before it got better. She decided to go soak in a hot bath for a while before the others got up. It helped the restless legs but did nothing for the strong cravings that she was having.

As she was getting dressed the nausea and stomach cramping started. She had gone through withdrawals a few times before and had sworn that she would rather die than go through this again. Feeling mad at herself for even being in this position she went into the kitchen and checked the schedule. Thank God, she thought, it wasn't her morning to cook breakfast. She quickly scanned the chart and noticed that she wasn't on kitchen duty for another three days, and she was grateful for that.

As the others came in getting their breakfast she started having chills and felt sick to her stomach. Running to the bathroom, she made it just in time. Stomach cramping, puking and diarrhea were hitting her simultaneously. One minute she felt hot, the next she felt cold. She knew that she was in for a rough go of it. She had been through this and knew this could go on for days. She hadn't got to the anxious, panicky stage yet but knew it would come too.

The tears hit as she sat on the floor in the bathroom. Her body needed that fix. As much as she wanted to resist, the urge was coming over her in waves and she could feel panic rising up through her whole body. She didn't know what to do. To go through this again felt like a death sentence. To keep using like she had been was also a death sentence. As she mulled this thought over in her mind she heard a slight tap on the door.

Rayna opened the door slowly, "Amanda, are you alright?" she asked, knowing already that she wasn't. Technically, when people entered rehab, they were supposed to be completely detoxed for at least three days. Unfortunately that usually wasn't the case and most who entered had used within minutes before their arrival, with comedowns full blown on their second day. The Rehab lost a lot of clients during this time. They would suddenly bolt, often times leaving their belongings behind, to hit the street and find their drug of choice.

"I just don't think I can do this," Amanda sobbed. "I hurt so fucking bad already. I just want to die," she said, tears rolling down her face.

Rayna knew this was true. She had been there herself. The opiate/heroin addicts had the hardest withdrawals and there was nothing easy about this harsh reality. "Well, I think we should get you ready and head over to County Health. We have an arrangement worked out with them and they will be able to help you out with some Suboxone. It will help you get through this rough spot. You'll see." She had seen Suboxone do wonders for helping people with withdrawals and since they had been able to hook people up through the County Health Clinic their overall success rate had gone up considerably.

Amanda had heard of Suboxone but had never really tried it herself. It always sounded a little too good to be true but she hoped that it helped as much as people said. Thinking that she had nothing to lose and grasping at anything to help ease the pain, she threw her shoes on and followed Reyna to the car.

The intake process itself didn't take too long. Much of it was a repeat of the intake at the rehab the day before. After Amanda had filled out the paperwork and they had taken her vitals, a nurse came in and gave her Suboxone, in two strips.

"Put them under your tongue and let them dissolve. Try to hold your spit for as long as possible. It's optimal to hold your saliva while they dissolve for at least 20 minutes," the nurse explained. "The longer you can do that the better they will work. We started you on a higher dose today to help through this rough spot and will keep you at that for a week. Next week, depending on how you are doing, we will probably decrease you down to one strip a day. The only requirement while you are on the program is that you have to test clean when you come in and you must attend group counseling every Wednesday. Group is from one to three in the conference room at the back of the building."

Watching the timer, Amanda let the Suboxone dissolve in her mouth. It didn't taste too bad; kind of reminded her of a lemon with a little bit of a spoiled flavor. It wasn't great but was doable. Twenty minutes felt like a long time not to swallow and when the timer finally went off she felt like she was choking to death trying to hold it all in.

She gathered her paperwork and walked back out to the car, where Rayna was waiting. Although it had only been a matter of minutes she was already feeling better. The nausea, stomach cramps, and body aches, were quickly going away. "It's pretty amazing isn't it? How fast it works to make you feel better?" Rayna asked. Not waiting for an answer, Rayna continued. "The other thing that is amazing about Suboxone is that it actually blocks the cravings. It allows you to focus on recovery without having to fight the urges and cravings on a daily basis. I have seen a lot of success with Suboxone."

On the drive back to the Rehab she continued to feel better. Although her stomach still felt a little queasy it was manageable and she was actually starting to feel hungry.

"You know Amanda, I was looking at your intake this morning and I noticed that you dropped out of school in your senior year. One thing we are really encouraging our clients to do, is to study for the GED test while you are here. We have found that it helps our clients to be busy and productive and setting small goals and achieving them while you are here will help you in your road to recovery. I would like you to think about it and if you are interested we have a volunteer teacher who comes in three times a week, for two hours a day and tutors in the different subjects that are needed to pass the test. He comes in at three this afternoon."

Amanda nodded her head in agreement. She did want to get her GED and knew without it she really wasn't employable. The Tribe required a high school diploma or GED for every position, even low end, entry-level jobs. Without it there was really no way to get a job and she did dream of one day having a job and supporting her children.

When they returned to the rehab she noticed that everyone was gone. She looked at the schedule and saw that there was a NA meeting being held at a local church, two blocks away. She warmed up some oatmeal that was left from breakfast, ate it and surprisingly her nausea was gone. She decided to change out of sweats and put on some real clothes and try to make herself a little more presentable.

She slipped on some jeans and could see that they were way too big. The last few months had taken a toll on her body. She was down to 118 pounds which was the lightest that she had been since about the 7th grade. She had never been a big person and was somewhat petite; her average weight was around 135. The last time she had gotten clean her weight had climbed up to 155 pounds and had bothered her a lot.

Although people would tell her that she looked healthy, she just felt fat and dowdy at that weight.

The ugly track marks on her arms were what she hated most. Amanda knew that these scars are sometimes permanent. It was like a constant reminder of her bad choices. She only hoped that in time they would fade away and be less noticeable. Luckily her skin tones were brown. If she were fairer, she thought, they would stand out even more. She slipped on a long sleeve henley, grabbed her make up bag and brush and went into the bathroom.

The mirror reflected the dark circles under her eyes. Her face looked hollow, but she still had pretty decent color in her cheeks. She decided that she didn't look as bad as some of the other girls that she'd been running with, who looked like "death walking." She brushed her teeth and washed her face and started putting on make-up. She wore very little make-up, mostly because she wasn't very good at applying it. Just a little foundation, eye liner, mascara and eye shadow and she was finished.

As she brushed out her hair she noticed how thin it had gotten. She had always been proud of her long, thick hair. It still fell past her butt but the ends were straggly and thin. She would try to get a trim when she got the chance. Pulling it up in a bun, she decided that she didn't look half bad, considering the last few months.

When Amanda walked into the main room she saw that Rayna was the only one there. "I think I'm going to walk over to group and catch the last hour," she told her. "I mean if that's okay?"

"Sure, I guess that would be okay. You are on the honor system though. I'm trusting you to go there and not get lost along the way." Rayna didn't want to belabor the point. It was just that she had been burned too many times and nothing surprised her anymore. The one thing she knew about addicts, especially since she had been one herself, was that they could look you right in the eye and lie their ass off.

As she walked the two blocks to the church she was surprised at how good she felt. Earlier that day she felt like she was dying and now was walking to a meeting; all her aches and pains gone as well as the nausea. But more than that, was that she wasn't thinking about a fix. It was weird to her and almost too good to be true. She felt a little anxious waiting for the other shoe to drop.

When she walked into the meeting, everyone turned around and stared at her, making Amanda feel a little uncomfortable.

"Good morning. Find a seat and join us," the lady running the meeting told her. She was older, with short blond hair and a little on the heavy side. "My name is Linda and I have been running the women's group meetings for about three months. Today we are talking about surrender."

Linda continued speaking. "Surrendering yourself to a higher power, accepting what is and accepting the past but moving on from there. I don't know anyone in recovery who doesn't wish they had done things different, or wish they could change decisions or choices that they have made, especially those made in an altered state of being high or drunk. In recovery we learn that we must accept ourselves and while we can't change our past behaviors we can learn from them."

"One part of this process and a helpful tool for recovery is to identify triggers. A trigger is a response to something, which could be emotional, environmental, anything that makes you want to use. Each person has their own triggers, although you may find that there are some triggers that you all might have in common. Before the next group I would like each of you to identify and write down at least 5 triggers. You can write down more but I want you to identify at least 5 and bring it back to the next meeting."

Amanda hung back as everyone left the meeting and introduced herself to Linda. They talked the usual; drug of choice, reasons for coming to rehab, motivators to stay clean. Linda shared with her that she was also a recovering heroin addict and had been clean now for fifteen years. She worked nights at the casino but volunteered to do the women's group meetings three times a week. She explained to Amanda that volunteering helped with her own sobriety. "You know even after fifteen years I still worry that I could easily fall back into addiction so I make a conscious effort daily to protect my sobriety."

Amanda left and found Barbara outside of the building waiting to walk back with her. "Hey cuz, how are you feeling?" Barbara asked.

"Much better since they hooked me up with Suboxone. I am still hurting a little but honestly it's much more manageable and I don't feel like I'm on the verge of dying," Amanda answered.

"Well, you're lucky that they have something that will help. They don't have anything for dope comedowns. I got here and slept for about 4 days straight, ate everything in sight and was bitchy as hell," Barbara said, referring to last week when she was coming down from methamphetamine. Laughing they started walking towards the rehab.

Once they got back they ate lunch and Amanda checked the schedule and saw that she was on cleaning duty for the bathroom. She looked at the clock and saw that she had an hour and a half before the GED tutor would arrive, so she decided to tackle her cleaning duties now. There were two bathrooms in the rehab and because they were cleaned on a daily basis, the chore wasn't that hard and took her less than thirty minutes.

She decided to go into the main room, which was where meetings and classes were held. The room had three long tables with chairs placed around them. There were two computers in the corner, both hooked up to a printer and one bookcase with paperback books, magazines and some hardback school textbooks. On one side of the room there was a chalkboard and behind it there were cabinets full of art supplies, fabric, a sewing machine and an assortment of craft materials. She knew that much of the supplies and books were donated by people in the community. A double-door led into another room set up more like a family room with a comfortable sectional sofa, a love seat and a television hooked up to a DVD player. A small case held DVD's, some board game— Monopoly, Yahtzee— and a few decks of cards.

There were still twenty more minutes before the GED study group started so she decided to go out and have a cigarette while she waited. It was quiet right now. Many of the residents had been there long enough to qualify for day passes so that they could leave for several hours and do shopping, walk to the beach, go to a movie or anything else that they needed or wanted to do. The only requirement was that they had to be back at a designated time and had to provide a clean urine sample if asked.

She was on a thirty-day blackout, meaning that she couldn't have visitors, or leave the premises unless accompanied by one of the rehab staff or make or receive phone calls. She knew that Rayna had made an exception earlier that day by letting her walk to the NA meeting alone, but that was rare. She wished she could call home and talk to her mom and kids but knew that was not possible. And if she tried to sneak a call that could be grounds for being terminated from the program.

Amanda sat on the bench outside, enjoying the unseasonably warm day. When she saw a Toyota Prius pull up and park and a man get out, she figured that must be the tutor. He wasn't as old as she expected and looked only to be in his late twenties, early thirties at most. He carried a load of books and his laptop and she quickly walked over to open the door for him.

"Thanks for the help. Wasn't sure I was going to make it," he laughed. "I'm Jim. I come here three times a week to tutor." Eyeing her up, he could tell that she hadn't been here long. She looked a little malnourished with dark circles under her eyes. She was a very pretty young woman and if he had to guess he would bet that her addiction was to opiates. He had been volunteering here for the past six months and saw that meth took more of a toll on the women than the opiates.

Jim enjoyed the time that he spent tutoring at the rehab. He loved teaching and currently had a job teaching seventh and eighth grade. That was rough and probably the hardest age of students to teach. Many of them were smarty, had attitude and it felt like they were constantly testing him. The difference between teaching children and adults was huge to him. He enjoyed teaching adults who were there because they wanted to be there, not because they had to be there. Most the students that he taught at the rehab were pretty down and out but they were sincere in their desire to learn and improve their circumstances.

Many of his co-workers had tried to warn him, when he started volunteering at the rehab, that he would be scammed and that his students would try to take advantage of his kindness. And while that happened at times, it really didn't bother him. He was kind and generous by nature, had been lucky enough to have been born into circumstances that afforded him what he needed and then some, and he liked the idea of giving back.

Two more of the rehab residents came in, one jumping on the computer and one grabbing a practice test that she had been working on.

"Good afternoon, ladies. Go ahead and start working on your practice tests while I do an intake and pre-test on our new student," Jim said, while motioning Amanda to come over and sit at the table closest to him. "And your name is?"

"Amanda," she answered.

He explained that the intake was short and mostly for his own purposes so that he could track his students and have an idea of what type of help that they would need in passing the GED test.

From the intake he learned that she was twenty-four years old, had two children, was from Hoopa and had dropped out in her senior year, while pregnant with her son. She told him that originally she had planned on returning to school after giving birth but it had never happened. He was a little surprised when she scored as high as she did on the pre-test. Her math skills were a little low but in all other areas she scored a passing or above score. His assessment was that in a few short weeks he could have her ready to pass the test. The majority of the students he worked with at the rehab started at a much lower level. The only frustration that he sometimes felt was that many of his students weren't there long enough to make the progress that he would have liked to see them make.

21

The rest of the evening went pretty smoothly. After dinner she watched television for a while and then went to her room, pulled out her notebook, and wrote a letter to her mom and kids. She missed them and it was going to be a long month not being able to call or see them. Once she made it through the thirty blackout days she would be allowed to have visitors and she hoped her mom would be able to bring her kids over to visit.

She turned to a new page in her notebook and wrote at the top, "What Are My Triggers." Although she knew what triggers were, she had never really thought about what hers were. It didn't come as easy as she had thought and wasn't something that jumped right out at her.

The first one, she guessed, would probably be hanging around with other people who were using. Somehow it was easy to feed into other's addiction when she was with them. And in the past when she had been clean for any length of time it only took being around other people who were high and she would be joining them in no time.

The second one, she decided, had to do with economics. The poorer she was and the more she struggled to meet basic needs the more she wanted to use, which didn't really make sense because if there weren't resources for food and basics then there was even less available for drugs. And even if it didn't make sense, it was the truth. It was easier to hustle for the high and then the rest really didn't seem that pressing or important anymore.

The third had to do with patterns and routine. There were certain times that she used. It was pretty ingrained in her mind, which was usually the first of the month when she got money, or holidays, or birthdays, or, and she was ashamed to admit it, her mom's payday. Anytime there was opportunity, it had quickly become routine.

That was basically all she could come up with right now. Luckily she had another day to think about it. When she hit the sack she slept pretty hard for the first part of the night but around four, woke up feeling sick. Her head and body hurt, she was shivering and felt like she might even have a fever. She was nauseous as hell and ended up running to the bathroom, puking up her dinner and everything else she had eaten that day.

It was obvious to her that the Suboxone had worn off. It would be three hours before Rayna would be at work and able to provide Amanda her daily dose. She went back to bed but couldn't go back to sleep. She was sick, antsy and was starting to crave a fix bad. By six she decided to get up and go into the kitchen. No one was up yet so she quietly made coffee and paced the floor waiting for seven o'clock.

At five minutes before seven she heard a car pull up. Knowing that it had to be Rayna she felt relief wash over her. She had made it and was grateful that Rayna was punctual. Even a few extra minutes seemed overwhelming.

The minute Rayna unlocked the door and came in she saw that Amanda was waiting and correctly guessed that the Suboxone must have worn out sometime in the middle of the night. She went straight into the office and unlocked the safe where they kept all of the medicines for the residents. She grabbed two strips of Suboxone and handed them to Amanda. "You know Amanda, many of our residents who are on Suboxone divide their dose and take one in the morning and one in the evening. You might want to try that this time and see if that helps get you through the night a little better. Everyone has their own method; what works best for them."

"That sounds good. I've been awake since four with comedowns hitting me hard," Amanda said, while putting a strip of Suboxone under her tongue.

Within twenty minutes her body calmed down and she started to feel like she was going to make it. With no meetings or classes this morning she decided to go back to bed for a while. She was tired from getting up so early, and within minutes she was out, falling into a deep sleep. She had weird dreams, some bordering on nightmares. When she woke up she realized that it was ten-thirty and that she had been asleep for around three hours.

It was quiet and she realized that everyone must be on their day passes or out in the living room. This was her second day clean and already she was starting to have a different perspective on things. Taking the cravings out of the equation really did help her to think in a different way. For months her sole focus in life had been getting high, and that was where all of her energy had gone. Now that she wasn't getting high and wasn't craving a fix she felt a little lost. She felt nervous and needed something to direct her energy towards.

She pulled her journal out from under her bed and flipped to the page that she had been working on about her "triggers." The fourth one, she decided, was stress. Stress from her kids being sick, or acting up, or a friend mad at her, or fighting with her ex. Once she started feeling pressure of any kind, it was her first instinct to get high. It was like her stock answer to everything. Even though it never solved anything, once she was high none of her problems or issues seemed to bother her anymore.

She had to dig deep for the fifth one. She thought hard about it but her mind kept coming up blank. She was almost to the point of giving up and deciding that she only had four triggers. Then it hit her. Boredom. There was a certain amount of energy and adrenaline that came with the hustle. You had to talk to people, sell people on your hustle, do whatever necessary to come up with the money for the fix. When she started feeling bored or restless she would direct her energy into getting high and for a while it brought a certain amount of excitement with it.

That night she took her second strip of Suboxone, as Rayna had suggested, and she slept through the night. She was looking forward to the next day; with meetings and GED tutoring on Mondays, Wednesday and Fridays, those days seemed to pass faster and easier. Tuesdays and Thursdays she had too much time on her hands and would feel anxious and bored. Not good for someone in recovery. She fell asleep smiling. A few days ago she doubted that she was going to make it clean for even one day; and here she was two days clean. Maybe this time...

Chapter Four

Waking to the alarm, Bev groaned. It was only Wednesday, hump day, and she already felt exhausted. It wasn't easy waking up every morning, getting two little ones up and ready, delivering them to school and then getting to work by eight. She had done it for years when her own kids were young but somehow it had seemed easier, maybe because she was younger and had more energy back then.

She thought of her daughter, over in rehab, while she showered. She knew that she wasn't allowed to make calls yet, not for thirty days, but expected she would probably start getting letters soon. Actually not hearing from her was a good sign. If she got a call, she would have been worried because that would probably be a call saying she wanted to come home and to come get her.

Today she had one major worry that she still hadn't figured out how to handle. Her utility bill was due by five o'clock today or by tomorrow morning there was a good chance that her lights would be shut off. With all of the problems and stress she had been dealing with for the last year, this was just one more thing to worry about in a long line of problems. Every day there was a different challenge: food, toiletries, car payment, insurance, electricity. The list went on and on and there just never seemed to be enough money to cover everything.

Any resources that had been available to her were now gone. Dealing with her daughter's addiction had drained any savings, however meager, away. It was still a week from payday and she had already used up her two payroll advances for the year. It felt like for the last year she was always swallowing her pride and asking family or friends to borrow money. Or trying to get advances or loans, or sell something or hock something. It made her feel like a loser and many times well-meaning friends and family always felt the need to give her advice or lecture her on being more careful with her finances. It wasn't like she was out gambling it away or going on shopping sprees. As a matter of fact she hadn't bought herself anything new for at least two years. Even her shoes and work clothes were the same ones that she had been wearing for years. It was more of a matter of survival for her, her daughter and her grandchildren.

As hard as it was, she knew what she had to do but there really wasn't any other choice this time. She was going to have to call her daughter, Ashley, and ask her to pay the bill for her. This was a last resort. Ashley was the hardest person for her to go to and if she could get the money anywhere else she would. It almost wasn't worth the lecture and disdain that she knew would be coming. If it were just her, she would prefer to live without electricity for a week. But with the kids that would be too hard and she could possibly lose custody of them if Indian Child Welfare found out.

She knew that it was now or never. If she didn't catch Ashley before she went to work then it probably wouldn't get paid today. Besides she wanted to get it over with before she started getting the kids ready. Taking a deep breath she picked up the phone and dialed the number.

"Hello," Ashley answered. Feeling put out the minute she saw the number flash up on her cell phone, she could only guess the nature of this call. Her mom only called her if she needed some kind of help or had a problem with her sister, Amanda.

"Good morning. Hope this isn't a bad time. I need a few minutes to talk and I need a big favor." Bev swallowed hard. The long silent pause said it all.

"I'm getting ready for work Mom. I have to be at the hospital for my shift by eight. What's up, this time?" Somehow Ashley knew it had to do with her sister, or her sister's kids. It almost always did. She felt sorry for her mom but on the other hand was tired of her mom being a doormat. She was sick of her sister's problems taking center stage and she wasn't buying in to it anymore. If her sister chose to do drugs then that was her problem and she didn't want any part of it. Tough love wasn't something that Ashley had a problem with.

"I have a shut off notice for my power bill that has to be paid by today. I was wondering if you could pay it and I will pay you back next week on my payday. I hate to ask. You know I wouldn't ask if I didn't have to but I'm in dire straits and am really hoping that you can help me out." Her voice sounded unnatural and her speech a little too fast. She braced herself for what was coming.

"Wow, really Mom." Ashley, shaking her head, could feel the resentment boiling up inside of her. "Why don't you have the money to pay it? I mean really, you know that it has to be paid every month. It's not like an emergency situation, like your car breaking down or something. I just don't understand why you can't budget your money better."

"I'm sorry and yes, you're right. I do know that it has to be paid every month. Things have just been tight. Your sister went to rehab on Monday and I had to buy a few supplies for her and Melanie needed a new pair of shoes. She had outgrown hers. I'm not asking you to give me the money. I'm just asking for a loan." Bev took a deep breath and waited. She knew her daughter would relent and loan her the money. She just had to show her disapproval first. It wasn't the first time that she had, had to borrow from her and probably wouldn't be the last. But the one thing in her favor was that she had always paid her back when she said she would.

"Well I guess on my lunch break I could run over to the PG&E pay station and pay it. How much is it anyhow?" Ashley asked, trying to sound less irritated. She didn't want to be a total bitch about it and of course she would help her mother.

"It's ninety-eight dollars. I really do appreciate you helping me out Ashley and I promise I will get it back to you next week. Is anything else new?" Bev really was grateful and felt relieved to know that her utility bill would be paid today.

"Not much. I've just been working a lot of hours at the hospital. I plan on going to Hawaii at the end of the month with a few friends. We'll be gone for a week. I'll call you before I go." Ashley answered, sounding rushed and ready to get off the phone.

"That sounds fun. I'm so happy for you babe. You work hard and deserve a nice vacation with your friends." Bev really was sincere in wishing her daughter a nice vacation. She really couldn't remember the last time she had taken a real vacation herself, but her biggest hope in life was that her daughters would have a better and easier life than she had and in the case of Ashley this was coming true.

Ashley hung up the phone feeling a little less annoyed and with the slightest twinge of guilt. It wasn't that she didn't care about her mother, her sister or her sister's kids. She just didn't have any tolerance for people making bad choices and inflicting all of their consequences on everyone else. In the past, several times, she had tried to intervene on her mother's behalf but that had backfired quickly. It served no purpose for her to go out on a limb and try to help her mother weed the problems out of her life. Her mother, for whatever reason, was an enabler who would move heaven and earth to make sure that her sister had whatever she needed to get by, including drugs and as hard as it was to watch, there just wasn't much anyone could do about it. Her mother was an adult and was going to do whatever she felt that she needed to do.

Having grown up with a lot of dysfunction around her, at an early age, Ashley had made up her mind that as soon as she graduated from high school she was going to move out of the Valley, go to school and make a different life for herself and that is exactly what she had done. Her drive and focus was readily apparent to all, even as a small girl. Once she made up her mind to do something, nothing could stop her.

In school, she had studied hard and put all of her energy into getting good grades. By eighth grade she had decided that she wanted to be a nurse so she worked hard to get good grades in high school, applied for and received many scholarships and started the nursing program right out of high school. She graduated with her Bachelor's in Nursing Studies at the age of twenty-four and for the past two years had been working at a hospital on the Coast. She worked in pre-op and post-op, preparing patients for surgery and then caring for them after surgery, while they were in recovery. She liked her job and it worked well for her. She didn't spend very much time with the patients; just long enough to get them ready for surgery and then again to get them ready for discharge or to be moved to in-patient. Never enough time to get to know her patients very well and she preferred it that way. Getting close to people wasn't her forte. For a lot of reasons she preferred to stay guarded and kept her distance.

To boost her income she often picked up shifts at a nearby nursing home. It worked out well for her because the nursing home let her pick up shifts that worked well with her hospital schedule. A lot of her friends didn't quite understand why she had chosen the nursing home for a second job but she really enjoyed the time she spent there. Growing up she had been especially close to her grandparents, great aunts and uncles who often told her that she had an old soul. For whatever reason she had always felt more comfortable with older people and when she was at the nursing home, it really was the only time that her soft side came out. When one of her patients passed away she did go through a period of grief, at times. But on the other hand she knew that she had helped care for them in their final days and got a great deal of comfort from that.

On her way to work she thought about her sister. She had basically lost all faith in her sister and felt angry with her most of the time. They were only two years apart and had grown up with a normal amount of sibling rivalry but for the most part had gotten along pretty well. At the ages of twelve and fourteen, they had lost their only brother to a car accident. He was seventeen years old and they had idolized him. He was handsome, smart, athletic and funny. Most of their competitiveness with each other centered on him and their need for attention from him.

Even now, twelve years later, the pain was still there, duller maybe, but always there. They had equally adored their brother and he, them. The three of them had bonded at a very early age. Their father was an alcoholic and his behavior was always unpredictable. Some of the time, when drunk, he could be loving, happy and funny. Other times he could be mean, angry and abusive. Most of his drunken anger was taken out on their mother. As Ashley got older she realized how much her brother had protected them and she was grateful. Many nights, during their father's drunken rages he would do his best to shield them from the ugliness that was going on in the next room. He would find ways to entertain them or make a game out of hiding in a closet. He made them feel safe and more than that, he made them feel loved.

His death had taken a toll on the whole family. Their father passed away eighth months later, basically drank himself to death. The guilt he felt for his son's death consumed him and he was never able to overcome it. The night of the accident, he had been too drunk to pick his wife up from work, so he had sent his son. It was storming that night and raining very hard. The car they owned was a "rez ride." Because it was not running well it was only used to get around locally, to school, store, and work. The tires were bald and slick. It hadn't been registered for years and of course had no insurance.

Waiting for their mom to get home and start dinner that night, they had heard sirens but never dreamed that it was just a precursor to the nightmare that they would soon be facing. Soon after, her uncle pulled in honking the horn and looking frantic. She could hear him yelling for her dad to get in the truck; that there had been an accident. No one came back for hours and as she and her sister sat waiting; they both started crying. She waited to hear the siren heading back out of the Valley to the hospital on the Coast, as was normal when there was an accident in the Valley. The fact that the ambulance never went back out was a bad sign and they both knew it.

Hours later, when their parents returned home, the look on their face when they walked in the door said it all. She knew, before they even told her, that her brother was dead. She remembered the next few weeks like a bad nightmare. She had got through it by just closing herself off and felt numb. She wanted to cry but couldn't. It would have been a relief but tears just wouldn't come. She knew that some of her family members thought that she was a little strange because she seemed so emotionless but that was how her brain dealt with tragedy and when her father died her reaction was much the same.

Her sister, Amanda, on the other hand was the complete opposite. She had cried for days, was inconsolable and welcomed all the hugs and condolences that were offered. Their lives were drastically and irrevocably changed at that point. While she withdrew and buried herself into her studies, her sister took solace in alcohol and drugs, even at the young age of twelve. Later, while in college, she learned that they had both been traumatized by the loss of their brother and then their father and could have greatly benefited from grief counseling but that wasn't something offered in their rural area and frankly just wasn't how they dealt with death.

Pulling into a parking spot she sighed deeply. That was in the past and there was nothing she could do to change what had happened. Today she had a busy day with her OR schedule and needed to be sharp and focused and at lunch she would run to the pay station and pay her mom's electricity bill.

Chapter Five

Amanda looked at the alarm clock, rolled over and started climbing out of bed. She was excited and anxious at the same time. She had made it one month and her blackout was over. Today her mom, uncle and her kids were coming to visit her. It was a beautiful day and once a month there was a planned luncheon where family members could come and visit for the day.

It hadn't been easy, even with the Suboxone, but she had made it over the hump and was finally feeling better, both physically and mentally. At times, especially at night, she felt deep pangs of guilt and regret for what she had put her family through. With every day clean, her clarity was coming back and in some ways that was good but in others it made her face things that had been buried for a long time.

Taking a quick shower she tried to figure out what to wear. She had put on about twenty pounds in the last month and while she knew she looked better it also limited her clothing options. The clothes that she did have were all starting to feel a little snug. She was trying not to trip about her weight gain but unfortunately she was reminded of it every time she got dressed.

She paid special attention while doing her hair and putting on her make up. Jim had said that he might stop by and she had to admit that the thought of him coming to the luncheon made her happy and maybe a little bit excited. Although he was her tutor she was starting to have a crush on him and wasn't sure yet if she truly had feelings for him or if she was just mistaking his kindness for something more. And then again, he was the only male that she had been around for thirty days and most of the residents at the rehab seemed to vie for his attention.

It was a long morning and she knew her family would not be arriving until around noon. Pacing back and forth looking out the window, it was a few minutes after eleven when she saw the Prius pull up. She walked out to meet Jim and again had mixed emotions. He wasn't her usual type. For starters he was white and she had really never dated or been with anyone outside of her race. And she had never really gone out with anyone who had it so together. He was smart, kind and had his life on track. He was always really nice to her and seemed to pay more attention to her than the other residents that attended his classes. But she didn't want to mistake that for being more than it was. After all, he could do better and what did she have to offer? She was a recovering junky with two kids and a long list of problems. Still, she was glad that he was coming today and the thought of getting to spend a little time around him made her happy.

Jim got out of his car and Amanda saw that he had a little bag in his hand. "Good morning. Are you excited to see your family today?" he asked.

"Yeah, excited and nervous I guess. It feels like a long morning. I just wish they would get here already." Although laughing, he could tell that she was nervous and rightly so, he supposed. She had gone through some major changes in the past month and hadn't had any contact with her family for thirty days.

"I hope you don't mind but I bought a couple of little presents for you to give your kids. I kind of thought that you might want to give them something and knowing that you haven't been able to go shopping or anything, I took the liberty," Jim said, a little hesitantly. It had seemed like a good idea but now he was feeling a little awkward.

Amanda smiled and grabbed the bag from him. Opening it she saw a baby doll that came with a bottle, pacifier and a little rattle. Digging a little deeper she pulled out a ninja turtle riding on a motorcycle. "Thank you. It's perfect. How did you know what to get them?" She was truly touched and it reminded her that there were still good people in the world. After living on the dark side for so long she sometimes forgot that.

"Well I do have a niece and nephew around the same age. I'm not totally inept at buying children presents, you know," he said, with faked sarcasm.

She reached out and gave him a hug. "Thank you. That's the nicest thing anyone has done for me in a long time." The hug felt good and awkward at the same time. They had become good friends and she didn't want it to get weird between them. Especially since her emotions were mixed and she wasn't really sure how she felt about him or how he felt about her.

He pulled away first but his eyes looked kind and reassuring. "I'm proud of you. You have come a long way in the past thirty days. I know

32

that your family is going to be proud too. I also wanted to give you the good news. I've talked to the local college and they are going to be holding their GED testing in two weeks from today. You've worked hard and I don't think that you are going to have any problem passing it. And after that maybe you should consider taking some college courses. You're smart and can do anything that you set your mind too."

"Thanks. Give yourself credit, too, though. There is no way that I would have been ready without all of your help." He was so confident in her that it made her feel good about herself. She had never really had anyone believe in her so completely before. It actually felt good but she also felt some pressure. She didn't want to disappoint him, if she didn't pass.

He could see the self-doubts flash in her eyes and suspected the cause. It was funny how in tuned he was with her and although they had only known each other for one short month, he felt like he had known her much longer.

"You will do fine and a lot of people don't pass the first time. That is why they let you retest up to three times in a year for a small fee. Just do the best you can and if you don't pass the first time don't give up. You will pass and you will get your GED," Jim told her confidently.

He was a good distraction and the next hour passed quickly. Seeing her mother's car pull up she took a deep breath and ran and flung open the door. Unbuckling their seatbelts she scooped up both of her kids, hugging and kissing them at the same time. Her son was receptive, hugging and kissing her back but she noticed that her daughter pulled back a little. Always more reserved than her brother she hung back, more content to watch and wait.

By then her mother and uncle had gotten out of the car. Amanda threw her arms around her mother and noticed that she looked better. Healthier and less tired than when she had last seen her. Knowing how much stress she had caused her mother she again felt some pangs of guilt. "Hi, Mom. I'm so glad that you could come and bring the kids. I have really missed you," Amanda said, choking up with emotion.

"I missed you too, honey. You look so good." And it was true. It was the best that she had seen her daughter look in years.

"Uncle, I'm so glad you came too. I missed you so much." Reaching up, she gave him a big hug and kiss.

"I missed you, too, Honey Bumpkins." Her uncle fondly replied. That had always been his nickname for her even though she couldn't remember him calling her that in years.

After giving them a tour of the rehab, they moved into the big dining room and sat down. A few of the other women had family members visiting too. Barbara walked in and looking around at the different families and sadness veiled over her eyes. Amanda knew her well and could tell that she was disappointed that no one had come to visit her even though she had invited several of her family members. She knew that Barbara didn't have much support from her family and she felt even more grateful to her mother and uncle for making the effort to come over today.

Amanda gave her kids their presents. "Oh boy, a ninja turtle. Thanks Mom." Michael gave her another big hug and then ran off to the couch in the living room to play. Her daughter smiled big, looking at her baby doll. Amanda looked down the table and gave Jim a big smile and mouthed a silent thank you to him. He smiled back and nodded his head in acknowledgment. He had stopped and bought the presents on impulse but now was glad that he had. Although he was there to visit all of the residents and their guests, more than that he was watching her and how she interacted with her children, mom and uncle. He was drawn to her and felt curious about her and her life. He noticed that her kids treated her more like a big sister and their grandmother more like a mother and he wondered if that bothered her. He was noticing too many things about her lately and it was starting to freak him out. He quickly made his rounds saying a hurried good-bye to everyone and quickly left.

Amanda felt a little deflated and disappointed when he left. She had hoped he would at least stay and eat and noticed that when he said good-bye to her, he seemed distracted and almost like he was in a hurry to get away from her. As it was she didn't have much time to think about it. It was time to eat and the residents were expected to dish up the food and serve their guests.

After eating Amanda and her mother went and sat down on the bench outside. Her uncle excused himself, saying that he was going to sit in the car for a little while and take a "cat nap" before he drove them back over the hill.

"You look good, Amanda; happy and healthy. Really, the best that I have seen you look in a long time. I'm so glad and so relieved." Beverly told her daughter.

"I feel good momma. The first few days were hard and at times I didn't know if I was going to make it. I'm so sorry, mom. Sorry for everything I have put you through. All of the stealing, lying and all of the demands and stress that I put on you. I love you so much and wish I could take it all back; all the pain and turmoil that I have caused you." Amanda's voice was cracking and it was all she could do to hold back her tears. "I have so many regrets and so much guilt."

Her mother put her arms around her, hugging her, both of them close to tears. "Amanda, we all make mistakes in life and we all have regrets. I have them too. I look back at when you kids were little and I wish I had protected you, your sister and brother more. I wish that I had put a stop to things that were going on and instilled more stability and security into your lives. But we can't change what happened. We can only move forward and try to do better. I don't want you to live with guilt. It's a wasted emotion, anyhow. I'm proud of you and I feel in my gut that you are going to make it this time. Before you just weren't quite ready, but this time you are. I can tell. Have you made plans about what you are going to do when your 90 days are up?"

"Well, I'm thinking that I would like to stay at the sober living house for at least three months after I'm done at rehab, and then well... I don't really want to go back to Hoopa." Watching her mother's face for a reaction, she continued on. "I would like to find a job over here, find a place and bring the kids over here with me. I appreciate you taking care of my kids but you should have a life now. You worked hard and raised us and then have raised my kids. I want you to do some things for yourself now."

Bev wasn't surprised. When she saw how well her daughter was doing she knew that it would only be a matter of time before she wanted her kids back. She was okay with that. She loved her grandkids but she was tired and as long as her daughter stayed clean, she had complete faith in her mothering abilities. It was only when she was using that she acted selfish and irresponsible.

"Well I would fully support that as long as you find a decent place and have the means to pay rent and living expenses. Hell, maybe I'll even move and join you," laughing she gave her daughter a big hug. "As much as I hate to, we are going to have to head home soon. You know Uncle doesn't like to drive at night. I've loved seeing you and I couldn't be more proud. I will call you in a few days now that you are able to get calls."

Amanda walked her family to the car and gave them all one more hug and kiss. Watching them pull out she wiped away tears. It had been an emotional day with the excitement of seeing her family and now the let down and low with them leaving. She was tired and ready for bed. And at the back of her mind her thoughts were on Jim and why he had left so abruptly. Everything seemed good up to the time that he left and she was more than a little disappointed that he hadn't stayed longer. Little did she know that on the other side of town, he was staring at the television, his mind a million miles away. He was as surprised as anyone with his reaction today. He wondered what was up with him anyhow. Why was he so taken with this girl? He had never had this reaction to any of his students before. Pouring himself a drink he decided to let it go. He had a headache at this point and maybe he was just overthinking the whole thing or maybe he was just tired.

The ride home was quiet. Both kids were asleep in five minutes and Ben and Bev were each deep in their own thoughts. Her thoughts were of her daughter and her grandchildren and the possibility of having a life where maybe she would have time to do some of the things that she wanted to do, like travel or visit friends or go to the casino and play bingo. His thoughts were of earlier days; when he was young and carefree. At times he missed those days and lately had been reflecting back on his life more and more.

Chapter Six

It was the eve of her GED test and Jim was coming by to do some last minute studying with her. She was nervous and having a lot of self-doubts. Although she had gotten fairly decent grades in school it was hard for her to gage if she was ready or not. After all, the schools on the reservation had some of the lowest testing in the state so she wasn't really sure if her fairly decent grades were up to par compared to other schools. Jim seemed to think that she was ready so she would just have to believe him.

Out of the three women studying for their GED, she was the only one that had done well enough on the pre-test to have a chance of passing the test. Because of the cost it wasn't prudent to take the test until they were ready. She was lucky because Jim had called her tribe's education department and they were paying for her test.

After almost two hours of studying, Jim closed the prep book and pushed it away. She looked up surprised and waited to see why he was quitting.

"You know, you've studied hard all week. You're ready. I know you are. But now it's time to take a deep breath and relax for a little while. Come on. Let's go out to eat. You don't have to check back in until ten so we still have a couple of hours and I'm hungry." Jim smiled at her with a look that he wasn't going to take no for an answer.

"Um, okay. Can I have a few minutes to get ready?" She was happy that she would get to go eat with him and their relationship had become increasingly more comfortable.

"Yep. But don't take all night. I'm starving. Besides you look fine," Jim said, looking admiringly at her. She was growing on him more and more and the dinner invitation helped extend the evening with her.

She hurriedly brushed her hair, put it up in a bun, grabbed a sweatshirt and went out to the car where he was waiting.

"I hope you like Chinese food because that is where I was thinking of going. If you don't though, we could go somewhere else. After all, this is your pre-celebratory dinner," he said, hoping that she liked Chinese food because that was what he was hungry for.

"I love Chinese food." Amanda told him.

Dinner was good although there was one awkward moment at dinner when they were ordering their food and Jim had started to order a glass of wine and ask if she wanted one. He quickly retracted and ordered an ice tea. Feeling a little bit embarrassed he hoped she hadn't noticed his faux pas.

"You know it's okay to have a glass of wine around me. And besides I never was a drinker. I hate alcohol." Amanda had no desire to drink wine or any other alcohol beverage for that matter.

"It's fine. I'm not that much of a drinker anyway, just an occasional glass of wine or a drink sometimes with dinner. But I wouldn't want to put you in a bad situation at your residential program or myself either for that matter. It would be poor judgment on my part," he explained.

She had spent a lot of time thinking about Jim and wondering about his life. She felt a little shy asking but was growing more and more comfortable around him so she decided to just dive in. "Tell me about you. It seems like you know so much about me but I don't really know anything about you. Like where did you grow up? What's your favorite color? Do you like sports? You don't have to answer. I'm just curious, you know. We spend a lot of time together and I was just wondering," her voice faded off. "I don't even know when your birthday is or how old you are?"

"Okay, well I'm an open book. Don't really have anything to hide. My birthday is February third and I'm twenty-nine. Going to hit the big three-O in a few months. I was raised in Southern California. My dad is a corporate lawyer and my mother a nurse. Although when my sister and I were little she was a stay at home mom. She didn't really go back into that field until we were both out of the house. There's nothing too exciting to tell. Just a normal childhood. Attended school, was a Boy Scout, played soccer in high school. Took a two-week vacation somewhere every summer. You know just normal stuff. Oh, and my favorite color is green." Jim was glad to share, and it was true. He did know more about her, than she about him.

"That sounds wonderful," she said with wistfulness in her voice.

He felt a little taken aback. "What do you mean? I mean it really was just kind of ordinary."

"I just mean that it sounds great and actually it sounds anything but ordinary from where I'm sitting." He had a look on his face that was mixed with shock and she didn't know if she had offended him or not. "Where did you go on vacation?" She asked curiously.

"Oh, we went to Florida, Hawaii, Yellowstone, Washington, D.C. You know regular vacation destinations. Although one year, when I was fourteen, we went to Paris," Jim stated, matter-of- factly.

"Wow. I always wanted to take a vacation like that. Our vacation consisted of camping and fishing, either at the river or up in the mountains. Those were fun. Don't get me wrong but I haven't really had a vacation like you're talking about. I really do want to take my kids to Disneyland. Have you been?" Laughing, she caught herself. "Of course you have. That was a dumb question."

"Well, since I was raised in Southern California, um, yes. As a matter of fact I have been to Disneyland a few times. Very touristy but every kid should go there at least once," Jim answered.

Dinner was good and they got back to the rehab right before ten. She loved having a little more freedom now. It felt so liberating to be able to make a phone call or go out to dinner. Or even go to the store for that matter.

"Thank you so much for dinner. I really do appreciate all the time you have put in on this GED test. I have wanted to take the test for years but always felt too scared to try. You're a good teacher. I bet the kids in your class love having you for a teacher," Amanda said, with a certain amount of awe in her voice.

"Some do and some don't. Seventh and Eighth graders are a hard bunch but I love what I do and feel lucky that I have been able to do something that I enjoy and have some influence in shaping these young lives. I knew from a very early age that I wanted to be a teacher. My parents weren't exactly thrilled at first. I think my dad wanted me to be an attorney like him and my mom had her heart set on me going into a medical profession. But once they got over their initial disappointment I think they realized that this was the best choice for me," Jim said, thinking about how lucky he was to have a job he loved.

"What about your sister? What does she do?" Amanda asked, trying to imagine what his sister was like.

"Well my sister is a nurse, much to my parent's delight, although right now she is a stay-at-home mom." He could sense the fascination that she had when he talked about his life. He hadn't really thought much about it and realized that he had probably taken for granted the lifestyle that he had been brought up in.

39

"So I will pick you up at seven thirty sharp. At eight they lock the doors and begin the test. I know that you're nervous but try to get a good night's sleep. It will help in the end." He walked her to the front door and gave her a hug. The hug lasted a little longer than their customary hug; almost as if neither of them wanted to be the first to let go. She finally pulled away and turned around quickly. The feelings between them were becoming obvious and even though there was some excitement about it, mostly she felt scared.

Sleep didn't come easy that night. She was nervous about her test. Nervous about her feelings for Jim. Nervous about life in general. Everything just seemed to be happening so fast. Five weeks ago she never dreamed that she would have been clean this long, studying for her GED and having feelings for someone who seemed completely out of her league. It was almost like she was watching her life from the outside, like a bystander and sometimes she had to remind herself that it was all real. She finally fell asleep around two and when the alarm went off at six, her first instinct was to turn it off and go back to sleep. The realization soon hit though and jumping up she got in the shower and started getting ready.

Looking out the window, she saw the Prius pull up at seven twenty-five. One thing about Jim was that he was never late and usually a few minutes early. She slid into the car and he grabbed her hand and gave it a quick squeeze.

"Nervous?" he asked.

She laughed, with a voice barely audible, "Very. But I've gotten to the point that I just want it over. For better or worse, I'm ready to take the test and know where I stand. Does that make sense?"

"I guess I can understand that. You have put a lot of time and energy into this. Just think of all of the free time that you will have after today. Have you thought about what you're going to do with all of your extra time?"

"No. Not really. In a little over three weeks I will be able to get a weekend pass and I want to go home for the weekend. And in another month I have to start looking into moving to a Sober Living House. Other than that I really haven't thought about it. I was thinking about maybe applying for a job out at the casino. I hope to get my own place eventually and move my kids over here with me." But at the same time it seemed so far out of her reach and overwhelming.

He could sense what she was feeling and now was definitely not the time to try to figure it all out. He wished he hadn't brought it up and quickly changed the subject. "It's a beautiful day and now is not the time to stress yourself out. One day at a time, right? I will be back at noon to pick you up for lunch and don't worry. You are going to do fine."

She got out of the car, walked towards the school and noticed a sign that said "GED today" with an arrow pointing down a hallway. Taking a deep breath she started walking towards the only open door in the long hallway. She was so nervous that she felt like puking. Overcome with doubt she suddenly felt shy and backwards and started wondering if she had made a big mistake.

The room was a regular classroom and there were four other people already there. Taking out her ID card she gave it to the lady administering the test and signed her paper. Finding a seat in the back, she took a pencil out of her purse and said a silent prayer. After listening to instructions for the next ten minutes, the test was finally passed out. Taking a deep breath she picked up her pencil and started.

Time passed really fast and much to her relief she knew more of the answers than she thought she would. After the first half hour the realization hit that she might actually pass and as she went through the test she started relaxing and the answers came easier and easier.

At noon, she walked outside and saw Jim sitting under a tree reading a book. He didn't notice her at first and as she walked towards him she smiled. He was such a good person that it made her want to be a better person too. Although she wasn't exactly sure why, she wanted to make him proud of her and she sometimes wondered what he would think if he knew her before, when she was high and using.

"Well, how did you do?" Even though he didn't want to show it, he had been feeling nervous for her, too. He knew how important this was to her and he really hoped that she passed this first go around but didn't want her to be disappointed if she didn't.

"I think that I did pretty good. I was so nervous but then as I started the test I realized that I knew most of the answers. It was math and you know that isn't my best subject; but it was like I knew how to do the problems and before I knew it I had finished that section," Amanda told him, slightly animated with relief and excitement.

He was happy to see how relaxed she looked now, compared to earlier.

"I went ahead and brought a picnic lunch. An hour isn't that long and I didn't want you to have to rush through lunch or stress about being late getting back to the test. Besides it's a beautiful day," Jim said, while motioning her to sit down on the blanket that he had spread out.

"I love picnics. What a great idea." Looking into the bag, sitting by his side, she started taking the food out of the bag, sandwiches from the deli, chips, drinks and a couple of candy bars. Ever since getting clean she craved sugar. She wasn't sure why that was but other recovering addicts with her at rehab also craved sugar.

"This looks good but God, I'm going to get fat if I keep eating at this rate." It was kind of a joke but on the other hand had a lot of truth in it.

"Do you worry about that? I've heard you make comments like that several times," Jim asked curiously.

There was a pause, while she thought about that. "I guess I do. I have been around a lot of people who have ballooned up when they got clean and got really heavy. I don't want that to happen to me," she answered honestly.

"You know maybe you should think about exercising. I go to the gym almost every morning. It is just part of my routine. And it would be good for your endorphins and serotonin levels. Anyhow, just a suggestion. I believe that the gym offers a free month membership. I could ask them if you're interested," Jim offered.

"Okay. It would probably be good for me. I am so out of shape. I haven't done anything physical for a long time. In high school I was pretty athletic. I played volleyball, basketball and softball. Until I got pregnant, that is," she said, picking up her sandwich and taking a bite.

He wanted to ask her more about that. He was curious about her life and wanted to know more about what she was like before she came to rehab but for now he would wait. Not sure if there were old wounds or fresh wounds or any other skeletons in her closet, he didn't want to stir up emotions today. Today the only thing she needed to focus on was her test.

The hour passed quickly and before they knew it, it was time for her to go back and finish her testing. The afternoon went easier with the testing on English and Social Studies. Those were her better subjects and at the end of the day she was reasonably certain that she had passed those sections.

"So, thank you everyone for coming to test today. Results won't be available for around sixty days. And remember; don't give up if you don't pass the first time. A schedule will be posted on our website if you need to retest." The woman administering the test gathered up all of the tests and put it in a folder.

She felt happy and relieved. It was over and even if she didn't pass at least she would know what she needed to work on. The Prius was parked in the corner of the parking lot and when Jim saw her walking out he pulled over to the front of the building and picked her up.

"I was thinking of taking you out to dinner again but decided against it." Seeing the disappointment flash across her face he quickly went on. "I would rather do something tomorrow instead. And I figured you must be exhausted today anyhow. I know the mental toll that all-day testing takes on a person. "

"I really didn't think about it but you are right. I actually am really tired. So what are we doing tomorrow?" She was actually pleased at the thought of spending a whole day with him.

"It's a surprise. I will pick you up at ten and dress casual," Jim told her teasingly.

"Oh, God. I hate surprises," she said, without much conviction in her voice.

When they got back to the rehab she noticed the head boss was there which was very unusual for the weekend. She was in the office with Rayna and although she couldn't hear what they were saying, by the tone of their voice and their animated movements she could tell something had happened. Going quickly into her room she saw Barbara standing by her bed, packing a suitcase. Her heart dropped in her chest because it was apparent that whatever happened had to do with Barbara.

"Barbara, what happened? What's going on?" Amanda asked.

Turning around, she could tell that Barbara had been crying. "I had a dirty test so I have to leave. Honestly I only used once and of all the days that they tested me, it had to be today."

"When? I mean, how did that happen? You've been doing so good," Amanda said, suddenly feeling sick to her stomach.

"I don't know. I was just feeling so bored today so I decided to go for a walk and ended up downtown. Do you remember Earl? He's related to us somehow. I don't know how exactly but I know he's a cousin. Well he was driving by and recognized me so he stopped and I jumped in with him. We drove out to the casino and before we went in he pulled out a bag of dope and offered me a line. At first I said no. But I watched him do a line and the next thing I knew I was snorting up one too. I regretted it as soon as I did it but it was too late then. Oh, God, I'm such an idiot. The minute my PO hears about this I will definitely be going to jail." Barbara's voice trailed off and she was obviously on the verge of crying again.

Hugging Barbara, tears ran down Amanda's cheeks. She knew first-hand how hard it was to resist when someone was putting it in your face.

And she knew the consequences weren't negotiable. A bad test at rehab was an automatic out. No second chances. Just pack your bag and leave.

"I'm so sorry Barbara. What are you going to do now?" Amanda asked, worried about her cousin.

"I got a hold of my brother Vic and he is coming to pick me up. No worries, cuz. I'll be okay. You just keep doing good. Your brother would be so proud of you. Don't forget that," Barbara said, sounding braver than she felt.

Picking up her suitcase, Barbara gave her one last hug. "I love you cousin. I'll get a hold of you when I can."

"I love you too Barbara. Please be careful and take care of yourself. And thanks for everything. You helped me through the tough times here. I'm not sure what I'm going to do without you," Amanda said, tears now coming to her eyes too.

As soon as Barbara left, Rayna knocked on the door and announced that all residents had to meet in the main room in five minutes. One of the other residents had left a week ago, after completing ninety days, leaving only eight residents at the rehab.

"So as everyone knows, Barbara had to leave tonight. Because of the circumstances everyone is going to have to do a test tonight. This is orders from the boss so I'll pass out the urine cups and wait in the office for you to turn them in." Rayna handed out the cups and hoped that no one else had a dirty test. She always felt bad and in some ways like she had failed, when stuff like this happened.

The whole process took about fifteen minutes and thankfully all of the residents tested clean. Exhausted from the day, Amanda went and crawled into bed right after she turned her urine test in. She felt sad and drained. The happiness of finally taking the GED test was tarnished with the sadness of Barbara's departure. Having a family member at the rehab with her had made her feel less alone and then there was the reality of how easy it was to slip up. It was easy to think that it could never happen to you but the truth was it could happen to anyone of them. Sometimes she felt like she was a hostage to her addiction and she hated the constant battle against it. She wished she could change what had happened to Barbara but, knowing that wasn't possible, she fell asleep fast and slept hard, exhausted from the test and then the upheaval created by her cousin.

Chapter Seven

Amanda woke up feeling excited yet nervous, happy yet sad. Barbara's sudden departure had left a cloud hanging over her head and looking over at the empty bed she realized how much she already missed her cousin. But, on the other hand, she was excited for the day. She really didn't like surprises but was starting to trust Jim and knew that whatever he had planned would be well thought out and something that she would enjoy. That was his personality and she knew him well enough to know that he didn't do things by the "seat of his pants." She tried to imagine what might be in store for her today but her mind kept coming up blank.

After showering, she pondered what to wear. What did casual mean anyhow? Not having a very big wardrobe she finally settled on a pair of jeans, a cami tank with a button up flannel shirt and a pair of tennis shoes. Hoping she wasn't underdressed she put on her make up and started brushing out her hair. Relieved that her hair was beginning to look thicker and healthy again, she decided to wear it down.

At ten o'clock sharp she looked out the window and saw a black ford F150 pull up. It took her a few seconds to notice that it was Jim, behind the wheel. She grabbed her purse and walked outside to greet him.

"Good morning. I didn't recognize you in a truck. Where's the Prius?" Amanda asked.

"I left it home today. I don't drive this very often, only because it doesn't get the best gas mileage, especially compared to the Prius. But today I thought we would take this out," Jim explained.

She opened the truck door, climbed in and put her seat belt on. It was a nice truck and she marveled how immaculate it was, inside and out. Jim started it up and backed it out of the driveway.

"So, what are we doing today?" Amanda asked. The suspense had been with her long enough.

"Well, I'm not exactly sure but I thought that we would start with a drive up the Coast. Maybe up to the redwoods, maybe stop at the beach.

I don't have a set itinerary although I do have a place picked out for lunch. It overlooks the ocean and has the best seafood in this whole area. Does that sound okay?" Jim asked, suddenly feeling a little nervous. He didn't even know if she liked seafood or not.

"That sounds great. I love going to the beach and I love driving through the redwoods. And I love eating seafood. Sounds like a win-win all the way around." Laughing, she felt relaxed and happy and although it was November, the day was warm and the sun shined brightly.

As they started driving north she told him about Barbara having a dirty test. "I just feel so bad for her. She worked so hard and was doing so well."

"Why do you think she did it? Use again, I mean?" Jim asked, knowing that it must have been a hard night for her with her cousin's sudden departure.

"I guess the temptation was too much for her. Sometimes it's hard to resist when it is right there in your face," she explained.

"I'm not going to pretend to understand. I guess I can't comprehend why someone would choose to do drugs, knowing that the consequences are so high." He wanted to understand but really didn't comprehend the struggle to stay clean.

"Well, that's addiction. If it was that easy, to give up, I mean, there wouldn't be addicts. I hated myself for using again. I knew better and I knew the costs that would come with it but I did it anyhow. At first, it was a matter of one more time but honestly there never is a one more time." Her voice trailed off, as she thought about it.

"I guess. Like I said I don't really understand all of the components of addiction. The only exposure I have had to substance abuse is my work at the rehab. And the people that are there aren't actively using. In the time that I have known you I have only seen the person that you are now. Clean and sober, I mean. It's hard for me to imagine what you were like before you came to rehab. And if you don't want to talk about this I understand. I'm not trying to be nosy or pry into something that isn't any of my business." He wanted her to be comfortable discussing it with him but he wasn't going to be pushy about it.

"It's fine. I don't mind talking about it with you. I trust you." Flashing him a smile, she took a deep breath, deciding how much she should actually share with him. Something told her that she needed to break it down slowly and not overload him all at once. She didn't want to completely scare him off.

Continuing, she took a deep breath and chose her words carefully. "When I look back even two months ago it's hard to believe how down and out I really was. I was bad. My whole focus in life was how to get another fix. When you're an addict it really does take all of your time and energy to get high. I mean, I guess if you were rich you wouldn't have to stress so much and hustle all of the time. But the money would have to be endless because there's no such thing as having enough."

"How did you start? Like how old were you and what did you use?" Jim asked, curiously.

"When I was twelve I started drinking and smoking pot. It started at first just on weekends when I was with some of my cousins and friends. They were a little older than me and I liked to hang out with them. We had lost my brother and then a few months later my dad," she paused for a minute thinking about the pain of that. "And I guess I liked how it made me feel. It just kind of made everything numb and nothing hurt so bad when I was high. That wasn't too bad, in the sense that I wasn't getting high every day but when I was fifteen I started using pills; first, Norco's and Klonopins but then one day someone gave me an Oxycontin and that was the beginning of the end. Everything changed then and I wasn't doing it anymore because it was fun or anything. At that point it went from being a want to a need and everything went downhill from there."

"Wow. You really were just a little girl still. I picture twelve-year-old girls talking with friends and giggling about boys. It must have been really hard on you to grow up so quickly and enter into this adult world when you were so young and not emotionally ready for all of that." It struck him that she was the same age as his students when she started using.

"I've never really thought about that but I guess so. When I was seventeen I got pregnant with my son and I did quit while I was pregnant but I was maintained on Methadone. I'm not sure I could have done it on my own but I was so excited and happy about having a baby and it was the one time that I really tried. I had dreams of being a mother and a wife, and even though I never married my kid's father, I did have visions of us being a family and raising our kids together. But that never really happened." Feeling a little emotional, she ended there.

They pulled off the highway into a rest area/picnic area; he pulled in and parked. Several other cars were there too with people walking the shoreline and enjoying the sunny day.

"Let's get out and walk in the sand for a while. Maybe because I'm from Southern California, I find it relaxing to walk in the sand and watch the waves. It's so powerful," Jim said, excited at the prospect of spending time at the ocean.

"Were you a surfer? I can totally see you as a surfer dude." Although laughing, it totally seemed plausible to her.

"Umm, somewhat. I did surf some but I didn't live at the beach surfing daily. I would have liked to but my parents wouldn't let me." Still pondering what she had told him, the mood seemed somewhat somber now.

He got out of the truck and stripped his sweatshirt off and sat down at the picnic table and pulled off his shoes and socks. "Come on, shoes off. You can't really appreciate this unless you walk barefoot in the sand."

Amanda sat down next to him and took her shoes and socks off. She contemplated taking her flannel shirt off. It really was too hot to wear long sleeves but she almost always kept her arms covered up. The track marks made her so self-conscious and although they had improved in the last month, they still were noticeable. In the end she decided to take it off. If he was truly her friend then he would have to accept that part of her and eventually he would see it anyhow. Watching her, he wondered what was going through her mind. He knew she was contemplating something, could tell by her hesitation but was clueless about what the problem was. It took several seconds before he noticed what she was always so careful to hide. Her eyes met his and she knew that he saw the black marks running up the veins on her arms. Although he recovered quickly she couldn't help but notice that brief look of shock that flashed across his face. Turning away quickly she stood watching the ocean. Her face felt hot and shame washed over her body. She was fighting hard not to cry but could feel tears welling up anyhow.

He walked up behind her, spun her around and put his arms around her. Nudging her face up towards his, their eyes met. "It's okay. I'm not judging you." Pulling her closer, he held her in his arms and at that point she lost the battle and tears started rolling down her cheeks. He held her for several minutes before the tears finally stopped and reaching up she started wiping them away with the back of her hand.

He had never really thought about it before. Although he had known from the beginning that she was addicted to opiates he had never really thought about what method she used them. The thought of this beautiful young woman sticking needles in her arms shocked him more than repelled him and at that moment he knew that he had fallen in love with her. Anything she had done before didn't matter. All he wanted, right then, was to reassure her that everything was going to be okay and if he could take the pain and shame away from her and bear if himself he would gladly do so.

He didn't know who was more surprised when he kissed her. It felt like he had lost all control and was powerless against it. She kissed him back, hesitantly at first but quickly she became hungry for more and they stood on the beach locked in a kiss for several minutes. She was the first to pull away and stood frozen for a minute looking at him. This was way out of her comfort zone and although it felt so good and so right, it also seemed surreal.

Jim looked embarrassed and uncomfortable. "I don't know what to say. I didn't plan that. It just kind of came out of nowhere." He wasn't sure if she was happy, mad, upset, fuming or what was going on in her head. She just stood there expressionless, looking at him in a way that was making him really uncomfortable.

"It's okay. It wasn't all you. I did kiss you back. I'm just a little surprised. That's all." She wanted to lighten the mood. She hated seeing him look so uncomfortable and unsure of himself. It wasn't natural for him. Walking towards him, Amanda put her arms around his neck and kissed him with all of the passion and bottled up emotion that she had been carrying around for months. This time he pulled away first. "Okay, now we're even," she said. Holding hands they started walking towards the waves.

They walked up the shoreline, holding hands. Both lost in their own thoughts, neither of them spoke. After about twenty minutes he motioned for her to sit against a piece of driftwood while they watched the waves coming in and going out.

Not able to handle the silence any longer he spoke first. "I don't know where that came from. Honestly, it wasn't planned and although I have suspected that I had feelings for you for a while now, I really had no intentions of making a move on you today."

Amanda turned towards him, grabbed his hand and looked in his eyes. "I'm glad you did. I've known for a long time that I was falling for you. But I don't know if you know what you're getting yourself into. I'm a mess and in the time that you have known me you have only seen the better side. But there's a whole lot more and I guess what surprises me the most is why? You are such an amazing person. You have a great life and I can see you with a teacher or counselor, you know, someone more like you, someone who has their life together. From your side, this just doesn't make sense to me. I don't know what I have to offer you. I'm a single mother of two kids. I'm a recovering heroin addict who hasn't even been clean for two months. Right now I don't know what kind of future I have. Don't know how long I'll stay clean. Don't know how I'm going to care for my kids. I have sold my soul more times than I can count just to get a fix. If you are smart you would run away from me as fast as possible and that's the truth."

"Like I said, it wasn't planned and I don't know why I'm so drawn to you, but I am. I feel like I have known you forever and even though I know what you're saying might be true, it just doesn't matter to me. Everyone makes mistakes. People turn their lives around every day. I know you can be the person that you want to be. Maybe you couldn't before and maybe it was just the pain and that is how you coped. But that was then. Now you have a chance to make a fresh start. The first thing you have to do is decide to forgive yourself. What's done is done and it's in the past. What I see when I look at you is a beautiful, kind, smart woman and that's all I see. So for now let's just take it one day at a time. Maybe this is going somewhere and maybe it won't but let's at least give it a chance," Jim told her with conviction. Everything he said was exactly what he felt and he only hoped that she understood what he was saying.

The rest of the day was lighter and she was grateful for that. She loved the restaurant that they ate at and was shocked that she didn't even know it existed. It had a beautiful view and after eating seafood that was cooked to perfection, they started back home. They kissed every chance they got and he wanted her like he had never wanted anyone before. But he didn't want to rush it. Besides, if he took her to his place there were too many time constraints. It was Sunday and she had to be back at the rehab by ten. Maybe next weekend she could get a weekend pass and stay all weekend with him. He would just have to wait.

That night she slept sound and truly felt happier than she had in her whole life. She felt like Cinderella and only hoped that it lasted.

Chapter Eight

Looking at the clock, Beverly wasn't surprised to see that it was four in the morning. This was the fourth night in a row that she had woke up in a panic, having the same recurring nightmare that left her unsettled and unable to sleep. Although the dream itself wasn't exactly clear, the general theme was the same. Images of family members that were now gone flashed in her dreams but with distorted faces. The ones of her son especially bothered her. At other times flashes of her daughter being carried on a stretcher played into the dream. Some of the time she looked dead and other times she would sit up on the stretcher holding her hands out towards her mother and crying in an unnatural, high pitched wail.

She got up, went to the bathroom and then walked down the hall to check on her grandkids. Covering each of them back up, she took a deep breath and walked back into her bedroom and turned the television on. Too early for the news, she opted for a silly old movie that she could watch mindlessly. Ever since waking up she felt disturbed and unsettled. Hopefully she would fall back asleep before too long. Since it was Saturday she could actually do that and the kids would normally sleep until nine on the weekend unless she woke them up earlier.

Sleep finally came again around five thirty and when she woke back up she was surprised that it was nine thirty. Deciding that she better check on the kids, she found them sitting on the couch watching television.

"Hey, good morning. How come no one came in and woke me up?" Beverly asked her grandchildren.

"We went in your room grandma but you were sleeping hard. Snoring even," Michael answered, in his teasing voice.

"Snoring. No way. I don't snore. You're just making that up," Beverly said, laughing at her grandson's observation.

Melanie looked up from the television. "You were, Gramma. You were snoring loud," she relayed to her grandma, in all seriousness.

"Well if you guys say so. Anyhow, I think I'm going to cook you two a big breakfast for letting me sleep in," Beverly said, as she walked towards the kitchen to make coffee.

Although she felt a little better, she was still tired and had just been feeling so blah lately. Maybe it was just middle age catching up with her or maybe stress. Whatever it was she felt that she was stuck in a rut and just couldn't shake the depressive mood that had been plaguing her lately.

"After breakfast, I think we are going to get ready and go visit Aunty Dee today," Beverly told the kids, knowing they would be excited. Aunty Dee was her mother's sister and the last one alive out of her mother's siblings. She was eighty-seven years old and even though she couldn't get around very good anymore, she had a sharp mind, was quick with her wit and outspoken with her opinions. Although she had married, she was never able to have children of her own so she filled that void with her nephews and nieces. They had all grown up especially close to Aunty Dee and she was the one that they always ran to for advice, love and comfort. Sometimes that came in the form of a lecture but at times that was needed too.

Before cooking breakfast Beverly started a fire in the woodstove. The house was cold and now that it was November she needed to keep a fire going most of the time. That was the hardest part of winter for her. Without a man in the house or at least an older boy, she had to worry about buying wood, splitting it, cutting kindling and starting fires. The house really didn't have any other source of heat. She had bought a couple of space heaters but they only warmed the immediate area and if she left them on for very long her electricity bill would go sky high. The cost of buying wood really put a strain on her financially and her only hope was that someday she could get a kerosene stove.

Once the house was warm and everyone had eaten a big breakfast it was hard to think about leaving. It was a gray, dreary day and looked like it could start raining anytime. But she hadn't been up to see her aunt for a while and knew that once she made the effort she would be glad that she had.

It took until almost noon to get the kids and herself ready and on their way. Her aunt lived on the other end of the Valley and up the creek and it only took about ten minutes to get to her house. Beverly had called her aunt the day before and let her know that they would be dropping by.

When they pulled into the driveway, one lone shaggy dog came running to the car to greet them. It was a mutt and must have been around 70 years old in dog years but it was Aunty Dee's baby and constant companion.

"Boomer," Michael called out. "Come here boy." The dog ran over to Michael and waited for him to pat his head. Melanie hung back. Even though she had been around Boomer several times, she was somewhat timid and scared around dogs; especially big dogs like Boomer.

Seeing the scared look in her eyes, Beverly swung her up in her arms and carried her towards the house. "It's alright, Mel. You know grandma isn't going to let anything hurt you."

The door swung open and Aunty Dee peeked her head through the door. She had shrunk with age and if she reached 5 foot now; that would probably be a stretch.

"Hi Aunty. I'm so glad we got to come up today. I've missed you so much." Reaching up she gave her aunt a hug and swung Melanie down on the floor. "Kids, tell Aunty Dee 'hello.' "

Both kids murmured a "hello" and then ran into the living room.

Following the kids inside, Aunty Dee scooped up a box out of the kitchen and carried it into the living room behind them. "Guess what kids? I have a project for you. I need this box of acorns cracked. I have a couple of little hammers ready and after I lay some newspaper on the floor, I will show you how to crack them. If you get this whole box done, I'm going to give you a dollar each for helping me."

"That's nice of you, Aunty, but you don't have to pay them. They should do it just because you need it done and I'm sure they would be glad to help you. Right kids?" Beverly said in a tone that didn't leave any room for argument.

"That's right, Aunty. You don't have to pay us," Michael said, trying to hide the disappointment in his voice.

"I know that I don't have to but I want to. Someday maybe I won't have anything to give you for helping me but today I do and I want to give you something for helping your old aunty out," Aunty Dee said, smiling down at the kids, whose faces immediately brightened.

While Aunty Dee spread newspaper out on the floor and showed the kids how to crack acorns, Beverly walked around the living room. It looked the same now as it did when she was a little girl. Every corner was filled with projects. One corner had a big storage shelf full of basket materials. After years and years of gathering, the shelves were jam-packed and sagging from the weight. Coffee cans lined the shelves, filled with willow sticks and roots, bear grass, maidenhair fern, yellow moss and porcupine quills. Everything was meticulously sorted by size and organized in a way that the rest of the house wasn't.

Having gathered with her aunt when she was younger, she appreciated all the work that it took to have a supply that big. On one shelf were tubs to fill with water for soaking the materials and then projects at various stages. There was one baby basket started, several medallions in various stages and one tobacco pouch that was almost finished.

On the other wall were all of her quilting materials. Yards and yards of materials, scissors, a quilting hoop, batting, thread and everything that a person would need to make a quilt. The sewing machine was set up away from the wall and aimed so that Aunty Dee could watch television while she sewed. Knowing her aunt so well, Bev knew that she never missed her afternoon soap operas and had been watching them since probably they were first aired.

Beverly let out a sigh of regret, wishing that she had learned these skills when she was young. She had plenty of time then and opportunity but no interest. And now at almost 50 she regretted not learning more and wished she had paid more attention. She knew some of the basics but hadn't really practiced enough to truly master the art.

"Come on dear. I have a pot of tea made for us and I thought we could sit in the kitchen and visit while the kids are busy." Aunty Dee was excited to have company. Most days she spent alone and loved to have someone to talk to and visit.

"Okay, Aunty. It's a perfect day for tea, isn't it?" Beverly sat down at the kitchen table and rubbed her hand on the oil linen tablecloth. Always proper, her Aunty, and while the house was somewhat disheveled there were always the little touches like tablecloths and flowers on the table.

"So what is going on? You look tired and I can always take one look at you and know when something is wrong. Ever since you were a little girl, your face and expressions are like an open book," Aunty Dee asked, concern showing in her eyes.

"Well, yeah. I'm a little tired, I guess. For the last two months things have really been a lot better and I keep thinking that I should feel better too; happier, you know. But I just feel so depressed and in a rut and I can't break out of it. I feel this impending doom and I'm having a hard time finding joy in anything right now." Then in detail, Beverly told her aunt about the recurring nightmares that she had been having. "I wake up the same time, around four every morning and the dreams bother my soul. It takes me a long time to go back to sleep, if I do at all."

"Well honey, I've been on this Earth for a long time. Sometimes I think too long but the one observation that I do have is that drugs are going to be the end of us, if something doesn't happen soon. Alcohol was bad enough and we certainly lost a lot of people to that. But what is going on now, with the younger generations and drugs, is breaking everyone down. You've got grandmothers and sometimes great-grandmothers raising little kids while the parents are getting high. Nobody respects anyone anymore. People will steal from their own family to get high. It's like it robs these young people of their soul and all they think about or care about is drugs. I believe that your house is full of negative energy right now. You had so many problems with Amanda, for so long and even though she isn't there anymore, all of the negative spirits and energy are still in your house. I'm going to give you some root and when you get home you need to burn the root and pray. Smudge your house and get rid of all of the bad that is in it. I'm fairly certain that your nightmares will stop after that but if not then I think we should ask the Shakers to come to your house and pray and get rid of the evil." Aunty Dee had seen this happen before.

"I haven't really thought of that, Aunty, but you're right. When I think about it now there does seem to be a negative atmosphere." Beverly hoped that her aunt was right. It would be so good to get a good night's sleep and feel some peace in her soul, something that she hadn't felt in a long, long time.

"Now as for you.... I think some of the problem is that for years you have put your life on hold and have lived from one crisis to the next. All of your energy and time has been spent on Amanda and all of her problems, demands, issues, threats, all of it. And even before that you had your husband to deal with. I won't speak ill of the man since he is dead now but the reality is that he didn't treat you good either. Now you have been raising grandchildren and honestly you haven't really had any life of your own. For the moment things are better but you're so worn out and beat down that you don't even know how to enjoy it. Tell me, Bev, when is the last time that you have actually done anything for yourself?" Aunty Dee asked.

"I don't really know. Too long to even remember, I guess. I've just felt so tired and well hopeless and I don't even know where to start anymore. I feel like I've gotten older and life has just passed me by. It seems that I have been operating on survival mode for longer than I can remember." Beverly voice cracked and she was trying hard not to cry.

"Of course you have dear. You are a survivor; I know that. And I know how truly bad it has been. From where you sit, you think you're older now and have lost out on opportunities. But from my perspective, you are young and have a lot of living left to do. You need to start being kind to yourself. I know that you blame yourself for the problems in your kid's life and you have done your best to fix it but your kids are older now. They are not babies and they made their own choices. That's not your fault and you don't have to feel responsible for their mistakes," Aunty Dee told her niece gently, but firmly. Her niece had always been such a kind person but often had the tendency to let her family walk all over her.

Beverly mulled this over for a minute. "I guess I do feel guilty. I just think that if I had provided them more security and sheltered them more from the abuse that their father dished out then maybe things would have turned out differently. Even with Ashley. She's successful on the surface, but she can be so cold and callous. I'm sure it's just self-protection but she seems so hard."

"Maybe, although I suspect that it is all a cover and one day it will come to a head. She'll be all right in the end. She's smart and driven. We have always known that she will do well in life. And Amanda, well I think that she will be okay in the end too. She has taken a rough path but now she's doing well and while she is not as driven as her sister, she is smart and caring and she'll make it. But then that leaves you. And it is time that you start figuring out the life you want and then going for it. Life is too short to have regrets and living in the past isn't really living at all," Aunty Dee said, voice trailing off.

"You're right Aunty. You always are. I knew I would feel better after talking to you. You always have a way of cutting through the nitty gritty and getting to the heart of the matter. So I was wondering about Thanksgiving. I was thinking about having a big dinner at my house. I am hoping that both of the girls can come up. And then you, Ben and really any of the family that wants to come. I think it would be a good distraction right now and would give me something to focus on." Beverly had been thinking about this for a while and until now hadn't really committed to the idea but the more that she thought about it the more she liked it.

"I think that sounds good, Beverly. I'll make the pies. That way you can just concentrate on the dinner. Plus I know that you're not really into baking pies." Aunty Dee said, pleased that her niece was going to host Thanksgiving this year.

"Yes, you are right. I just never had the knack like you and Mom. By the way, who are you making a baby basket for?" Beverly asked, knowing that her aunt never really made baby baskets anymore unless someone in the family was having a baby.

"Oh that's for Jessie. You know Larry's daughter. She's not due until February but I decided to get a head start on it. My hands aren't as strong as they use to be so it takes me longer than it used to. That and my eyes," Aunty Dee answered, glancing towards the kids in the living room, checking their progress.

"Little Jessie? Wow. I didn't know that she was old enough to have kids?" Beverly hadn't seen her for a while but last time she had seen her she was still a very young girl, or so she had thought.

"She's young. She'll turn seventeen in January. But she has a lot of support from her family and the dad's family, " Aunt Dee explained.

"I really wish that I would have paid more attention and done more with basketry. I really regret now that I didn't try harder, you know, when you and mom tried to get me interested in weaving," Beverly said, wishfully.

"Well it's not too late, you know. As a matter of fact it might actually help you to feel better about things. Working on a basket is therapeutic in a lot of ways. If you want, you can start coming up once a week or on the weekend and we can work on it. You can come up more but I know that's not easy with the kids right now." Aunty Dee was actually glad that she showed interest now and it would give her company, too.

"I would love that, Aunty. Wednesdays might work out, as a matter of fact. I could probably ask the kid's other grandmother to keep them from the time school gets out at three, until I pick them up around eight-thirty or nine. I probably won't be able to start until after Thanksgiving but I definitely want to do this." She felt excited at the prospect and happy to have something to look forward to.

The afternoon went by fast but by five she knew it was time to get the kids home and start dinner. By now the fire was probably out and the house would be cold if they got home too late. Before they said their good byes, Aunty Dee handed her a piece of root, "tonight burn root and pray. Walk around in each room with it. This will get rid of the bad and hopefully you will be able to sleep all night again. No more nightmares. Call me next week so we can make all the final plans for Thanksgiving."

When they got home, not feeling like cooking a big dinner, Beverly threw a frozen pizza in the oven. While the kids watched TV, she lit her root and walked through all of the rooms, praying, just as her aunt had told her to do. She loved the smell and felt more at peace when she had finished.

That night she slept soundly through the night and woke up at seven feeling well rested and refreshed. She took out her notebook and pen and started making a list for Thanksgiving Dinner. After years of holiday drama, she knew this year could be different and she hoped that this year they would have a normal, calm, Thanksgiving dinner.

Chapter Nine

Jim was distracted more than he was comfortable with this week. Time seemed to be going at a snail's pace and he just wished that the week would be over. After talking to Amanda they had decided that she was going to try to get a weekend pass and stay with him. He was used to being in better control of his feelings but at this point was feeling impatient. Maybe the fact that he hadn't been with a woman for several months had something to do with it.

After much debate they had decided to keep their budding romance from anyone at the rehab. He thought that they should just face it head on and let Rayna and the other staff know that she was going to spend the weekend with him. "After all, everyone is suspecting that something is going on anyhow, so why keep it a secret. We are two consenting adults," Jim said, trying to persuade her.

"I understand that but believe me, staff at the rehab will frown upon it. Number one, they openly discourage rehab residents from getting into any relationship for at least the first year of sobriety. They believe it will lower the chance of remaining clean and sober. And second, you're a tutor here and I don't want to be responsible for you losing your job here." Amanda was just as adamant and knew that there would be repercussions if they found out.

"Okay. But you do know that I volunteer here, right? I don't get paid for the time that I'm here so it's not like I'd be losing my job. I have a real job. If I have to quit to be with you, then so be it." On this point he was adamant. He really didn't feel like he needed anyone's approval of his feelings towards her.

"Well, let's see how this weekend goes. Maybe after this weekend you will decide that you don't even like me. Then what's the point? They would lose a tutor for nothing. I'm just saying to give it a little time, that's all," Amanda said, wondering how someone so smart, could be so naive.

"Really? You think I won't like you after this weekend? Are you that bad?" He said jokingly, trying to lighten the mood a little.

"Maybe," She said, laughing. "I don't even know anymore."

"Well there's not much chance of that. But if you want to keep this private until after the weekend then I will go along with that. But then we tell them. I'm not going to sneak around like a little kid or somebody who has something to hide," Jim said.

During the next week while he was at the rehab tutoring, their contact was limited. After all she had already taken the GED test and without knowing whether she had passed or not there wasn't much point to keep studying for it. They were so comfortable together when they were alone or away but now when he came by the rehab it felt awkward. She was trying to act indifferent and blasé towards him but it felt so unnatural.

On Wednesday when he came at three, she was waiting out front for him.

"Do you think I could use your cell phone for a little while? I want to call my mom and check on her and my kids." She had run out of calling cards and didn't want to call collect. She knew her mom had limited finances and it didn't seem fair to put more of a burden on her. Besides, there really was no privacy to talk in the office.

"Sure. Talk as long as you want," he said, reaching in his pocket and handing her his phone.

Walking out to the back she dialed her mom who still had one of those little prepaid Verizon phones with a flip top. It served its purpose, she guessed, since her mom wasn't really one to get on Facebook or the Internet but she had been trying to get her to upgrade for months now. She would have preferred to wait until evening and call her on the home phone but Jim would be leaving before her mom got off of work.

"Hello." Her mom answered on the fifth ring.

"Hi Mom. I was starting to think that you weren't going to answer. Do you have a minute to talk?" Knowing that her mom was still at work, she hoped that it was a good time to call.

"Hi, honey. I can take a break and talk a minute. Whose phone are you on?" Beverly asked.

"This is Jim's phone. He's the tutor here that you met when you came over," Amanda quickly explained.

"Oh yes. I remember him. I almost didn't answer because I didn't recognize the number. I thought it was a bill collector or something." Although they both laughed, they both also knew the truth in that.

"How's Michael and Melanie?" she asked.

"They are good. We went to Aunty Dee's last weekend and they cracked a box of acorns for her. They had a good day up there. I'm so glad you called. I've wanted to talk to you about Thanksgiving. I'm going to host the family dinner this year and I'm really hoping that you and Ashley can make it. I was thinking that I could either buy you a bus ticket or if Ashley is coming, ask her if she could pick you up. It would only be about a half hour out of her way," her mom paused a minute, waiting for an answer.

"I have been thinking about coming home for Thanksgiving. I'm not sure about riding with Ashley though, Mom. She really doesn't like me and I'm pretty sure she isn't going to go out of her way to pick me up." She felt sad about her and her sister's relationship but she had gotten over it a long time ago. Ashley was such a bitch to the whole world and didn't seem to have any feelings towards family.

"Well, it wouldn't hurt to ask and of course she loves you. She's your sister. You know Ashley. That's just her." Beverly really couldn't defend Ashley much. Everyone in the family thought of her as mean and uptight. But they just accepted that about her and tried not to cross her.

"I haven't asked for a pass yet but I'm pretty sure it will be okay. I'll call you early next week and let you know for sure if I can come and I'll check the bus schedules in the meantime. How's Uncle, by the way? I had a dream about him last night. I don't really remember what the dream was about but I woke up thinking about him." Amanda didn't add that the dream was disturbing, although she wasn't sure why.

"He's okay but he's just getting over a cold so he stayed away for a few days. He must be feeling better because I saw him downtown earlier and he invited himself to dinner tonight," Beverly answered, noticing her supervisor walking towards her open door.

"Well, he must be getting better if his appetite is back." Smiling, thinking about her Uncle, it hit her how homesick she was getting.

"Well, babe, I better get off. I've got someone walking in my office. Be sure to call me next week though so we have time to figure out your ride home and back. Love you." Beverly quickly hung up before Amanda could answer and put her phone in her purse, not wanting to get a write up for taking personal calls at work.

Amanda hung up and all of the sudden was looking forward to Thanksgiving. This was the first year that her mom had hosted the family dinner in a long time. She couldn't really remember the last time but decided that it must have been six or seven years ago because it was when Michael was a baby.

Sitting outside, finishing her cigarette, she wondered how much of that had to do with her. Alcohol, drugs and holidays don't mix very well and usually brought out the worst in everybody. For herself, she hadn't really enjoyed the holidays for a long time and suddenly was looking forward to it.

The rest of the week was uneventful. Amanda had settled into a routine at the rehab but often was bored. There were only so many meetings that she could attend during the week and trying to find something to do the rest of the time was becoming increasingly difficult. There were always chores that were required at the rehab but even those didn't take more than an hour a day. Many times she felt restless and while she could leave during the day, without money there weren't many places to go.

On Thursday afternoon she filled out a pass request and took it into Rayna. She was requesting a forty-eight hour pass, from Friday at five to Sunday at five. She hesitated on the line asking where she would be during this time. While not wanting to lie about it, she still thought it was better not to let them know that she would be staying at Jim's.

"So your request states that you're going to stay at a friend's house this weekend. Is that local or out of the area?" Rayna asked, while still scanning the request.

"It's local. Just with a friend. And I'm going to be requesting a pass during Thanksgiving also. My mom is hosting a family Thanksgiving dinner this year and I am really hoping to go home and be there to help her with stuff." Amanda felt nervous under Rayna's stare. Feeling like she could see right through her, her hands started sweating and her heart started racing. When she was high she could lie her ass off but now it was hard and while she wasn't exactly lying, she was trying to avoid any prying or directly asked questions about where she would be staying.

"So is this friend Jim?" Rayna asked, hoping that they really didn't think that she was that stupid.

Not making eye contact, Amanda froze momentarily. She didn't really want to answer but now that it was out there point blank, she didn't have much choice. "Uh huh," she answered, her voice not much more than a whisper.

"Well, I was suspecting that maybe there was something going on but wasn't really sure. I don't know what to say except that I really can't give you an answer right now. I would like to talk to Jim and think about this first. I'll let you know by tomorrow morning." Rayna wasn't really sure what to do in this situation. This was the first time that she had come across something of this nature and was more than a little unsure of how to handle it.

Leaving the office Amanda felt more than a little disappointed although she expected this type of reaction. It was a hard realization that staff had final say and could basically deny her request and the ramifications that might be placed on Jim actually bothered her more than anything else. Wishing again that she had a cell phone, she would have liked to warn him or at least give him a heads up so that he knew what was coming.

Going into her room, she heard Rayna shut the office door and knew that she was probably calling Jim. She was right and within thirty minutes he pulled up outside and went into Rayna's office, firmly shutting the door. The brief glimpse of him showed a man with a determined look on his face but instead of looking upset, as she had expected, he looked somewhat calm and amused.

"Well, as I told you on the phone, I have a request for a weekend pass from Amanda to apparently stay the weekend with you," Rayna explained. "I haven't really come across this situation before so I am a little at a loss on what I should do. Those of us who are paid staff, here at the rehab, sign clauses when we start working here that we will not get involved in any type of staff/client relationship. Apparently because you are volunteer staff that was never done and except for the agreement for us to perform a background check on you, we really don't have any other paperwork done. So I guess I would just like to appeal to your better judgment and ask if you really understand what you are getting yourself into?"

The look on Jim's face was mixed with amusement and disbelief. "I appreciate what you're saying but I'm a grown ass man, perfectly capable of looking out for my best interests. Sorry if I'm coming off sarcastic but it's not like I'm in some perverted affair with one of my middle school students. Amanda and I are both consenting adults. Yes, I happen to be a tutor here and yes, she happens to be a resident here and in the process of working together we have developed feelings for each other. Plain and simple."

"It's not really a legal or moral issue that I'm trying to press here. We really stress to the residents, if they are not in a relationship when they enter rehab, to not develop one when they are here. Honestly, we encourage them to steer clear of relationships for at least one year after becoming clean. And for a very good reason. It's a lot harder to stay clean, than to get clean. Let's say that after a few weeks you both decide that this isn't working. Or let's say that in a few weeks or even months you decide that this isn't working. The first thing that she is going to do is start using again, self-medicating for whatever pain that she might feel if the relationship doesn't go well." Rayna was trying hard to keep calm and talk in low tones but frustration was showing on her face.

"Okay, I understand what you're saying. But the problem is that we are past that. We have already started a relationship and I think that we are both too far in to stop now. I have real feelings for Amanda. I didn't expect this to happen; didn't plan it; but it happened and whether she gets a pass this weekend or not, in the end we will be together." His face had softened somewhat. Some of the things that Rayna said did make sense but he couldn't change how he felt.

"Okay. I'm going to go ahead and grant her request. I can only do so much to help our residents succeed. I just hope that you will educate yourself on addiction and recovery. There's a really dark side that goes along with addiction that I'm not sure you understand. How would you feel to know that the woman you care for has maybe been involved in theft, robberies or given head to the local dealer for a bag? Not pretty things but believe me not uncommon in the drug world. And when you look at the statistics for a recovering addict to remain clean, well it's not very high, especially when the addiction is to heroin." Rayna hated to put such a negative spin on the whole situation but she wanted him to understand what he was getting into.

"I don't know as much as you do about it. I will be the first to admit that. And no, I haven't thought about the ugly things that you are talking about. But what I do know is that addiction is a disease. So whatever has happened in the past, the good, the bad and the ugly, I'm not going to hold it against her. Amanda's a good person; smart, funny, kind. That's basically what I see when I look at her. So thanks for the advice but I'm going to take my chances," Jim replied. He was done with this conversation and his tone reflected that.

"Okay. Well, I've done my part. And good luck. I mean that with all sincerity. You're a nice guy who obviously cares about people. And she's a nice person too. There really is a kindness and gentleness about her. I hope that you both find happiness with each other. But I'm done with the lectures." She still had her concerns but she hoped that he wouldn't find those out first hand. The movie "Pretty Woman" flashed in her head and she hoped that maybe Amanda would be the Cinderella of rehab. Closing the door after he walked out, she laughed to herself at her analogies.

Jim walked into the main room and found Amanda standing by the table, looking worried and upset. He felt bad that she had let herself get so worked up about this. But she was at the mercy of the rehab, whereas he wasn't. "It's fine," he told her, in a whispered tone. "You don't have to worry, she's approving it."

"Okay." She wanted to know more and ask him what they had discussed, but she knew that now wasn't the time and there were other residents nearby. She took a deep breath and her body visibly relaxed.

"I'll see you tomorrow. Have a good night," Jim told her, before heading back out to his car and leaving.

After Jim left, Amanda went to her room. Now that her pass was approved the reality of staying with him for the weekend started sinking in. While she was excited about the prospect, all of the sudden she felt really nervous about it too. Self-doubts started plaguing her. She hadn't really been with anyone, in a sober state anyhow, in years. Having sex with someone when you're high and having sex with someone you care about, when you're straight, was completely different and she knew it. The latter was much better but also took a lot more thought and planning. The former was never planned, it just happened and usually in a way when good judgment wasn't part of the equation.

After dinner she read a book until she got tired enough to fall asleep. She had already decided that she would pack her bag tomorrow. It was going to be a long day and she needed all the distractions possible. That night she dreamed of her uncle again but like the last dream there was nothing really concrete that she could remember about it. Only the conscious thought that she had dreamed of him when she woke up.

At home, her mom was picking up the phone to call Ashley. She knew with her oldest daughter, everything was in the timing and calling in the evening, after she was home from work and had time to relax for a little while, was usually the best time.

"Hello," Ashley answered.

"Hi, Ash, it's Mom. How was your day?" Not wanting to dive right in, Beverly thought she would make small talk first.

"Long, but okay. Is everything okay?" Ashley wasn't used to getting calls from her mom for no reason.

"Everything is fine. I just wanted to talk to you about Thanksgiving. So this year I'm going to host the family dinner and I'm hoping that you can come up." Beverly had dived in faster than planned.

"Are you sure you want to host the dinner? That sounds like a lot of work and then there is the usual holiday drama with some of the family.

I just wonder why you would want to put yourself through that." Ashley could think of a million other things that she would like to do on Thanksgiving rather than go home.

"I just think it would be a nice thing to do. In the past there was always so much going on with Amanda and all of her b.s. And this year things are better so I would like to host the dinner. And I haven't had a turn in a long time, which hasn't been fair to Aunt Sally or Aunt Millie. And Uncle is really glad that I'm hosting it and specifically said he hoped that both you and Amanda would come." She knew Ashley would have a hard time saying no if her uncle wanted her to come. It was like bringing in the "big guns" and she knew it but that was how bad she wanted this to happen.

"Well, if I come up it would only be for the day," Ashley relented. "I took on some extra shifts at the nursing home during the holidays so I would have to be back out here on Thursday night." Ashley guessed it wouldn't hurt to come up for one day. Besides she really wanted to see Aunty Dee and Uncle Ben. They were her favorites and she missed them.

Taking a deep breath, Beverly went on. "So I was also trying to coordinate a ride for Amanda to come up too. Maybe you could bring her up with you and then we can figure out another ride for her on Sunday?"

"I'd rather not. I'd be happy to buy a bus ticket for her but I don't really want to drive to the rehab, pick her up and then ride with her all the way to Hoopa. Sorry, Mom, but I can't do that. You know we haven't really talked since our blow up and I'm not going out of my way to do her any favors until she apologizes to me. I will buy her a ticket though if you need me to." Ashley felt like that was more than fair and didn't give much more thought about it.

"Okay. Well, I will call you next week and give you a better time frame of when we're eating," Beverly said, knowing better than to push Ashley in to giving her sister a ride. As a matter of fact, she knew that if she pushed too hard, Ashley would end up not coming and Beverly only hoped that when she got there and saw the positive changes in Amanda that she would come around and maybe soften a little.

"Okay. Bye Mom. See you next week." Ashley hung up the phone. She guessed it would be good to go home and see the family. She wasn't much of a holiday person; too many years of drama had taken its toll. Thinking back to her youth, she couldn't remember a holiday where her dad or one of her family members hadn't gotten drunk and acted up. Oh well. That was the past and she wasn't going to dwell on that anymore.

Chapter Ten

Amanda woke up Friday morning feeling sick to her stomach. Anxiety was running high and she was having serious doubts about the weekend. She still didn't understand why Jim was interested in her and although she really liked him and was genuinely attracted to him, she was scared that she was going to blow it somehow and he was going to drop her like a hot potato.

It took a while to decide what to wear and pack her bag. She was in serious need of some new clothes. Everything just looked old and dingy and she had worn it a thousand times before. More than that, she wished that she had some new, cute underwear, bras and something decent to sleep in. All she slept in was sweats and big t-shirts and somehow that just didn't seem like the right attire for this weekend.

After everything was packed and she had cleaned her room, it was only ten o'clock. Needing something to keep her occupied for the next seven hours, Amanda went into the study room and started pulling out art supplies. In one bin were some beads, beading needles, thread and leather. She hadn't beaded in years and wondered if she still knew how. Deciding that she would make a keychain for her uncle she picked out black and red beads and started rolling her leather. She didn't have the keychain ring but knew that she could find one of those at home. Surprisingly it came back to her very fast and by three o'clock when Jim came in for tutoring she was over half way done.

"Hey. How are you doing? That's beautiful. I didn't know you could bead." Not really waiting for an answer, he gave her a wink and walked into the study room.

She watched him from the next room and was amazed and a little dismayed at how calm and self -assured he was while she on the other hand was having an agonizing day. "Typical man," she muttered to herself. Gathering up her supplies she put them in her room and went into the bathroom and started packing toiletries that she might need over the weekend. She had taken a long shower earlier, shaving her legs, underarms and last minute grooming.

Going back into the main room she could hear the conversation going on in the study room. He was working with two of the residents and she could hear him giving them instructions and all of them laughing and joking around. She knew that some of the residents mistook his friendliness for flirting. Being in an all- female institution, they all craved and vied for his attention when he was present. There was a time, when she would have been jealous but she felt secure in a strange way that she didn't quite understand.

After a long day it was finally five o'clock and as he gathered up his paperwork and laptop, she went into her room and grabbed her bag and met him outside in the parking lot. As soon as he unlocked the car door she jumped in the passenger side and threw her bag in the back seat. Jim slid into the driver's seat, looked sideways at her and gave her a big smile. "So it's finally Friday. I don't know about you but for me it's been the longest week of my life."

"Yeah. I agree with you on that." At this point she just wanted to get this first time over. She had never been more nervous in her life and the anticipation was just making it worse.

"You look so nervous. You're not having second thoughts are you?" The last thing he wanted was for her to feel like she was being forced into something. While he would be severely disappointed if she had changed her mind, he would have accepted it and given her more time.

"No. Not really. I'm just feeling really nervous. I just want this to be perfect for you, I guess, and I'm a little afraid of disappointing you." She felt dumb for saying it, but it was the truth.

"Seriously, you don't have anything to worry about. I don't think there is anything that you could do that would disappoint me." He loved that part of her; she was somehow naïve and innocent and at the same time had a vulnerability that made him feel extremely protective of her. He had been with other women in his life; ones that had been important to him too, but had never felt about them what he was feeling for her.

His place was about three miles from the rehab and although it wasn't exactly beach front, it was overlooking the ocean. It wasn't a very big house but it was really cute and she immediately loved it. After parking the car, he grabbed her bag and led her up the walkway to the front door. He unlocked the door, flipped on the lights and motioned her to come in. "Be it ever so humble, there's no place like home." He wrapped both arms around her and kissed her long and hard. "Sorry, but I couldn't wait any longer. Now I'll give you a tour."

Inside the front door was the living room. She was surprised how well decorated it was and had pictured him living in more of a bachelor pad. But he had actually fixed the place up very nice. There was a comfortable looking sectional couch with lamps on either side. On the wall was a big screen television. Some nice pictures hung on the walls and the front window had floor length drapes.

Further on was a long dining room that led into the kitchen. The kitchen was spotless and had all modern appliances, a tile floor and cabinets that were painted white. The dining room had a high table with four stools, one on each side and a matching hutch against the wall. The hutch looked like it served as a desk at times with paperwork and mail neatly piled on it. Off of the living room was a door that led to a bathroom, which again was clean and super organized. Next to the bathroom was another door that had stairs that led to the next level. At the top of the stairs was an open room that was the one bedroom in the house. It was a big room with a large window that looked straight out over the ocean. There was a big lounging chair, facing the window and she could imagine him sitting in it, watching the ocean. There was a high, big bed in the center, a big chest of drawers, a hamper and some assorted weights in the corner. Through a door on the opposite side there was a big master bathroom with a huge bathtub and a separate shower with glass doors.

"Oh my God," she gushed. "I love this bathroom and the tub is so big." She was in complete awe of his house but the bathroom, by far, impressed her the most. Everything looked so clean and was in its proper place. It looked like a home on a television show. There didn't seem to be clutter anywhere. "I love your house. It's not what I expected."

"What do you mean? What did you expect?" he asked curiously, as he sat her bag down on the bed.

"I don't know exactly but I guess that I thought it would be more like a bachelor pad or a man cave. You know, maybe messy with dirty dishes in the sink and cluttered. Some empty beer cans sitting around or poster girls hanging on the walls."

"Well, that might have been true in my college days I guess, but I outgrew that a while ago. But thanks. I'm glad that you like it. Do you want something to drink or are you hungry? I didn't even think about stopping and getting food."

Walking towards him with a mischievous look in her eyes, she replied, "Hmm. I'm hungry all right. Starving as a matter of fact." Wrapping both arms around him, her mouth met his with the hunger that had been pent up for a long time. They stood there making out for quite some time. He didn't want to ravish her all at once and he wanted to savor every second of their first time together. Plus, something told him that he needed to take things slow and even though she had advanced on him first, he could feel the nervous energy emanating from her body.

Lowering her to the bed, he started slowly undressing her. Their eyes locked and he slowly started kissing her while fumbling hurriedly to get out of his own clothes. What started out slow and controlled soon turned fast and frantic. He felt like he had waited a lifetime for her and now was impatient to have all of her, to himself. Sex with him was by far the best she had ever had and being straight and clear-headed made it that much better.

Afterwards, lying entwined in each other's arm, neither spoke for a few minutes. They were both lost in their contented state and nothing seemed awkward about the long pause of silence. He was the first to speak, "so for the record, you didn't disappoint me at all. Just saying."

Smiling, she laughed and answered, "I'm glad. You didn't disappoint me either. As a matter of fact, just the opposite." Shifting her head on his shoulder so that she could see his face, she continued. "Seriously, you were amazing. I really didn't know sex could be so good."

"I aim to please, but really don't give all the credit to me. You were pretty wonderful yourself." Reaching over and kissing her, the atmosphere was happy and relaxed.

Lying in bed, talking and making out for another hour, he was the first to get up to walk towards the bathroom. "So we haven't talked about dinner yet. I don't know if you're hungry but I am starving and if I'm going to keep my strength and stamina up this weekend, I'm going to have to have some fuel."

Not lost on his innuendoes she laughed. "Well, we better get some food in you then and lots of it because you definitely are going to need to keep up your strength and stamina this weekend." She loved his sense of humor and they easily joked around together.

"So what are you hungry for? Do you want to get dressed and go out or bring something back? I'm open for suggestions," Jim asked, walking back out of the bathroom.

"How about having a pizza delivered?" Amanda suggested. "The thought of getting up and going somewhere right now sounds dreadful."

"Wow. I like how you think. Pizza it is. What kind do you like?" It hit him that as close as they had become there was still so much he didn't know about her. Like her favorite pizza.

"It doesn't really matter. I like pepperoni, combination or Hawaiian. I'm not really picky when it comes to pizza. It's kind of a treat. We don't have pizza parlors in Hoopa so we only usually eat it once in a while when we go out to the Coast, which isn't all that often." Amanda explained.

"Okay, well let's order half pepperoni and half Hawaiian. And a couple of salads and bread sticks," Jim said, trying to remember what else they had that he could order.

"Aw, you are hungry. Poor baby," Amanda said, with emphasized sarcasm.

Sitting on the edge of the bed he looked up the number to his favorite pizza place on his phone and placed an order. "I am hungry. I worked hard today, teaching ungrateful brats. Then I had some extracurricular activities to take care of this evening." Laying back down he pulled her towards him.

"Oh, is that what this is called? " Laughing she started planting kisses all over his face. "How much time do we have before the pizza comes?" she asked.

"They said it would be about thirty minutes. Why? Are you in a hurry for something?" He asked, eyeing her hungrily.

"Well, I was thinking about that big bathtub you have and how good it would feel to soak in a hot bubble bath." She loved hot baths and the thought of soaking in that big tub was more and more inviting.

"That sounds like a good idea. Maybe as soon as the pizza is delivered I'll join you," he offered.

Sitting up in the bed she started looking around for her clothes. He was so comfortable walking around naked in front of her. She wasn't there yet and suddenly felt overwhelmingly modest and her mind started racing trying to figure out how she was going to get from the bed to the bathroom.

"Is something wrong? I thought you were going to take a bath." Turning to look at her he wondered if she had changed her mind.

"Okay, this is going to sound really stupid but I don't think I can get up and walk around naked in front of you." She laughed when she said it but he had already learned to recognize the difference between her real laugh and her nervous laugh.

"Seriously? I mean I just had my hands and mouth on just about every part of your body and now you're shy about being naked in front of me." He was shaking his head in mocked disbelief but actually he found it cute and endearing.

"I know. I'm sorry. I told you it was stupid. I flunked gym because I refused to dress down or shower in front of people," Amanda explained, looking away, still feeling embarrassed about the whole thing.

Standing up, Jim walked to the closet and retrieved a robe hanging from a hook. He held it out to her and turned around while she stood up and wrapped it around herself. Turning back around he gave her a quick kiss. "You don't have to be sorry. I want you to be comfortable. I tend to be somewhat of a nudist at home but it's okay if you're not. No worries, okay?"

"Okay." Her voice was barely a whisper. "Thanks." Walking over to her bag, she pulled out a bottle of vanilla-scented bubble bath, a cami shirt and a pair of panties. That was about the best she could come up with in the way of sexy lingerie but it was by far better than the old comfy gray sweats and oversized t-shirt that she usually slept in.

She walked into the bathroom and started a hot bath, pouring bubble bath under the running water. Noticing a candle on the back of the toilet, along with a book of matches, she lit the candle and turned the light off. She pulled her hair up in a bun on the top of her head, stepped out of the robe and into the hot, bubbly water.

It was the biggest bathtub that she had ever been in and she absolutely loved it. She turned off the water and lay back in the tub and let out a deep breath. As her body started relaxing, the door opened and Jim walked in.

"I was just going to tell you that the pizza is here, but wow, that looks so inviting. I haven't really used the bathtub often and never with bubbles," Jim told her, waiting for an invitation.

"Are you kidding me? I think I could live in this bathtub. As a matter of fact I might not leave it all weekend. Come on in, the water is great," Amanda answered, motioning for him to join her.

"Oh, really. Well, you would turn into a prune if you lived in the bath." Slipping off his shorts he stepped into the bath, and positioned himself behind her. Lying back against him, his arms circled around her. "This is really nice though. I wonder why I haven't used it more often. And I love the bubble bath. What flavor is it?"

"Can't you tell? It's vanilla. They say it lowers anxiety and makes your skin soft at the same time. It's my favorite." She loved taking a bubble bath with him. He washed her back and laid kisses all along her neck and shoulders. This was a first for both of them and she could have stayed there forever but after thirty minutes their hands and feet were starting to wrinkle.

He got out first, wrapped a towel around his waist and started out the door. "Come on downstairs when you're ready. "

As much as she wanted to stay in the bath, she could smell the pizza and decided that she was hungry. She dried off, slipped into her cami shirt and panties and put his robe back on before walking downstairs. He got plates and silverware from the cupboard and carrying in two Pepsi's met her in the dining room. Loading up their plates with pizza, salad and bread sticks, they walked to the couch and sat down.

"So any preference on what to watch on television? Your choice." Holding the remote out to her, she shook her head no.

"I don't really care. Whatever you want. I'm not that into TV." It was true. At home they only had two channels. A lot of people in the Valley had satellite now but that would have been an extra expense that they just couldn't afford. Her mom had bought a lot of DVD's for the kids over the years and that was usually what was playing at their house.

"Yeah. Me neither. I'd rather read although I do like watching football and basketball games." Settling on a music channel, they sat eating and talking.

"So," she asked, "what are your plans for Thanksgiving next week? Are you going down south to your parents?" "No. I just plan on staying here. School gets out early on Wednesday but that doesn't really leave much time to travel anywhere by Thursday. What about you?"

"I actually plan on going home for Thanksgiving. My mom is hosting the family dinner so I want to go home and help her and visit my kids." A brief look of disappointment flashed across his face although he recovered quickly. He had envisioned maybe spending the holiday with her, here at his house; having a quiet, romantic Thanksgiving dinner. At times he forgot that she had children and of course she needed to help her mother.

The disappointed look wasn't lost on her. "Why don't you come home with me? My family would love to have you and the thought of you being home alone on Thanksgiving makes me feel bad." The minute it came out of her mouth, she instantly regretted it. If she wanted to chase him away, then this would probably be the fastest way to do it. She couldn't think of any holiday in her whole life, where there hadn't been some kind of drama. Kicking herself, she silently prayed that he wouldn't accept the invitation.

"Really? Your family wouldn't mind? I mean it sounds great but I wouldn't want to intrude," Jim answered, hesitantly.

"Of course they wouldn't mind. They would be happy to have you come to dinner. The more the merrier." Smiling on the outside, inside she was slowly dying a thousand deaths. Her mother had always told her to think before she spoke and in this case she was absolutely right.

"Well, if you're sure. I've always wanted to go to Hoopa. We could leave Wednesday afternoon. School gets out at one that day so we could be on the road by three or so. There is a motel there, right?" He was excited. He hadn't been looking forward to spending the holiday alone and he loved road trips and going somewhere new.

"There is a motel but I'm going to ask my uncle if you can stay with him. He lives right down the hill from our house and has an extra bedroom. He would probably love the company. I would prefer you stay with me, at my house, but it's probably too early for that," Amanda offered, knowing that her uncle would be amenable to letting Jim stay at his house.

After they had almost polished off the pizza they laid on the sectional and put a movie on although neither of them had much interest in what was playing. Stroking her hair a thought suddenly came to him and he kicked himself wondering why he hadn't thought of it sooner. "So I'm sorry for not bringing this up sooner but are you on birth control? I was so caught up in the moment that I didn't even think about using protection but I do have condoms and, well…" he paused, not sure what else to say. He was a little upset that he had been so careless earlier.

"It's covered. I'm on birth control shots so no worries. And I don't have anything else you have to worry about either. But thanks for not asking. As a matter of fact this is the first time I've had sex in months." Amanda wanted to reassure him and did appreciate him not asking about anything else. Maybe he didn't realize the high-risk lifestyle that she had been living, but she knew.

"Well, me neither, as a matter of fact. But I'm ready to make up for lost time." Pulling her on top of him on the sectional, this time when they made love there was nothing fast or frantic about it. They took their time, explored each other almost methodically and when they were finished, they fell asleep in each other's arms.

The rest of the weekend went faster than either of them would have liked. The majority of their time was spent in bed: making love, talking and laughing. She loved how comfortable and relaxed she felt with him and by the end of the weekend she could freely walk around naked in front of him without any thought about it. He loved her sense of humor but more than that, he loved how he felt when he was with her.

On Sunday as five o'clock approached their mood turned solemn and they both were sad and sorry to see the weekend end. Loading her bag in the truck he felt depressed and hated to see her go. While he understood that this is how it had to be, he wasn't used to having to conform to the dictates of others. She, on the other hand, accepted it for what it was and while she would have liked to stay longer, knew that it wasn't possible.

"I hate that you have to be on a curfew and follow so many damn rules. Have you looked anymore into moving into one of the Sober Living houses?" Jim asked, frustration in his tone.

"I have. There are some openings right now but I would really like to have a job lined up somewhere first. The cost to live in the houses is 400.00 a month." She had thought of it often and while it seemed far off, her ninety days were coming up fast and she was going to have to decide soon what she was going to do. "I really do hope to eventually have my own place and move my kids over here with me. If I did pass my GED I'm sure that would help with my job search."

"Will your mom be okay with that?" He had watched that dynamic first hand and wondered if her mom would be as receptive to it as Amanda seemed to think.

"I think she will support it. She never wanted to raise more kids but she did what she had to do. But I know that it is harder on her than she lets on. I'm sure she'll miss them but as long as I am clean and have my life together, I think that she will be okay with me taking them back." Although she had only spoken briefly about this with her mom, she had never worried about her mom not wanting to give her kids back, if she was clean.

"I'm glad. And I think that you're right. I'm sure it's not easy for her and it will probably take some time for the kids, you and your mom to adjust to the new changes but in the long run it will be worth it for all of you," Jim said, thoughtfully.

"Yeah, it will be good. I do think that I have my work cut out for me though. Right now my kids treat me more like a big sister than a mom, which I can't blame them, especially my daughter. She's pretty much been under my mom's care since she was born." At times that had bothered Amanda, but the only person to blame was herself.

"Well, lucky for them that they've had your mom to care for them." He really didn't know what else to say.

"And I'm sorry about curfew. I would love to stay with you another night too. But when someone is in recovery, they really do have to be accountable and have firm limits set around them. I'm no different. Truth be told, I don't really trust myself yet either. The Suboxone helps but I worry all of the time about relapse. It feels like a dark shadow lurking after me all of the time." She hated this conversation with him. It was uncomfortable but on the other hand, her addiction was like a white elephant in the room. It wasn't something that they talked about often but it was something that at some point needed to be acknowledged, at least in her mind.

"Well, I don't want to put a downer on the weekend. I'm grateful for the time we have had and I'm looking forward to the times that we are going to have. I'm proud of you. You are going to make it just fine." He pulled over a block from the rehab and leaned over and gave her one last, long kiss. Again, she sensed that he really didn't understand the dynamics of addiction or the lifelong implications that came with it. In the back of her mind it bothered her. She was falling in love with him but didn't know if he would truly ever understand her addiction and the impact it had on her, on a daily basis.

As they pulled into the rehab, she grabbed his hand. "Thanks for everything. I have had the best weekend with you." She wanted to say more, tell him that she hoped that she never disappointed him and that she wanted to be a better person because of him but she didn't know how so she just left it at that.

As he watched her walk into the rehab, he smiled. He was too far in and he knew it. Shaking his head he wondered how this woman had gotten under his skin in such a short period of time but she had. It was exciting and scary at the same time. For the first time ever, he dreaded going home to an empty house and when he walked into his house alone, he already missed her.

She walked in and used the phone to make a collect call. "Hi Mom. I was wondering if it would be okay for Jim to come over for Thanksgiving. And maybe you could ask Uncle if he could stay with him so he doesn't have to stay at the motel."

Because the call was collect they kept the conversation short. Although her mother had said it was fine for her to bring Jim over for

Thanksgiving, she could clearly hear the misgivings in her voice, subtle as it was. She expected it. They were private and not really used to bringing outsiders into the mix.

That night she replayed the whole weekend in her head. All in all it was a good weekend. Her feelings for Jim were deep and real. She only hoped that they would survive Thanksgiving weekend intact and again chastised herself for inviting him over.

Chapter Eleven

By Wednesday afternoon Beverly had decided that she had bit off more than she could chew. The idea of hosting Thanksgiving dinner had sounded a lot better than the reality of it. She was already tired and there was still so much to do. She had done all of the shopping but there was still the house to clean and she wanted to do whatever prep work she could do today that would make tomorrow easier. She was expecting about twenty to twenty-five people, all family members, but now she felt added pressure with Amanda bringing a friend home. He seemed nice enough but having a guest outside of the family and someone they really didn't know made everything seem harder.

She hadn't really planned on making a big dinner tonight and if it was just them she would have settled on something easy like sandwiches but with company coming she felt obliged to cook something more fitting for a first time guest. She had about three hours to get everything done and dinner started. Ben had taken the kids down to his place and she was grateful for that.

By four o'clock everything was almost in order with the exception of Amanda's room. Her bedroom basically had been closed off since she had left for rehab and it was the one last job that Beverly needed to tackle before she started dinner. Ben had put a lock on the door when Amanda had left and it had been too soon; wounds too fresh for Beverly to try to clean it up then. Now with Amanda on her way home it had to be done and couldn't be put off any longer.

Beverly opened the bedroom door and the cold air hit her in the face. As she looked around the room, she realized it was worse than she had imagined possible. It had the atmosphere of a drug den and she felt instantly nauseated just walking in there. She went back into the kitchen and grabbed trash bags, Clorox wipes and a bucket of hot, soapy water. Deciding to strip the bed first, she went and loaded it all up in the washing machine and started the load.

Pop cans that served as ashtrays lined the dresser and the top of the dresser had a black residue all over it, along with wax from melted candles. After discarding all of the cans and trash on the top of the dresser, she took rags out of the hot water and scrubbed the top of the dresser, trying to get the black film and wax off of it. She opened the top dresser drawer and found several blackened spoons, Q-tips with the ends cut off and several needles that were uncapped and looked used. There were more empty little baggies, blackened with residue, than she could even count. Everything got thrown away, with the exception of the needles. Not knowing what to do with them, she put them in her bathroom on a top shelf until she could properly dispose of them in a Sharp's container.

Throwing the bedding into the dryer, she glanced at the clock. She was relieved to know that she still had a little more time before Amanda and Jim got there. As she ran the vacuum, she noticed several burn marks scorched into the carpet. Probably from Amanda nodding off, she thought to herself. At five the room looked decent. If she had more time and energy she would have liked to shampoo the carpet and wash the curtains but in the short hour that she had had to clean the room it didn't look half bad. Once the sheets and blankets were dry she would make up the bed and at least it was livable without too many reminders of past activities that had taken place there.

She had decided on lasagna for dinner. It seemed safe; something everyone liked and could be stretched a long way in case others dropped by. It was just going in the oven when she heard Ben and the kids pull up.

"Grandma, we're back. Is Mom here yet?" Michael ran in ahead of his sister and uncle

"Not yet, Michael, but soon. Your mom called a little while ago and they should be here any time," Beverly answered.

"Come on Michael. Let's carry some wood and fill the wood box up for your Grandma," Ben said. He noticed earlier that her woodpile was getting low. It was frustrating because there was a time where he would have gone up the hill and knocked two loads out by himself but lately he was tired all the time and felt breathless with just the slightest exertion.

Beverly had just finished the salad and was putting garlic bread in the oven when she heard the dog barking and knew that Amanda and her friend must have pulled in.

"Okay kids. I think your mom is here. Be on good behavior, okay?" After wiping her hands on her apron, Bev walked towards the door.

Amanda opened the front door and walked in first. "Hey. I'm here. Hi kids." Michael was first to run over and jump up in her arms.

"Wow, Michael. You're getting so big. You are going to pass me up before you know it." Hugging and kissing him, she swung him back down and swooped up Melanie. "Hi baby. You're getting so big too. It's almost your birthday and you'll be my big four-year-old girl." Melanie smiled shyly while peeking over her mom's shoulder at Jim, who was standing in the doorway.

After setting her daughter back down, Amanda turned towards Jim and pulled him forward. "So kids, this is Jim. Do you remember him? You met him when you came over to see Mommy?" Both kids glanced over at him with curiosity in their faces.

"Hi," Michael offered.

"Hi Michael. What grade are you in?" Jim felt a little out of place, not because he was uncomfortable around children but because everyone had stopped talking and was staring at the two of them. He knew he was being scrutinized all the way around. Kids included.

"I'm in first grade." Pushing his sister forward, he continued. "This is Melanie, she doesn't go to real school yet. She's in Head Start." Used to letting her brother talk for her she quickly backed away and scrambled to get back behind her brother.

"Hi honey. I'm so glad you made it. We've missed you so much." Bev hugged her daughter and again was pleased at how good and healthy she looked now, even from three weeks ago, when they had last seen her. It was a vast difference from the woman who had left eight short weeks ago.

"Hi Jim. It's so nice to see you again. Welcome to our home." Beverly said, while giving him a hug too.

Ben, who had hung back in the living room while everyone greeted each other, finally stepped forward, first giving Amanda a hug and then shaking hands with Jim. "Uncle, I'm so glad you're here. I've been dreaming about you a lot lately. Are you okay?" Amanda had always had a connection with her uncle and although the dreams were never bad, her sixth sense told her that something was going on.

"I'm fine, Honey Bumpkins. You don't need to worry about me. Your little ones keep me on my toes," Ben answered.

"I'm sure they do, Uncle. They are so lucky to have you next door." Amanda smiled, thinking about when she was little. She loved having her uncle next door when she was growing up.

"So why don't you take your things in your room and we'll get ready to eat." Beverly was quick to see the panicked look in Amanda's eyes and realized that she hadn't told her daughter that she had cleaned her room. "I hope you don't mind that I got your room ready. All that is left is for you to make your bed back up."

As Amanda walked down the hall with Jim carrying her bag, she led him to the bedroom. She opened the door and let out a sigh of relief. The room was a little cold but looked one hundred times better than when she had left to rehab. Jim closed the door behind them and spun her around. "I hope it's okay if I sneak in a kiss while we are in here."

"Yes." She answered laughing. "It has been about thirty minutes since we last kissed but then we have got to get back out there. You can't hide in here all night."

As they walked back out into the living room, for the first time she noticed how badly the house needed a makeover. The walls could definitely use paint and the carpets were past any help that shampooing could offer. After spending time at Jim's immaculate house, all of the sudden she felt self-conscious about her mom's house. She wondered if he noticed or paid attention to details like that.

When they got into the living room, Jim immediately walked over to the bookshelves where her mom had displayed pictures of Amanda, Ashley and their brother when they were babies all the way up to high school. "I'm going to help with dinner. Make yourself comfortable and if you need anything just holler," Amanda told him, unsure of whether to leave him or not.

"I'm sure I'll be fine." He could sense that she was nervous and he just wanted to put her at ease. He was comfortable in new situations and didn't feel out of place at all. "Is this you? You were such a cute baby."

Walking over to look at the picture, she replied, "Yes. That's me with my dad holding me."

Looking at the picture, he could see a strong resemblance between Amanda and her daughter. He had thought so before but now seeing pictures when she was younger, it was even more so.

Walking into the kitchen, Amanda could smell the lasagna cooking. "Wow, Mom, that smells delicious. What can I do to help?"

"Well if you could set the table; everything else is about done. I'm just waiting for the bread to be done and then we'll be ready to eat," Beverly told her daughter.

Pulling out plates, she noticed that nothing matched, not even two plates were the same. Shaking her head she wondered what had gotten into her. She had never worried or thought about these things before.

"By the way, Mom, thanks for cleaning my room before we got here. I really didn't think about it until we came through the door and then I was horrified. I'm sorry you had to clean up such a mess." Amanda knew exactly what shape the room was in when she left.

"It's okay. I think it was probably better for me to do it than you anyhow. I wouldn't want anything that was in there to set off triggers." Beverly answered honestly and had earnestly been reading anything available on addiction and recovery.

"Well, I appreciate it and you are right. Even though I feel good right now, I don't want to take any chances," Amanda said, grateful to her mother.

Dinner was good and the atmosphere relaxed.

"Thank you so much for dinner, Beverly. That was the best lasagna I've ever had. I only hope that Amanda has picked up some of your cooking skills," Jim said politely, although it was absolutely true. Everyone laughed, including Amanda, because it was a well-known fact that Amanda didn't cook. At least not when she could help it.

"Good one, Jim. You should know by now that my cooking is limited but I am anxious to learn. I never really had any interest before," Amanda said, laughing at Jim, who had unknowingly told a joke.

"Well, honey, you're still young. And you always master anything that you set your mind to; so this won't be any different." Ben was quick to defend his niece. They all knew why the interest wasn't there earlier but he had always seen the potential in Amanda and had complete faith in her.

"Thanks, Uncle. You always have my back. Oh, I made you something." Walking across the living room she grabbed her purse and pulled out the keychain that she had beaded for him.

"I didn't have a key ring but I will find one while I'm here and put it on." Amanda said, while handing her uncle the keychain.

Ben held the keychain up in the light and twirled it around and around. "Oohh. I love it. Thanks, babe. And it's my favorite colors too."

She was glad that he liked it but knew that he would. He was such a genuine person who truly appreciated presents that were made for him. It was easy to want to spoil him.

Amanda started clearing the table off while her mom went to get the kids ready for bed.

"Well, Jim, you ready to head down the hill with me? I go to bed early and with us out of the way these two women can start baking and getting ready for tomorrow." Ben stood up and put on his coat, giving Jim a couple of minutes to say his good-byes.

Jim walked into the kitchen and gave Amanda a quick hug and kiss. "Well, I'm off. I will see you in the morning. Don't work too hard."

"Okay. Have a good night. Although I think you men get off too easy." As she walked him to the door, she called out, "Uncle, be sure to tell Jim some Injun-devil stories, okay?"

Chuckling, Ben answered, "I don't know. I don't want him awake all night on his first night here."

Beverly came out after getting the kids to bed and put on a kettle of water. "Let's sit down for five minutes and have a cup of tea and figure out our game plan for the night."

"Okay, Mom," Amanda answered.

After sitting down at the table, Beverly took out a list of the menu and handed it to Amanda. "So, here what I plan to serve tomorrow. Aunty Dee is making the pies but I thought if we could bake cornbread and boil eggs tonight, then that would speed things up tomorrow morning. And then we could start dinner rolls tonight and a small batch of cinnamon rolls so that tomorrow morning we can have hot cinnamon rolls with our coffee. I was hoping to eat around one o'clock."

"That early? Don't we usually eat around three or four?" Amanda asked.

"Well, normally yes. But Ashley is coming up and she has to be back out on the Coast by five for work so I have had to push it up a little earlier," Beverly explained.

"Well, that makes sense. Honestly, Mom, I'm surprised that she agreed to come. It's the first time in years that Ashley is coming home for a holiday. What prompted that?" Amanda was skeptical that her sister would actually show up.

"Well I pulled the big guns out and told her that Uncle really wanted her to come up. You know that neither of you can ever refuse him." Nodding her head in agreement, Amanda knew that this was absolutely true.

"Good one, Mom. I didn't know you could be so devious." Amanda had to hand it to her.

They spent the rest of the night cooking and visiting. Beverly did most of the cooking while Amanda followed behind, cleaning up and assisting her in whatever she needed.

86

"So, Amanda, tell me about Jim. I have to say I didn't see that one coming. Is he recovering too? I mean, I know he's a teacher but I thought maybe he volunteers at the rehab because he is recovering himself." Beverly broached the subject carefully. She of all people knew that Amanda could clam up and then there was no getting anything out of her.

"No, Mom. He's not recovering. As a matter of fact he is extremely straight laced with little if any exposure to substance abuse. He's just a really nice guy who wanted to help people, so he volunteered at the Rehab. He's really smart, kind and a great teacher," Amanda told her mom.

"Well that's great. What a wonderful thing to do." Beverly was impressed and happy to hear that he wasn't in recovery himself. "You sound a little hesitant though. Is something wrong?"

Amanda looked away and out of nervousness started biting on her nails. "No. Not really. I'm just still a little confused, that's all. He just has it so together. He has a great house, a good job, a great life. I'm just not sure how I fit in. I feel like a charity case and I just keep waiting for him to come to his senses."

Beverly contemplated what her daughter was saying. "So, in other words you think you're not good enough for him. Well, my dear girl, I can tell you right now that isn't true. You're beautiful, smart and kind. And don't try comparing his world to ours. We are different and you know this. We have our own culture and our own standards that we go by. Don't try comparing yourself to standards that aren't our own. We don't put all of our value on materials things and we don't base success on the face value of a job. Something brought you two together, some connection was there, so don't overthink it." Getting up Beverly walked over and gave her daughter a hug.

"Thanks, Mom. You're absolutely right. I probably have been overthinking it. I guess we better get busy. What time do we need to get up and get dinner going in the morning?" Amanda asked, anxious to change the subject.

"I was thinking that we need to get up around 6. The turkey is big, around twenty-five pounds so I would like to get it in the oven by seven at the latest," Beverly answered.

"Wow, that is big. How many people do you think will be coming?" Amanda asked.

"I think about twenty. And, Cousin Harold just got home and is going to come too." Beverly knew this news wouldn't go over well with Amanda.

"Oh God." Amanda exclaimed. "He's out of jail?"

"Yes, I guess he got out three days ago. Aunt Millie said he would be coming to dinner. I knew that you wouldn't be thrilled but he is family so there wasn't much I could do about it." Beverly understood her daughter's reaction. Harold was unpredictable and it was anyone's guess how he would behave.

"Yeah, I know." Amanda hated to be around her cousin, Harold. In the past when he came to family dinners he always came drunk and belligerent. Most of the drama and fights that happened at the holiday dinners were started by him.

By half past twelve they had everything done that could be done. "Good night Mom. I usually get up early at the rehab but in case I oversleep please be sure to come in and wake me up."

"Good night babe. I'm really glad you came home for the weekend. It's good for the kids, too." Beverly stood up and gave her daughter a hug before turning off the lights and retiring to her room.

Lying in her own bed that night it took her a long time to go to sleep. Whether it was being back in her bed that night or just being back in the Valley, her mind kept going back to the last few years of her life. All the time that she had spent hustling and being high felt wasted now and more than any other time she was full of regrets. She wished for so many things, but mostly that she would have done things differently and handled life differently. Around three in the morning she cried herself to sleep.

At six her mom came in and sat on the edge of her bed. "Amanda. Come on honey, time to wake up."

Sitting up and stretching, Amanda felt disoriented at first but after a couple of seconds realized that she was home. "Good morning. I'll be out in a few minutes." She slipped into a pair of yoga pants and a long-sleeved henley, went to the bathroom, washed her face, brushed her teeth and pulled her hair up. Although better than when she fell asleep, there was still a depressive air hanging around her.

Her mom showed her how to roll out the cinnamon rolls and then together they pinched off dough to rise for dinner rolls. While her mom got the stuffing into the turkey, Amanda baked the cinnamon rolls. By seven, the turkey was in the oven and everything was on schedule.

"Well, we have a little window of time now to drink some coffee and sample the cinnamon rolls. Pretty soon we will start the fruit salad, green bean casserole and then around ten we can start peeling potatoes." Beverly poured two cups of coffee and carried it to the table.

Within ten minutes they heard Ben's truck pull up and Amanda got up to get her uncle and Jim coffee and rolls.

"Good morning. Perfect timing I'd say." Ben, always the morning person, looked chipper and happy today.

Amanda handed her uncle a cup of coffee. "Here you go Uncle. Here's your coffee, just like you like it. Blond and sweet."

"You know it babe. Just like my women." Ben took the coffee while everyone started laughing. It had been a long-standing joke since Amanda was a little girl.

Handing Jim his coffee, Amanda asked, "So, how was your night? Did you sleep well?"

"Actually, I slept very well. It's so quiet here. Once I hit the bed I was out." Jim sat down at the table and pulled Amanda towards him. The circles under her eyes didn't go unnoticed by him, nor did the puffy eyes. He knew her well enough now to know when she was feeling stressed, although he could only guess why.

"Hey baby, are you doing okay?" His voice was soft and gentle while his eyes searched hers.

"Yeah. I'm good. I didn't sleep very well, that's all." She put on her best smile, trying to convince him that everything was okay.

By noon, everything was pretty much ready. The turkey was cooling and everything else was ready to go, with the exception of mashing the potatoes and making gravy. Ben and Jim set up one long table that Amanda covered with a tablecloth. They had decided to set up the food buffet style. There wasn't really enough room to have a sit down dinner so they had decided that this would be the best option for serving everyone.

With everything ready, Amanda ran and showered, wanting to get ready before anyone arrived. She took a dress out of her closet and decided to wear it with her boots. She had not seen some of her family for a long time and wanted to look her best. Jim had gone next door and changed into a pair of slacks and a beautiful teal colored sweater.

As Amanda walked into the living room, a wide smile beamed across Jim's face. "Wow. You look beautiful. I don't think I've ever seen you in a dress before," he told her admiringly.

"Thanks, but shut up. You're embarrassing me." She was joking but it was painfully true. She had always felt uncomfortable if anyone complimented her.

"Well, I'd think that you'd be used to it but okay. Actually you look horrible. Is that better?" Jim asked, teasingly.

"Yes it is." Both of them laughing, she walked over and brushed her hand over his sweater. "By the way, you look pretty good yourself," Amanda said, looking at Jim appreciatively.

"Thank you. And for the record I don't mind compliments." He was teasing and the mood was light. Her mom and uncle were both laughing and it didn't go unnoticed by them, how compatible Amanda and Jim were together.

At twelve-thirty sharp, cars started pulling up. Ben had left a little while earlier to pick Aunty Dee and her pies up. Within a ten-minute span, the house was packed with family. As Amanda went around the room with Jim introducing him to everyone, he tried to mentally keep track of names and who belonged to whom. There was Aunty Sally and her husband Fred and their four kids who were eleven, thirteen, sixteen and nineteen. Then there was Aunty Millie, her boyfriend Andrew and two of her kids who were twenty and twenty-two. Her son, Harold, was not with them and Amanda silently breathed a sigh of relief.

Ben and Aunty Dee pulled up and several of the boys went out to help carry pies in. Jim was immediately taken with this spry, elderly woman who commanded attention from the whole group. Last to show up was Ashley. Jim would have known immediately that she was Amanda's sister. There were enough similarities in their features and she had the same dimples that Amanda had. But where Amanda's expression was soft and thoughtful, Ashley's was guarded and seemed harsh at times.

Beverly was the first to greet her eldest daughter. "Ashley. I'm so glad you made it. How was the drive?" Giving her a big hug, she noticed how stiff and unyielding her daughter felt.

"Hi, Mom. It was okay. Not too bad. I had a late shift last night so got a later start than I had planned." Scanning the room, Ashley spotted Uncle Ben and went over to him next. The hug that she gave him was heartfelt. "Hi, Uncle. I've missed you so much."

"I've missed you too Ash. You'd think you lived farther away for how little we see you. I'm really glad that you came up today. You look great." Ben felt nothing but love for his niece, Ashley. Knowing how hard growing up had been for her, he easily overlooked her uptight temperament and knew it was all a front.

Making her rounds talking to family she finally came over to Amanda. "Ashley, this is my friend Jim. Jim, my sister Ashley." Amanda

90

made the introductions and noticed Ashley looked a little surprised, taking Jim in. Obviously he wasn't Amanda's usual type.

"Hi, Ashley, nice to meet you." Jim offered his hand, which she briefly shook.

"Nice to meet you too." Ashley wondered if he was from the Rehab too. He didn't look the type but she knew by now that you can never tell. Addicts came in all forms.

After Aunty Dee said a prayer, Amanda and Ashley made plates for all the aunts and uncles who were seated at the table. After they were served, everyone else lined up to dish up their plates. Amanda fixed plates for Michael and Melanie and seated them at a small table in the living room and then got back in line with Jim.

With two chairs left at the table, Aunty Dee urged them to sit down. All eyes at the table were watching Jim with curiosity. Aunty Dee was the first to finally ask what the others wanted to know. "Well Jim. Tell us about yourself. How did you and Amanda meet?"

"Um, well, I'm a volunteer tutor at the rehab. I help the residents prepare for their GED, well I mean the ones who didn't graduate from high school and I'm a teacher at the middle school, seventh and eighth grade. I'm from Southern California and moved up to this area two years ago. I guess that's about everything. Anything else you want to know?" Jim answered easily.

"No. I guess that's it. For now," Aunty Dee answered, while the rest of the table laughed.

Dinner was good and everyone was feeling full and relaxed. Amanda and Ashley went into the kitchen and started carrying pies and whipped cream to the table. Hearing a warrior cry outside they both knew whose voice was behind that yell.

Opening the door, their cousin Harold walked in. "Hey. I made it. You didn't start without me did you?" His voice was loud and boisterous and everyone turned to watch his entrance.

Harold's mother, Aunt Mille, was the first to answer. "Harold, I told you to be here by one. We already ate dinner and getting ready for dessert."

"I'm sorry, Mom. Had to make a few stops on my way." Harold was a handsome twenty-five year old man with a long braid and a beautiful, perfect smile. He was tall and was intimidating just by virtue of his size. He had lots of tattoos covering his arms and neck that he had gotten from his various stints in prison.

Beverly got up and started walking towards the kitchen. "It's okay, Harold. There's plenty of food left. I'll make you a plate. Go ahead and sit down," she said while motioning towards a now empty chair.

"Thanks, Aunty Bev. You're the best," Harold said, while taking a seat.

Sitting down, everyone nearby could smell the alcohol on him and the room went uncomfortably quiet. Looking around the room, Harold zoned in on the one person he didn't know. "Who are you?" He asked, aiming his question at Jim.

Jim immediately stood up, moving closer and stuck his hand out. "Hi. I'm Jim."

Harold shook his hand and smiled big. "Oh, Ashley. You finally got a man, huh? I always knew you would be the one to bring an Oakie boyfriend home. You always thought you were too good for an Injun."

Ashley's mouth flew open in protest but she quickly decided against saying anything. Growing up with Harold all of her life she knew that there was no winning with him. Once you got him going, he wouldn't stop and would just keep throwing out nasty insults, especially when drunk.

"That's not Ashley's friend, Harold. This is a friend of Amanda's and he came up with her to join us for Thanksgiving." Aunty Dee smiled reassuringly at Jim while she spoke.

"Amanda. Ha. So are you her connection or something? How'd you hook up with Amanda?" Harold asked, looking at Jim a little more closely now.

Amanda's was fuming and she could feel her face getting hot. Ashley was insulted and the look she threw at Harold showed no love lost. Harold didn't miss a beat. He loved getting a reaction from his cousins.

The whole family looked at Jim, watching his reaction but as upset as everyone else was, Jim looked calm and unfazed by the jabs from Harold.

"Actually Harold, I met Amanda at the rehab. I'm a tutor there and we've become friends. I am really happy that I got to come over today and join your family for Thanksgiving." Jim spoke politely, knowing it was best to not say anything confrontational to Harold. It was obvious that he was drunk and spoiling for a fight with someone.

Harold looked around the room and his eyes met Amanda's. "Oh. You've been at rehab again huh, Amanda? I wondered why you were getting fat. Never fails, people go to rehab and come back fat."

92

"Harold Duane, you had better watch your manners and apologize. You sound drunk and we all know that you just want to stir everything up when you're drunk." Aunty Dee had had enough and wasn't going to put up with him embarrassing the family like this.

Jim felt bad for Amanda and Ashley and could see immediately that the whole family reacted to Harold. He was so used to seventh and eighth grade students who liked to push his buttons that he was practiced at not reacting. More interesting to him was that Harold's mother, Millie, had just kind of disappeared and it was Aunty Dee and Ben who were dealing with Harold's bad behavior.

"Okay, Aunty Dee, I'm sorry. Sorry Amanda and Ashley. You know me. I'm just playing. Sorry Jim. No offense. I'm just the family asshole." Harold walked to his pickup truck, climbed inside and took another shot of cheap vodka, chasing it down with a beer. Always the misunderstood martyr when he was drinking, he opened another beer and thought back on how unfair life had always been to him.

With Harold outside for the moment, the group ate dessert and tried to get the atmosphere relaxed again but no one was feeling it. "Come on, let's not let one little mishap put a damper on our lovely dinner." Aunty Dee tried to lighten the mood, although even she realized that it was an uphill battle. "Bev and Amanda worked hard making a wonderful dinner and we aren't going to let Harold ruin it."

The kids were the first to relax. They started chasing each other and playing. Sitting at the table the adults started talking and joking around with each other while Amanda and Ashley started the ominous detail of cleaning up all of the dinner dishes. Aunt Millie finally came back in from one of the back bedrooms and joined the group. She was quiet and Jim thought that she looked sad and upset, but not knowing her well, wasn't really sure if he was reading her right or not.

Just as things started to settle down, Harold stumbled back through the front door, looking a little more hammered, then when he had walked out thirty minutes earlier. "Hey. Where's my plate. I thought someone was making me a plate."

Amanda carried out the plate that had been made for him earlier and set it down in front of him along with a fork.

"Thanks cuz." Harold started eating like a person who was starving and hadn't eaten in a long time. "I don't know why the fuck we are celebrating Thanksgiving anyhow. Do you guys ever think about that? It's stupid, if you ask me."

"Well, Harold, we aren't really celebrating Thanksgiving. But it's a holiday where we can all get together and enjoy a meal together." Ben knew to keep it short and simple. When drunk, Harold could easily misconstrue anything anybody said, and often did.

"Well, at least we have a pilgrim here with us this year. Aeeeee. Just kidding, Jim." Harold laughed but he was eyeing Jim with mistrust and suspicion.

With the dishes almost done, Amanda decided to walk out on the front porch and have a cigarette. She had hoped that she and Ashley would have visited a little more while cleaning up but Ashley seemed distant and uninterested in having a conversation with her. As a matter of fact she kept looking at her watch and Amanda could see her mentally counting the seconds until she could leave.

Jim decided that maybe he would join Amanda on the porch, hoping that out of sight, out of mind, Harold would focus on something besides him. "Hey, babe, how's it going?"

Turning towards him she gave him a faint smile. "I'm okay. A little embarrassed that you had to see the holiday circus though. Sorry about Harold. He's the family jerk that always like to make a scene wherever he is."

"It's no big deal. And it's certainly not a reflection on you. He can say whatever he wants to me or about me. I deal with smarty kids all day long and believe me they can throw out the insults and be really mean. I've learned not to react because that's normally what they are looking for. I'm just sorry that he had to say hurtful things to you and he definitely was taking jabs at your sister." Jim tried to reassure her and reached out and stroked her arm.

"You're too sweet. I really don't know why you're so good to me." She felt relieved that he wasn't upset and leaning towards him, pulled his face towards hers and kissed him.

Pulling back when he heard the front door open he wasn't surprised to see Harold stumbling out the door and down the steps. "God, get a room already. Aeee. I'm getting a beer. Do either of you want one?" The question was asked more in a form of a dare and it wasn't lost on either Jim or Amanda.

"Sure, I'll have one," Jim answered.

"No thanks, Harold. You know I'm not a drinker." Amanda would have walked back in the house but she wasn't going to leave Jim alone with Harold so she lit another cigarette and waited while Harold walked to his truck and retrieved two cans of Coors. Throwing one at Jim, he popped his open and drank half the can in one drink.

"Thanks Harold. I was getting thirsty." Jim opened his beer and took a drink.

"So, how serious are you two? And Amanda, what made you go to rehab?" Harold asked.

"I just needed to go. It was getting crazy. You know how that is." Amanda answered nonchalantly. She didn't want to go into personal details with Harold. Not when he was drunk.

"Oh. I thought I heard Mom saying that you went because you overdosed and almost died. In front of your kids even. What happened? Did you get a bag of bad stuff or what?" Harold asked.

Amanda's only wished at that moment that the earth would open up and swallow her up. This was something that she had never talked about with Jim, and although she turned away quickly, not before she saw Jim's face register a look of surprise. Harold noticed it too and knew he had struck a nerve.

"I don't really want to talk about it right now, Harold, and maybe you should mind your own business." She was mad and felt completely exposed and humiliated. "What were you in jail for the last time anyhow, Harold?"

"Don't try to change the subject little cuz. I'm only asking because I love you. I'm just glad you're okay. I heard that if the ambulance didn't get here when it did, you'd be gone right now." Pretending concern, he walked towards her, trying to pull her into a bear hug.

"Well, thanks for your concern but I'm fine." Amanda pulled away as fast as possible and walked back in the house, leaving Jim and Harold alone to finish their beer.

"Gee, that was awkward. I didn't mean to say anything wrong. I just thought that since you guys were a couple she would have told you about that." Shaking his head, looking puzzled, Harold guzzled the rest of his beer and went back to his truck to get another beer.

Seeing that as a good time to exit, Jim went into the house. Not finding Amanda in the living room or dining room, he sat down on the couch and watched the kids playing on the floor in front of him. He was a little surprised that she hadn't told him about her close brush with death but wasn't going to give Harold the satisfaction of seeing that it bothered him.

Amanda had gone into her room. Needing a minute to regroup herself, she took a deep breath and looked in the mirror. She had known that it was going to be hard coming home, especially the first time but with the added pressure of having Jim with her, it was getting to be too much. She had planned on telling him about her overdose, someday but not yet. Hearing a knock on the door, she opened it expecting to see Jim but instead it was her sister Ashley.

"I'm going to take off now, Amanda. I just wanted to say 'bye.' " Ashley felt bad for her sister. She might not understand her sister and her issues but she did understand family drama issues.

"I'm sorry about Harold. Don't let him get to you though; just keep up the good work." She wanted to be supportive but just didn't know what to say. She wasn't comfortable talking like this and just wanted to leave and get back over the hill where she felt safe and didn't have to deal with any of this.

"Good bye, Ashley. I'm really glad that you came today." She wanted to hug her sister but that just wasn't Ashley and she knew it. She would just keep it at that and be grateful that her sister had even bothered to come in and tell her good-bye.

Amanda walked back into the living room and found Jim sitting on the floor, coloring with Melanie. It was a heartwarming sight and she walked over and joined them. Making eye contact with her, he asked, "is everything okay?"

"Yeah. It's fine. I was just saying good-bye to Ashley. What are you guys doing?" Amanda asked.

"Oh, Melanie is teaching me to color. Isn't she the best little artist?" Jim said, as Melanie smiled at her mom, proud of her picture.

"Yes, she is quite the artist." Amanda smiled at her daughter. She often felt like it was her daughter who she had let down the most and sometimes it was hard to get over the guilt of that.

By six o'clock everyone had left and one of her uncles had driven Harold home, after much fighting and arguing with him over the keys. The only one left was Ben and he left soon after, claiming to be tired and wanting a nap.

"Don't worry about me, Ben. I'll walk down later and really, don't feel like you have to get up and entertain me. I'll probably go to bed early too," Jim told him.

The rest of the evening they watched movies with the kids, all four of them cuddled on the couch with blankets. Her mother had excused herself right after Ben left and had just wanted to take a hot bath and go to bed.

Both kids fell asleep on the couch around nine and Jim, yawning himself, decided to walk down the hill and go to bed.

Amanda walked him to the door and they kissed good-bye. She didn't know if it was her imagination or not but she felt like everything had been strained since Harold had delivered his blow. Again, it felt like the white elephant in the room and she knew that it was something that they were going to have to talk about sooner or later.

"Good night. I'll see you tomorrow. Maybe we can take the kids out and I'll give you a tour of the Valley," Amanda offered.

"Sounds good. Try to get a good night sleep. You and your mom did an awesome job making dinner and I'm glad that you invited me. I'm proud of you, by the way. I know this wasn't easy but you handled everything great." Smiling at her, Jim closed the door and walked down the hill.

Out of pure exhaustion, she slept hard all night. He was right. It wasn't easy but she had made it and tomorrow they would be spending the day with the kids and if they had any alone time she would tell him firsthand what had happened.

Chapter Twelve

A good night's sleep did Amanda wonders and when she woke up she felt recharged and hopeful again. Looking at the clock she was surprised to see it was already eight o'clock. She could hear voices coming down the hall and realized that her mom and Jim were visiting in the dining room. Wondering how long he had been there, she got up and joined them.

"Good morning. How long have you been here?" she looked around and noticed that her kids weren't up yet.

"Good morning, Sleeping Beauty. I got here about fifteen minutes ago. We thought we would let you sleep in." Jim stood up and walked over, giving her a quick morning kiss.

"Nice," she answered, looking a little suspicious at them both, wondering if they were talking about her or not.

"Jim was just telling me some funny stories about some of his students," Beverly nonchalantly answered, knowing what was going through her daughter's mind.

Amanda poured a cup of coffee and joined them at the table.

"So, your uncle suggested that we take the kids and go up the hill and get a Christmas tree. He said he hasn't done that in a few years and thought it would be a good outing. What do you think?" Jim loved the outdoors and was excited about the prospect.

"That sounds like fun. I haven't done that since I was a little girl. Did he say what time he wanted to go?" Amanda asked, excitedly.

"He said we should try to head up the hill by ten thirty or eleven. We are going to take my truck up since I have more room than his single cab. Bev, there's room for you if you want to go with us," Jim said, extending the invitation.

"No, no. I'm looking forward to a day by myself. I might even go to the casino and gamble for a while. Thanks for inviting me though." Beverly smiled at Jim and appreciated how thoughtful he was. She was excited about having a break from the kids. She loved her grandchildren but really hadn't had a day to herself for a long time.

Jim stood up, carried his cup to the sink and washed it out. "I'm going to go gas up and then go by the store and get some snacks to take up the hill. Is there anything in particular that the kids would like?" He asked, directing the question to both Amanda and Beverly.

"Maybe some Capri Suns and a few waters. I'll make turkey sandwiches from the leftovers so if you could get chips and drinks that would be great." Checking the time on the microwave, Amanda decided that she had better start getting ready and get the kids up, who she knew would be excited. They had never gone up and got a Christmas tree before.

"Okay. We'll be by at ten thirty to pick everyone up." Bev and Amanda both turned and watched Jim walk out the door.

"I have to say, Amanda, I really like your friend. He's such a thoughtful person. I'm glad that you brought him home for Thanksgiving." Beverly smiled at her daughter.

"Yeah. He's a pretty great guy Mom." Changing the subject quickly, she added," I'm going to shower and get dressed and then I'll get the kids up and start getting them ready." She was glad that her mom liked Jim but really wasn't ready to talk about it yet.

"Okay. I can start waking them up and feed them if you want." Beverly offered.

"No. I'll do it. You deserve a break. I know it hasn't been easy for you to take care of them all of the time. I am really grateful for all that you do. I really am hoping that in time I can move them out on the Coast with me. It won't happen overnight but I'm hoping within the next year it will all work out," Amanda told her mother, hoping that the news would go over well.

"It will work out. Just don't push yourself too hard. These things take a little time but it will happen. And you know how much I love your kids. They mean everything to me. You'll see someday when you're a grandma." Beverly reached out and squeezed her daughter's hand.

"Okay, but hopefully not for a very long time." They both laughed and then something crossed her mind that had been bothering her. "I've been meaning to ask you about uncle. Is he okay? He seems to be tired a lot." Amanda had meant to mention this last night but never got the chance. "He also looks like he's losing weight."

"I've noticed that too. He hasn't said anything but does complain about being tired a lot." Beverly had been feeling worried about him, too, but she hadn't wanted to say anything to Amanda about it and cause her unnecessary worrying. He was the rock of their family and the thought of something happening to him was unthinkable.

After Amanda had showered, she went in to her kid's bedroom, sat down on Melanie's bed and gently shook her. "Kids, wake up. Guess what? We're going to go up the hill and get a Christmas tree today. Would you like that?"

Michael was the first to jump up. "Yah. That sounds great Mom. Are we going to cut it down and everything?"

"Yes, babe. We are going to ride up in Jim's truck and find the prettiest tree we can. Uncle is going too. Does that sound fun Mel?" Her daughter smiled and nodded her head yes.

"Okay, well, we better get up and get moving. We don't want to get left. I'm going to make you a bowl of cereal first and then we need to find you some warm clothes. There's probably snow up the hill so you need to dress warm and bring a hat and gloves," Amanda told her kids, before going in and pouring their cereal.

Excited, both kids jumped up, ate their breakfast and then ran into the bedroom to get dressed. While they ate their cereal, Amanda made turkey sandwiches for the adults and peanut butter and jelly sandwiches for the kids. Beverly heated water and filled up two thermoses; one with coffee and one with hot chocolate. "The one thing I remember about getting Christmas trees is that it can get really cold so hopefully a hot drink will help keep everyone warm," Beverly said, trying to remember the last time she had gone up to get a tree. It had been years when her husband was still alive and her children were little.

"Good idea. Thanks, Mom. The last time I remember going up the hill to get a tree must have been twelve or thirteen years ago. I think I was eleven because Dad was still alive." She didn't add that the day had started off exciting and fun but halfway through the day, seven or eight beers later, the outing turned sour. Too many times, what started off as fun ended bad and just thinking about it made her start feeling anxious. Pulling herself together she mentally reminded herself that the past was the past and today she wanted to make good memories for her children.

At ten thirty sharp they heard the truck pull up and the kids went running out while Amanda gathered up a few bags she had packed: one with the food she had made and one with dry clothes and a few small blankets for the kids. The one thing that she did remember was getting wet and cold after trudging through the snow. Jim walked in and helped her carry out the bags to the truck. He looked happy and was as excited as Michael and Melanie.

"Good morning, Uncle." Amanda greeted him. "This was a great idea. Thanks for thinking of it."

"You're welcome babe. I thought this would be a good outing for the kids and I know that Jim wanted to get up into the mountains while he was over here." Ben and Jim had spent quite some time visiting and Ben really liked him. More than that though, he saw the kind of person he was and knew that if Jim and Amanda made it as a couple, that her and the kids would have stability and security. He loved Amanda like a daughter and only wanted the best for her. The thought of someone taking care of her and her kids gave him comfort and he just hoped that they were as compatible as they appeared.

Jim had already moved the booster seats into the back seat of his truck and Amanda strapped both kids in before taking the seat between them and buckling her seat belt.

"Ben, do you want to drive? You know where we're going better than I do," Jim offered.

"Nope. I'm happy to co-pilot," Ben answered.

Heading down the highway and past downtown, Ben showed him the turn off that led up the hill. The road was fairly well maintained and the first five miles they climbed steadily up. While there were no shoulders to speak of, there were wider spots to pull off every so often. At one point, Ben had him pull over and stop at one of the wide spots. Looking out the window, Jim could see the whole Valley. "Wow, what a beautiful view." He was in awe and reaching beneath his seat he pulled out a camera, jumped out of the truck and started snapping pictures.

"Are you a photographer, Jim?" Ben asked curiously.

"No. Not professionally, anyhow. But it is a hobby of mine. I have taken several classes in photography just for the fun of it. I wanted to take pictures yesterday at Thanksgiving but since I was a guest and just meeting everybody, I didn't want to make anyone uncomfortable," Jim answered. Nodding his head in agreement, Ben thought that it was probably better to wait.

Jim got back in the truck and they went two more miles before they got to the snow. The road had a lot of track marks, showing that quite a few trucks had gone up ahead of them this morning. "A lot of people go up for trees on Thanksgiving weekend," Ben explained. "If you wait much longer and we get much snow, then it is impossible to get up to the good trees."

They drove about thirty minutes more, until they came to a prairie. Several trucks had pulled over and parked in a clearing and footprints led off into the wooded area of trees.

"Go ahead and pull over. This looks like a good place to walk in and look for our tree." Ben pointed to a spot where the snow wasn't too deep. Jim had already put the truck in 4WD, not wanting to take any chances of getting stuck. Not with the kids anyhow.

They all jumped out of the truck and the kids squealed in delight. Scooping up snow, they made snowballs and snow angels. Jim got out his camera again and started snapping pictures of Michael and Melanie while they played. Amanda and Ben both smiled, watching how much fun they were having.

After giving them time to play, Ben finally called out "Okay. We had better go look for that perfect Christmas tree. Come on kids." As they started walking towards the tree line Ben asked, "Amanda do you want a Silvertip or a bushy Fir?"

"I want a Silvertip, Uncle. We haven't had one of those in years. I love how elegant they look." Amanda had always loved the Silvertips but in recent years they had taken whatever someone brought them.

Glancing over at Jim, Ben asked, "what about you Jim? Which do you prefer?"

"Um. I don't know, Ben. But we don't have to get me a tree," Jim said, not expecting to get a tree too.

"Nonsense. We're up here. Might as well get a tree for you too," Ben answered.

"Don't I need a permit or something?" Jim asked. The last thing he wanted to do was get in trouble for illegally taking a Christmas tree.

Ben and Amanda both started laughing. "No. It's fine. We can cut them on the res. Now if you went to Forest Service land, then yes, you would need a permit. And if you get stopped on our way back to the Coast, then I can show my tribal ID and tell them I got it here on the square. No worries," Amanda explained.

Trudging through the snow was a little slow with the kids. After the first ten minutes, Melanie got tired of walking so Jim carried her on his shoulders. They saw several prospective trees but none really jumped out at them. Suddenly, Amanda saw the one she liked. "What about that one?" She asked, as she pointed to the one that had caught her eye. Walking towards the one she was pointing to, Ben slowly walked around it, looking it up and down and from all angles.

"That is a pretty tree and it looks like the perfect size for the house. What do you think kids?" Ben asked. Michael ran around the tree several times, yelling. "Yeah, that one, that one. Can I help cut it down?" Ben looked up at Melanie, sitting on Jim's shoulders. "What about you, Mel. Do you like this one?" Melanie looked down at her uncle and smiled big. "I love it." She answered, nodding her head yes.

"Well, it looks like everyone is in agreement, so I guess this is the one." Ben was carrying a little hatchet and a small hack saw. He chopped the tree trunk first and then let Michael help him saw the blade back and forth. Jim snapped pictures of Ben and Michael cutting the tree down and of Amanda and Melanie watching.

"Okay, one tree down, one to go." Ben was having a good day. He loved being up in the mountains and was really enjoying spending time with Amanda, Jim and the kids today. He didn't want to rush them but he was starting to feel really tired and already out of breath. Luckily, Jim found a tree soon after. He went for a much smaller tree and explained that in his little house, he didn't need a very big tree, especially since it was just him there.

"What about you, Uncle? Don't you want a tree for your house?" Amanda asked, as they were walking down the hill dragging the trees back towards the truck.

"No babe. You know I never put a tree up. I don't even have ornaments." Ben loved the holidays but wasn't into decorating or putting trees up.

"Uncle, if you don't have a tree then where will Santa Claus leave your presents?" Melanie asked, very seriously.

Surprised, they all turned to look at Melanie. Usually so quiet, Jim thought to himself that that was the most he had ever heard her say at once. It was obvious that she was giving this a lot of thought.

"Well, Mel, Santa always leaves my presents under the tree at your house. I think that he knows that Uncle goes to your house every Christmas morning. But thank you for thinking about that for me." Ben chuckled to himself. He really loved these kids and somehow was getting sentimental in his older years.

With Ben and Jim dragging the trees through the snow, Amanda carried Melanie on her back. Finally back at the truck, they all got in and Jim started it up so that they could warm up. Amanda poured warm drinks for everyone and handed out the sandwiches and then they sat in the truck having their picnic. There was only one mishap when Michael spilled his hot chocolate on the seat and floor. Amanda gasped, worried that Jim would be upset. After all, he kept his truck immaculate and it was an expensive vehicle.

"It's fine," he said, not the least bit fazed. He took out some paper towels and wiped the seat and floor. "It's just a truck. A little hot chocolate isn't going to hurt anything."

"I'm so sorry," Amanda apologetically replied.

"Really, it's okay." Glancing at Michael, who was looking super guilty, he patted his arm. "It was an accident, Michael. It's okay. Look, it's already cleaned up. Now come on, who wants to have a snowball fight?" Jim, Michael and Melanie chased each other, throwing snowballs at each other and then they made snow angels. Ben and Amanda stood by the truck watching them play. Ben appreciated how patient and kind Jim was to the kids. The only male influence that had consistently been in the kid's lives was him and it was nice to see them warming up to Jim.

Snow started falling, so they decided it was time to head down the hill. Amanda stripped the wet, cold clothes off of the kids and dressed them in the clothes that she had brought for them. Both kids fell asleep on the way down the hill. After dropping Ben off at his house they took the kids home and unloaded the truck. Michael woke up and ran in the house while Jim carried Melanie in and both kids sprawled out on the couch. They found a note on the table from Beverly, telling them that she was going to Bingo with her cousin, Jan, and would be home around midnight.

"Thanks for taking us out to get a tree. I don't know who enjoyed it more, the kids or Uncle, but it was fun. I'm glad we got to do that." Smiling, she reached out and rubbed his arm. With her mom gone until late, she hoped to put the kids to bed early and have some quality, alone time with Jim.

"You're welcome. I really enjoyed it too. It really is beautiful here," Jim said, appreciatively.

"Do you want to take a hot shower? You must be cold in those wet clothes," she offered.

"My clothes are down the hill so why don't you shower first while I run and get them." He looked towards the kids wondering if they would be okay while he ran down the hill.

Reading his mind, she answered before he even asked. "They will be okay for a few minutes. I'll put a movie on before I jump in the shower. They're so worn out that I doubt that they will even move off of the couch. As a matter of fact, I'm hoping to get them to bed early, so me and you can have some alone time." Looking slyly at him, there was no doubt in his mind what she was thinking.

"Hmmm. I like the sound of that." Reaching out, he pulled her in his arms and kissed her. "I'll be back shortly. Have you thought about dinner? I was thinking of just going to get fast food. What are our choices?" He had only been downtown once and didn't see too many eating establishments.

"Well there aren't too many choices and I doubt anything will be open past five. The best bet would probably be the deli at the store. They have chicken or hot deli food like that," Amanda told him, glad that she wouldn't have to cook dinner tonight.

"Well, after I shower I'll run down and get something for dinner. You worked so hard yesterday on Thanksgiving dinner that today you should take it easy," Jim said.

"Thanks. You're always so sweet," Amanda said, smiling at him appreciatively.

After she turned on a movie for the kids, she jumped in the shower. The hot water felt good hitting her skin and she finally felt like she was thawing out.

Jim decided to shower next door. Ben had built a fire and was already sitting in his recliner dozing off. Deciding to just head to the store now, so that once he was back he wouldn't have to leave again, he sent Amanda a text telling her he would be back soon.

Driving downtown he saw a pickup by the side of the road with a load of wood and a for sale sign on top of the load. Beverly's low woodpile hadn't gone unnoticed by him and he had heard Ben saying several times that he needed to get up the hill and cut her some wood. He pulled in alongside the truck thinking he would at least ask the price.

The guy in the driver's seat rolled down his window and looked at him suspiciously.

"Hey, I was just wondering how much for your load of wood?" Jim asked. He could see the man eyeing him and his truck up, while mentally calculating what he could get for the load. He didn't want to go too low, if he could get more but didn't want to go so high that he didn't make the sale.

"Well it's a mixed load of Fir and Madrone, so I want one hundred twenty-five for it." The man watched Jim's face for a reaction.

"Okay. That seems fair, I guess. Can you deliver it for me?" Jim asked.

"Sure, as long as it's in the Valley. If it's further than that I'll have to charge more." Looking at Jim, he just assumed that he was from Willow Creek. He hadn't seen him around the Valley before.

Jim started giving the directions and the man knew exactly where he was talking about. "Oh, you mean Bev's house? Okay, I can deliver it there. How do you know Bev?" More than anything he was curious about why this white man was buying wood for Bev's house.

"I'm a friend of Amanda's. I'm just over for the weekend but I know that she will be needing wood soon." Taking money out of his pocket Jim paid for the wood.

"My name is Henry by the way. I'm Amanda's cousin on her dad's side. How is Amanda doing? I heard she had gone to rehab," Henry asked.

"She's doing really well. She just came over for the weekend to visit her mom and kids." Jim said, forgetting how closely everyone was related in this small community and knew everyone else's business. Growing up in the city the only people he knew were a few neighbors.

"Glad to hear it. Amanda is a sweet girl, not like her sister Ashley. Now she's the mean one. I'm really happy that she's doing better. She looked horrible the last time I saw her. All sucked up, looking like death walking and hustling everyone. Well, anyway, I will go ahead and deliver this load. As a matter of fact I will even stack it for you." Henry was happy with the sale. If it had been anyone local he would have charged eighty dollars. He wondered if he should have held out for more but then decided that at least he had made forty-five more than he expected so it was a good day.

Driving on to the store, Jim had to think about what Henry had said. He had seen her on her second day at rehab and while she was skinny he hadn't noticed anything that different. Not in the category of "death walking" any way. Shaking his head he also wondered what he meant by "hustling everyone." Pushing it to the back of his mind he decided that he wasn't going to dwell on it. After all, he knew there were issues before but that was in the past and the less he knew the better.

Jim arrived back at Bev's house and Henry had just finished throwing the wood out of the back of his truck and was busy stacking it. He carried in the groceries and Amanda met him at the door. "Oh my God," she gushed. "I can't believe you bought a load of wood for my mom. She's going to be so happy." Throwing her arms around him she gave him a heartfelt hug.

"Oh, good. I was hoping that it would be a good surprise. Ben seemed to be worrying about it and had said several times that he needed to get up the hill and cut her wood. I really appreciate everyone's hospitality so I wanted to do something back." Smiling, he was glad that she was happy. He had been trying to think of what he could do to show his appreciation, and this just seemed more practical and needed, then say a bottle of wine.

Jim couldn't decide on what to buy for dinner so he had bought a variety of things; frozen pizza, fish sticks, deli chicken, chicken strips, potato wedges, cereal, milk, juice for the kids and cookies. He knew he had gone a little overboard, probably because he was hungry himself but decided that whatever they didn't eat tonight could be used over the weekend. After they had eaten and she had bathed the kids, they sprawled out on the couch and watched movies. It was a relaxing night and by nine thirty both kids had fell asleep on the couch, while watching "Home Alone."

Amanda stood up and grabbed Jim's hand and led him down the hall to her bedroom. "I'm so glad to finally have some time with you. Hmmm, I've missed you," she said, as she started unbuttoning his shirt and planting slow, long kisses on his neck.

"I've missed you too," he answered, while his hands quickly glided over her body undressing her. The sex was good, as usual, and she was grateful that neither of her kids had woke up, something that they never had to worry about before. Lying against his chest, with his arm wrapped around her, she took a deep breath and decided it was time to talk about the "white elephant." It had been bothering her ever since Harold had told him about her overdose and she didn't want him to think that she was trying to hide something from him.

Taking a deep breath, she started. "So, I wanted to talk to you, while we are alone about what Harold said yesterday. You know about the OD. I guess it's something that I'm still coming to terms with and well, um, you looked kinda shocked or surprised and I just don't want you to think that it was something I was trying to keep from you. I really did want to tell you about it myself but it just never seemed like the right time. But I wish that I would have told you myself before Harold did."

Shifting around, it was obvious to her that he was already uncomfortable with this conversation. "I'm sorry that I didn't do a better job hiding my reaction yesterday. I guess mostly because I hated giving Harold the satisfaction of seeing that he had struck a nerve, so to speak. But again, that was in the past. I mean, you don't owe me an explanation or anything."

"Well, maybe I don't but somehow it feels dishonest and while it's not my favorite topic I just don't want to feel like I'm keeping some big, dark secret from you." She was trying hard to be honest and wished that he would ask questions or somehow interact a little more. An uncomfortable silence fell over the room.

"So even though I have told you how bad my addiction was, I'm not sure that you can even imagine what that means. And before I checked into rehab I was in a very low and dark place. It's like, you know that you're doing wrong, messing everything up but you feel powerless to stop it. The addiction takes over and that is all you care about. Anyhow, I really wasn't trying to kill myself. I'm no doctor but I think that my tolerance had gotten higher and higher. The amount that used to get me high and make me feel good didn't anymore. And from what I was told, the bag of heroin that I had that night was maybe stronger than what I was used to. So I shot up two times, closer together than usual, because the first high just wasn't doing the job. That's all I really remember. Apparently my mom heard noise and came in to check on me and found me out cold. She yelled at my son to run down the hill and get my uncle and she called 911. When my uncle got here, they said I had no pulse and wasn't breathing so he started doing rescue breathing. The ambulance took about fifteen minutes to get here. Once they gave me Narcan I came to really quickly. It was hell though. Narcan is like detoxing all at once and my whole body hurt so bad and I felt so sick that I almost wished that I had died. But at that moment I made the decision to go to rehab. It wasn't the pain or being sick that did it. It was the look on my mom and uncle's face and the scared look in my kid's eyes. All of the sudden I had a moment of clarity and I could see all of the pain and heartache that I was causing the people that I loved the most and who loved me the most. My innocent babies witnessing their mom essentially dead and at that moment I knew that things had to change." Her voice was starting to crack at the end and she took a deep breath, trying not to cry.

He was silent for a while, taking in what she was telling him and carefully choosing his response. In some ways he felt pressured to say the right things back and he wasn't sure what the correct response was. "Well, I'm not going to pretend to understand or have first-hand knowledge of what you're telling me. I don't know exactly what to say except that I'm glad you made the decision to go to rehab and as awful as it all sounds, if that's what it took then I guess in some ways it was a positive thing. And, I guess that I'm just really happy that someone was here to save you. To think that I may never have met you or have you in my life is a horrible thought to me," he paused for a minute before he went on, " I love you." This was the first time he had said this out loud to her but at that moment he knew it was absolutely true.

109

"You love me?" A look of surprise crossed her face and then looking up into his eyes, tears came to her own. "I love you too," she answered. It wasn't until the words came out of her mouth that she realized just how much she loved him.

Her mouth met his and they kissed passionately. Amanda pulled away suddenly, jumped up and slipped her clothes back on. Jim sat up looking at her confused. "What's up?" He asked.

"Don't you hear one of the kid's crying?" She asked.

"Actually, I didn't. I guess I was a little caught up in the moment." He laid back down wondering if he should get up and head down the hill or hang around in case the kids went back to sleep and they had more time together.

She correctly guessed what he was thinking and told him before she walked out, "I really want you to stay the night with me tonight, up here."

"Will that be all right? With your family, I mean," he asked.

"Yes. It will be fine. I am a grown woman, with two kids. I think my family knows we're having sex." She was teasing him and he laughed with her.

"Well if you're sure. I don't want to wake up with a shot gun to my head," he joked back.

"No chance of that. The biggest reason I didn't have you stay here the first few nights was that I wanted to give the kids a chance to get to know you first," Amanda explained.

Jim nodded his head in agreement, got up and slipped his pants on. "I think I'll go stoke the fire up."

Amanda got her kids moved into their beds. Shortly after they heard Bev pull up outside. The minute she came through the door, Amanda could tell that she had won, by the smile on her face.

"Did you win?" Amanda asked, even though she already knew the answer.

"I did. I won a regular game and didn't have to split with anyone. Five hundred dollars! I am so happy and relieved. Now I can actually buy some Christmas presents and I wanted to order a load of wood so Ben doesn't have to go out and try to cut a load," Beverly said, excitedly.

"Well, then you are going to be even happier because Jim already bought a load and had it delivered today." Amanda then told her mom about Jim seeing Henry selling a load by the side of the road and had bought it for her. "It is a mixed load of Fir and Madrone and Henry even stacked it for you."

"Oh, Jim. Thank you." Beverly walked over and gave him a hug. "That's so nice. I don't even know how to repay you for such a nice surprise."

"No repayment is necessary, Beverly. I really appreciate all your hospitality and wanted to do something to show my gratitude." Jim was so glad that he had bought the wood, even if it had been on a whim. It felt good that such a small gesture on his part could bring so much happiness.

"You don't even know what a godsend that is for me and the kids. And I really didn't want Ben to go and try to get a load for me. He's not as young as he used to be, but he is so stubborn. Once he gets a mindset to do something he will do it come hell or high water." Beverly was truly happy. The money and the wood eased a lot of her burden and she let out a sigh of relief. Things really were looking up.

By midnight they all retired to bed. It had been a long day and within ten minutes Amanda was fast asleep wrapped in Jim's arms. She loved sleeping in the same bed, with his arms wrapped around her. It made her feel safe and loved and tonight she felt like all her dreams were coming true.

Chapter Thirteen

The rest of the weekend flew by. Saturday, they put the tree up and let the kids do the majority of the decorating. Most of the ornaments were on the bottom half of the tree but they had worked so hard decorating it that Amanda didn't have the heart to move any of the ornaments around. "I think it looks perfect," Jim told them while grabbing his camera and snapping pictures of the kids standing by the tree.

That night, Jim took everyone up to Willow Creek for dinner. Since they had the kids, they decided on the pizza parlor. A lot of other people had the same idea so the wait was long but Jim got quarters from the cashier and kept the kids occupied with video games. Bev and Ben were relieved to turn over the duties of entertaining the kids to Amanda and Jim for the night. They were young, energetic and had the stamina to keep up with the kids, better than either of them did.

Sunday, around one, they started packing up and loading the truck, getting ready to leave. Amanda had to be back at the rehab by five o'clock and Jim wanted a little time to wash clothes and get ready for the workweek. It was hard leaving and Amanda was wracked by guilt. Both kids were clinging to her crying and by the time they left she was in tears too.

"Don't worry, honey. They will be fine once you're gone," Beverly reassured her.

Ben had walked up too, to see them off. Shaking hands with Jim, he too hated to see them leave. "You're welcome back anytime Jim. You always have a place to stay." Normally a very private person, both Amanda and Beverly were a little surprised at the extended invitation he made.

Giving his niece a big hug, he held her tight for a minute. "Bye, babe. I love you and I'm proud of you. Keep up the good work." Ben released her and she had tears in her eyes. "Bye, Uncle. I love you too."

Lastly she gave her mom a hug and kiss. "Bye, Mom. Thanks for everything. I really had a good weekend. I'll call you tomorrow."

As they drove out of the Valley, it took her a minute to regain her composure. Even though she knew it was for the best and loved her new life on the Coast, it was hard to leave her kids.

Giving her some time, Jim didn't talk until they were almost to Willow Creek. "I really enjoyed myself this weekend. You have a great family and your kids are awesome. I can see why it's so hard to leave them, but you're doing what you need to do for them and yourself. You do know that, right?"

"Yeah, I know," she answered. She was glad that he understood how she was feeling. "It's just hard. I really miss them and feel like a loser sometimes for letting them down like I have."

"Well, I don't have kids but I can tell you that kids are resilient and forgiving. And as they get older they will understand that this is something that you did for them." He was trying to be supportive but wasn't sure if what he was saying was comforting or not. Deciding that now was a good time to change the subject, he had something that he wanted to ask her.

"So in a couple of weeks the school is having their Christmas Dinner for staff. I'm not sure where they are holding it this year but normally it's either at the casino or one of the fancier hotels. And…" he paused for a brief second, "I was wondering if you would go with me?"

"Wow, really. You want me to be your date?" She was touched that he wanted her to go with him. "I would love too. Is it formal? I'm not sure what I would wear." Mentally going through her wardrobe she couldn't come up with anything that would be appropriate for a Christmas Dinner.

"Well, I don't think it's exactly formal but it is festive and everyone does get pretty dressed up. But next weekend we can go shopping." Before she could protest, Jim continued. "I wanted to take you shopping anyhow and then you can help me pick out something to wear. I'm not the best shopper." He knew that she needed to get some new things and also realized that her finances were limited. He had wanted to offer earlier but also knew how proud she was and didn't want her to feel like a charity case. There were a lot of things he wanted to buy her and do for her but he also knew her well enough to realize that he had to tread lightly and gradually work up from small gestures.

"That sounds great. I'll get my per capita check next week too and wanted to buy some Christmas presents." Her Mom had just shared the news with her, the day before.

"What's a per capita check?" He asked.

"It's a payment that the Tribe gives to its membership. It's based on our timber revenues and money from our enterprises, or something like that. I'm not exactly sure how they calculate it but we normally always get it in December. On good years we get a check in August for school clothes too," Amanda explained, the best that she could. "Anyhow, this year it's five hundred dollars, which is better than last year. I get half of my kid's money too, but I'm going to give that to my mom." Amanda had been relieved when her mom had told her about the checks coming out. Without it she really had no way to buy Christmas presents.

"So next weekend we will spend a day shopping and then the following weekend is the dinner. I'm hoping that you can get an overnight pass. The dinner usually gets over around ten or eleven but I thought we could gamble awhile before we go back to my place." Jim told her, already looking forward to next weekend. The overnight was contingent upon her getting a pass but there really was no reason for them to deny it. After all, she had always made it back in time and had never had an issue with a dirty test.

They talked all the way back to the Coast, mostly about her kids, her mom and her uncle.

"I really did enjoy myself. Your kids are great. They are really well behaved for their age and smart and funny. Melanie is just about the cutest little girl I have ever been around," Jim said, with complete sincerity.

"Thanks. They really liked you too, especially my Uncle Ben. Just for the record, he doesn't always warm up to people that fast, especially non-Natives." She hoped he didn't find that offensive but it was the truth.

"He's a great guy. So interesting. I could talk to him for hours. We talked about history and the culture. I learned a lot from him." Jim was pleased that Ben liked him because the feeling was mutual. He had complete respect for her uncle.

"I'm glad. You know the first night, when we got there, I was feeling a little embarrassed and self-conscious," she confessed.

"Really? About what?" he asked, not quite understanding.

"Well, I just hadn't really noticed before what bad shape our house was in and how shabby everything looked. And then when I was setting

115

the table, it hit me that absolutely none of our dishes matched. Your immaculate house kept flashing in my head." She laughed, but in an embarrassed way.

"Are you kidding me?" He looked sideways at her, with a puzzled look on his face. "Well I hope that you didn't feel like that on my account. I really didn't notice and I don't pay attention to things like that. Yes, my house might be in better shape but then again it's just me. I don't have kids or family there. As a matter of fact, except when you stayed the weekend, I really haven't had anyone else in my house. There's no comparison. I'm not home most days and normally am just there to sleep and maybe watch television for a while. "

"I guess I didn't really think about it like that." And she hadn't.

"I loved your house. It had life to it and had all the signs of children and people actually living in a home. And for the record, I'm not a snob like that." He spoke firmly but gently. He didn't want to belabor the point or hurt her feelings but he wanted her to understand that he wasn't the kind of person who would look down on someone over dishes not matching, or houses that might need a little work.

"You're right. I'm sorry. And really I didn't mean to imply that I thought you were a snob. I know you well enough to know that that isn't true. I guess it's my own insecurities," Amanda admitted, hoping to smooth it over.

"I really hope that someday you will appreciate your worth. You are kind and sweet and everyone who knows you sees this. I guess some of your charm is that you are so beautiful and you don't see it. It's just genuinely you." If anything frustrated him at times it was her low self-esteem. More than once he had wished she could see herself through other's eyes.

The rest of the trip was lighter with him telling her stories about his childhood and places that he had been. After pulling into the rehab he kissed her and held her close to him for a minute. "I really did have a great time. Thanks again for inviting me," Jim told her, while still holding her close.

"I'm glad you came. I had a great time too," she answered. Reaching in the backseat she grabbed her duffle bag and opened her door to get out.

She was just getting ready to shut the door when he called out, "I love you. I'll talk to you tomorrow."

Quickly replying, "I love you too," she closed the truck door. Although she absolutely meant it, it still felt weird and awkward to say out loud.

The week passed fast. She saw him briefly when he was there doing his tutoring and Wednesday night they went to dinner after he had finished at the rehab. They decided that they would go up to Oregon to shop for clothes and Christmas presents. "If you can get a pass we can get a room and stay the night. If not, then we will make a fast turn-around trip," Jim told her. Hopefully she could get a pass but if not, at least they had a back-up plan.

Thursday, she walked into the office and filled out an overnight pass. Rayna quickly read the request, signed it and handed it back. "So Amanda I'm going to go ahead and approve this. You have shown responsibility every time you've gotten a pass; you've never been late or had a dirty test. I was just looking at your file and your ninety days will be up on January tenth. Have you made any more decisions about what you are going to do then?" Rayna asked, half expecting that she would be moving in with Jim.

"Well, I really want to move into a sober living house but I don't know how I would pay for it without finding a job first." Amanda didn't want that burden to fall on her mother, sister or uncle. She had already decided that if she couldn't find a job and pay her own way then she would go home and try to make it work there.

"Well, I really hope that works out. I would hate to see you go home already, only because the rate of relapse increases then. You know if you got on General Assistance that would help cover most of the cost. Or, do you think that maybe your Tribe would help?" Rayna knew that other tribes had helped clients in the past and she had learned to be creative in helping clients find resources to pay for rehab and sober living housing.

"I guess I could check. I hadn't really thought about asking the Tribe to help. I would rather not be on GA, only because then you owe them and they will bill you forever. I know others who owe thousands of dollars now, for assistance they received when they had no income." Amanda really didn't want to go on General Assistance if it meant racking up a monthly bill that she would end up owing to the state.

"Well, you have a little more than a month to work on it but the time sneaks up fast. If you need me to do anything to help, like writing a letter, or help you with a resume for a job search, just let me know," Rayna offered.

Saturday morning Amanda woke up early and packed a bag. She was excited to go shopping, something she really hadn't done in years.

In the past few years when she had any type of money it went for drugs, never for clothes or presents. Jim picked her up at eight and walking out to meet him, she climbed in the truck and threw her bag in the back seat. "I thought you would be driving the Prius today. You know to save on gas."

"Well, I almost did but I was watching the weather channel and there's a chance we might hit snow so I decided to bring the truck. That way I don't have to worry about putting chains on," Jim explained.

The drive was good and uneventful. They listened to CDs and he told her about some of the other teachers at the middle school. By noon they were in Medford. "I already made reservations at a hotel but we can't check in until four, so I was thinking that we could go eat lunch somewhere and then hit the mall. How does that sound?" Jim asked.

"That sounds good," Amanda answered. "I am starting to get hungry." One of the things she loved about going places with Jim was that he always had it planned out and there was never stress about finding a place to stay, or getting lost. He just handled everything so smoothly and she could just relax and enjoy the trip. It felt good to travel and not worry about breaking down or have the ability to eat at a restaurant without having to worry if there was enough money. It was a type of security that she had never had before and one that she truly appreciated.

They decided on an Italian restaurant for lunch. Jim let her pick what type of food she was hungry for and she confessed that she had a weakness for pasta.

After eating, they drove to the mall and found a parking spot. "So how do you want to work this? Would you feel better shopping by yourself or do you want me to go with you? I'm going to warn you, I'm not the best clothes shopper and I don't want you to feel rushed," Jim explained, wanting to do whatever would make her the most comfortable.

"I don't know. What do you prefer?" Amanda threw it back on him. She had always felt intimidated shopping but on the other hand she didn't really want him standing around while she tried clothes on.

"Well, why don't you go look for clothes for yourself first and then we can meet and go shopping for Christmas presents. Really, you will probably do better shopping for clothes by yourself, without me hanging around." Pulling out his wallet he took out five, one hundred dollar bills and handed it to her.

"What's this for? Seriously I'm not buying a prom dress; just a nice dress and shoes." She tried handing him his money back.

"I told you that I wanted you to shop for yourself. Buy yourself clothes, shoes, a purse, whatever. This is partly your Christmas present and I want to do this. I'm not taking no for an answer." Jim had expected that she would protest which is why he waited until they were at the mall to give her the money.

"I don't know what to say. I feel funny taking this much money." She looked at him but could see the determination in his eyes.

"Look, I have a good income and I have nothing really to spend it on. Just myself and basic bills, so please, just go shop and enjoy. How about we meet at the food court, in say, two hours, and then we'll shop together," Jim said with decisiveness in his tone, leaving no room for argument.

"All right. Thank you. I haven't shopped for so long, I hope it comes back to me," Amanda said, jokingly and rolled her eyes at him.

"Don't worry. It's just like riding a bike. You'll get the hang of it," Jim said, winking at her before turning and walking off in the opposite direction.

Since her main objective was finding a dress for the dinner, she started with that. After looking through several stores she eyed a red velvet A-line dress. It looked festive and sexy, but in a classy way versus a slutty way. Trying it on, she looked in the mirror and knew it was the one. It fit just right, hung nicely and she felt good wearing it. Next, she found a pair of black heels. She tried them on, decided they were comfortable enough and something she could wear without falling down.

After that she bought more practical clothes that she desperately needed right now; jeans, warm shirts, a pair of boots, underwear, bras and a few night shirts to sleep in that were cute and sexy. Looking at the big clock in the middle of the mall she noticed that it was ten minutes until their arranged meeting time. She carried all of her bags to the food court and started scanning the crowd for Jim. It was crowded today with all of the Christmas shoppers. She was a careful shopper, used to being frugal and still had sixty dollars left from the money he had given her.

Approaching the middle of the food court she saw him sitting on a bench and smiled to herself, thinking how handsome he was and how lucky she was. There was no question that he would be there. He was so stable and dependable. She never had to worry about drama when she was with him.

"Wow. You got a lot of bags there. Did you have enough money? I didn't want you using your own money; that's for your Christmas presents." Looking over all of the bags that she was carrying it was hard to believe that she could have gotten all of that with the money he had given her.

"Are you kidding," she told him. "I still have sixty dollars left of the money you gave me."

He shot her a look of disbelief.

"Really. I can show you the receipts if you don't believe me." She started pulling the receipts out of her pocket.

"No, that's okay. I believe you. I guess you are a good shopper. So I bought myself something to wear to the dinner and a pair of shoes and it took me almost the same amount of time to buy that as it took you to buy all of this. I'm impressed," Jim said, with exaggerated astonishment. "Let's go put this in the truck so we can start buying presents." They walked out to the truck and Jim locked all of the shopping bags up in the truck.

"So who do you want to buy for first? The kids or your mom and uncle?" Jim asked.

"Let's start with the kids. Who all do you have to buy for, by the way?" Amanda asked, curious about his Christmas list.

"Well, my mom and dad, my sister, brother-in-law and my niece and nephew," he answered.

They decided to go to a toy store first and ended up spending two hours shopping there. "Oh my gosh," Amanda exclaimed. "There is so much here it's almost overwhelming." She walked up and down the aisles, weighing out one present over another. Jim on the other hand, picked his presents out much faster; a Monster High doll for his niece and a Lego set for his nephew.

"How did you pick something out so fast?" Amanda asked, still having a hard time choosing.

"Well, I don't have as much pressure as you do. I'm not the parent. Their parents will buy them a lot and generally go a little overboard so I called my sister and asked her what to get. I didn't want to duplicate," he explained.

"I guess that makes sense. Well, now you can focus on helping me." She grabbed his hand and started leading him up the aisles with her. In the end she got her daughter a big set of Disney princess dolls, a tea set, some books and a cash register that came with fake money. For her son she got a Lego set, a fishing pole, an electric train and a big SpongeBob pillow.

"So what am I getting your kids?" He asked. "I am at a loss as to what to get them."

"I don't know. I guess we could look around some more," she answered.

"I wanted to ask you if you thought they would like something like a Wii or an X box?" Jim had been thinking about it since he had been there at Thanksgiving.

"I don't know. I mean, of course they would like it but I'm not sure my mom could handle hooking it up or knowing how to help them with it, if there were problems. She really struggles with electronics. Besides, that's too much anyhow." She was touched but she knew that her mom would stress about it.

"Okay. So the other option I was thinking about was getting them each a Nintendo DS Gameboy. They are easy to use and it could entertain them when they ride out to the Coast or have to wait at the doctor's office. You know times like that," Jim said, putting his sales pitch on.

"It's nice that you want to buy them something like that but that is pretty expensive." She didn't know the exact price but knew that they were probably a couple hundred dollars each and again felt a little funny about the money that Jim was spending.

"Well, that is what I want to get them. They are such good kids. Couldn't we just say that Santa brought them?" He was trying hard to persuade her.

"Gosh. That just seems like a lot. I don't know." Biting on her fingernails, she was feeling awkward right now. "Can I think about it?"

"Sure." He sounded a little disappointed but he wasn't done yet. He would give her some time and then bring it up again. "It's been a long day. Why don't we go check in the hotel and rest for a while? We still have tomorrow to shop."

"That sounds good. I am getting a little tired," Amanda conceded.

After he checked them into the hotel, they carried their bags up to the room on the second floor. The room was one of the nicest that she had stayed in. "Is this a smoking room?" She asked, but noticed that there weren't ashtrays anywhere.

"No. This is a smoke-free hotel. I'm sorry I didn't even think about that," he apologized.

"It's okay. I'm trying to cut back anyway. If I start feigning too bad I can always step out on the balcony." The more she was around Jim the more conscious she was about smoking.

After they had settled in he sat on the edge of the bed and pulled her over to sit on his lap. "So, have you decided about the Gameboys?"

"No. Not really. It's a nice gesture but it just seems like a lot of money. And then, paying for my clothes today. Your always so blasé about it but to me it's a lot of money and it just makes me feel weird, you know." Not wanting to sound unappreciative, she hoped that he understood what she was trying to convey.

"Well, I love you and I want to take care of you and your kids. It's as simple as that. I'm trying hard not to push because I know that it makes you uncomfortable; but it's just money. I'm by no means a millionaire but I do have resources and I'm not offering to do anything that I can't afford or that is going to break me." He didn't want to tell her that he had a trust fund that had been set up when he was born, by one of his grandparents. Figuring that would freak her out, he decided that he would keep that to himself for the time being.

"Gosh. You're so persuasive. I really do appreciate all that you do. I just don't ever want to take it for granted. Things happen and money can come and go. I've never had the means to just go out and buy anything I've wanted and nothing has come easy. I have watched my family struggle to put food on the table more times than not. I just don't want you to ever feel like I'm using you or that I'm with you for what I get out of it. I love you for a lot of reasons but your money isn't one of them," Amanda explained. She really did appreciate all of his gestures but would love him anyhow.

"I know. That's one of the things I love about you," he murmured, while nuzzling her neck.

Moving her off of his lap and onto the bed this time when they made love there was more intensity than in the past with an added component of an emotional connection between two people who knew and understood each other and were growing more and more in love. As she lay in his arms she felt complete, maybe for the first time in her life. They fell asleep and both slept hard, exhausted from the trip and shopping. He stirred first, waking her up and at first she was disoriented and groggy.

"Wow. What time is it?" he asked her.

Looking at the clock by the bed, she answered, "It's eight. We slept two hours." Sitting up, rubbing her eyes, she still felt a little disoriented.

"What do you want to do for dinner?" He asked, stomach rumbling.

"I picked lunch. This time it's up to you," she murmured.

Pulling a menu out of the drawer, he scanned it. "Well, if it's my choice I pick room service."

Picking up the phone he ordered two steak sandwiches with fries, two green salads, a glass of wine for himself and an ice tea for her.

Dinner was delivered about thirty minutes later and after eating a leisurely dinner they took a shower. She put on one of her new nightshirts. It was pink, silky and soft. She loved it. "Wow, I like it," he said appreciatively. "It's a far cry from your usual sweat pants and oversized t-shirt."

"I know. Right?" She laughed and playfully pushed at him.

Propped up in bed, he pulled out a pile of his student's essays and started grading them. She watched television and tried not to disturb him while he worked. Taking a strip of Suboxone out of her purse, she took out a little pair of scissors and cut a strip. She was down to one strip a day and sometimes one strip even lasted a day and a half. She looked at the clock and mentally started timing twenty minutes while it dissolved.

After twenty minutes she finally swallowed and grabbed a drink to wash the taste out of her mouth. He had watched her routine before but had never really paid attention. "So what exactly does Suboxone do?" He asked, curious about how it worked.

"Well, it blocks opiates for starters. If I tried to use something, which I have no intention of doing, then I wouldn't get anything out of it; but more importantly it stops cravings." Amanda was pleased that he was showing interest and asking.

"How long do people usually take it? I mean do the cravings eventually stop or…?" Jim asked, his voice trailing off.

"I'm not sure. I guess it's different for everyone. They say some people have to take it for life. Others take it for months or up to a year I guess. When you go off it you have to wean off over a period of time, I've been told," Amanda answered.

"Oh. I'm just curious. I never really heard of it before." Giving her a reassuring smile, he went back to reading his essays.

"I really hope that I can get off of Suboxone within a few months." She wanted him to know that. "It's my goal to not be dependent on anything, you know."

"Well, I'm sure that you will make it a reality." He grabbed her hand and brought it to his lips and kissed it. "You are such a strong woman. I'm really proud of you." She smiled to herself. Even though it seemed corny, it made her feel good.

The next morning they woke up to the sound of rain. It was dreary and cold and they both would have loved to stay in bed and have a leisurely morning but they still had shopping to do and he knew that they could hit snow on the way home so didn't want to leave too late. While she got ready he walked to the breakfast buffet and got them coffee, fruit and a couple of pastries. Loading everything in the truck they went back to the mall. She relented and he bought each of her kids a Nintendo DS Gameboy along with several games that he chose based on age and gender and spent a lot of time reading the package before deciding which to buy.

Their style of choosing presents was completely different. She bought practical gifts. For her mom she bought a robe, slippers and a jacket. For her uncle she bought a flannel shirt, wool socks and a pair of gloves. Jim bought more on a whim. For his mom he bought a bottle of expensive perfume and for his dad some Cuban cigars and a leather satchel. He bought his sister a book and his brother in law a leather wallet along with a gift card for both of them.

"I have three presents left to get and I'm not sure what to get Ashley. She's hard to buy for." She had been giving it a lot of thought but nothing was coming to mind. "I want to buy something for Rayna and I need to get something for Aunty Dee."

"Okay. Well we still have a few hours. I think we should get on the road by one at the latest so we can be sure to make it back by five," Jim said, while looking at his watch.

While she went into one of the stores, he browsed around at one of the Verizon kiosk, looking at new phones.

She finally decided on a scarf for Rayna, who wore bright scarfs almost daily. For her sister she bought a picture frame, a scented candle and a pretty make up bag. For her aunt, she bought slippers and a bubble bath set. The last person she needed to buy for was Jim and that was the hardest. She didn't have a clue what to buy him. She had one hundred sixty dollars left, so she decided that she would have to be creative about what she bought him; something thoughtful and meaningful without being expensive. And it was hard because he was with her. Deciding to wait and figure out something when he wasn't with her she walked out to the bench where he was waiting.

"Okay. I'm done. How about you?" Amanda asked, but already knew that he was ready and anxious to hit the road.

"I'm ready. I think we should go through drive-thru and eat on the road. This storm seems to be getting worse." Jim answered, looking towards the sky, which was looking more and more ominous.

After they had gone through drive-thru and were on their way, he finally handed a bag to her from Verizon. "So I hope you don't get mad at me but I bought you a phone." He spoke without looking at her. "I know that you can't have it at the rehab so I'll keep it while you're there but this way you can call your mom and kids and when you apply for jobs you'll have a number that they can reach you at."

Opening the bag, a big smile crossed her face. It was an iPhone and she instantly loved it. "Oh my God. I love it. Thank you." She was too excited to protest. She had never had anything other than a ten dollar pre-paid flip phone and had always wanted a good phone that she could get on the internet, Facebook and all the other cool things she saw people doing on their phones.

Unbuckling her seatbelt, she leaned across the center console and planted a big kiss on the side of his face. "Thank you. I really do love it."

"I can see that. I'm really glad but put your seatbelt back on. You never know about other drivers." He was laughing and joking but serious at the same time. "So, I put you on my plan. It has unlimited calling and texting. I'm not sure how much data it has but I don't use much data on mine so hopefully it's enough." He had bought it on a whim and had been a little worried that she would protest about him spending too much. He was glad she hadn't and was happy that she was so thrilled about it. Being with her had opened his eyes to how much he took for granted.

The drive home took a little longer than expected. They hit snow on one pass and had to put the truck in 4WD until they got over the top and down towards the bottom of the hill. She played with her phone most of the way and he teased her about being like a kid with a new toy. Arriving back at the rehab at four thirty they kissed good-bye and she reluctantly gave him the phone to hold on to for her. "Please keep my new baby safe," she told him jokingly, as she got out of the truck.

"I will. Don't worry. I'll see you tomorrow at three." She had asked him to keep her presents at his house. "Sometimes things disappear at rehab. I just don't want to chance having anything mysteriously walk off." He hadn't really thought of that before but then again this was a rehab, not a sorority house, he reminded himself.

Chapter Fourteen

Friday night, they went to dinner and made plans for the next day. "So I got a pass for tomorrow night, "Amanda relayed to Jim. "I wasn't sure what time you were picking me up so I just said 'sometime tomorrow morning until Sunday night at five.' Does that work?"

"Yep. That sounds good. I will come by around nine tomorrow morning and pick you up. I was going to ask if you wanted to get your hair done or nails done, pedicure, you know, girl stuff." He wasn't sure if that was something she would like to do or not but had decided that it wouldn't hurt to ask.

"I hadn't really thought about it." Thinking that maybe he wanted her to look more polished in front of his co-workers, she tried not to feel insecure about his offer.

"I think you look perfect but I just wanted to offer. You know, just pamper you a little bit," he said, reaching across the table and kissing her.

"I mean, I guess. I just don't really know what I would want done with my hair." It wasn't something that she had really considered.

"Well, I don't mean cut it. I love your long hair. I especially love it when it falls all over my naked body. Hmm," he said, sensuously and sincerely.

"I see where your mind's at," she told him. "I love that too."

"I can't wait until tomorrow night. You're going to look so beautiful in your new dress." Jim was getting worked up just thinking about it but there was something else on his mind that he needed to tell her.

"So, I normally don't like to talk about past relationships. I'm a firm believer that the past is the past and I don't dwell on it." He took a drink of water and paused for a minute. She started feeling nervous wondering what he had heard and immediately assumed the worse. "So, I apologize in advance but I wanted to prepare you before tomorrow night. So, a few months before we started dating, I broke up with a woman who is one of the secretaries at the school. Last year I actually took her to the

Christmas dinner and we went out for a few months. It didn't take me long to figure out that the woman is psycho. Actually, that is an understatement. How do I put this nicely? Well let's just say that she's a crazy bitch." He paused again for a moment, giving time for this bit of information to sink in.

"Okay. So is this crazy bitch going to nut up when she sees me with you?" Amanda asked, jokingly, but soon realized that he wasn't laughing.

"Well I don't think she'll nut up exactly. But she can be pretty nasty and I'm not sure what she is capable of. In the least she will probably try to put you down and make you uncomfortable. I will try to steer clear of her, but unfortunately she has no shame and will probably keep popping up wherever we are." He seemed a little embarrassed and Amanda wondered if there was more that he just wasn't telling her.

"Okay. Well thanks for the warning but I'll be okay. I'm a 'rez' girl, you know. Believe me I can handle whatever she throws at me. What does she look like by the way? So I will recognize her if she comes at me in the bathroom or something." Again, she was joking but he wasn't on board with her humor tonight. Of course he had dated before her. He was handsome, smart, funny, generous and kind. She was sure lots of women at his work liked him and wanted to hook up with him.

"Well, she's actually not bad looking on the outside but the inside just makes her ugly. She's on the tall side, slim, blond. She resembles a Barbie doll in some ways. On first glance, she actually is kind of pretty but believe me it doesn't take long before the ugly side of her comes out," he said, with a look of disdain when he described her.

Feeling a little intimidated by his description she was quiet for a minute. "So, how old is she?" She asked.

"She's twenty-seven. Her name is Tiffany. Anyhow, it's over. I don't have any feelings for her, except maybe pity. When I broke it off with her she was very angry. Apparently, she had been telling people that we were going to get married even though we had never talked about it and I had never even considered that." She was looking a little stressed as he told her about Tiffany and although it wasn't his favorite subject, he wanted to prepare her, just in case. He knew Tiffany well enough to know that she would take cruel pleasure in putting on a show and exaggerating their relationship. "Anyhow, I just thought that I should let you know. You know the old saying, 'A woman scorned.' "

"Okay. Well thanks for the heads up. Are you sure you want to go? Maybe it would be better not to give her the opportunity." She was feeling nervous now and intimidated before she had even seen this woman.

"I want to go and I have a lot of co-workers who I want you to meet. They've heard me talk about you enough. I want them to see that you're real and not an imaginary girlfriend that I have made up. It will be fine and we will have a good time, I promise. It is at the casino, by the way, so we can gamble a little after the dinner." He almost regretted bringing Tiffany up but had given it a lot of thought and knew that it was better that she knew beforehand rather than being blindsided at the dinner.

She made an appointment at a hair salon to have her hair done, a manicure and a pedicure. She actually had had nails done once, when she graduated from eighth grade and had hated the feeling and they didn't last long. She figured that being the tomboy that she was, she was just too rough on nails. But it had been ages since she had done anything like that and she was actually looking forward to it. Besides, if she had competition at this dinner then she better look her best.

He picked her up at nine on Saturday morning and they drove to his house.

"So my appointment is at one. I've never had a pedicure before." She was getting excited about the whole beauty appointment and just hoped that her hair came out okay.

"That works out. We have time to have breakfast and hang out before your appointment. Do you have a driver's license? I was thinking that you could just take the Prius to your appointment." That way he could go get a haircut at the barber shop and they could meet up again, after she was done.

"Actually, no I don't. I can drive and have driven a lot but I never did get a license," she answered, a little embarrassed.

"Oh. Okay. I just assumed that you had one. Well, I'll drop you off and then you can text me when you're done." He was a little surprised and wondered how she had gone so long without getting a license. "How is it that you never got a license? I just thought it was kind of a rite of passage as a teenager, you know, to get a driver's license."

"Yeah. I guess it seems strange but I have pretty much only driven around Hoopa, for the most part. I've driven to the Coast a few times. I just never went out and took a test. Luckily, I guess, I have never been stopped." She hadn't thought of this as unusual before but he was right. At her age, she should have a license by now.

"Well, I think next week we should get a driver's handbook and schedule a test for you. Then after the written, you can use the Prius to take a driving test." He had been thinking about letting her use the Prius to go job-hunting, but not without a license.

"Okay. Hopefully I pass. That would be embarrassing if I didn't." She laughed nervously and again it struck him how little confidence she had in herself.

"You will pass; if not the first time, then the next time." He put his arm around her as they walked into the house.

In the corner was the tree that they had cut down at Thanksgiving. She hadn't been over since he had put it up and she immediately walked over to it in complete awe. "This is the prettiest tree I have ever seen." And it was true. It was covered in tiny white lights and it looked like every ornament was strategically placed. There was an angel on top, made out of crystal. The tree looked elegant and it was hard to believe that he had decorated it by himself.

Coming behind her, he circled both of his arms around her waist and pulled her towards him. "I was hoping that you would like it. I haven't really ever put a tree up before and had to go buy ornaments and the angel for the top. I wanted to surprise you and have it decorated before you came over."

"It's absolutely beautiful." Turning around she encircled his neck with her arms and their lips locked in a long kiss. As his hands started unbuttoning her jeans, he whispered, "God, I've missed you all week." Lowering her to the couch, their bodies melted into one as they had passionate, unhurried sex. Afterwards they lay in each other's arms, both spent for the moment, feeling completely relaxed and happy.

"Well it's almost eleven. I propose that we shower, eat breakfast and get ready to go to your appointment." It was a dreary day outside and if it wasn't for the dinner, he would have just as soon stayed with her all day, watching movies and doing basically nothing. Maybe tomorrow, he thought, and looked forward to the prospect.

After she had run a bath, he jumped in the shower and they both dressed and went downstairs. He made them breakfast burritos while she cut fresh fruit and poured them orange juice. She was getting more comfortable in his kitchen and was starting to know where he kept everything. Sitting at the table, eating breakfast, they read the newspaper. He read the headlines while she on the other hand looked through the Want Ads. The job listings were dismal at best. There were only a handful of Help Wanted ads and many of those were for nurses or some other professional position that she wasn't qualified for. "Do you ever think of going to school? You're so smart and it would really benefit you, in the long run." Jim asked, looking over the top of the newspaper, at her.

"No. I haven't really thought about it much. I'm not even sure what I would go to school for. My sister has done well with her nursing degree but that definitely isn't for me. I have a weak stomach and hate the sight of blood," Amanda answered.

"Well, there are lots of areas that you could go into; computer science, teaching, law, business, art, just to name a few. I've seen how good you are on computers. Think about it. There are lots of resources for financial aid if you decided that you wanted to go to school." He knew that she could do well in school and also hoped that by taking some classes, it would help boost up her self-esteem.

"Okay. I'll think about it. Thanks for always believing in me. You're truly the best person I know." She meant that and sometimes wished that he had been in her life sooner, before she had really gone off the deep end.

"Ditto. I feel the same about you. I look at you and you're so beautiful, inside and out. You're kind, smart and sensitive. I love everything about you. I don't know any more what my life was like before you. It seems meaningless up to that point." It just felt right to say it and he hoped she really heard what he was saying. Tears came to her eyes and a look of sadness veiled over her face.

Jim quickly pulled her into his arms and embraced her. "What's wrong? Did I say something to upset you?" He asked, confused.

Amanda quickly wiped her tears away. It took a minute to answer. "It was beautiful. I love you so much. I'm just scared that I'm going to disappoint you. Sometimes I'm just scared that you don't really know me," she explained, struggling to compose herself.

"I think that I do." Kissing her he continued. "But it's almost time to go. Today is going to be a good day so let's just focus on that." He knew by now not to bombard her with too much emotional sentiment at once. She had a hard time accepting that she was worthy of love and he suspected that it had to do with something from when she was growing up or things that happened when she was on drugs. He knew that she could probably benefit from some counseling but just didn't know how to broach the subject yet.

Before they left, she retrieved her new phone that was on a charger on the kitchen counter. "You had me so distracted all morning that I forgot all about my phone."

"I wondered. I kind of thought that would be the first thing you asked for. Glad to see that I rated above the phone," he said, teasing.

They drove to the Salon and he dropped her off. "Text me when you're ready to be picked up. I'm going to go get a haircut and do a couple of errands."

She felt awkward at first, walking into the Salon. She was definitely out of her comfort zone but the lady at the desk was pleasant and friendly and led her to a chair. "So we are going to start with the pedicure, then the manicure and last we will do your hair. You have beautiful hair, by the way."

"Thanks. So I'm going to confess that I've never had a pedicure. I'm not really sure what to do." She decided to just put it out there.

"It's fine. We will take good care of you." The desk lady smiled at her reassuringly and within a few minutes her feet were soaking in a basin of warm water. When the pedicure was done, she looked down and admired her toenails. They looked perfect. The lady painted them a burgundy red and on the two big toenails, there was a diamond looking stone glued on. She had never seen fancier toenails and giggled to herself while looking at them.

Next, was the manicure. She ended up getting a red that matched her dress with gold, festive flakes mixed in. It almost looked a little gaudy to her but decided that since it was the holidays she was going to go with it.

Moving to a different station, in front of a big mirror, the lady started brushing her hair out. "So what are we doing today? Are we cutting your hair, styling it, or both?" The hairstylist asked.

"I'm not really sure. I want a trim but just an inch or two but I need it styled. I'm going to a Christmas dinner tonight and I would like some type of hairstyle but I'm not good at this so I'm not sure what I want. Could you suggest something?" Amanda had been dreading this part of the appointment because she truly didn't know what she wanted done to her hair and was open for suggestions.

"With your long hair we could do all sorts of things. Let me think about it a minute."

The stylist walked around the chair looking at her hair and touching it a few times, deep in thought. "Do you want to wear it up or down?"

"Well, I would like the back down." She knew Jim loved her long hair and preferred it down versus up in a bun.

"Okay. I have a great idea. Trust me, you're going to look beautiful." The stylist grabbed a water bottle and started spraying water on Amanda's hair and combing it out. "Have you ever cut your hair?" she asked.

"Once. When I was twelve my mom cut it short," she answered, leaving out that it was when her brother died and as customary the whole family cut their hair.

It took almost two hours but in the end it turned out great and was worth every second and every dollar. The stylist had braided the front in tiny sections from the front to just past the back of her head. Then she spent a lot of time curling sections of the long hair in the back. The end result was very elegant looking and she loved it. She felt more like she was going to a prom then a Christmas dinner. She texted Jim to pick her up and in about ten minutes he was there.

"Wow. You look beautiful. I love it," he exclaimed, looking appreciatively at her.

"Thanks," she answered, looking away. Knowing how hard it was for her to take compliments he didn't say more.

"So it's almost five and drinks and hors d'oeuvres start at six and dinner at seven. Meaning we better get our butts in gear and start getting ready." He knew that he wouldn't take very long changing but imagined that she would need longer.

She grabbed her make up bag and went upstairs to the bathroom, taking her time to carefully apply her make up. The pressure was on, as far as she was concerned, ever since he had told her about Tiffany. Tonight she would have to step up her game because she had no plans on letting "Barbie doll Tiffany" outshine her. He was her man now and Tiffany was going to have to get over herself.

At ten minutes before six, she walked downstairs where he was waiting. She looked good tonight and she knew it. Looking up the staircase at her, a big smile crossed Jim's face. "Wow. I don't know what else to say except, "wow." You look absolutely beautiful." And it was true. Her red velvet dress fit snug and accentuated her curves, looking sexy and suave. The heels went perfect with the dress. The only thing missing was jewelry and she had wished that she had a necklace, earrings or something that matched.

As if on cue, he pulled a long skinny box out of his pocket. "So there is one thing missing," handing her the box, he went on, "Merry early Christmas."

"Seriously. You've been spending so much on me. I don't know what to say." Her hands were shaking as she opened the box and the excitement she was feeling was hard to contain. Peeking inside she saw a gold chain with a diamond in a teardrop setting hanging on the bottom. It was delicate and beautiful. She had never really owned a piece of fine jewelry before. "Thank you. I feel like a princess. You're always spoiling me and doing nice things for me." He took the necklace and turned her around while he fastened the clasp.

"I'm glad you like it. I knew it would look beautiful with your dress." Amanda put both hands up to his face and pulling him towards her gave him a long kiss. It could have gone on and on but he finally broke away. "Well, we better make a move or we might end up blowing off the dinner and going back upstairs," Jim said, pleased that she liked the necklace so much.

The drive to the casino was quiet. She was lost in thought, wondering what she had done to deserve so much happiness. Thinking back to the vast difference three short months ago it almost seemed unreal now that things could be so wonderful.

"You seem lost in thought. Penny for your thoughts," Jim said, glancing over at her appreciatively. She really did look beautiful.

"I'm just thinking how happy I am and how wonderful you are." She told him. Giving him a smile, she ran her fingers along the diamond pendant, wondering when he had bought it.

Deciding to use valet parking, he pulled to the front of the casino and went around and opened her door and then gave the valet his key. Tucking the valet ticket into his pocket, he put his arm around her as they started walking towards the Banquet room at the back of the casino.

They walked in and already there were quite a few people there. A bar was set up on the end of the big room and everyone was gathered around it. Holding her hand, they walked to where everyone was assembled. As they got closer to the bar, she saw Tiffany. She knew by his description, that it was her. And if that wasn't enough, the daggers that Tiffany was throwing at her would have tipped her off. Jim ordered a rum and coke for himself and a coke for her. Holding their drinks Jim led Amanda to one of the groups and started introducing her to his co-workers. She greeted everyone that she was introduced to with a big smile and shook hands with each of them. Although she was nervous, tonight was his night and she wasn't going to let him down.

Strategically, he made the rounds with her but had managed to steer clear of Tiffany. He knew that Tiffany was watching them and wanted to send her a clear message. As far as he was concerned this nonsense with Tiffany had to stop. They had been broke up for six months now and it was time that she accepted it. He hadn't told Amanda that he had found a letter in his desk, the day before from Tiffany, professing her love for him and begging him for another chance.

Even though he was always attentive and openly affectionate to Amanda, tonight it was even more so. Either his arm was around her or he was holding her hand and he kissed her often. When it was time for everyone to be seated for dinner, much to his surprise this year there was assigned seating. Of course, he found himself seated between Amanda and Tiffany and he knew that was no coincidence. If he could have changed seats without causing a scene he would have, but by the time he realized what was happening it was too late to do anything about it.

"Hi Jim," Tiffany coyly said. "Whose your friend?"

"Amanda, this is Tiffany. Tiffany, this is my girlfriend, Amanda." Jim said introducing them. He could see Tiffany's eyebrow lift when he used the term girlfriend and he knew it was a little cruel but he didn't care. Tiffany needed to move on.

"It's nice to meet you Tiffany. Are you a teacher too?" Amanda had decided that she would play dumb and pretend like she had no idea who Tiffany was.

"No. I'm one of the school secretaries. Surely, Jim has talked about me." Tiffany couldn't believe that Jim hadn't mentioned her or their relationship.

Looking at Jim very innocently, Amanda replied, "I don't remember him talking about you. But then again he tells me so much about his co-workers and I'm not that good at remembering names."

"I'm a little surprised, Jim that you didn't tell her that last year you brought me as your date to this dinner. Or that we dated for quite some time." Gloating, Tiffany watched Amanda's reaction to see how she would digest it.

"Well, Tiffany, there wasn't really any reason to mention it. That's past history." Jim shot her a look of disdain and then turning towards Amanda, rubbed her cheek and murmured, 'I'm more interested in the present."

Leaning over and kissing him, Amanda replied, "Oh, baby. That's so sweet. My life just started when I met you." She was pouring it on thick. They both were but if that was what it took, then so be it.

"Well, Amanda, just a tip. Jim is pretty fickle. One minute he'll sweep you off your feet and profess his love for you, the next minute he'll dump you so fast it will make your head swim." Tiffany stared hard in Jim's eyes as she said it, just daring him to say something back.

"Okay. I'm not going to sit here and be uncomfortable the whole dinner, Tiffany. You have been exaggerating our few dates to everyone. What I have with Amanda is nothing like what I had with you. There are many nice men out there who would love to be with you, so why don't you get back out in the dating pool and find somebody?" Jim didn't mean to lose his temper but Tiffany always had a way of bringing the worst out in him.

To that Tiffany had no answer. Jim turned his attention back to Amanda and the other people sitting at the table. After introducing Amanda to the rest of the table, casino staff started serving dinner and for the moment everyone was busy eating and making small talk.

In between courses, Amanda excused herself to go to the bathroom, which was out in the main part of the casino. On her way back from the bathroom, she heard someone calling her name. Looking around she spotted her cousin Barbara. "Barbara! I'm so happy to see you. Are you alright?" Amanda was excited to see her cousin. She had thought of her daily, since she had been kicked out of rehab and often worried about her. She knew how rough it could be on the streets and also knew that Barbara didn't have any kind of real support from her family.

"I'm doing okay. I came here with a few friends to gamble and hang out for a while. You look beautiful, Amanda. What's the occasion?" Barbara asked.

"So I don't have much time but I'm here with Jim, at his school's Christmas dinner." She smiled slyly at her cousin. Barbara had known that Amanda had a crush on Jim, even before Amanda had acknowledged it herself.

"I knew it. There was always chemistry between you two." Barbara shook her head in disbelief but genuinely felt happy for her cousin. Amanda was a good person and deserved a good guy like Jim. "I'm so happy for you."

They talked a few more minutes. Amanda gave her her phone number and made her promise to call. Saying their good-byes with promises to keep in touch, Amanda headed back into the banquet room while Barbara headed towards the bathroom.

Amanda sat down at the table at the same time that Tiffany stood up. She looked towards Jim and Amanda and announced, "I'm going out for a minute." Not sure why she felt the need to share this information, Jim just looked blankly at her.

As they watched Tiffany walk away, Jim looked apologetically at Amanda. "I'm sorry if this is uncomfortable. I didn't see this seating arrangement coming. They have never had assigned seating before. We can leave, if you want."

"Absolutely not. I'm not giving Tiffany the satisfaction," Amanda whispered. "I think we should just enjoy ourselves and this great dinner.

Screw her. We aren't leaving." Leaning over, she kissed the side of his face and rubbed her hand on his outer thigh.

"God, I love you," he whispered back. Grabbing her hand, he held it in one place. "You're making me want to head home right now and get you out of that dress."

Tiffany walked in the bathroom, cell phone to her ear. Talking loudly to a friend, she ranted, "Can you believe the nerve of him. He brought some chick to the dinner and they've been all over each other all night." Pausing while she listened to the person on the other end, she didn't notice that a woman was standing by the paper towel dispenser watching her. "I didn't know he was dating anyone else. Her name is Amanda. I haven't seen her before. She's an Indian girl and I don't know what the hell he's thinking." Pausing again for a minute, she looked in the mirror and started fluffing her hair. "No. She's not very pretty. As a matter of fact she just looks trashy. I just wish he would come to his senses. You can't tell me that he is over me. We had a good thing. Do you think he's just trying to make me jealous?" She asked the person on the other end of the phone.

Barbara didn't move. As soon as that bitch hung up she was going to let her have it. Finally noticing Barbara, Tiffany quickly hung up the phone. Barbara stared hard at Tiffany. "Bitch, I know you weren't talking about my cousin, Amanda."

Turning her back on Barbara and getting ready to walk out, Tiffany snidely replied, "Mind your own business. Nobody was talking to you."

Barbara shook her head. There was no way in hell that she was going to let this fly. "My cousin is my business. Jim has been in love with her for months and they are very happy together."

"Well, sorry, but he was mine first. It's obvious that this whole thing is an attempt to make me jealous. I feel sorry for your cousin because in the end she will be the one with a broken heart." Tiffany started walking towards the door but not before Barbara got the final say.

"You are nothing but a stuck up, phony bitch. What they have is real. But I'm warning you, if you mess with my cousin, I will hunt you down and fuck you up bad. I'm not playing. Amanda is my family and I won't let anyone mess with her." It took all of Barbara's restraint not to slap this woman.

Feeling a little nervous, Tiffany walked out at a fast pace and went straight to a security guard. "Excuse me but there is an Indian lady in the bathroom who was threatening me." Giving the security guard a description, he radioed for back up. Tiffany pointed Barbara out, at one of the slot machines and three security guards approached her.

Tiffany walked back into the banquet room with a smug look on her face. "You might want to go out and help your cousin. She tried to jump me in the bathroom." Tiffany said, blinking her eyes and looking innocently at Jim.

"How do you know my cousin?" Amanda demanded.

"I don't know her but she was listening in on a private conversation and then tried to jump me over it. Nice Jim. What a classy family your little girlfriend has." Tiffany looked at Amanda gleefully.

By the time Jim and Amanda got out to the main part of the casino, there was already a sheriff walking through the front door and heading towards Barbara and the security guards. While the security guards were talking to the officer, Amanda and Jim talked to Barbara. "What happened? Tiffany is saying that you threatened her." Amanda talked in low tones while Jim was trying to listen in to what the security guards were saying to the Sheriff.

"Well, I was drying my hands and this blond chick came in and was talking hella crap about you. Saying that you were trash and that Jim was just trying to make her jealous, so when she hung up I jacked her up about it. I didn't lay a hand on her. I just told her that if she messed with you that I was going to fuck her up." Barbara explained, very animated and it was obvious to Amanda that she was high.

Jim and Amanda stood by while the officer took Barbara's statement. The security guard went into the banquet room and returned with Tiffany, who was going to give her statement next.

"Man, this isn't going to go well," Amanda told Jim. "Barbara's going to go to jail."

"Do you think so? I mean it's her word against Tiffany's. And she didn't really hurt her or lay a hand on her." Jim didn't think it was that serious, not for someone to go to jail over.

"Well, who do you think they are going to believe? A blond little Barbie doll, or the rough looking Indian girl." She felt bad and responsible, since Barbara was taking up for her.

There was no point in answering because as much as he didn't want to see it, the prejudice was becoming increasingly apparent. The sheriff and security guards were hovering over Tiffany, consoling and reassuring her. After they took Tiffany's statement, the Sheriff walked back over to Barbara, handcuffed her and informed her that she was under arrest. By now, there was a large crowd gathered around them, trying to see what was going on. As the sheriff walked Barbara towards the front door, she turned and called to Amanda. "Love you cousin. It's all good, don't worry. I'll be fine. Write me."

Amanda was visibly upset and had big tears threatening to break free. Jim put his arm around her and pulled her in, close to his body. "I know you're upset. We don't have to stay. I don't mind if we leave now." And he didn't. Maybe coming to this dinner had been a bad idea.

"It's up to you. They're just now serving the entrée. Maybe we should just go back in. I don't want you to look bad by leaving abruptly." That was a big offer on her part and he appreciated it.

Walking back in, Tiffany was animatedly telling the rest of the table what had happened. She stopped mid-sentence when they sat back down. The entrée consisted of prime rib, red skinned mashed potatoes and stir-fried asparagus. Much to Tiffany's annoyance, Jim and Amanda ignored her for the rest of the meal. He politely made small talk, with the other diners seated by them and they decided not to wait for dessert to be served.

"Let's go gamble for a while before we go home." He told her, as they stood up to leave. The "go home" was not lost on Tiffany and she wondered if they were living together. Feeling frustrated by his lack of attention, she ordered another drink and watched them walk towards the casino.

They played slots for about a half hour but neither of them were having much luck and both were feeling tired. The whole "Barbara" incident had definitely put a damper on the evening.

"Are you ready to go?" Jim asked, suddenly feeling tired.

Shaking her head yes, she didn't tell him that she had been ready hours ago. The fact that Barbara had gone to jail had only been part of what had bothered her this evening. There was no denying that Tiffany was drop dead gorgeous and he initially had been attracted to her. She was so completely opposite of Amanda and somehow that bothered her.

Driving home, the mood was somber. "I feel really bad about Barbara going to jail. How long do you think they will keep her?" he asked.

"I don't know. She had told me earlier that she had a warrant for a probation violation so probably thirty days for that. As far as threatening Tiffany, I would be surprised if that one stuck. I don't see the DA's office actually pursuing that." She answered.

"I would hope not. Tiffany has a way of exaggerating everything and I'm sure it wasn't as bad as she made it out to be. If there's anything I can do to help, I will," he offered.

"I don't know what you can do but I think tomorrow I will go down to the jail and put some money on her books. You know, so she can order from commissary." She couldn't put much on her books but even twenty dollars would be something.

It didn't go unnoticed by Jim that Amanda knew much more about this, than he did. "Have you been in jail before?" He asked, curiosity getting the best of him.

A little surprised that he asked, she paused for a moment. "Yes, once I had to do ten days. It wasn't fun."

"Oh. Do you mind me asking for what?" Jim asked, trying not to sound too surprised.

"It was for possession and drug paraphernalia." She didn't want to elaborate. It wasn't something she was proud of and she had had a really hard time in jail. She wasn't hardcore like some of the other women and for a while she had actually felt traumatized from the whole thing.

When they got home they went straight upstairs to bed. He kissed her good night but this was the first night that they slept together without making love. It felt strange and she wasn't sure if he was tired or if it had something to do with the "Barbara/Tiffany incident" or the fact that she had been in jail before. It bothered her and she lay in bed for hours before finally falling asleep. He went straight to sleep, his brain too tired to digest the events of the evening. But at five in the morning he woke up and was wide-awake. Moving to the chair, in front of the big window facing the ocean, his brain started processing the previous night. After sleeping he could think with more clarity and it struck him how unfair it was that the security guards immediately took Tiffany's side before even talking to Barbara. She could have made up anything and they would have believed her. Prejudice was a hard concept for him but in this instance it was plain and simple and he couldn't deny it or excuse it.

And as far as Amanda going to jail before, well what did he expect. He knew there was a past that wasn't always pretty, in terms of her substance abuse. He had said it didn't matter, so it was unfair now for him to judge her on things that happened when she was using. By the time she starting waking up at eight, he felt good about life again and had a better perspective on everything in general.

Climbing back into bed with her, he kissed her and let his hands roam over her body. Looking in his eyes she knew that whatever had bothered him the previous night was over and all seemed right again. She smiled and felt happy. She hated feeling that disconnect that she had felt the previous night and climbing on top of him, she showed him all of the sweet passion that she felt for him.

They stayed in bed most of the day, only getting up to get something to eat once. In the afternoon they both fell asleep and when they woke up again it was fifteen minutes before five. They both jumped up and rushed around, putting her things in her bag and he got her back to the rehab right at five. After kissing her goodbye he promised to pick her up on his lunch break, the following day and take her to the jail to put money on Barbara's books.

Chapter Fifteen

The following weekend Amanda got another weekend pass to stay with Jim. They spent the whole day Saturday wrapping presents. Jim had bought gift bags for his presents but he did help her wrap presents for her kids. She still hadn't bought a present for him yet but had decided that she was going to wait until she got home. She wanted to buy him something from Hoopa; some type of native piece, although she hadn't decided what that might be. She was torn between buying him a necklace, a basketry car hanging, a piece of pottery or an art piece for his wall.

They had discussed their plans for Christmas and she was going to go home on the twenty-third and be with her kids and family for the holiday. He was going to stay home because his mother and father were driving up and spending a week with him at Christmas.

"I really want you to meet my parents while they are here. What do you think about me coming up the day after Christmas, staying the night and then the next day you and the kids can come over and stay here for a few days." He didn't want to spend his whole Christmas vacation without her and now would be a good time for her to meet his family.

"Where would we all stay? I don't think we could all fit in your house with your parents here." Amanda wasn't sure she was ready to meet them but besides that, his house was a one bedroom.

"Oh, my parents have already booked a room at the Hilton." He laughed. "I certainly wasn't planning on cramming everyone in my little house. But there's plenty of room for the kids. I can get a blow up mattress and make a bed for them upstairs, with us."

"Okay. I guess that would work out." She hadn't even considered that his family would be staying in a hotel. A week at a hotel just seemed like a big expense and it cut down on actual visiting time

"I know that you're nervous to meet my parents but they really are nice people and I know that they are going to love you." He had expected her to put up a fight but he could see her yielding and knew he was winning the battle at this point. "Besides, the thought of being away from you for more than a few days is unbearable to me."

"Aww. That's so sweet. I was thinking the same. Okay, you win. I just hope that they like me as much as you think they will," she added nervously.

"Trust me. They will love you," he reassured her.

The rest of the weekend went by fast. After wrapping presents he ran and got take-out from the Chinese restaurant. After they ate, they made a bed on the couch, turned off all of the lights except for the Christmas tree lights and watched Christmas movies. At two in the morning they finally fell asleep, before "It's a Wonderful Life" was over. It was a relaxing weekend and there was nothing she loved more than laying in the dark, watching the blinking lights on the tree.

The next day, Amanda packed the presents in a box and tried to make it as compact as possible. Tuesday morning she was going to catch the bus to Hoopa. That would give her two days to get ready for Christmas and help her mom. After hosting the Thanksgiving dinner, they had decided to have a smaller Christmas dinner with just Amanda, Bev, Michael, Melanie, Uncle Ben and Aunty Dee. It was unclear if Ashley was going to join them or not.

Jim was going to take her to the bus station on Tuesday morning and then come home and get ready for his parents who he was expecting Tuesday afternoon. "I'm so glad to be off of school for two weeks," he had told her. "I'm really ready for a break from my students. I'm not sure what is going on but it's been a rough week. "

"I can't imagine having to deal with that many twelve and thirteen year olds all day like you do. I think I would go crazy," she said. Giving him a hug, she continued, "You're such an amazing man. I bet your students love you."

"Well, sometimes they do and sometimes they don't. Teaching children that age definitely isn't for the faint of heart." And that was putting it lightly, he thought to himself.

Sunday afternoon, while she was gathering her things together, he grabbed her and pulled her to the bed. "One for the road," he said laughing. "But really, this is our last chance until I come over on Friday." This would be the longest stretch that they had gone without being intimate. Although he would see her Tuesday, when he drove her to the bus station, their time would be limited. Thinking about it, she missed him already and it made her wonder what she would ever do without him in her life. Besides the fact that she loved him, she had come to depend on him and felt lost when they were apart.

He dropped her off at the rehab and she decided to wash clothes and write a letter to Barbara. Since Barbara had left the rehab, she still only had one roommate. It was quiet because her roommate, Leona, stayed in the main room watching television, most of the time. She couldn't imagine anything worse than sitting in jail on Christmas and she felt bad for her cousin, Barbara. Although she knew that she would have gotten picked up eventually, if it hadn't been for Tiffany, she probably would have been on the run for several more months.

The next two days dragged by slowly. She was bored to tears and it was raining so she couldn't really walk to meetings without getting drenched. Several of the women had finished their ninety-day stint the week before and around the holidays there really wasn't anyone standing in line to come to rehab. After the first of the year there would probably be an increase in women entering the rehab. It made sense that people didn't want to be on a black out during Christmas.

They had put up a small tree at the rehab and there were only two residents who would actually be there on Christmas. Rayna and one of the other workers were going to be there and they were planning a small dinner. When Jim picked Amanda up Tuesday morning to take her to the bus station, Rayna extended an invitation for him to join them. He declined, explaining that he had out of town guests coming and would be spending Christmas with them. Amanda felt relieved that he couldn't go, even though she hated feeling jealous and insecure.

He casually mentioned it on their way to the bus station. "So that was nice of Rayna to invite me to Christmas dinner. Very thoughtful." Amanda didn't realize that she had rolled her eyes and made a face when he said it, until it was too late.

"What? You don't think that was nice?" He asked, looking puzzled.

"I'm sorry," she said apologetically. "Of course it was nice. I just don't want her or any of the residents getting any ideas."

"Okay." He started laughing. "I mean, I do work there and am around her and the residents three times a week. What's so different about this?"

She paused a minute to figure it out herself. "Well I think that before everyone just felt like you were off limits but now that you're in a relationship with me, they look at you differently. It's kind of like, if you could be with an addict like me, then maybe they have a chance. And you're so handsome and sweet. I know a lot of those girls have crushes on you."

"Really? Which ones? Maybe I will go to the dinner after all." He was teasing her and she reached over and slapped his arm.

"Shut up. I guess I should have kept my mouth shut." She was laughing at him now but she knew there was truth in what she said.

"Well, I kind of like the fact that you're jealous but believe me, you have nothing to worry about. There is only one woman that I am interested in." Reaching across the seat, he grabbed her hand and kissed it. "I'm going to miss you. This will be the longest three days of my life."

"Well, at least your family will be here to distract you," she said, although she agreed. It was going to be a long three days.

Going in the bus station, Jim bought her bus ticket and carried the box of presents to check-in for her. He had insisted that she bring the game boys with her and had wrapped them himself and had written 'from Santa Claus" on the gift tags. Her other bag she carried on with her. She hadn't taken a whole lot of clothes since she would be back on Saturday.

They stood by the side of the bus and kissed and said their good byes. She felt emotional and had to keep reminding herself that it was only for a couple of days.

"I love you. Have a good time and relax." He worried and almost hated to send her alone. He knew how hard it was for her to go back and hoped that this time it would be less traumatic than last.

"I will. I love you too. I'll see you on Friday. Text and call me a lot," she said, while holding up her phone.

"You can be sure of it. Probably so much that you'll get sick of me," he answered.

They both laughed as she boarded the bus. Taking a seat mid-way to the back, she picked a window seat. She was surprised that there weren't more passengers on the bus, being so close to Christmas. Stretching out in her seat, she slept most of the way to Willow Creek. As the bus pulled in she saw her mom and her kids standing by the car, waiting for the bus. Watching them out her window she smiled to herself. They looked so happy and excited. This Christmas was going to be different. The last few Christmases she hadn't been at her best. She had worried more about getting high than making sure that her kids had a good Christmas. She was ashamed at how selfish she had acted.

After exiting the bus, she ran towards her kids, and hugged them. "Hi kids. Are you all ready for Christmas?"

"Yes. Only two more days, Mom. We have a calendar that you pull a little window out and it has a treat behind it. There are only two left and then it's Christmas." Michael was excited and could barely contain himself. "And on Saturday, Grandma took us to see Santa Claus and he gave me and Mel a present and a big candy cane."

"You guys got an early present. You're lucky." Amanda had forgotten that the tribal Christmas dinner had been last weekend. "Hi, Mom," she said, while giving her mom a hug. She waited while the driver unloaded the big box with the wrapped presents and then she loaded it in the car with her bag.

When they got home she took everything to her room and opened the box and took out all of the presents to put under the tree, except for the "Santa Claus" presents. She added her presents to the few that were already under the tree.

"So, Mom, who do we have coming over for Christmas?" Amanda asked, trying to figure out what all they needed to do, over the next few days.

"Well, Uncle Ben and Aunty Dee and then just us. Ashley isn't going to make it after all. She decided to take a shift at the nursing home on Christmas and then for New Year's she is going to Cancun with a couple of her friends. She did send some presents up though," Beverly answered.

"I didn't really expect her to come up for Christmas since she came up for Thanksgiving. How is Uncle, by the way?" Amanda asked.

"He's okay but I'm really trying to get him to go to the doctor and get a good check-up. There isn't anything specific going on but a lot of little things. Like he's really tired all the time and his color doesn't look good. He also hasn't had much appetite and he looks like he has lost some more weight." Beverly was more worried than she let on but her brother was so stubborn and she had been nagging him as it was. She had decided to give it a rest for a few days, until Christmas was over.

"Is he coming up tonight?" Amanda asked, a little surprised that he wasn't already there.

"No. He said he would come up tomorrow for Christmas Eve and then on Christmas because he had a few things to do today." Beverly explained. "So we don't have much to do until tomorrow and since it's just us we can do everything at our own pace. No time schedule for anything. I thought tonight we could just visit and relax."

"That sounds good. Are you off work tomorrow?" Amanda asked.

"Yes. The chairman actually gave us the day before Christmas and the day after Christmas off. I'm so glad because with school out I was having a hard time finding childcare for Michael. Ben watched him two of the days and then his other grandparents watched him one day," Beverly said.

"So I haven't had a chance to talk to you about this before but Jim is coming over on Friday and we wanted to take the kids back to the coast with us on Saturday to stay for a few days. I'm not sure what day we would be bringing them back yet." Amanda hoped that her Mom would be agreeable and enjoy having a little break.

"Okay. I think that will be good for the kids. They will be so excited to go with you and Jim. They seem to really like him," Beverly said. "And that will solve the problem of finding a babysitter next week. I'll be off on New Year's Day. Do you have plans while you have them?"

"No plans exactly but Jim's parents are up and Jim would like me and the kids to meet them," Amanda answered.

"Wow. That's nice. It must be getting pretty serious if he wants to introduce you and the kids to his parents." Beverly was happy for her daughter although it seemed to be moving faster than she would have thought.

"Yeah. I'm pretty nervous. I really hope that they like me. So we will be at Jim's house and I guess his parents are getting a room at the Hilton, for the week. Obviously they are pretty well off. I know a week at the Hilton must cost a pretty penny," Amanda said, still having a hard time wrapping her head around that.

They ate an early dinner and after putting the kids to bed they sat in the living room visiting and talking until the wee hours of the morning. Amanda showed her Mom her new phone and the necklace that Jim had given her. She told her about the Christmas dinner and about Barbara's run in with Tiffany.

"Gosh, that Tiffany sounds absolutely awful. Jim is such a nice guy. It's hard to imagine him being with such a bitch," Beverly observed.

"Well it didn't last more than a few months. She is drop dead, model like, gorgeous and I think that was the initial attraction but he says that it didn't take long to see her true colors." Amanda explained in detail what Tiffany looked like. She wished she could say she was an ugly witch with a big wart on her nose but the truth was, she was really pretty and that couldn't be denied.

"The one thing I know about Jim is that he is deeper that what is just on the surface. He's a good man with a big heart. That's why he is such a perfect match for you." Beverly knew this to be true. She could only hope that his parents were as open minded and kind as the son that they had raised.

They went to bed around one and woke up the next morning around nine and started getting busy. Amanda mopped and cleaned the house while Beverly started baking some pies and desserts.

"So at work they gave us a prime rib. It turned out to be a lot bigger than I thought it would be, but it's going to be so good and besides we haven't had a good roast forever," Beverly said.

Throughout the day Jim texted Amanda off and on, giving her an update on what he was doing and asked about the kids and what she was working on. She really wished he were with her; it was still hard to be back in the Valley. Early afternoon her mom gave her a grocery list of all the last minute things they would need. The store would be closing early for Christmas Eve and wouldn't open again until the day after Christmas so this was the last chance to get any last minute items that they might have forgotten.

The kids went with her to the store and while she drove there she laughed to herself thinking about Jim and the fact that he would be horrified that she was driving downtown without a license. It hadn't even seemed unusual to her until he had pointed it out. True to his word, he had gotten her a Driver's handbook to study and she was going to take a written test after the first of the year.

Going to the store was hard. She saw a lot of people that she would rather not see and even getting out of the car she was approached by two different people asking if she wanted to buy Norcos or Dilaudids. "No thanks," was all she answered. It didn't do any good to say that she was clean now because people using didn't want to hear it. She knew, because she had been the same. The second person even went on to whisper who was holding the "black," in case she was interested.

She tried getting in and out of the store as fast as possible, but there were long lines with everyone getting their last minute food and holiday items before they closed at five. One thing she didn't miss was the high grocery prices. On the coast the prices were much lower; sometimes half the cost of what they paid at the only store on the reservation. Even a gallon of milk here was almost five dollars.

That night, Uncle Ben came up for dinner and spent the evening. Amanda made Crab Louie and stir-fried shrimp with vegetables. Beverly made salmon dip, using the smoked salmon that they had canned during the fall. Amanda was so happy to see her uncle but she too could tell that he had lost more weight. "Uncle, you're fading away. You better go to the doctor and get checked," she told him.

"I will, after Christmas. I think I have an ulcer. But I went up the hill and picked some tea and I think it's helping. Besides, I hate going to the doctor. Every time I go they just find something wrong," Ben answered.

"Okay. But promise me that you'll go, okay? I mean it. We could never get by without you," Amanda told him, and she meant it.

"Aww right, Honey Bumpkins. I'll make an appointment and go, right after the first of the year." He knew better than arguing with Amanda. She would nag and beg until he agreed to go and he hadn't been feeling well, so maybe it was time.

After dinner they let the kids open one present each, as was their custom on Christmas Eve. Amanda handed Melanie the present that held the tea set and for Michael she picked the Lego set. She wanted them to open something that would keep them occupied for a while. They were both excited and a little on the hyper side this evening.

While they were happily playing with their new toys, Amanda, Beverly and Ben drank hot chocolate and played Yahtzee. It was a relaxing evening and the only thing missing, as far as Amanda was concerned, was Jim. Outside it was raining and storming and it was a perfect night to be home, with a good fire going and playing games with family. While the kids played in the living room, Beverly put on "How the Grinch Stole Christmas." The kids liked the cartoon version better than the movie version. "Okay kids, when this is over it is bed time. Santa can't come if you're awake," Beverly told her grandkids.

When the movie was over, Amanda helped the kids pour a glass of milk and put out a few cookies. Although they both protested and said that they weren't sleepy, they went to bed fairly easy and within ten minutes they were both out. Amanda did one last clean up and then went out on the porch to smoke a cigarette and call Jim.

He answered on the third ring. "Hi babe. How's your Christmas Eve?"

"It's good. Uncle Ben is here and we made seafood for dinner and we've been playing Yahtzee," she told him, missing him even more the minute she heard his voice.

"That sounds nice. We are having dinner out, at that little seafood place that I took you to. We're just ordering dessert. How's the kids?" he asked.

"They're good. They got to open a present tonight so they were happy and busy. Actually I just got them to bed," she told him.

"I miss you. I wish I was there with you," he told her, in whispered tones.

150

"I wish you were too. I miss you so much. Are you having a good visit?" she asked.

"Yes. It's good. My parents can't wait to meet you." He had told them about Amanda and they were genuinely happy for him but maybe a little surprised when he had told them that he planned on marrying her. But they had expected it in some ways. After all he was almost thirty years old and they were anxious for him to start a family and for them to get a few more grandchildren. His mother was a little skeptical about him being a stepfather. She knew that wasn't an easy role for most people. But then her son wasn't "most people" and he truly loved children, obviously since he had chosen a profession of teaching.

They talked a few more minutes and she told him she would call in the morning after the kids woke up and opened their presents. Uncle Ben left shortly after and said he would come back up early. "The best thing about Christmas is watching the kids open their presents," he had said, before heading home.

By midnight, Amanda and Beverly had both gone to bed. Amanda fell asleep fairly fast and slept hard. She dreamed all night and although when she woke up she didn't remember exactly what she had dreamed about, she felt happy.

She heard someone in the living room building a fire and knew it must be her uncle. He was always thoughtful like that and probably wanted the living room to be warm and cozy before the kids got up to open their presents. Amanda joined him in the living room and he had a roaring fire going and had already started coffee. Soon after, Beverly joined them and within ten minutes the house came alive with the kids running out of the bedroom, all excited and ready to open presents.

Amanda passed out the gifts and all of the adults sat and watched the kids open their presents first. Amanda took pictures with her phone and had promised Jim that she would send him some and even took a few videos on her phone. They were the most excited about their Gameboys from Santa Claus and it was almost overwhelming for them to receive so many gifts. Ashley had bought them several outfits and a pair of rain boots each. While they were less excited about those presents, Amanda was grateful because Ashley always bought them nice clothes and always made sure they were the right size. Uncle Ben had bought Michael a Swiss army knife and for Melanie he had made a little girl's regalia necklace. It was ten strands of pine nuts but made small for her. It was beautiful and Amanda knew that he had put a lot of work

151

into it. She let Melanie try it on but then went and put it up to save for her.

"I love it, Uncle. When did you work on that?" Amanda asked him.

"Well, I started picking up pine cones last year. I figured she could wear it during the dress show on Sovereign's Day and at different events." He was pleased that they liked it.

"I really want to make her a dress. I haven't tried before but I was going to ask Aunty Dee to help me get one started." Amanda had been thinking about this for a while and had decided that even though it would take months to do, it would be worth it and she had a lot of spare time right now anyhow.

Beverly and Ben really liked their presents from Amanda. Beverly hadn't really had anything new for so many years and she was ecstatic with her new coat. And likewise Ben was appreciative of the warm flannel shirt and gloves that Amanda had gotten him.

Amanda opened her presents last. Ashley had bought her a pair of boots and a purse that matched. They were nicer than what she could have bought herself and she was thrilled. Because she and Ashley wore the same size, she knew that they would fit perfect before she had even tried them on. Her mom had bought her a sweater, a pair of jeans and a short, satin robe. "Thank you, Mom. I'm so glad you got the jeans a size bigger so they fit," she said laughing. "And I love the robe. So sexy." She reached over and gave her mom a hug.

Her uncle handed her a gift bag and she pulled out something wrapped in tissue paper. It was a necklace that matched Melanie's except some of the strands had beautiful long pieces of abalone that sounded so pretty when they hit against each other. It was delicate and beautiful and she absolutely loved it. Holding it up she twirled it and watched the light hit the beads. "Oh Uncle, thank you so much. It's the prettiest necklace that I have even seen." She knew better than to go on anymore because her uncle, much like herself when it came to compliments, was already looking uncomfortable.

"I'm glad that you like it, babe. I thought that when Melanie gets old enough to dance, she could wear it in the pit." He had spent a lot of time making these necklaces, gathering the pinecones, cutting the abalone pieces himself, and he was glad that they liked it. He wanted to give her and Melanie something that they could have forever and that had meaning.

While the kids played with their new toys, Beverly made waffles and started getting her dough ready for rolls and seasoned the prime rib.

Amanda started gathering up all of the wrapping paper and boxes and put it in a pile, to burn outside later. The pace this morning was leisurely compared to Thanksgiving and Ben took a nap in the chair by the fire while the kids played. Amanda really couldn't think of a more relaxing Christmas and neither could Beverly. While she cooked she occasionally had flash backs to the last few Christmases which had been nothing but drama with Amanda, who had begged and threatened for money, immediately sold her presents to get high and had taken zero interest in the kids that day. The difference was huge and almost too good to be true.

Around ten, Amanda sent pictures to Jim of the kids opening their presents and then went outside and called him. They talked for about ten minutes, wishing each other a Merry Christmas and talking about the next day when he would come over.

Hanging up, Jim thought of how different their Christmases were. He and his parents had stayed up late, drinking wine and he didn't get up until around nine. This morning when his parents arrived they had Champagne and fancy croissants, that his mom had brought up from down south. The few presents that they opened were expensive and luxurious and there was none of the excitement or magic of children opening presents, nor were there any practical, much needed gifts that Amanda and her family appreciated and were grateful for. Instead of planning to prepare a dinner, they had made reservations that evening at an expensive restaurant that required coats and ties for men and women dressed in their finest. While he was enjoying himself, he missed what Amanda and her family had. He had loved the Thanksgiving dinner with her family and liked the closeness of being with a big family and the simpler nature in which they celebrated.

Amanda went and got Aunty Dee around two that afternoon. She had called her the week before to order a car hanging for Jim's truck so she went in to pick it up and to help carry some food and presents out to the car.

Aunty Dee held out the basket car hanging that she had made. The design was black and made with maidenhair fern and the bottom had black and white beads with Dentalium hanging down for the dangles. "This is perfect Aunty Dee. It's exactly what I had in mind. How much do I owe you?" Amanda asked, still admiring the car hanging.

"Well honey, since you're family, I was thinking thirty dollars. And I put some root in the basket." Aunty Dee always felt funny charging family members, so she had knocked the price down to half of what she normally got.

"Well thank you Aunty but that's too cheap." Amanda protested, while handing her a fifty-dollar bill. She knew the value and wanted to give her aunt a fair price.

"Are you sure, honey? I don't want to break you. I know how tight everything is around Christmas. "Aunty Dee appreciated the offer but would have been happy with thirty dollars. After all, it was enough for her bingo buy-in on Sunday.

"I'm sure, Aunty. Thank you. It really is beautiful." She was impressed with the fine work that her Aunty could still do, even with her bad eyesight.

Amanda loaded up the presents, two pies and a big fruit salad that Aunty Dee had made. Then she helped walk Aunty Dee to the car and they drove back to Beverly's house.

The dinner was outstanding, especially the Prime Rib. They ate so much that they were stuffed and decided to wait on dessert until after they had time to digest their food a little.

Aunty Dee was pleased with the slippers and bubble bath that Amanda had given her. Beverly gave her a house robe that buttoned up the front and had two big pockets in the front. Ever since any of them could remember, she always wore this type of robe, usually most of the day, unless she had to go somewhere. Ben had got her a new bible, in large print and a beaded book marker that he had bought from someone set up in front of the grocery store.

Aunty Dee had so many family members that there was no way that she could buy something for each of them and they didn't expect her to. She did bring a big tin of popcorn and a movie, "The Sound of Music," as her gift to all of them. "It was always one of my favorites," she told them.

"It was always one of my favorite movies too," Beverly said. She put it on and they all retired in the living room to watch it. Melanie lay on her mom's lap playing her Game boy but within fifteen minutes she was fast asleep. Michael sat on the floor and played with his train set, while Ben also fell asleep in his favorite chair by the fire. Beverly looked around the room and felt nothing but peace and contentment. It had been a wonderful day and she couldn't think of anything that would have made it better. Towards the end of the movie, Amanda went to the kitchen and made dessert plates for each of them. After eating dessert, Ben drove Aunty Dee home and then retired to his house.

"Let's not worry about cleaning up tonight," Beverly said. "All of the food is put up and we can clean up tomorrow. Do you know what time Jim will be here?"

"Not exactly. He said mid-afternoon but he is going to text me when he leaves," Amanda answered.

"This has been the best Christmas I think I have ever had, Amanda. Thank you for all of your help and thoughtfulness in making it such a special day for everyone." Beverly wanted to give her daughter encouragement and credit for all of the miraculous strides that she had made in the past few months.

"It was nice, wasn't it?" Amanda agreed. "I think about the last few Christmases and how selfish and awful I was. I really don't know how you put up with me. I look back on that time and it's like I was a monster out of control. I don't ever want to be that monster again. This is so much better." She had tears in her eyes and just thinking about it made her sick to her stomach.

"Well, it's in the past and now that you know how good life can be. I'm confident that you'll never go back to that. There were reasons that it happened though and things that you had to come to terms with. Are you getting any counseling now? You know, to explore why it happened so that it never comes back to haunt you again?" Beverly had thought of this often. She knew that there were traumatic things that had happened and she often worried that these ghosts could pop up again to haunt her daughter.

"Well, not exactly. I go to a lot of group counseling and NA meetings but as far as one on one counseling, no. I haven't really had anywhere to go for that. But I do know from group that my using was an attempt to mask the pain that I was feeling for a lot of reasons." Amanda didn't feel the need to expand. Her mother, of all people, knew the trauma and events that had happened, not just to her but her mom and sister as well.

They both retired to bed around eleven and just as she got into bed, Jim called. "I just wanted to say good night and that I love and miss you. I can't wait to come over tomorrow."

"I can't wait either. We had such a good Christmas but the one thing missing was you. I love you so much and appreciate everything you have done for me and my family. I don't know why God blessed me by bringing you into my life but I feel like the luckiest person in the world." It was hard for Amanda to be so sentimental and express her feelings but tonight she felt like she had to say it.

"Aww, that's the sweetest thing anyone has ever told me. That has totally made my whole Christmas," Jim answered and it was true.

Hanging up she went to sleep smiling and couldn't wait until tomorrow night when she would be sleeping in his arms.

Chapter Sixteen

Jim arrived at three o'clock sharp and with him came a new round of excitement. For Amanda, the excitement was her happiness at seeing him. For Michael and Melanie it was because of the presents he brought for them. They had never received so many presents; Christmases and birthdays normally had been more modest in their short lives. Ben had come up about an hour before and after Jim unloaded everything from his truck, they sat in the front room exchanging presents. For Michael, Jim had bought a remote truck and a Nerf gun set with soft bullets. For Melanie he had bought a doll from the movie "Frozen" and a box of art supplies, crayons, color books, safety scissors, paste, stickers, colored pencils and construction paper. Amanda hadn't really expected him to bring so much, since he had bought them Gameboys and she wondered when he had shopped for these presents.

After watching the kids open their presents, they all insisted on Jim opening his presents next. Beverly gave him a crocheted hat with Indian designs; something all of the men in Hoopa wore. Ben gave him a book, "In the Land of the Grasshopper Song," which he thought Jim would enjoy because it included local history, which they had sat up and talked about, at length. Amanda gave him her presents last. He opened the basketry car hanging first and was so impressed that Aunty Dee had made it. Although he didn't know much about local basketry, he could appreciate how fine the work was. The other present she got for him was a coffee cup, made out of local clay, with local designs carved into it. Something, she hoped that he could use at work maybe.

"Thank you, everyone. These are wonderful gifts." He was truly touched and really hadn't been expecting presents from all of them. He handed out his gifts, starting with Beverly. Beverly opened the top of the gift bag and pulled out the tissue paper. Wrapped in the tissue paper was a beautiful shawl and when she held it up to admire it, a gift card to Target fell out.

"Oh Jim, this is absolutely beautiful." She said, holding up the shawl. Picking up the gift card, she pulled it out of the little envelope and saw that it was for $100.00. "Thank you." Beverly wanted to protest that he had given her too much and she felt a little uncomfortable, but she didn't want to seem ungrateful. "Thank you so much." This would come in handy, with Melanie's birthday coming up in two weeks, she thought.

"You're so very welcome Beverly," Jim answered. He had always been taught that giving a gift card was lazy and not thoughtful but he knew that she struggled on her modest earnings and hoped that this might help in some small way.

Next, he handed Ben a large gift bag, which Ben begrudgingly accepted. Opening the top, he pulled out a black Carhartt jacket. "This is really nice. Thank you." Although he didn't say much, he put it on right away. It was a perfect fit and obvious to all, that he liked it.

The grand finale was Amanda's presents. She really didn't expect anything. After all, he had already given her a phone and a diamond necklace. Smiling big he handed her a small wrapped present and a gift bag.

"Which one should I open first?" She asked, teasing him and feeling excited about the possibilities.

"Start with the gift bag," Jim told her.

Opening the gift bag she pulled out a framed picture of Michael and Melanie standing by the Christmas tree. The picture was a 5 x 7, in a pretty silver frame. It was a great picture and looked like it had been done professionally. "Wow. This is a great picture. It looks like it could have been taken in a studio." Next she took the small, long, wrapped present and ripped the paper off. Opening the top of the box she saw a diamond link bracelet. The diamonds were small, with gold links between them. It was beautiful and delicate and as much as she loved her necklace, this was even better. "I love it," she said while giving him a big hug. "It's the most beautiful bracelet that I have ever seen." And that was the truth. Smiling big, again she felt like the luckiest person in the world.

Jim went out to the truck to get his overnight bag and a couple of bags of groceries. "I hope you don't mind if I brought some food with me. It's so much cheaper on the coast and since I have a big appetite I decided it would be worthwhile to stop and pick up a few things before I drove up."

Setting the bags down on the kitchen counter, he followed Amanda down the hall to put his overnight bag in her room.

Beverly unloaded the groceries that he had bought which were a mixture of necessity items, like milk, bread and eggs, along with snack items, like cookies, crackers and popcorn. He had bought a lot for an overnight stay but she had learned that it was just his nature to be generous and she appreciated the gesture and the thought.

Down the hall, Amanda and Jim were locked in a kiss. "Do you think anyone would miss us if we didn't go out for a while?" He asked her jokingly.

"I'm pretty sure that everyone would miss us." She told him, planting a few more kisses on his face before grabbing his hand and leading him back down the hall to the living room.

Beverly had put on a pot of beans earlier that morning and for dinner made Indian tacos. Ben stayed for dinner and afterwards they sat in the living room, visiting and enjoying the warm fire. Outside it was threatening to rain again and a cold front had moved in, giving them a chance of snow on the valley floor. The kids sat on the floor, each entertained playing by themselves with their new things. Melanie loved the art supplies that Jim had gotten her and was busy for hours. He was impressed with how well behaved they were. His niece and nephew were rambunctious and really couldn't play more than five minutes by themselves and seemed to need a lot of attention and constant entertaining.

It was a relaxing evening and Jim was really enjoying the atmosphere. Nothing was rushed and all of them were content to just sit and visit. "Mom, tell us some stories." Amanda urged. "I know Jim would love to hear some of your stories."

"Okay. I guess I could tell a few. Which one do you want me to tell?" Beverly asked her daughter.

"Well my favorite is Coyote dancing with the stars," Amanda told her.

Beverly told several Coyote stories and then "Rough Nose," which was one of the kid's favorites. When she was done, Jim was completely mesmerized. "Thank you, Beverly. That was great." And he meant it. He loved the culture and the tight family ties. He had a couple of aunts and uncles on both his mother and father's side and a few cousins but they lived some distance apart and they rarely saw each other growing up. He couldn't really think of anything that had been passed down for generations and virtually any type of oral history was non-existent.

At ten, Ben went home and said he would be back in the morning to drink coffee and see them off. Melanie had fallen asleep on the floor, so

Jim carried her to her bed and Amanda got Michael to bed. Beverly went to her room and after stoking up the fire, Jim and Amanda retired to Amanda's bedroom.

"Alone at last." He teased, while they both fell onto the bed.

Pretending to yawn big, Amanda said, "I'm so tired. I just want to go to sleep now. Good night."

"Yeah, right," Jim answered. "You're not getting off that easy."

"I'm joking. I've missed you so much. I couldn't wait for you to get here." Unbuttoning his shirt, she started planting kisses down his chest. When they did finally fall asleep, their arms and legs were intertwined with her head lying against his chest. Neither stirred until morning when he woke up first and quietly climbed out of bed, slipped on some sweat pants and a t-shirt and went out to start a fire. Never living in a house with wood heat, he was getting better at starting a fire and cutting kindling. The house was already getting cold and when he opened the wood stove there were only a few hot coals left. He got a fire going and made coffee and, about thirty minutes later, Ben walked in and they poured coffee and sat at the table talking. By eight, Beverly got up and joined them for coffee. Amanda soon followed and by nine, both kids were up, running around excited about the trip they were taking.

They visited for another hour and then reluctantly started getting ready; packing clothes, shoes and toys so that the kids had something to play with at Jim's house. Jim really enjoyed visiting Amanda's family and would have gladly stayed longer if his parents weren't over on the coast waiting for him to return. Amanda would have liked to stay, too, because his parents were on the coast waiting.

By eleven they were loaded up and both kids were strapped in their seats with their Gameboys to keep them occupied on the two-hour drive to Jim's place. They made good time and by one they were pulling into Jim's driveway. He had told his parents that he would call them as soon as he got home and everyone settled in.

Amanda gave Michael and Melanie a tour, while Jim unloaded all of their bags and belongings and carried them upstairs. Upstairs in the bedroom, Jim had set up a blow up bed and had made it up with sheets and blankets. The kids were excited at being somewhere new and different and ran up and down the stairs several times. Amanda hoped that they settled down before his parents came over.

About a half hour later, Jim called his parents and let them know he was back and that they could come over any time. Amanda turned on the television and put a show on for the kids.

160

"I bought groceries before I left and tried to get stuff that the kids would like. You might want to look through the fridge and cupboards and see if there's anything else that we need. We can always go shopping later if we need to." Jim told her.

"Okay. I'm going to look for something for their lunch. Are you hungry?" she asked.

"A little maybe. Why don't we cook a pizza? That's easy and I know that they love pizza," he suggested.

While she put the pizza in, a thought crossed her mind. "So what have you told your parents about me?" She really didn't know what to expect and her anxiety was quickly rising.

"Well, I told them that I had a girlfriend that I wanted them to meet and I told them how great you are and that I hope someday to marry you." He omitted that he and his mother had gotten into a brief disagreement about him becoming involved with someone who already had children. His mother couldn't help but voice her opinion about how hard it was to have a ready-made family. She backed off when she saw how fast he was to defend his girlfriend.

"Do they know how, or I guess I should say, where we met?" she asked.

"Well, I told them I had met you at the rehab." He didn't tell them that she was a resident there and they seemed to assume that she worked there and he knew it was unfair to not correct them but decided that it would all come out eventually. His reasoning was that once they met her they would see how great she was and he hoped that it wouldn't matter then.

"Oh, good," she said, visibly relieved and before he could further explain there was a knock on the door and Jim's parents were coming through the door.

"Honey, you're back." Turning towards the door, Amanda saw a woman who looked mid to late fifties. She was an attractive woman, although not overly beautiful. She was of medium height and build, had short brown hair and beautiful green eyes. She looked very well maintained and had the air of someone always in control and in charge. Her husband walked in behind her and was tall, distinguished looking with brown hair, blue eyes and just a hint of gray starting to show in his hair and beard. He had kind eyes and a laid back personality which was contradictory to his courtroom personality. Of the two, it was obvious that Jim favored his father in looks, with the exception of his green eyes, which was definitely from his mother. But personality wise he was definitely more like his father—laid back and easy going.

After greeting her son and giving him a hug, the older woman turned to Amanda and seemed to take her in, in one look. Without waiting for Jim to introduce them, the woman stuck her hand out and said, "Hi. I'm Helen and you must be Amanda."

Shaking her hand and smiling back, Amanda felt tongue tied at first and was only able to mutter, "hello." The father came over but instead of extending his hand, he hugged her and introduced himself. "Hi Amanda. I'm Phil." Not waiting for an answer, he went straight to Michael and Melanie who were sitting on the couch, staring wide-eyed at these strangers who had walked in.

"Hi. What's your names?" Phil asked.

"I'm Michael and this is my sister Melanie." Michael offered, looking towards his mom to see if it was okay.

"And how old are you?" he asked.

"I'm six and my sister is three but she will be four soon. We are going to have a birthday party when we get home," Michael told him.

Phil talked to Michael and Melanie a few more minutes. It was apparent to Amanda that he enjoyed children, much like his son.

Helen went into the kitchen and made coffee, poured a cup for herself and her husband and then seated herself at the dining room table. Amanda was getting more uncomfortable by the minute. Helen was definitely eyeing her up and although shewas not rude or unpleasant, was not openly friendly either. When Melanie needed to go to the bathroom, it was a good excuse to escape for a moment and take her upstairs. Taking her time, she dreaded going back downstairs but knew that she couldn't put it off much longer. After finding a different show for the kids, she once again joined the group in the dining room.

"So, Jim," his mother asked, "what do you want to do for dinner tonight? We could go out but not with the children; so, do you want me to cook something here?"

"I guess we could cook something here. Or we could barbeque," Jim offered.

"That sounds good to me," Phil interjected. "Buy some t-bones or New York steaks."

"Phil, you know you shouldn't be eating so much red meat," Helen scolded. "I swear, Jim. Your Dad would eat steak every night if he could."

"Well, Mom, he's on vacation. Let him eat his steak. You can always put him on a diet when he gets home." At times Jim didn't know how his father had put up with his mother for so many years. Everyone who knew her understood that she was a control freak, especially to those closest to her. Jim knew one of the things that attracted him to Amanda was that she wasn't controlling. As a matter of fact, she was basically the opposite.

Although Jim offered to go to the store and buy the steaks, Helen insisted on going instead because she wanted to pick out the steaks and buy veggies to go with it. Once they were gone, Amanda took a deep breath and relaxed a little.

"Sorry about my mother," Jim apologized. "She has always been a little overbearing."'

"Oh. I hadn't really noticed," Amanda lied. "She seems nice and very devoted to your father." In no way did she want to come between him and his mother and knew that it was better to just grin and bear it.

"I guess she means well and it works for her as a charge nurse, but honestly it wears me out. When I was a teenager I couldn't wait to move away and be on my own. She really didn't allow me or my sister any kind of freedom and was extremely hard on us." Jim had never really opened up like this before and she was touched.

"I'm going to go upstairs and change. How long are your parents here for?" she asked, hoping that they weren't going to stay the whole week.

"They are leaving Monday morning. They want to be home by New Year's Eve and plan on spending several days getting home. My dad doesn't like to drive more than five to six hours at a stretch," Jim explained.

Going upstairs, Amanda went into the bathroom and took out the last strip of Suboxone and threw the package away. It certainly was different with his parents here and she missed the relaxed atmosphere that they normally had together. Changing into something less casual than the jeans she was wearing, she redid her hair and make-up and slipped the diamond necklace on.

Amanda grabbed sweatshirts for the kids and they joined Jim, who was starting a fire in the barbeque, in the backyard. Minutes later, Helen and Phil came back with several bags of groceries. Leaving the kids outside with Jim, Amanda went into the kitchen to see what she could do to help.

"So, Amanda, I'm going to throw some potatoes in the oven and I got some fresh veggies to stir fry and salad stuff. Oh, and I stopped at a bakery to buy some fresh bread." Helen pulled out a bottle of red wine from one of the bags and grabbed four wine glasses from the cupboard.

163

"No wine for me Helen. I'm not really a drinker. But thank you," Amanda told her.

"Oh. Okay." Helen looked momentarily puzzled and then her face lit up. "Are you pregnant?" she asked, part of her excited and the other part hoping not.

"No. I'm not. I just really don't like drinking," Amanda explained, hoping that she didn't sound rude.

"Okay. Well we aren't big drinkers but we do like to have wine with our dinner." Helen put one of the wine glasses back and then carried out two glasses for Phil and Jim, who were both still outside.

"So, what would you like me to do?" Amanda asked,

"Well, why don't you make the salad and I'll start cutting the veggies up," Helen answered.

While Amanda worked on the salad, she noticed that Helen glanced over from time to time and seemed like she was biting her tongue trying hard not to instruct her how to make the salad. It made Amanda uncomfortable; like she was making the salad wrong. She was glad when she was done and could escape back outside with Jim and the kids.

Smiling, Jim came over and standing behind her, put both arms around her. "Are you okay?" he asked her, noticing that she was quieter than usual and a little withdrawn.

Smiling back, she answered, "I'm okay. Just have a little bit of a headache." Which wasn't a lie.

"I have Tylenol in the upstairs bathroom. Do you want me to go upstairs and get you one?" he offered.

"No. I'm okay. I'll go up in a little while and get one." Not wanting to tell him that his mother was causing her headache, she just hoped to get through dinner and then she could excuse herself to get the kids to bed.

Dinner was good and Amanda was pleased that the kids were on their best behavior at the table. She really did give her mom the credit for her kid's good manners and behavior. After dinner, she excused herself to go upstairs and get Michael and Melanie bathed and in bed. By the time she came back down, Helen and Phil were just getting ready to leave. Saying their good-byes they made plans to come and spend their last day with Jim, before departing on Monday.

"If it's nice I was hoping we could go play a round of golf," Phil told Jim. "Maybe spend the afternoon on the green."

"That would be fun for you two," Helen chimed in. "You haven't been able to golf together for years."

"Well, maybe." Jim said, glancing towards Amanda. "Let's see how it looks outside tomorrow."

Helen didn't miss the questioning glance he threw at Amanda and hated seeing her son act so whipped. "Amanda and I can spend the day getting to know each other better. Right, Amanda? We'll find something to do with the kids for a few hours."

"Of course," Amanda muttered. She knew to say anything else at this point would just make her look bad.

"Well, it sounds good but let's see how the weather is tomorrow. You know how unpredictable it is on the coast," Jim said, not wanting to commit until he had time to talk to Amanda alone.

Later, after Helen and Phil had left and they were lying in bed, Jim broached the subject, feeling Amanda out about the golfing plans.

"I'm not really that excited about going golfing tomorrow but I know it would mean a lot to my dad. Will you be okay with my mom for a few hours?" Jim asked, basically unsure and not completely comfortable leaving her with his mom yet.

"Absolutely. You should go golfing with your Dad and have a good time. You don't have to worry. We'll be fine." Amanda knew that there was no way to win on this. There was no way she could tell him that his mother scared her to death.

"Okay. You're the best. And Monday we'll take the kids somewhere and do something fun. I promise." Reaching over he gave her a kiss and felt relieved that his mother and girlfriend were getting along so well.

The next morning when Amanda woke up and looked out the window she immediately felt disappointed. She had prayed hard that it would be raining today but the sun was shining bright and looked like it was going to be a beautiful day.

They had a late breakfast and by noon they were all bathed and dressed. At twelve thirty Helen and Phil arrived.

"We figured that you had already eaten so we stopped and grabbed a bite on our way." Helen explained.

"Come on, Jim." Phil stated. "Let's hit the green. It's a great day for golfing."

Jim grabbed his clubs from the front closet and Amanda walked him to the front door to see him off.

"Bye, honey. I'll text you in a little while. We shouldn't be more than a couple of hours." Jim kissed her goodbye and charged out the door. He was obviously excited about going golfing.

"Amanda, I'm going to put on another pot of coffee and then we can sit and visit. I'm so glad that we finally have a chance to get to know one another better," Helen said brightly.

"Okay. Let me put something on for the kid's to watch." Nervously she scanned the guide and selected something that would keep them both occupied while she and Helen talked.

Helen poured them both a cup of coffee and motioned for her to sit down at the dining room table. "Do you take anything in your coffee? I drink mine black. I'm a big coffee drinker and prefer a dark roast."

"I like a little cream and sugar but I'll get it," Amanda answered, before Helen got up.

After stirring her coffee she joined Helen at the table. Something seemed amiss and she felt a lump forming in her throat and butterflies hitting her stomach.

"So, Amanda, I'm really glad that we have a chance to talk alone," Helen, said, emphasizing the word "alone."

Amanda looked up from her coffee, not sure how to answer. She felt like a fly, getting caught in a spider web.

"I'm not one to beat around the bush. I'm a little outspoken and I'm going to cut to the chase. Yesterday when I went upstairs and used the bathroom I saw a wrapper discarded in the trashcan. I wasn't really sure what Suboxone was so I took the wrapper back to the motel room with me and spent the evening looking it up, on the Internet. I know that my son isn't using Suboxone so I can only assume that it is yours. So, I'm going to ask you point blank. Are you an addict?" Helen took a drink of her coffee and waited for an answer.

Feeling a little blindsided, Amanda took a deep breath trying to decide the best way to answer. "I'm in recovery." Feeling a little confused, she continued, "Jim said that he had told you that we met at rehab."

"Jim said he met you at a rehab where he volunteered. I just assumed that you worked there or something. He didn't mention that you were a resident there." Helen felt a little annoyed with her son but it was understandable that he wanted to keep that information to himself, so to her it was forgivable.

"I'm sorry about the misunderstanding. But yes, I am a resident there," Amanda explained.

"Jim is my only son and my youngest. He has always been such a kind person who sees the best in everyone. That's part of what makes him such a great teacher. But because of his kindness he sometimes can be gullible and can be taken advantage of. I don't know what to say. I don't want to hurt your feelings but I had much higher hopes for my son and always hoped that he would pick a life partner that would have similar interests and background as him. Do you understand what I'm saying?" Helen was smiling but her eyes looked like ice.

"I think that you are saying that you don't want me with your son," Amanda offered. "I really do love him, you know."

"Well, of course you do, dear. Why wouldn't you? He's handsome, smart, kind, has a good job and he has lots of money. But of course you probably know that," Helen chided.

"What do you mean lots of money? I mean I know that he's comfortable from his teaching job." Amanda shook her head, not fully understanding.

"Well, maybe I shouldn't say anything but Jim was a trust fund baby. His paternal grandparents set up a trust fund when he was born, and as they were quite well off, it is substantial. Basically he doesn't have to work but he loves his job and teaching." Helen wasn't sure if Amanda was telling the truth or not.

"Well, it wouldn't really matter to me if he didn't have a dime. We're in love. You don't really know me or what kind of person I am, to decide if I'm right for your son or not." Amanda wasn't giving up that easy.

"Well, let's look at what I do know. You have two children, and obviously was a teen mom. You are a recovering addict. I'm not sure what you were using but my guess would be heroin. So forgive me but right there is enough to raise some red flags." Helen wasn't backing down either. After all, her son's future and happiness were at stake.

"I'm not sure what to say. I love Jim and care deeply about him. I don't plan on doing anything to hurt him," Amanda calmly stated.

"I don't think that you plan on hurting him and I'm sure that you do love him. But unfortunately, the reality is that this is a disease that you will more than likely struggle with all of your life. If you truly care about Jim you would cut him loose and let him find someone that he can be happy with; someone more in his league. Just think about it, that's all I'm asking. If you are truly as nice as Jim says then I know that you will do the right thing." Helen was done. She was hitting below the belt but in her mind she knew that she was saving her son a lot of heartache.

Turning away, Amanda walked into the living room to check on her kids. Her face was burning hot. She had dealt with mean people in her life but never on this level and frankly she didn't know how to deal with it.

"Come on kids. We are going to go outside and take a walk. It's too nice of a day to stay inside." Grabbing her cigarettes she ushered the kids to the door and outside.

"Where are we going mommy?" Michael asked.

"There's a park a few blocks away. We are going to go play and have fun," Amanda said, with enthusiasm that she wasn't really feeling.

They stayed at the park for three hours. She would have stayed longer but the kids were getting hungry. On their way back from the park she got a text from Jim letting her know that they had just finished golfing and would be home soon.

"Perfect timing," She said to herself. A block from the house she watched Jim and Phil pull up and unload their golf bags. Jim walked in the house and then exited a few seconds later and started walking towards them.

"Hi. Where have you guys been?" he asked, scooping Melanie up and giving her a piggy back ride and then leaned towards Amanda giving her a kiss.

"It's such a beautiful day that we went to the park," Amanda answered.

As he looked at her, he could immediately tell that something was wrong and his instinct told him that it had something to do with his mother. Amanda avoided his stare. She was undecided on whether to tell him about his mother or not. She didn't want to come between them. But if he asked point blank or pushed she knew that she would probably break down and spill all.

"So is everything okay?" he gently asked.

"Yeah. Everything's fine," she answered.

"You're lying. I can take one look at you and know something's wrong." Looking up he saw his mom and dad getting into their car. Backing out of the driveway, Phil stopped and rolled down his window. "We're going to go back to the hotel and rest for a while. Your mom isn't feeling well. I'll call you later."

Jim knew that there was no way in hell that they would have gone back to the hotel "to rest" on their last night's visit. After they walked into the house he put something on the television for the kids.

"Hey guys, me and your mom will be outside in the backyard for a minute. Okay? Watch the show and we'll be back in soon." Grabbing Amanda by the hand, he led her out the back door.

"I can tell that something happened while I was gone and I'd be willing to bet that my mom said something or did something to upset you. So you might as well tell me and please don't try to sugar coat it.

168

Just tell me the truth." Reaching out, he stroked her hair away from her eyes and waited to hear what she had to say.

Lighting a cigarette, she told him what had transpired while he was gone. She didn't sugar coat it, nor did she embellish it, just told him exactly what was said, word for word. She had replayed it in her head so many times that afternoon that it wasn't hard.

"Wow. I'm so sorry. I'm sorry about what she said, but I'm also sorry that I wasn't honest with them in the first place. I should have just told them the truth. I knew my mother would have issues with you, if she knew that you were a recovering addict and I guess I thought that if she got to know you first, then it wouldn't be so important. I'm sorry for my part in this." His voice was shaking and this was the first time ever that she had seen him visibly upset.

"It's okay." She told him. All of the sudden she felt tired and just wanted to go to bed.

"No. It's not okay. I'm sorry." He pulled her against him and held her tightly for several minutes. He finally let her go and they walked back into the house to check on the kids.

"I've got to run an errand." He told her. "Should I pick something up for dinner?"

"No. There's plenty here. I'll cook something while you're gone. Please don't go fight with your parents," she implored. "I really don't want to be the cause of a family squabble. It makes me uncomfortable."

"Don't worry," he answered. He stopped long enough to give her a kiss; he grabbed his keys and walked out the door.

While he was gone, she made some grilled cheese sandwiches for the kids and warmed up leftovers for her and Jim. He was back within an hour. They ate a silent dinner, each lost in their own thoughts. She wished he would tell her what happened but decided not to push. He would tell her when he was ready.

After getting Michael and Melanie to bed, she went into the bathroom and ran a hot, bubble bath. She felt emotionally exhausted and drained. Several minutes later he joined her in the bath.

"So I did go and confront my mother. She hadn't told my dad anything about it and he was quite upset with her as well. I'm not going to lie and tell you it was all roses and sunshine. But we do have an understanding now." He didn't tell her that it was quite ugly and he had even threatened to cut his mom off, until she could accept that Amanda was part of his life now.

169

"Why didn't you tell me about the money?" she asked. That had been nagging at her in the back of her mind. She assumed that it was because he didn't trust her enough to share that with her.

"Basically, I'm a little embarrassed about it. I didn't do anything to earn it, or deserve it. I was just born into lucky circumstances. It's something that I really don't talk about and I don't really give it much thought. I'm sorry. I wasn't trying to hide it from you," Jim said, sincerity in his voice as he spoke.

They went to bed early that night, both of them tired after all of the emotional upheaval of the day. Amanda woke up at four in the morning and couldn't go back to sleep. Grabbing a little throw blanket, she sat in his chair looking out at the ocean. Helen's remarks kept going over and over in her head and her soul felt wounded. All she had wanted was for his parents to like her and now that would probably never happen.

Chapter Seventeen

Jim wasn't surprised that his parents had left Monday morning without coming over to say good-bye. He knew better than anyone how stubborn his mother could be.

Phil called before they left. "I love you, son. Don't worry about your mom. She will come around. I like Amanda and she has beautiful children. I trust your judgment and in the end we want you to be happy. As difficult as your mother can be, she wants you to be happy too, so just give her some time. We are going to hit the road soon." Phil had wanted to go by the house and say good-bye but Helen was still upset and didn't want to stop, although he suspected that embarrassment had something to do with it.

"I love you too, Dad. I'm glad you came up and thanks for always being there for me. I'm sorry that the visit had to end this way," Jim told his dad. In many ways he felt relieved that his parents had headed home. He knew how hurt Amanda was over his mother's remarks and that it would take time to heal those wounds.

On Monday they spent the day with Michael and Melanie, as Jim had promised. They went to the zoo and park, had lunch at a burger joint and then went to the movies. By evening, the kids were exhausted and went to bed early. Amanda and Jim stretched out on the couch and watched a movie, tired too.

"So, babe, have you figured out what you are going to do yet?" Jim asked.

Amanda knew exactly what he was talking about. She only had two more weeks at the rehab before she had to move, either to a sober living house or back home.

"No. Not really, but I think I'm going to have to go back to Hoopa, at least for the time being. I really can't afford to live in the sober living house without a job," she answered.

"Well, I have another option. You could move in here with me. I missed you last week when you went home for Christmas and it made me realize how much I like having you here. I don't want to push you but I hope that you'll consider it."

"Really? I would love nothing more than to live here with you, but are you sure?" she asked excitedly.

"Of course I'm sure. I wouldn't have asked if I wasn't sure," he stated, looking pleased.

"Okay. As long as you're not offering out of pity," she answered.

"Well you should know by now how much I love you. I have told you multiple times that I want to spend my life with you. I've wanted to ask you for a few weeks now but I don't want to do anything that might mess your sobriety up. So, before you decide I would like to make this offer too. If you feel it would be better for you to live in a sober living house for a few months then I would like to pay the monthly cost. You know I can afford it and I want you to make a decision based on what is best for you, not decided by finances," Jim explained.

Wiping tears from her eyes, she was almost too choked up to talk. "I don't know what to say. You always treat me so good."

"You don't have to decide tonight. You can sleep on it if you want," he offered.

"I don't need to sleep on it. I want to be here with you. I'll be fine; but just to make sure, I will keep attending meetings and going to group. And I still want to find a job and carry my weight around here." She felt like a burden had been lifted.

"Okay, but please promise me that if you start struggling, you will tell me and let me help." He wanted her to trust him.

"Okay." Amanda agreed. "I promise. So I was wondering what you wanted to do for New Year's Eve."

"What do you mean? I really don't have plans but do you have something in mind?" he asked, confused.

"Well, we never talked about when we were taking Michael and Melanie back to Hoopa and I wasn't sure if we were doing that before New Year's or after," she paused.

"I haven't really thought about it but I'm open to ideas. I'd be happy to take you out on New Year's Eve or I'd be fine with just staying in. But tell me what you would like to do?" he asked.

"Well, for the past few years I've gone out on New Year's and not in a good way. I got high and went on a run for days, you know, using New Year's as an excuse. This year I would like to be home with my kids and have a quiet, New Year's Eve. And maybe invite Uncle Ben over and play games and do normal family stuff. My mom will probably go to the New

Year's Eve Marathon Bingo. She has always wanted to do that but since she had my kids she never got a chance," she told him; he could hear the regret in her voice.

"I think that sounds great. I would love nothing more than to spend New Year's in Hoopa with your family, especially with your Uncle Ben." And that was absolutely true. He had never really enjoyed going out on New Year's Eve; too many people and too much drinking and he would much prefer staying home and having a quiet evening spent with her family.

Before going to bed she called her mom and told her the news. "So, we are going to come home on Thursday and stay until Sunday. If you want, you could go to the bingo marathon. And I was hoping Uncle Ben would come up and spend New Year's Eve with us."

"That would be great. I'm not positive about bingo yet. I will have to see if there is someone I can ride with but it will be great to have you and Jim come over and stay," Beverly said, excited about the possibility of going to bingo. But if it didn't work out, that would be okay, too. "We need to plan Melanie's birthday for the following week, while you are here."

"Yeah, we need to do that. She wants a princess party but we need to decide where we are having it and who we will be inviting. I have some other news, too," Amanda told her mother excitedly. "So Jim has asked me to move in with him. Well, he also offered to pay my rent at the sober living house if I preferred but I would much rather live with him and I think that I can do it."

"Oh honey. That's wonderful. I'm so happy for you both." Beverly was happy and relieved. She had worried about her daughter coming home but on the other hand there was no way that she could squeeze out the four hundred dollars a month fee. She also knew that the visit with Jim's parents had not gone well and as much as her daughter tried to sound like it didn't bother her, she knew that it did.

"I'm really happy, Mom. Happier than I've ever been. We will see you on Thursday. The kids are so lonesome for you and uncle already." She hung up the phone and they soon went upstairs to bed. It had been a long day and she knew that the kids would get up early in the morning.

The next few days went smooth and since Jim's parents had left, the atmosphere was once again relaxed. By Thursday, Michael and Melanie were both getting homesick and anxious to get back to the Valley. They stopped at a grocery store before they left and picked out food for New Year's Eve and New Year's Day. Amanda had decided that for New

Year's Eve they would have finger foods and snacks that they could munch on throughout the night. For New Year's Day they decided to have a buffet of seafood and they bought crab, shrimp, muscles and clam strips. They made it to Hoopa by two and Beverly and Ben were both there, waiting for them.

Both kids ran up to their grandma, hugging her and then to their uncle. Ben picked Melanie up and carried her in the house while the rest followed.

"So, I found a ride to bingo and I'm going to leave soon," Beverly told them. She had her bingo dabbers setting on the table, ready to go.

"I'm glad you're going, Mom. I hope you win. Are you staying the night on the coast or are you coming back tonight, or I guess early morning?" Amanda asked, knowing that the marathon wouldn't get over until three or four in the morning.

"Since it's not raining or snowing, we are going to come home when it gets over. I should be home by five at the latest. Ben is sponsoring me so I'm hoping to win for both of us." She really couldn't have afforded the buy-in for the marathon, which was one hundred twenty-five dollars, but her brother had offered to pay her way.

Jim and Ben carried in the groceries, suitcases and bags of toys that they had taken over for Michael and Melanie. A car pulled up and honked and Beverly grabbed her dabbers and purse and flew out the door. "Bye. Love you. Wish me luck." She called out before she closed the door.

"Bye, Mom." Amanda called out. "We will be making good medicine for you to win tonight."

Amanda went into the kid's bedroom and unpacked their clothes and put their toys away. They were happy to be home, in their own surroundings and both of them attached themselves to their Uncle Ben. Michael gave his uncle a recap of everything that they had done on their trip.

By early evening Amanda had made nachos, chips and dip, opened a jar of smoked salmon, cut up cheese and put crackers out. She pulled out a crib board and a deck of cards and they took turns playing crib. Although Amanda had told the kids that they could stay up until midnight, by ten o'clock both Michael and Melanie were sound asleep. At five minutes before midnight, Amanda opened a bottle of Apple Cider and poured a glass for Ben, Jim and herself. Even without a clock they would have known when it was midnight by the sound of M80's and gunshot fire going off. After a long kiss at midnight, they raised their glasses and made a toast. "Here's to the best year ever and to all the good things waiting to happen," Jim said. "I'll second that," Amanda chimed in.

It was the best New Year's Eve she could remember. The last few New Year's Eve seemed like a blur and remembering back to her childhood, they were always full of too much drinking which led to fighting and drama. There would have been a time when she would have found tonight too boring for her liking but tonight she appreciated what she had and everything seemed perfect.

Although they were tired, none of them wanted to go to bed. They were enjoying each other's company; laughing, joking and visiting.

At one thirty, Amanda was curled up on the couch by Jim, and Ben was sitting in the rocking chair by the fire watching a movie when she heard a strange noise. In the corner of her eye she saw her uncle stiffen up and slump towards the floor. Startled, she jumped up before Jim realized anything was going on.

"Oh my God. Uncle, are you all right?" Amanda yelled. By now he was lying on the floor with convulsions hitting his body.

"He's having a seizure. Is your uncle epileptic?" Jim asked. He had once had a student who had seizures at times and knew to roll his head to the side so that he didn't choke.

"No. He's never done this before." Amanda stood in shock, watching. This was the scariest thing she had ever seen and her uncle looked like he was dying. Tears streaming down her face, she watched as Jim moved the chair back away from him and turned his head to the side.

"Amanda, call an ambulance," Jim yelled at her. Still in a daze, she couldn't move. "Amanda, call an ambulance, now," his voice demanded.

Snapping out of it, she grabbed her phone. It took her three times to punch the numbers in correctly. When she finally got a dispatcher on the phone, she had trouble giving directions to the house. After several minutes she hung up. "The ambulance is about fifteen minutes out. God, I wish they would hurry." Her voice was almost hysterical by now.

The seizure stopped after five minutes and while they waited, Jim put a pillow under Ben's head and covered him with a blanket. At one point Ben started coming around and kept trying to sit up but Jim gently pushed him back down. "Ben, you've had a seizure. The ambulance is on its way but I need you to just lay still for now," Jim told him, reassuringly but firmly at the same time.

Amanda watched and was amazed how calm and capable Jim was in a crisis. She was freaking out and don't know how she would have handled it, if he hadn't been there. Fifteen minutes felt like fifteen hours and when the ambulance finally rolled in she felt relief wash over her. They only stayed long enough to take a quick set of vitals and start an IV, before they loaded him up and took off over the hill.

"I've got to find someone to watch the kids," Amanda told Jim.

"Do you have any family you can call?" he asked her.

"I'm going to try to call their grandparents and see if I can drop them off," Amanda answered. Dialing them up, she prayed they would answer. On the seventh ring, the kid's paternal grandmother answered the phone. After explaining what had happened, the grandmother told her to bring the children right over and she would start making up a bed for them. After wrapping blankets around the sleeping kids, Jim carried Michael out and Amanda carried Melanie out and they drove a few miles down the road to her ex in-laws and carried them in. Neither of them ever really woke up, except Michael once, but he was in a sleep daze and never fully coherent.

"Do you think we should stop and get anything from the house?" Jim asked. "Before we head out?"

"I don't know. I guess I better get my purse and maybe a change of clothes." She had done this before, in different circumstances and knew that sometimes the wait at the hospital could be several days.

Jim pulled up in the driveway and they jumped out and Amanda grabbed her purse while Jim grabbed their overnight bags, which were still sitting on the floor in her bedroom. Almost out the door, she turned and ran back into the kitchen and grabbed a phone book. "I'm going to call the casino on our way and try having mom paged. I know she will want to go to the hospital as soon as she can."

It took several tries to get through and finally the casino operator was paging her mother. She was on hold for almost five minutes and finally her mother answered. "Hello. Amanda? What's wrong?" Her heart was racing and all she could think of was that something happened to one of the children.

"Uncle had a seizure. The ambulance is taking him out," Amanda told her Mom. It took a few seconds before the news seemed to sink in. "Where are you?" Beverly asked.

"We are just going up Lord Ellis." Amanda said. "Do you want to meet at the hospital or do we need to come pick you up?"

"No. I'll just meet you at the hospital," Beverly told her daughter. "I'll find a ride and get there as soon as I can."

By the time they got to Blue Lake, they were right behind the ambulance. Following the ambulance into the parking lot, they parked while the ambulance backed into the bay.

"God. I'm nervous." Amanda jumped out of the truck and ran towards the back door of the ambulance. Looking around for her mom, she saw her in the waiting room, looking out the window. As soon as Beverly saw her daughter, she ran outside and joined her, waiting for the driver to open the back door and carry Ben on the stretcher into the emergency room.

"What happened?" Beverly asked, her daughter.

"We were watching a movie, everything seemed fine and then I looked over because I saw uncle kind of slump down and fall towards the floor from his chair. He had a seizure. Oh Mom, it was so scary. He was convulsing and looked like he was dying. His lips turned blue. It was so awful. We called the ambulance and by the time they got there he had started to come to, but he still seemed disoriented and dazed." Amanda spoke fast and nervous as she explained to her mother what had happened.

The paramedics rolled him out and into the emergency room. Both Beverly and Amanda followed them in to the little curtained off room while Jim walked through the other door that led into the waiting room. He knew that there was limited space and since he wasn't immediate family, wanted to stay out of the way.

After the paramedics had moved Ben into the hospital bed, they walked out of the room and a nurse came in and hooked him up to a machine to monitor his vitals. Looking around the room, Amanda noticed that he was more oriented now and looked like he had slept.

"How are you feeling, Uncle?" Amanda asked, walking over to stand by the side of the bed and hold his hand.

"I'm okay but I have a bad headache," Ben answered, his voice a little shaky.

"Well, the doctor will come in soon and hopefully will be able to tell us what is going on," Beverly told her brother.

"I don't really remember anything. One minute I was watching the movie and the next thing I woke up and I was in the ambulance. My whole body hurts though. I feel like I've been ran over by a semi-truck." And that was the truth. His whole body, especially his muscles, hurt worse than anything he could remember.

The nurse wrote his vitals down and walked out. They could hear her relaying the information to the doctor and he in turn picked up the phone and made a few calls. About five minutes later he popped into the room.

"Hello, I'm Dr. Johnson." The doctor looked to be later thirties and had such a confident and matter of fact attitude that they immediately felt more relaxed. "So, Mr. Brigham, I've ordered a CT scan of your head and abdomen and some lab work. How are you feeling now?"

"I have a bad headache and my body feels like I've been run over by a truck." Ben relayed to the doctor.

"I'll have the nurse come in and give you something for your pain. It's not uncommon to have a bad headache and muscle pain after a seizure. With your muscles' involuntary contracting during the seizure, you will probably be sore for several days. So, have you ever had a seizure before?" The doctor asked, while writing notes in a chart.

"No doctor. Never," Ben answered.

"Any past medical history of cancer, diabetes, or heart disease?" The doctor asked.

"No doctor. I've been pretty healthy," Ben answered, wishing that he would hurry up so the nurse could get him some pain meds.

"Okay. I will come back in after the tests are done and hopefully have some answers for you." The doctor said, before walking out the door and giving the nurse orders for some IV pain medication.

The nurse came in about five minutes later and administered morphine in his IV. "This should help your headache and body pain." The nurse explained. "I also put in a little Phenergan in case you get nauseous and it will help you relax a little too."

When the lab technician came in to take blood, Amanda stepped out to the waiting room to touch base with Jim and give him an update.

"How's he doing?" Jim asked, concern showing on his face.

"Well, the doctor ordered a cat scan of his brain and abdomen and some blood work. He has a really bad headache and says he feels really sore all over his body, which the doctor says is normal. The nurse gave him something for pain, so hopefully he'll feel better soon," Amanda told him.

"I guess they won't know anything until all the tests come back?" Jim said. "Should I go get you and Beverly some coffee?"

"Yeah, that would be nice. It's going to be a long night," Amanda answered. "I'm going back in but I'll come back out and touch base in a little bit."

When she got back in the room, Ben had been wheeled out. "They took him for his CT scan." Beverly told her. "They said he would be back in twenty minutes or so."

Amanda sat back down by her mother. "Jim went to get us some coffee." Nodding her head, Beverly was glad that Jim was here for Amanda. About ten minutes later the nurse came into the room and told Amanda that there was a gentleman in the waiting room who had coffee for them. Walking back out to the waiting room, Amanda got the coffee and could see down the hall, that they were getting ready to wheel Ben back to the ER room.

"I'm going to go back in but thank you. I'll come back out as soon as we hear something." Amanda turned and walked back into the ER. Jim sat down and watched her walking down the hallway. She was visibly upset and seemed so fragile right now that he felt worried. Although they didn't have any clear answers yet, his gut instinct was that there was something seriously wrong. Considering the weight loss, fatigue, breathing difficulties and now seizures, he knew that in all probability it couldn't be good. As she walked back into the exam room, Ben was just being wheeled back into the room. He was sleeping and although he opened his eyes for a minute, it wasn't long before he was sleeping hard again. Whispering to her Mom, Amanda asked, "Have you called Ashley yet?"

"No. Not yet. I thought I would wait until the doctor comes back in and gives us an update. I'm not even sure if she's back from her trip yet," Beverly answered in hushed tones.

Another twenty minutes passed before the doctor came in and sat down on the rolling, round chair. The look on his face, told both women that they had found something.

Reaching over he touched Ben's arm and gentle shook him. "Mr. Brigham, it's Doctor Johnson. How's your headache?"

Slowly opening his eyes and looking slightly disoriented, Ben looked around the room trying to remember what had happened. "I guess it's a little better now. I think the pain meds helped."

"Good. I thought it would help. So I just went and looked at the results of your CT scan and there is a mass in the left occipital side of the brain, along with a mass in your liver and possibly a small mass in the left lower lobe of your lung. Your blood tests show that you are very anemic and have very elevated LFT's. Do you drink alcohol?" Dr. Johnson had suspected that Ben had cirrhosis for probably some time now.

"No. Not anymore. I haven't had a drink for over 12 years," Ben relayed to him.

"Do you have a history of heavy drinking, before that?" Dr. Johnson asked.

"Yes. I was an alcoholic for around 20 years," Ben answered.

"Well Mr. Brigham, I'm not going to pretend that I have all of the answers tonight. We need to admit you to the hospital and do more testing. The House Doctor will take over your case and he will oversee your care, order tests and arrange for any specialists that might be needed for diagnosis and treatment. Do you have any questions for me?" Dr. Johnson asked.

Ben looked uncomfortably at the doctor with a look of panic. "How long do I have to stay here doc? I really don't like hospitals."

"I can't really say. Possibly several days though." The doctor knew that it would probably be more like a week but he wanted to give him time to digest what he had just been told. He knew his patient was very ill and didn't want to add stress on him until they knew exactly what was going on. "I'm going to call and find a room for you and work on getting you admitted."

"Is there any way I can go home and just come back for tests?" Ben asked, hopeful. He had never really believed in doctors and normally tried to avoid them.

"I'm sorry but no. Until we know the exact cause, there's a chance that you could have more seizures and we will be able to help manage your pain better if you are here." The doctor rose to leave and Beverly followed him out the door and into the hallway.

"Doctor, how sick is my brother? I mean is there more that you're not telling us?" Beverly asked.

"Well, I can't say a lot at this point, without further testing and I don't want to break patient confidentiality but I will say that I believe that your brother is very ill. We will know more in the next few days. You might want to talk to your brother about signing a release so that we can discuss his case with you and it might be a good idea for him to think about signing a document that appoints someone to make medical decisions for him, in case he becomes incapacitated." The doctor patted her arm and then went back to the side office to start making arrangements for Ben's admission.

As Beverly walked back into the room, she met Amanda walking out. "Mom, I'm going to go talk to Jim and let him know what is going on," Amanda told her.

Amanda found Jim still sitting in the waiting room, reading a magazine. Rising, he met her at the doorway and motioned her out in the hall. "The waiting room is pretty crowded. Let's go into the hall and talk."

"So the tests came back and the doctor said he has a mass in his head, liver and lung. What does a mass mean? Is that tumors and does that mean he has cancer?" Not waiting for an answer, she continued. "Anyhow, they are admitting him for maybe a couple of days."

"I'm so sorry, babe. I know it doesn't sound good but let's wait until they know for sure what's going on before jumping to conclusions. Okay?" He hugged her and stroked her hair for a minute. He could tell she was really stressed and he also knew that being up all night only added to that. It was already six in the morning. "How is he feeling? Is his headache better?

"I think so," Amanda answered. "They gave him some morphine and some other stuff, so he has been going in and out of sleep. I know he's scared. Not about being sick so much but about staying in the hospital. He hates hospitals and going to the doctor."

"Well, I'm glad that he's here so that they can get to the bottom of what is going on and give him the care that he needs," Jim said, trying to reassure her.

"I guess. Once they get him admitted I guess we can go home for a while and sleep and then I'll need to pick the kids up. I'm going to go back in," she said.

It took over an hour to admit Ben to the hospital. When he finally got settled into a room, he fell into a deep sleep.

"I think you and Jim should go home and check on the kids and get some sleep. I'm going to stay here. The nurse said that this chair makes out into a bed, so I'm going to try to sleep a little while Ben is sleeping. When I wake up I'll call Ashley," Beverly said.

"Okay," Amanda agreed. "I hate to leave you but I think you're right. I'll call later, after we get home."

She went out and found Jim pacing the halls. She thought how grateful she was that he was here and then filled him in on the plan.

"I'll do whatever you want to do." He pulled out a couple of twenties and handed it to Amanda. "Give this to your mom, in case she needs anything."

"Thanks. I'm sure she will appreciate it." She walked back into the room and gave it to her mom.

"That's so sweet. I didn't even think about needing anything. I have a little in the bank but I don't have my debit card. After I bought my bingo buy-in, it pretty much wiped out my cash," Beverly explained. "Tell him thank you and I'll pay him back on my pay day."

"I'll tell him, but I know he's not worried about you paying him back," Amanda told her. "I love you and tell uncle I love him, when he wakes up."

She had planned on staying awake on the way home to make sure Jim stayed awake while driving but not even five miles down the road she fell fast asleep. When she woke up, they were pulling into the driveway and Jim was gently shaking her arm and calling her name.

"Oh my God. I am so sorry. I planned on staying awake to help you stay awake," she told him.

"It's okay. I was fine. If I got too tired, I would have pulled over. I wasn't sure if we were going home or picking the kids up first, so I just pulled in here," Jim told her.

"It's hard to decide. I'm scared once we go in and go to sleep we won't be able to get up after a few hours but if we go get them now we won't get any sleep." She hadn't really decided what to do.

"I'll tell you what; I'll make sure that we wake up in a few hours. It's eight thirty now so I'll set my alarm for eleven thirty." He knew her indecisiveness had a lot to do with fatigue.

"Okay. That sounds good and I'm sure their grandparents won't mind." Yawning big, she walked down the hall to the bedroom and he followed. Within five minutes they were both sleeping hard and at eleven thirty when his alarm went off on his phone, it felt like they had only been asleep for a few minutes, instead of three hours.

"Let's jump in the shower. It will probably help us wake up a little," Jim suggested.

Amanda jumped up and started looking for clothes. She felt groggy with that "hungover" feeling. Her anxiety was high and emotions raw, with worry about her uncle. The fact that this was the first day of the year was not lost on her. She had had high hopes for having the best year ever and it seemed like an ominous start.

They took a shower together and although it wasn't really planned, after a few minutes of soaping each other up, they had sex. It was more of a quickie, not really in the romantic sense that both of them were more accustomed to but in some ways provided a release that they needed. Feeling more awake, either from the shower or sex, they quickly dressed and headed out to pick up Michael and Melanie.

As they pulled in to her ex in-law's house to pick the kids up, she noticed several cars there that she didn't recognize.

"Do you want me to go with you or wait in the car?" Jim asked.

"I guess wait. I'm not sure who is here," she answered, glancing curiously towards the house.

Before she got to the door, it swung open and Michael and Melanie came running out. "Guess what Mom? Dad's here," Michael yelled, proudly turning around and looking at his dad, who was following them out.

Amanda was a little surprised and caught off guard. She hadn't seen her ex for quite some time and wondered when he had gotten out of jail.

Watching from the truck, Jim knew in his gut that it was her ex; Michael and Melanie's father. Although they only hugged briefly, there was something familiar in their touch, like old lovers who knew each other well. Even though he knew it was foolish, he felt jealous. It wasn't like he didn't know that she had been in a relationship before; she had two kids. She had never really opened up and talked about her ex before and he hadn't really given much thought about him before. But now, watching them talking, he found himself curious and somewhat envious.

After a few moments, she turned towards the truck and smiled at Jim. After saying something to the man standing by her, they both walked towards the truck. Jim jumped out of the truck and walked towards the front of the truck to meet them.

"So Jim, this is Troy, Michael and Melanie's dad. Troy this is Jim, my boyfriend." She said proudly.

"Hi, Troy. Nice to meet you. You have great kids," Jim told him, while shaking his hand.

"Nice to meet you too, Jim." Troy answered. "So, I told Amanda that the kids can stay the weekend. I'm sure you guys are tired and stressed out over Uncle Ben."

"That's nice. We are pretty tired," Amanda answered. "We might run back to the hospital later but for the most part we will be around."

"Well I haven't seen them for quite some time. Almost four months. It will be good for us," Troy told them. He was checking out Jim with the same curiosity that Jim had for him. He had never imagined Amanda hooking up with a white guy but she looked happy and better than she had in years. He was happy for her and if this is what it took for her to do better in her life, then he was glad for her.

"Let me give you my cell number. You can call if you need me to pick the kids up or any kind of emergency." Amanda walked to the truck and pulled a pen out and wrote her number down.

Handing it to Troy, she gave him one more hug. "Thanks Troy. I really appreciate this."

"I'm glad to help. I know I haven't been there for the kids. I've been clean for four months now and I plan on doing right by them," he said regretfully, not just about the kids, but about Amanda too. She was the only woman that he had ever loved and his mind flashed back to earlier days when they were teenagers and madly in love. The four months he spent in jail had given him a lot of time to think and he had hoped when he got out that they could maybe rekindle what they had once had. But seeing her now, it was obvious that she had moved on and she seemed happy. She deserved that, he thought to himself.

Chapter Eighteen

On Sunday, Jim and Amanda got up early and headed back to the hospital. Amanda packed a change of clothes for her mom and before they left she dropped some clothes off for Michael and Melanie. It was a dreary, cold day and felt like it could snow anytime. They had both had a good night sleep and were well rested. Amanda was glad that Troy was stepping up and taking care of the kids so that they could go visit Uncle Ben without worrying about childcare arrangements.

"So, we haven't really talked about your ex much," Jim asked, hesitantly. "I guess I'm a little curious about him. I hope you don't mind me bringing it up."

"No. I don't mind. You're not jealous are you?" she asked jokingly.

"Well, maybe just a little," he answered, laughing.

"Oh please. That's so over," she said. "I care about him in a way that you care about an old friend and don't want to see anything happen to them. But in a romantic sense, I don't have those types of feelings for him, not anymore."

"I'm glad," he said while grabbing her hand and bringing it up to his lips. "What happened? For it to end, I mean."

"Well, for starters, I think we were just too young when we became a couple. We were fifteen when we started going out. At the time we were so in love that it seemed we would be together forever. You know, young love. When I got pregnant with Michael it wasn't planned but we were happy about it. Unfortunately we both had drug issues and it just got worse. On the one hand we enabled each other but after a while we both had big habits and at times we fought over drugs. After Melanie was born we both were spiraling down and then I caught him cheating, not once but several times, and that just pretty much ended us. But then again, our first love was always the drugs." She felt sad, thinking about how low they had both sunk. "He was a good person. He was kind and funny but in the end the drugs got the better of him. I'm glad to see him doing well and clean now. Sometimes it takes jail for people to kick their habit. He seems pretty determined now."

"Well, I hope he stays clean, for the kid's sake. I'm sure it would be nice for them to have their father in their lives," Jim said. It was still a hard concept for him to understand, putting drugs before one's children.

"Yeah, I hope he can stay clean too. When I see him it's like seeing a good friend that you only want the best for but again I don't think of him in a romantic sense at all," she reassured him.

"Good to hear," Jim answered. Although normally not insecure he knew there was history and a strong bond between Amanda and Troy since they had two children together. And, if he was honest, Troy was a nice looking guy and seemed pretty charming.

They arrived at the hospital and she carried in the change of clothes she had brought for her mother. Ben was sleeping when they walked in. Her mother was sitting in a chair, watching television. It didn't look like she had gotten much sleep. "Hi," Beverly said quietly. "Uncle is taking a nap. He was up a lot last night. How are the kids?"

"They're good Mom. Troy has them and offered to keep them this weekend." Noticing the worry flash across her mother's face, she quickly added, "don't worry Mom, he's straight."

"Good. That makes me feel better," Beverly said, relieved.

"So have they figured out what is going on with Uncle?" Amanda asked.

"No but the doctor did say that he was going to come in this morning and talk to us," Beverly answered. "I'm not sure what time and was scared if I walked to the cafeteria to get coffee that I would miss him."

"I'll go get coffee for you, Bev. Do you want anything else? A doughnut or bagel?" Jim offered.

"Maybe a bagel and cream cheese. Mostly coffee, though," Beverly said sleepily. It was never easy to get a good night's sleep in the hospital.

While Jim went to the cafeteria, Amanda sat by the bed watching her uncle sleep. He looked so fragile right now. Not like the strong, virile man that had been with her all of her life. As if he knew that someone was watching him sleep, he roused and slowly woke up.

"Hey. How long have you been here?" Ben asked, pushing the button on the side of his bed to raise the head of the bed.

"Not very long, maybe five minutes," Amanda answered.

"Well, don't watch me sleep. It's creepy," Ben said, teasing her.

"At least you haven't lost your sense of humor," Amanda joked back. A nurse came in and handed Ben several pills and a small cup of water. "I'll be back in a few minutes to take your vitals," the nurse told him, before heading back out the door.

"What do you think, Amanda? I think that nurse kind of likes me. Should I bring her home with me?" Ben asked.

"Well, she certainly is your type, Uncle. Blond and built," Amanda joked back, laughing. The whole family had always given Ben a bad time for his preference of blondes with big boobs.

Jim had just walked in with Beverly's coffee and bagel, when the doctor came in. Jim excused himself and went back out into the waiting room. The room felt small and judging from the doctor's manner, he sensed that he was coming in to deliver bad news. Out of respect for the family, he didn't want to intrude and felt it was important to let them have privacy.

Standing by the side of the bed, the doctor looked grim and cleared his throat before starting. "So, Mr. Brigham we got all of your test results back and I've been reviewing them with my partner this morning. We believe that you have primary liver cancer that has metastasized to your lungs and brain. I'm sorry. Although primary liver cancer isn't all that common, people with cirrhosis have a much higher risk of contracting this disease. I'm working on a treatment plan, although at this late stage there aren't many options and they will mostly be palliative. Do you have any questions?" This was the hardest part of the job and the doctor always hated when he had to deliver a blow like this, to his patients.

"Can I go home soon and how long do I have?" Ben asked. He had prepared himself for this possibility and wasn't really surprised. He had known for quite some time that he was sick. But he was more afraid of being stuck in the hospital, than he was of impending death.

"Well, I really don't want to venture a guess. The Oncologist might have a better answer. I can say that in similar cases the life expectancy is anywhere from three to six months but every patient is different." Putting his hand on Ben's shoulder he wanted to leave him with something comforting. "We will do everything possible to make sure that you are comfortable. As far as going home, I would like to keep you a few more days and give you another transfusion to address your anemia. Do you have any questions for me?" the doctor asked, directing the question to Beverly and Amanda.

"Is there any treatment, chemotherapy or radiation that could prolong his time?" Beverly asked.

"Unfortunately it's much too advanced. If we utilize any of those options it will be for palliative care only, to make sure that your brother is comfortable," the doctor answered.

"No, Beverly. I don't want treatment anyhow," Ben said adamantly. "I've watched too many people do that and the time that they had left was spent going back and forth to the hospital and feeling deathly ill the whole time."

"I'll be back later this afternoon and we will talk more about discharge medications and I will write a referral to Hospice," the doctor informed them, before walking out the door.

Although she tried hard not to cry, after the doctor walked out, tears started sliding down Amanda's cheeks. She felt bad about it, wanting to be the comforter, not the one being comforted.

"Please don't cry, Honey Bumpkins. I've had a good life. I've lived exactly how I've wanted and I don't have any regrets. It's just the natural course of life." Ben reached out and grabbed her hand. He was surprised how comfortable he was with the thought of death. He had always imagined that he would be scared or too weak to go through a terminal diagnosis but now that it was actually happening he felt calm and peaceful. His biggest concern was that he didn't want to be a burden on his family.

"I just don't know what we will do without you." Amanda said, smiling through her tears. "You have always been our rock."

"You will all make it, believe me." Ben told her. "So today I would really like everyone to go home. I would like to be alone and have time to digest this. And, Beverly, you need to rest. You have work tomorrow."

Although both Beverly and Amanda protested, Ben wasn't going to take no for an answer. Although accepting of his fate, he still needed time to process everything happening to him and he couldn't do that with his sister and niece there.

Amanda excused herself while her mom did last minute hovering over her brother. She wanted to talk to Jim alone before they left the hospital. She found him in the waiting room and motioned him to the hallway. "Can we walk out to the truck for a minute?" she asked, walking towards the door without waiting for an answer.

Jim knew before she told him, that Ben was terminal. He had spent a lot of time in the waiting room, looking up symptoms and correlating diagnosis on his phone. "So Uncle has liver cancer that has spread to his brain and liver," and as she told him the tears came back, although this time she didn't try to hold them in. Putting his arms around her, he held her tightly while she cried. "I'm sorry," was all that he said. There was nothing else to say; nothing that would change the outcome and they knew it. When she finally quit crying and was able to compose herself again, they walked back into Ben's room. Jim sat down in a chair and talked a moment about the books that Ben had given him for Christmas and about football. Ben was a die-hard Packers fan and Jim was a die-hard Cowboys fan, so they jokingly ribbed each other about their respective teams.

"Well, I guess we will hit the road now Uncle. I'm coming back tomorrow and stay until you get out," Amanda told him, in a tone that he knew he couldn't argue with.

"What about the kid's?" Ben asked.

"Troy has them. I'm going to ask him if he will keep them a few more days," she answered.

"I can't wait to get home. I have always hated hospitals," Ben grumbled.

"I know. But it's only a few more days and you'll be home," Beverly told him reassuringly. The whole family knew Ben's aversion to doctors and hospitals, which is probably why he had waited so long to seek treatment.

Jim insisted on taking Beverly and Amanda to breakfast before heading back over the hill. He knew that Beverly was probably hungry after being at the hospital for several days and he was pretty hungry himself. Amanda really wasn't hungry and felt too upset to eat but tried to be a good sport and ordered a waffle anyhow. When their food came she could only manage to swallow a few bites that seemed to get stuck in her throat.

"So Mom, have you talked to Ashley?" she asked.

"I called her on New Year's when Uncle was first admitted but haven't called her since. I wanted to wait until I knew more. She will be back from her trip tomorrow and is traveling today." Beverly had decided to wait until she was home before calling her and giving her the bad news.

"So, I'm going to talk to Troy when we get home and see if he will keep Melanie and Michael a few more days. I really want to come back and stay with Uncle at the hospital," Amanda told them, talking out loud as much as to Jim and Beverly.

"I'll have to head out early to make it back to work tomorrow. I can drop you off on my way," Jim offered. "It's hard to believe Christmas vacation is over already."

"I can keep the kids. We are already used to our routine. I would like Troy or his parents to keep the kids though when Ben gets discharged so I can drive out and pick you guy's up," Beverly said. "Once he's home we will have to figure out a schedule for his care. I talked to the doctor privately and he said that Ben's cancer is progressing very fast."

The rest of breakfast was somber. Although they were trying to put up a good front, the mood was depressed. The ride home was the same and for the first time in three months, Amanda was feigning for a fix. The realization hit her hard and made her anxious. After all that she had gone through to be clean, it disturbed her that she would even want to use again. She felt antsy and immediately started mopping and cleaning when they got home; anything to try to keep from thinking about it.

"Are you okay, honey?' Jim asked. "Why don't we watch a movie or go for a walk?" He wasn't exactly sure what was going on in her head and was clueless about the battle that she was fighting.

"Can we go to the Casino?" She asked. "I just want to clear my head and could really use a distraction right now."

"Sure. Anything you want," Jim answered. "Beverly, do you want to go too?"

"No. I think I'll go down and check on Ben's house and see if it needs cleaning. I also want to wash his sheets and blankets and make sure that everything is ready before he comes home. I won't have time during the week, with work and everything." Beverly needed a distraction too, but in a different way than her daughter.

The casino distraction started off good and Amanda even won one hundred dollars right off the bat. As she walked to the bathroom she saw several of her connections walking in the door and she made small talk with them for a minute before hurrying back to Jim and holding out the one hundred dollars to him.

"No, you won it. Keep it and buy yourself something," he urged. He didn't need the money and was hoping it would make her happy.

"No. Really, take it," she pleaded. Not wanting to tell him that she didn't trust herself right now with money in her pocket and itching for a fix, she held it out to him.

"Okay. I'll hold it for you and give it to you when we get home," Jim told her. He assumed that she was just scared that she would gamble it away.

They left soon after and on the way home stopped and picked Michael and Melanie up. They were happy and excited to see their mom and Jim. Troy came out and assured Amanda that he could keep the kids anytime. "We've had a great time. Bring them over anytime. I want to be here to help you with whatever you need." It was a sweet offer and Amanda was touched. This was the "old" Troy, the man he was before the drugs got to him and a moment of clarity came back. She knew that she had to stay strong and not give in during this stressful period.

When they got home she decided to take an extra strip of Suboxone and it helped. The rest of the night went smoother after that and she concentrated on washing clothes and packing a bag of essentials that she would need at the hospital. They would have to get up early and be on the road by six so that Jim could get to work on time. Going to bed early, she cuddled into Jim. Her body felt tired but her mind was in overdrive. She listened to him sleep and his breathing was almost hypnotic. The harder she tried not to think about things, the more overwhelmed she felt and it was after two before she finally fell asleep.

The alarm went off at five thirty and instead of jumping up and getting ready, Jim pulled her closer, while his hands roamed over her body. Half asleep she really wasn't in the mood. She still felt distracted and her body felt numb. It wasn't her usual reaction and she tried hard to fake it. Normally she loved nothing more than making love with Jim, but her mind was a million miles away. Her thoughts were on her uncle, Jim's parents, Tiffany and just about everything that had happened in the past three months. And in the back of it all was the devil she was fighting. Disappointment had hit hard, when she woke up and was still craving a fix.

Although things felt a little different, Jim assumed that it was because it was so early and she was worried about her uncle. When they finally got up, they hurriedly took a shower together and got dressed. She walked in to tell her mom good-bye.

"Call me and give me an update on Ben," Beverly told her. "And when they get ready to discharge him, call and give me a heads up so I can take off work and come pick you guys up."

"I will. And I will call and check in. Don't worry. Bye. Love you." Amanda told her as she walked towards the door to leave.

"Love you too," Beverly called out, while getting out of bed. She had to get ready and get the kid's ready and she knew after being on vacation and off of their routine for two weeks that it would be no easy task.

The trip out was quiet, with Jim occasionally making small talk. Amanda was content to listen to music and her mind wandered back to the past, when she was a little girl. She had so many memories of her uncle. He had been such a big part of her life and the thought of him not being around seemed unbearable. She was no stranger to the pain of death and losing someone you love but before it had come unexpected and there was no time to process beforehand. She wasn't sure if this would be harder or easier having had time to say good-bye.

It was seven when Jim pulled up to the hospital entrance. He hated to leave her but knew that he didn't have a choice. He had his students to think about and hated to use subs. It was more trouble than it was worth, with his students acting up and the classroom in total disarray.

"I love you. Please take care of yourself," Jim told her. "I'll call you when I get a break today."

"I love you too and don't worry, I'll be okay. Thanks for being here for me." Leaning over she kissed him goodbye before grabbing her bag and climbing out of the truck.

Ben was awake, sitting up watching television, when she walked in. "Good morning," he called out to her. "You're out and about early this morning."

He looked good this morning. His color was good and by looking at him it was hard to believe that he only had a short time left to live.

"Jim dropped me off on his way to work. He has to be there by eight. How was your night?" she asked.

"I slept like a baby," Ben answered. "I think they put something in my IV to help me sleep because I slept hard and feel a little drugged this morning."

Amanda put her bag in the little closet on the edge of the room and then pulled the recliner chair closer to the bed and stretched out and got comfortable on it. Close to eight a breakfast tray was brought in to Ben. "Here, help me eat this," Ben told her. "You know I'm not that big of a breakfast eater."

"I'm not that hungry, Uncle," she said, eyeing up the tray. "What did you get for breakfast?"

"It looks like scrambled eggs, turkey bacon, wheat toast, a little cup of fruit, a cup of coffee and some orange juice," he answered.

"Wow. Just like Denny's?" she told him, laughing.

"I'm just going to drink coffee and eat the toast so help yourself," Ben offered. "I've been feeling really nauseous since I woke up so I'm going to eat light."

Amanda reached over and grabbed the fruit cup and ate a few bites of the eggs. "The fruit is good, Uncle. Are you sure you don't want some?" She asked.

"No. I'm good. I would have eaten the bacon if it were real. I just don't know about turkey bacon. Too dry for my liking. I don't know why they had to take a good thing and change it," Ben grumbled.

"I know what you mean," Amanda said, sympathizing with her uncle. It was a silly thing to dwell on and they both started laughing at the same time.

"Look at us, putting all of this damn energy into bacon," Ben said, shaking his head.

The morning went a little slow. Amanda had packed a deck of cards and a crib board and they spent a couple of hours playing crib. Just before noon, the door flung open and both Ben and Amanda were surprised to see Ashley coming through the door. Rushing to the side of the bed, Ashley threw her arms around her uncle and gave him a big hug.

"Hey, Ashley. You're back," Ben said, while hugging her back. He could tell she was fighting hard to hold back tears and he was as surprised as Amanda was. Ashley was never one to show much emotion and it was a little unnerving to see her like this. "It's okay," he said, while holding her tight and patting her back.

"I'm sorry," Ashley said, while wiping her eyes. "I'm just really emotional today." Putting a smile on her face, she continued. "So, how are you feeling?"

"I'm okay. You know, I haven't really been feeling good for quite some time and I don't feel any worse today than I have been feeling," Ben explained.

Looking across to the other side of the bed, Ashley saw her sister sitting in the reclining chair. "Hi, Amanda. How's it going?" Ashley asked her sister.

"Okay. We were just playing cribbage and waiting for lunch," Amanda replied. Her sister looked good, tanned and healthy. It was obvious that the vacation had done her well. For a minute, Amanda felt a quick flash of jealousy but then dismissed the thought. This wasn't the past where Ashley was doing well with a good life and Amanda was doing bad, barely making it. She had a wonderful boyfriend, two beautiful kids and was finally getting her life together and for the first time she didn't feel jealous or inferior to her sister.

Ashley sat on the other side of her uncle and made small talk. Around twelve thirty his lunch tray was delivered. He picked at it and took a few bites of his soup and some type of casserole. He really had no appetite but knew that everyone would make a fuss if he didn't eat a little. He was tired and really wanted a nap. He didn't mind his nieces visiting but didn't feel like he could nap when they were there.

"So, girls, I'm getting a little tired and I think I'm going to take a nap. Why don't you go to lunch?" Ben suggested.

"Okay. We can take a hint," Amanda said jokingly. She knew her uncle would try to stay awake and visit if they were there and she could tell that he was tired.

"We'll take our time and let you sleep," Ashley told him, giving him a hug and kiss before walking out into the hallway. Turning towards her sister, she asked, "So, where do you want to go? We can go somewhere in my car. Or would you rather stay here and eat in the cafeteria?"

"Let's go somewhere. I'll be eating at the cafeteria tonight," Amanda answered. Her sister was being so open and friendly that she was a little surprised.

"Sounds good. There is a little restaurant down the street that I have eaten at a few times and is pretty good," Ashley said.

Getting in the car, Amanda noticed that the inside was immaculate and brand new looking. Ashley was the most organized, orderly person that she knew and she wondered what would ever happen if Ashley had kids. The restaurant was more of a small café and they walked in just as the noon lunch crowd was leaving. Sitting down at a small booth, the waitress handed them both a menu and poured water into their glasses. Amanda scanned the menu noticing that there were a variety of vegetarian choices.

"Any suggestions?" Amanda asked her sister.

"Well, I've been eating mostly vegetarian for the past month. I'm probably going to order a tofu burger. But they have really good soup and quiches," Ashley answered.

"Wow. You don't eat meat. What about eggs and cheese?" Amanda asked, somewhat amazed. The only vegetarians she had ever known were more of the hippie, tree hugger types.

"I eat fish and eggs. I've cut out red meat and pork but I will eat lean chicken breast once a week or so," Ashley explained.

"What prompted that?" Amanda asked, curious since her sister had always loved hamburgers, bacon and a good steak.

"Well, I did it partly for health reasons and I have a friend who I eat with quite often who is a vegetarian," Ashley replied.

"Girlfriend or boyfriend?" Amanda asked, thinking it must be a man, to bring this big of change in Ashley.

"It's a boyfriend," Ashley answered, grinning. "I'll tell you because I know you will keep asking questions. So, I met him at the hospital. He's a Radiologist and I have been dating him since before Thanksgiving. His name is Steve and he moved here from Sacramento last summer. That's who I went on vacation with. He's gorgeous, smart and funny. Really outgoing, which I know is the opposite of me but somehow it works."

Amanda couldn't help but feel really happy and excited for her sister. She hadn't seen Ashley this happy or animated in years and she was actually opening up; talking and smiling. Not the uptight, withdrawn woman that they had all grown accustomed to.

"I'm so happy for you. It must be love because you look great. I have news too. I'm moving in with Jim. It would have been this week but I've decided that I am going to stay with Uncle and take care of him. I don't want him to be alone and it makes the most sense for me to be with him since you and mom have work." Amanda had given this a lot of thought and had talked to Jim briefly about it on their way to the hospital this morning.

"Well, it does make sense and I know that Uncle would prefer it be you. You always were his favorite," Ashley stated, not in a jealous way but as fact.

The waitress came and took their order. Amanda settled on a dinner salad and a bowl of Clam Chowder while Ashley ordered a dinner salad and a garden burger.

"I'm going to go to the bathroom before our order comes." Ashley said, standing up and heading towards the bathroom.

Although Amanda was feeling better today, she still had moments of extreme anxiety and cravings. Deciding to wait until she got back to the hospital to take her Suboxone she mentally started calculating how many hours it had been since she last took part of a strip this morning. A sudden realization hit her and grabbing her purse she frantically started digging through it. Panic sat in as she realized that she had taken the little pouch that she carried her Suboxone strips in, out of her purse this morning and had sat them on the dresser beside the bed. Anxiety started running high. The last few days had been hard enough, even with Suboxone but now without it, she didn't know what she was going to do. Pulling everything out of her purse, she prayed that she would find them but soon it was apparent that she had left them at home.

"Hey, are you okay?" Ashley asked, as she sat back down. Her sister looked like she had seen a ghost.

"Yes. I'm okay. I'm just feeling a little sick to my stomach." Which was an understatement, Amanda thought. Somehow her mouth was still moving, making small talk with her sister but on the inside she was freaking out.

When their food came Amanda took a few bites, not wanting to bring attention to the distress that she was in at the moment. This was probably the best visit that she had ever had with her sister since they were little girls but instead of being able to enjoy it, she was mentally trying to find an answer to her situation. It was too late to catch the bus back up to the Valley and she didn't know anyone local that might have a hook up for Suboxone.

"So, do you want to go walk around the mall for a while? I don't have to be at work for a few more hours?" Ashley asked. "I guess we could go back to the hospital but I want Uncle to get a good nap."

"Okay," Amanda agreed, less than enthusiastic.

Ashley looked at her, trying to gauge what was going on. "Is everything okay Amanda? You seem a little distracted."

"I'm okay. Just a little tired I guess." For a moment, Amanda almost told her sister the truth but her sister was never this open and friendly and not wanting to rock the boat, she bit her tongue and decided against it. Besides, her sister didn't have time to drive her home and back; not with her work schedule anyhow.

They walked around the mall for an hour, window-shopping. Whoever Ashley's new boyfriend was had done wonders for her. Amanda had basically given up on ever seeing her sister so relaxed and open. It was the relationship that she had always hoped for with her sister and she almost had to pinch herself to make sure she wasn't dreaming.

On the ride back to the hospital the realization of their uncle's prognosis seemed to come back. "I'm going to work on rearranging my work schedule so I can come up and help you with Uncle." Ashley told her sister. "I've taken care of a lot of people who were terminal and towards the end Uncle Ben is going to need round the clock care. The main thing will be to make sure that he is comfortable and not in pain. I know a lot of the Hospice workers who come into the nursing home so I'm going to look into what kind of resources might be available for him."

"Thanks Ashley. It just seems so unreal that he has so little time left. I don't know how I'm going to tell Michael and Melanie. They are so used to being with him on a daily basis." Amanda wasn't sure what to tell them and how much they would understand about death.

"That's going to be hard but the Hospice workers have little pamphlets about how to explain death and dying to children. I'll try to get one for you," Ashley offered.

Ashley stayed for another hour before leaving to go to work. Amanda played a few more games of crib with her uncle and for a while it was a good distraction but by four in the afternoon she was really feigning out. She figured that some of it had to be in her mind because she had taken a small piece of a strip early in the morning. It was a little early to be feigning out this bad but knowing that she didn't have any with her was making it worse and panic was starting to set in again.

"Are you okay, honey?" Ben asked. He noticed that she seemed antsy and nervous.

"Yeah, I'm okay. Just a little restless." She wanted to tell him the truth but it seemed unfair to put that on him. He had enough to worry about.

Around five when the door swung open they expected to see a nurse and were surprised when Harold walked in the door. "Hey, Uncle." Harold walked to the side of the bed and gave his uncle a big bear hug. "I heard you were in the hospital and came by to see if you wanted me to break you out."

Ben laughed, while shaking his head "yes." "I was wondering when you were going to come and get me out of here."

"Hey Amanda. How are you doing?" Harold asked her warily. He hadn't seen her since Thanksgiving and wondered if she was still mad at him for being such an ass.

"I'm okay. You?" She was glad to see him in decent shape. He wasn't drunk and didn't smell like alcohol at all. And no matter what he did, she never stayed mad at him. He was family.

"Doing good. I haven't drank for almost a month now," he proudly told them.

"That's good. I'm proud of you Harold," Amanda told him.

"I'm glad," Ben told his nephew. "Part of the reason I'm in here is because of the drinking I did when I was young." He wasn't going to give Harold a lecture, but hoped that he understood that this was the reality and price he was paying for past behaviors.

The nurse came in with a dinner tray and Amanda thought now would be a good time to go out and smoke. "Harold, I am going to go outside and smoke. Do you want to join me or stay in here and visit?"

"I'll go out with you," Harold answered. He was normally hyper and didn't stay in one place long.

Because the hospital was a no-smoking facility, they jumped into Harold's pickup truck to smoke. Getting in Amanda couldn't help but notice several small empty baggies on the floorboard. "Um, sorry. I should have thrown those out. Are you still clean?" Harold asked, knowing the struggle himself, firsthand.

"Yeah. I'm doing okay, although today has been hard," Amanda told him.

"I know. I feel bad about Uncle too," Harold sympathized.

"It's not just that Harold. I forgot my Suboxone at home," she told him, without looking at him. She hated to admit how much she depended on it, making her feel weak inside.

"Oh shit." Was all that Harold answered. He knew first-hand how hard that could be and also what the implications were. Amanda hadn't really been clean that long and if he guessed correctly, she was probably still on a fairly high maintenance dose.

"Do you have any money? I might know someone out here who will sell you a few." Harold asked her.

"Yeah. I have some money. Even one would get me through until we get home, probably tomorrow," she told him, suddenly feeling hopeful that her cousin might be able to find her one.

"Do you want to ride? It's not very far," Harold asked.

"Okay. Let me run in and get my purse," Amanda answered. She would have preferred to stay at the hospital but didn't really trust Harold. He was known to take the money and run and she was too desperate to take that chance. Just sitting in his truck was making her feign out harder, with too many little signs of recent drug use showing.

Walking back into the hospital she grabbed her purse and told Ben that she would be right back. He raised his eyebrows a little surprised that she would leave with Harold and felt immediately suspicious, but then chided himself for not being more trusting. Amanda had changed and wasn't the same person that she was three months ago.

They drove to his connection's house and Amanda gave Harold twenty bucks. In Hoopa, Suboxone sold for ten dollars a strip but she didn't know what the going price was out here. Harold didn't come back for about ten minutes, while she anxiously waited. When he finally walked back towards the pick-up he had a big smile on his face and looked triumphant. Feeling relieved she let out a sigh of relief.

"So Amanda, this guy didn't have any Suboxone. He called a few of his friends but no one knew where to get any. That's what took so long. So I scored a bag of H for us. I know, I know, you're clean right now but just use a little bit. You know, enough to keep you from hurting but not enough to get high." Harold didn't want Amanda to be upset with him for using her money to buy heroin so he was trying his hardest to convince her.

"Oh my God!" Amanda exclaimed. "You know I can't do that Harold. I'm an addict. I won't be able to stop." Shaking her head, she was mad. The last thing she needed was this kind of temptation pushed in her face. It had been hard enough feigning out for days now and if she was truthful, probably for a little longer than that. Her cravings first started when she had the falling out with Jim's mom and it had progressively gotten worse.

"Just use a little bit to get through the night and then start back on Suboxone when you get home again," Harold told her, persuading her. At that point he started reaching under his seat, grabbing a spoon and a pack of needles. "I even got clean needles so no worries about that. And don't worry, I won't tell a soul. It will be our little secret."

Part of her brain was screaming "no" and the other part was screaming "yes." Watching him draw it up in the needle she started losing her resolve. She would just make sure that it was once. And she wouldn't get high; just use enough to keep from hurting and feigning. The minute they got home she would go right back on her Suboxone and would be more careful to never forget it again.

The minute the needle went in she knew that she had made a big mistake and instantly regretted it. In that split second, if she could take it back she would have. The high wasn't worth the guilt she was feeling. Not taking into account that she had been clean for almost three months, her tolerance was lower and she felt higher than she had anticipated.

On the ride back to the hospital, she nodded off several times and when Harold pulled up to the hospital entrance it was clear that he was not going back in. "I'm going to go visit some friends," he told her. "I'll come by and check on you in the morning."

"Okay. I'll see you tomorrow," Amanda said, as she grabbed her purse and climbed out of the truck. She berated herself all the way down the hallway and felt like the biggest idiot in the world. She wanted to cry but knew that, that wouldn't change what she did. And once again she felt the shame that had become all too familiar.

Chapter Nineteen

Swinging open her uncle's door, she was shocked to see Jim sitting by the bed, talking to Ben. Unfortunately, he was the last person she wanted to see right now and the guilt washed over her even more, if that was possible.

"There you are. I was wondering if you got lost," Jim told her, while rising to give her a hug and a kiss.

"Hey. I wasn't expecting you or I would have been here." Hugging him back she prayed that she didn't look as high as she felt. "I just went for a little ride with Harold."

Ben took one look at his niece and he instantly knew. It made him feel sick to his stomach and upset. Although Jim didn't say anything, the minute he found out that she had been with Harold his suspicions were high. He knew how vulnerable she was and he just didn't trust Harold.

"Well, I just wanted to come down and see if you needed anything. Plus it was a good excuse to come see Ben," he said, smiling at Ben, who he had become close too since staying with him.

"That's so sweet. Thank you, babe," she said, leaning over and kissing him. She thought that he was eyeing her suspiciously and hoped that she was just being paranoid.

"Where is Harold?" Jim asked.

"He let me off and was going to go visit a friend," she answered. "He is going to come back in the morning and visit you," she told her uncle.

"Well let's go grab a bite," Jim suggested. He wanted to talk privately. Ben had enough on his plate right now without dragging him into this. "Ben, do you want anything? We can order you something to bring back."

"No thanks. They bring me more food than I could ever eat. You two go eat. I'm going to watch the news and rest awhile," Ben told them. He was pretty sure that Jim knew and he wasn't looking very happy at the moment.

Jim grabbed her hand and pulled her towards the hallway. She felt like a little girl getting sent to the principal's office and was becoming more uncomfortable by the minute.

As they walked towards the car, he spun around, obviously shook up. "Amanda, what the hell's going on?" She had never seen him lose his temper or even raise his voice for that matter and it brought her back to earth, for the moment.

"What do you mean?" she answered.

Still looking pissed, he opened her car door and waited for her to get in. He wasn't going to make a scene in the parking lot but walking around the front of the car to the driver's side, it was obvious to her that he knew. Slamming the door, he turned towards her and took a deep breath. He needed to pull it together before he said something he would regret.

"You know what I mean. I'm not stupid and just looking at your eyes, it's obvious that you're high on something." His voice was calmer but still stinging with frustration.

She thought of denying it, or lying and saying that she had only smoked weed but decided against it. He deserved the truth. No one had ever believed in her as much as him or treated her so well. "I'm sorry," was all she could say at first. The tears started and it took her several minutes to compose herself. "I'm not going to lie to you." And from there she told him about feigning for days and forgetting her Suboxone. "I didn't want to use and then the temptation was there and I just felt scared and weak but the minute I did it I instantly regretted it. If I could take it back, I would. I feel like I let everyone down. I'm sorry." It was genuine and sincere and his heart broke for her.

"Why didn't you tell me? I would have left school and drove you back to Hoopa to get your Suboxone. I want you to trust me," he said, his voice catching. "And if you're feigning out, tell me. I would support you however I could."

"Because we never talk about it. It's like the white elephant in the room. The few times I have brought it up you have dismissed it and changed the subject right away," she stated, more in a factual way, then accusatory way.

He didn't know what to say to that. He started to protest but when he thought about it, she was right. "You're right. I'm sorry. I didn't mean to dismiss it. I guess I'm just not comfortable talking about it. It's not something I can relate to and I'm never sure what to say."

"It's not your fault. One of the things I love about you is that you can't relate to it. I love that innocence about you, in terms of drugs." She told him.

He let out a breath. He didn't know what to say and all of his anger and frustration were gone now. Although still upset about her using, he felt somewhat responsible now. "Let's go eat." He reached over and kissed her and while she still regretted what she had done, she felt grateful that Jim was understanding and no longer seemed mad at her. There was nothing he could say that would make her feel worse than she already did.

They ended up going to the pizza parlor and Jim told Amanda about his day, while they waited for their pizza. The students were restless on their first day back from vacation and it had been a pretty tiring day. When they were done eating, Amanda boxed up what was left of the pizza to take back to the hospital. "If there is anything that Uncle will eat, it's pizza," Amanda said. Jim nodded his head in agreement, knowing this was true. She felt better now than she had earlier. It was strange how hard that little bit of heroin had hit her. Mostly she was tired now. The day had taken an emotional toll on her and her brain felt frazzled.

"Should we go to Hoopa and get your Suboxone now?" Jim asked. He was tired but was willing to do whatever needed for Amanda to maintain her sobriety.

"No. The nurse told me that they plan on discharging Uncle by noon, tomorrow. I'll be okay. And you need your rest," she said sympathetically. It had been a hard day for him too.

"Okay, but promise me that if something happens and they don't release him tomorrow that you will call or text me. Please," he implored.

"I will. Thanks again, for everything." On the way back to the hospital she told him about Ashley's visit and the complete change in her sister.

"I guess she just needed to find love," Jim said, laughing while Amanda rolled her eyes.

"I guess. As corny as it sounds, it's true." Amanda said. She felt at peace and in spite of everything that had happened today, she felt closer to Jim than she ever had.

"I'm going to run in for a minute before I head home and say good bye to Ben," Jim said, while pulling into a parking space.

"Okay, but you can't stay long. You've been up since five thirty this morning and I know you have to be exhausted by now. I'm a little worried about you driving home," she told him.

"Hmm, I love that you worry about me but I'll be okay. I'll just stop and buy a red bull on my way home." Getting out of the car, they walked into the hospital, holding hands and laughing. Ben was relieved to see them walk in, hand in hand and looking happy. He had been worried since they had left and visions of them fighting and breaking up had played out in his head. Maybe it was selfish but it made him feel better and more at peace with his impending demise, to know that Amanda and her children would be taken care of. This worried him the most. He had been more like a father than an uncle to her over the years and felt responsible. It worried him how she would manage without him and he liked Jim. He was an honorable, stand up man who would take good care of Amanda, Michael and Melanie.

After ten minutes, Jim started yawning and Amanda urged him to hit the road. She walked him to his car to see him off. "I really love you," she said, while circling her arms around his neck and kissing him.

"I love you too," he replied. "And please, call me if you get in trouble again. I can be here in under an hour. Promise me."

"Okay. I promise. Don't worry though. I feel stupid for my lapse in judgment. I don't plan on making this mistake again." And it was true. She didn't want to go backwards, not now when she had worked so hard to get to where she was.

When she got back into the hospital room, Ben was sound asleep. Although it was only a little after eight, she was exhausted herself. Grabbing a pillow and blanket out of the closet, she made a bed on the recliner chair and turned the television off. She was asleep within minutes and had horrible dreams all night; nightmares about falling off a cliff and being washed out into the ocean. At five in the morning she woke up startled and it took her several minutes to orient herself. Ben was lying in bed, awake. He had tried to be quiet and didn't turn on the television so that she could sleep.

"Good morning," she told him, stretching and struggling to sit up. "Did you get to sleep?"

"I slept hard until around four. You don't have to get up yet. It's still early," Ben said.

"It's okay. I've been asleep since almost eight last night," she told him.

Since she was awake, Ben turned the television on and put the early morning news on. He didn't know how to broach last night with Amanda. He was still feeling disappointed that she had slipped and even though he knew that it was a battle she would fight throughout her life, he needed to know that she could be strong and resist temptations that would always be there.

"So, what happened last night? When you went with Harold, I mean," Ben gently asked her.

"Well, I didn't want to tell you and stress you out but I forgot my Suboxone and I have been feigning for days. I'm sorry, Uncle. I just started freaking out and having bad anxiety. I guess I didn't realize how dependent I am on the Suboxone to keep me clean." She didn't tell him that this morning she woke up still feigning. As much as she regretted it, in retrospect it felt good and if it hadn't been for the guilt she would have enjoyed it.

"You know, Amanda, the biggest problem is that you haven't learned coping skills. I know. My addiction was a bottle. Every time life dealt me a bunk hand that was how I handled it. I got drunk. I had to learn how to handle things sober and that's what I see you going through. There's good times and bad times and somehow you have to learn how to deal with the bad, without getting high," Ben told her.

"I know. But how? When you get upset, how do you deal with it, now?" Amanda asked, carefully thinking over what he was telling her. It was certainly true enough.

"Well, first of all I had to work on reprogramming my brain. If something went wrong I would immediately want to go get a bottle. So every time that happened I would go fishing or hunting. That was my outlet and after a while that became my normal and the urge to drown my sorrows became less and less. I also had a sponsor. Not officially, but I would call my friend, Hal, who was also recovering and it always seemed to help. He would encourage me or go hunting or fishing with me." Ben hadn't really had the urge to drink for years now. Even with what he was going through right now, he never even considered getting drunk.

"That makes sense," she said, thinking about who she had that she could call. Rayna, at rehab, maybe. "I guess what really makes me upset is that now it's ruined my whole sobriety claim. You know, yesterday morning I could say that I've been clean for eighty-two days and now I've ruined that. It would be lying to not start at ground zero again and I hate that."

"Yeah, that sucks but believe me, there will come a time when you won't even be counting anymore and you will actually have to stop and calculate how long you have been sober," Ben said. "At least that's how it worked for me."

She laid back on the recliner, thinking about what he was telling her. It all made sense listening to what he was saying but not as easy to actually apply when dealing with these demons. Ben didn't belabor the point. He knew that there was only so much you could say without it turning into nagging. He just prayed that this slip up was a one-time lapse and that Amanda would get back on track now.

Amanda fell back asleep until the nurse came in at eight to give Ben his medications and take his vitals. A few minutes later his breakfast tray came and she walked down to the nurse's station to get a cup of coffee for herself. Walking back to the room she received a text from Harold checking what time they would be leaving. The texts went back and forth until Harold finally got to the point of what he really wanted to know. "So I have a hook up for some Dilaudids, you know, in case it takes longer than you thought and if you are sick this morning." Amanda read the text and felt herself feigning again. She was hurting this morning and she wasn't sure how long until her uncle got discharged but she wasn't caving this time. "I'm not sure but I'm okay. Last night was really stupid on my part and I don't plan on doing that again," she texted back. Harold was disappointed. He had really hoped that she would want to use again this morning. It would have made his life easier. Now he would have to figure out a new plan on how to get high for the day.

Beverly got to the hospital by noon, having taken the whole day off. The nurse was just finishing giving Ben all of his discharge papers and prescriptions to take to the pharmacy when she walked in. "Good timing, Sis," Ben happily told her. He was relieved to be getting out of the hospital and had been antsy all morning waiting for the doctor to finish his discharge orders so that they could get on the road and get back to his own house.

The nurse went over the discharge instructions with Beverly and Amanda too, just to make sure that everyone was clear about follow-up appointments, medication schedule and supportive care that Ben would need.

Amanda received a text from Jim when they were leaving the hospital and didn't get a chance to answer right then. When she finally did remember, there was no cell phone signal and it was about an hour later when she finally answered. Little did she know that Jim was sitting in his class, watching his phone and getting worried when she didn't answer right away. He was still blown away that she had relapsed and it scared him how easily she had slipped up. He immediately felt suspicious when she didn't answer right away and that was new and a little unsettling.

When they got home they went straight to Ben's and unloaded the little bedpan and bag with his items from the hospital. The ride home had taken its toll and he was tired and ready for a nap. "Wow. It looks nice in here; better than when I left," he commented, looking around. "Thanks, Sis." Beverly had given the place a good cleaning, washed and dried his bedding and stocked the fridge. After getting him settled in his recliner, Beverly drove back up the hill. "I'm going to go home for a little while and do a few things before I pick the kids up from school and daycare. I have a pot of stew I put in the crock pot this morning that I'll bring down later."

Ben fell asleep within a few minutes and Amanda went into the spare bedroom. Her mom had already made up the bed with fresh linens. She loved this room because the window overlooked the river. The river was high right now and looked so powerful. She could stand there looking at it for hours. Feeling her phone vibrate, she checked and saw it was Jim.

"Hello." She answered.

"Hi, babe. Just wanted to see if you made it back alright and how Ben did on the way home," he asked. He sounded funny and she had the feeling that he was mostly checking up on her.

"We got here about fifteen minutes ago and Uncle is already in his recliner sleeping and my mom went up the hill. I'm just standing here watching the river but I'm going to go up the hill in a little bit and get some pajamas, clothes and things I will need while I'm down here," Amanda told him, trying to reassure him that she was okay.

"So, Friday there's no school, some kind of in-service that I really don't have to be at, so I was thinking I would come over Thursday, after school," he said. He probably should go to the in-service but had already been excused by his supervisor, feeling it was more important for him to go to Hoopa and support Amanda. They talked a few more minutes before hanging up, with him telling her he would call later in the evening.

When she got back from going to get her things, Ben was waking up. "Amanda, are Michael and Melanie home yet? I really want to see those little brats," he said. "I've missed the hell out of 'em."

"No. Not yet. Mom just left to go pick them up. What do you want to do? Are you getting bored? We could play cards if you want," Amanda offered.

"I'm okay. I don't want you to feel like you have to entertain me. I have a book that I'm reading right now," Ben answered. He wasn't bored but he was lonesome for the kids. He was used to seeing them daily and it had been five days since he had seen them, probably the longest stretch he had ever gone since they were born.

Amanda had picked up her Suboxone along with clothing and other items she would need at her uncle's and already she felt better. She made a solemn vow to herself to never forget it again. The result, she now knew, could be disastrous and she was more dependent on it than she had realized.

Around five, her mom pulled up and while she was unloading the crock pot of stew, the kids came running in ahead of her. Michael flung the door open and ran in with his sister right behind him. "Uncle. You're back," Michael said, running over and stopping by the recliner. Normally he would have jumped on him but his grandma had told him that Uncle Ben was sick and they needed to take it easy around him.

"There you guys are," Ben said, reaching out to give Michael a hug and then reaching over and swinging Melanie over on his lap. "I really missed you."

"We missed you too, Uncle. Are you still sick?" Michael innocently asked, looking his uncle over from head to toe. He didn't look sick.

"Yeah. A little bit," was all that Ben said, without elaborating. Beverly dished dinner up and everyone ate and then watched a movie, one that Ben had put on for the kids to watch. When it was over it was almost eight o'clock. "Well, we better get back home. These kids haven't been easy to get up for school this week. They got off their schedule during Christmas break," Beverly told Ben and Amanda.

"Thanks for the stew, Beverly. It was good as always," Ben said, although he hadn't really eaten more than a few bites and they all knew it. He just didn't have any appetite and was basically having to force himself to eat anything right now.

Amanda went outside and made a call to Jim before retiring for the night. The call was brief; Jim sounded tired and although she couldn't quite put her finger, on exactly why, she knew things had changed since her relapse. Their voices sounded the same but there was still a barrier there and she wasn't sure how to break it down and get back to where they were before this happened.

The next two days they settled into their routine. Ben slept quite a bit during the day and she figured that was probably due to his illness and the medication that they had given him. At night they had dinner with her Mom, Michael and Melanie and then would sit around visiting or watching movies. He enjoyed the evenings when everyone was there and sometimes reminisced telling them stories about things he had done in his crazier, younger days.

On Thursday evening Jim showed up and both Ben and Amanda were happy to see him. Amanda was getting bored and needed to find something to fill her time during the day and Ben just really enjoyed the company. Of course he came with groceries and books and magazines for Ben. He really was a thoughtful person and Amanda really appreciated that about him.

After unloading the groceries Jim walked back out to his truck to get his overnight bag and Amanda followed him out to smoke and to have a few minutes alone. She leaned over and pressed him against the side of his truck with her body, while giving him a long, passionate kiss. "God, it feels like I haven't seen you for a long time. I've really missed you," Amanda told him.

"I've missed you too. Are you okay?" He asked, eyes searching hers.

"I'm fine." She answered, knowing immediately what he was referring to. Turning away, she felt immediately annoyed. It was like being under constant scrutiny and it was obvious that he didn't trust her now. Although she couldn't blame anyone but herself it still made her feel annoyed.

"Okay. Just checking," Jim said, not really understanding that her annoyance was directed at him. He just assumed that she was stressed and a little moody. "How is Ben?"

"He seems okay. It's almost hard to believe that he is as sick as he is or has so little time left. The most noticeable thing is that he sleeps more and doesn't eat very much. He pretends to eat, mostly to make everyone happy, I think, but doesn't eat more than a few bites." Amanda explained. "I guess we better go back in and visit. Mom and the kids should be coming down soon. And Melanie's birthday is Sunday. With everything going on I almost forgot, but I'm going to have to get out to the coast and get some party supplies, presents and throw a party together on Sunday."

"Okay. What day do you want to go out? Tomorrow or Saturday?" Jim asked.

"Well, that's what I wanted to talk to you about. I wanted to know if we could take Uncle out for a ride, up the hill and into the mountains, one day. That's what he really misses doing and there isn't really a lot of snow right now. I just think he would really appreciate going for a ride up the hill and getting out of the house," Amanda explained.

"Of course we can do that. You know I will do anything for Ben. Maybe we can go to Eureka tomorrow and do the shopping and then go up the hill on Saturday. Where are you having her party?" Ben asked.

"I'm thinking of just having it at the house and inviting family. Of course I will have to invite Melanie's Dad and some of his family too. I would like to keep it easy and buy Take n Bake pizzas to serve, along with a cake already made, from one of the bakeries." She had about two hundred dollars to spend on the birthday, which wasn't a whole lot since it was for presents too. She knew Jim would help with the cost but it still felt awkward to ask him. He had already done so much, way more than Melanie's dad, Troy, had ever done.

"Well, let's just plan on going tomorrow. Will Ben be okay, without someone here, if we go tomorrow?" He hadn't thought of that earlier.

"I think so and I'll ask a few family members to check on him. It would work the best because Melanie will be at school and I can shop without her," Amanda said. She felt bad. With so much going on, the birthday had snuck up on her. The good thing though was that Melanie was easy. She didn't make big demands, at least not yet.

At dinner that night, she discussed her plans with Beverly and Ben. "I'll be fine by myself for the day. Really Amanda, you don't have to worry. I'm not a child, you know." Ben was getting a little impatient with all of the hovering. At least for now, he didn't need twenty-four hour care and secretly hoped he went before he got to that point.

"I know. You're right Uncle. We just worry about you because we love you," Amanda said, smoothing it over. "Mom, would you work on calling everyone and inviting them. I was thinking two o'clock on Sunday afternoon."

"Sure. I'll start working on that tonight when I get home," Beverly said. It would be a good time for the family to come and see Ben too, although she didn't say that.

That night Amanda slept hard. It felt good to be sleeping back in Jim's arms. For the moment things seemed good and now that he was there with her, he seemed reassured that she was doing okay and maintaining her sobriety.

The next morning they got up early and Amanda made coffee, gave Ben his medicine and made him toast and left the phone right by his recliner with her number and Beverly's number programmed in to speed dial. After showing him several times what number to push, she started to tell him goodbye and that they would be back soon.

"Wait." Ben said, pulling out his wallet and handing her two hundred dollar bills. "Get her a present from me and anything left, put towards the party."

"You don't have to give me that much, Uncle. You might need it," Amanda protested.

"It's just money, Amanda. I can't take it with me. Please just take it. I want to help," Ben said, firmly.

"Okay. Thanks Uncle. I love you." Amanda gave him a hug and kiss and started out the door with tears in her eyes. He was too good, not only to her but always to her kids. She couldn't imagine life without him.

The drive to Eureka started out quiet. Her thoughts were on her uncle and Jim seemed lost in his own thoughts, too. He wanted to talk and ask her questions about her relapse but he wasn't quite sure how. Clearing his throat, he finally got up the nerve. "So, I was wondering about the other day. I guess it has kind of thrown me for a loop and made me realize how little I know about recovery," he started. Amanda looked over at him and felt as uncomfortable as he did.

"Okay, sure. What do you want to know?" She asked.

"I don't know really. I guess mostly I have been worried about you and feeling really scared that it will happen again, only maybe worse or last longer," Jim said.

"Well, I mean, I forgot my Suboxone and I think that has a lot to do with it," she explained.

"I understand but you had mentioned that you had been feigning out before that. Do you want to talk about that?" Jim asked. He knew they were both uncomfortable but this had really been bothering him. He hated having this worried feeling all of the time; that she would slip again and he just wanted to understand how this happened.

"I don't know what to say. I had been feigning out, that's true. It started when I had the falling out with your mom and then with Uncle Ben getting sick, it just got worse. In the hospital Uncle Ben told me that he used to do the same thing, only with alcohol. I guess that I need to learn how to cope with things but, for so many years, using was how I coped so it is kind of ingrained. I'm aware of it now but I just don't know how to reprogram my brain." She wanted to be honest and give him the answers that he was looking for but she didn't have them herself yet.

"Would it help for you to go to meetings while you are home? Or counseling maybe?" Jim suggested.

"I guess. I'm okay with counseling anyhow. I don't really want to attend meetings when I'm home. I'll just see the same people I used with and that almost feels like that could be a trigger in itself." She had thought about attending meetings while she was home but just wasn't sure. She felt better laying low and not really seeing very many people. The hardest thing about being home was there were constant reminders in her face, everywhere she turned.

"Okay. I'm just worried, that's all. I love you and want to spend my life with you. I can't pretend to understand all that you are going through in your struggle and I guess it scared me. I had never seen you high before and it just didn't feel like the person I know." He didn't know what else to say, so ended there.

"I know. I'm sorry. I hope you never see that person again," she said and he noticed that she didn't make any promises and sounded unsure of herself, which didn't give him much confidence.

The rest of the day was lighter. They went to several stores, buying princess party supplies and they even found a piñata that looked like a big castle. She bought a beautiful princess doll that was almost as big as Melanie and she was going to let that be the present from Uncle Ben. It would be her favorite present and she wanted Ben to have the honor of being the giver of that gift. Jim bought Melanie a beautiful princess dress, shiny little shoes to match and a tiara. "She might as well look the part of a beautiful princess," he said. Amanda bought an assortment of other presents and then stopped at the dollar store and bought wrapping paper and gift bags. She also bought a bouquet of balloons that she would have blown up at the grocery store in Hoopa.

They had Chinese food for lunch and the last stop was to buy Take n Bake pizzas. "How many people are you expecting?" Jim asked.

"I'm guessing between thirty and forty, maybe a few more," Amanda answered, trying to decide how many pizzas to buy.

"Wow, that's a big party. I would have loved having a party like that, when I was little," Jim said. "I can't remember ever having more than ten people at most, at any of my parties, growing up."

"Our parties are always that big and that's just inviting family," Amanda said, thinking how unusual it would be to have so few people at a birthday party.

They got back right before three and Ben was in his recliner but told them he had several visitors stop by while they were gone. His other sisters, Sally and Millie had come over and stayed several hours. It was a good visit but he was glad when they left so that he could take a nap.

That night after dinner Amanda told Ben about their plan to take him for a ride in the mountains, the next day. As she expected, he was excited about the prospect. Michael and Melanie stayed the night and she made beds for them on the couch in the front room. Ben slept in his recliner at night, preferring to be close to the fire and television as opposed to his cold bedroom. He woke up often during the night and would watch television until he fell back asleep. From the bedroom, Amanda and Jim could hear him telling the kids stories until they fell asleep. "Your uncle really is an amazing man," Ben said. "I feel really lucky to have become friends with him."

"I'm glad too. He really does like you," Amanda answered, feeling a little choked up with emotion. She really didn't like to dwell on Ben's impending death and choose instead to focus on the present, and enjoy the time they had, right now, to spend with him. But sometimes it couldn't be dismissed and whether she wanted to or not, she had to face it.

The next morning, they got up by eight and after having coffee, Amanda got the kids up and fed them cereal. Ben was in high spirits and excited about heading up into the hills. While the kids ate, Amanda made more coffee and poured it into a big thermos and grabbed some juice boxes and string cheese for Michael and Melanie. Knowing that Ben didn't have the stamina to stay up the hill all day, Amanda really didn't think it was necessary to pack very much food. She put a jar of smoked salmon and crackers in her bag and figured that would get them by, if they got hungry.

Ben grabbed his 22 rifle out of the closet and a box of bullets. "Michael, today I'm going to teach you how to shoot the 22, okay?"

"Really?" Michael said, in awe. "I get to shoot it by myself?"

"Yep. I think you're getting old enough now. And I'm giving you this gun, but you can't have it until you're older. Until then your mom will have to keep it for you." Ben didn't have much but had decided to start giving away what he had now, while he was still able to.

"Thanks, Uncle." Michael said, running over and hugging Ben.

They went up a different road than when they had gone up for Christmas trees. "This road will loop back around and the elevation isn't quite as high so there shouldn't really be much snow," Ben explained, while giving Jim directions. Once they got to a clear spot, they pulled over and Ben put up a few targets and showed Michael how to shoot the gun. Michael was proud and excited that his uncle was finally trusting him to shoot the gun by himself. Up to that point he had only been allowed to shoot a bb gun but this was a lot better.

"You did really good Michael," Ben praised him. "But remember, you can only shoot the gun when you have an adult with you."

The whole trip took around three hours. They visited, laughed and had a great time. There was nothing rushed and they stopped periodically, letting the kids play in the snow, when they got up to a higher elevation. There wasn't as much snow as some years and had there been more snow, they could have never made the loop and would have had to turn around and go back.

When they got back, Ben was just starting to feel tired. It had been a perfect outing. "Thank you guys. I really enjoyed that. Thanks for taking me up."

"You're welcome Ben," Jim answered. "I always like going up in the mountains with you. I feel like I learn so much."

"I'm glad you enjoyed it Uncle. If the weather stays like this we can probably do it again soon," Amanda told him.

"That would be nice but really I'm hoping that we get more snow. We really need some snow pack so we don't have another drought next summer," Ben said. Last year the river had been lower than he ever remembered it being and that wasn't good for the fish. Fire season had also started earlier than usual.

After getting Ben settled in they took Michael and Melanie back to her Mom's. Amanda wanted to have time to wrap presents, stuff the piñata and make a few finger foods to go with the pizzas.

Jim helped her wrap presents and stuff the piñata and then they made little goody bags to give to the kids.

"Who all did you invite?" Jim asked, curious about the guest list.

"Well, I invited my Aunts, Sally and Millie and their families, and Troy, his parents and his sister and her kids. And of course I invited Aunty Dee and then all of us." She answered. "Mostly everyone you met at Thanksgiving. Oh and I invited Ashley and her boyfriend but I'm not sure that she will come up."

"Will Harold be coming?" Jim asked, with disdain in his voice.

"I really don't know. Of course he is invited. I couldn't very well invite everyone but him," Amanda explained, feeling a little funny that he had asked. She knew that Jim didn't really like Harold and she couldn't really blame him; but he was family, for better or worse and had to be included.

"I know I just hope that he can come in better shape than he did at Thanksgiving," Jim said.

"I know he's annoying but he's family and we are all used to him," Amanda replied, a little surprised. She had never heard Jim sound so judgmental and it bothered her a little bit.

"I'm sorry." Knowing he had crossed the line, Jim quickly tried to smooth it over. "I just worry about you, that's all and it seems from an outside perspective that he doesn't really have your best interest at heart."

"He's an addict. And he's been in prison quite a bit. A lot of guys who have done time for extended periods become pretty self-centered but it isn't his fault that I used. I take responsibility for that," she said adamantly.

"Okay. Again, I'm sorry. I'm just a little protective of you, I guess." He walked over and gave her a kiss. He didn't want to upset her but he had been mad at Harold ever since her relapse. A "real man" would have encouraged her to stay clean and maybe even offered to drive her home to get her Suboxone versus taking her out to hook up.

That night she made chilidogs for dinner and a bowl of soup for Ben with some crackers. She had noticed that he didn't eat more than a few bites at a time but as long as he was eating a little she wasn't too concerned. The doctor was ordering Ben a few cases of Ensure that they would have to pick up at the pharmacy on Monday when it opened.

That night they went to bed early. Tomorrow would be a busy day with the birthday party and Amanda planned on getting up by seven to start preparing for it. The days seemed to be passing by fast and she didn't like that. She wanted to slow the clock down but she knew that wasn't possible.

Chapter Twenty

Amanda groaned when the alarm went off at seven. She rolled over and planned on snuggling with Jim a few more minutes but soon realized that his side of the bed was empty. Jim had woke up at six and would have gone back to sleep but heard Ben stirring in the living room. He got up and stoked up the fire and made coffee. Amanda walked into the living room and found Ben and Jim drinking coffee, talking and watching the news.

"Good morning. Everyone is up so early," Amanda muttered, as she walked into the kitchen to pour herself a cup of coffee.

"Good morning." Ben and Jim both answered at the same time.

Grabbing a cup of coffee, Amanda joined them in the living room and sat down on the couch by Jim. She was still sleepy but mentally she was making a list of all of the things that she needed to do before the party started. It was hard to believe that her baby was four years old today.

"So what's on the agenda today?" Jim asked.

"Well, after I make breakfast, shower and get dressed, I want to go up to mom's and work on decorating and setting up everything for the party. I need to haul the presents, decorations, food and drinks up there," Amanda answered.

"What can I do to help? Besides loading and unloading all of the party stuff," Jim asked. "Oh, and can I give Mel her present early? I want her to be able to wear the princess outfit for her party."

"Yes, you can give her your present early and mostly I guess I need help decorating and hanging the piñata up." It felt good to have a partner and someone to share the workload with. Amanda hadn't had that in years. Even when she had been with Troy, they had never had that kind of relationship. It was always her doing all of the work and him running around, content to let her do the work by herself.

By ten o'clock she had made breakfast, gave Ben his medicine and they had loaded all of the pizzas, decorations, cake and presents in the truck.

"Uncle, we'll be back to get you a little before two. Try to get some rest. I know everyone will want to visit," Amanda told Ben, before leaving.

"No worries about that. I'll probably be asleep before you even get up the hill," Ben replied already feeling tired.

As they pulled in Beverly's driveway they were met by two excited children, who came running out to greet them. Their excitement couldn't be contained and they were jumping, screaming and running in circles. Jim enlisted their help and pretty soon had them both making trips, carrying in anything that he could find that was unbreakable and light enough for them to handle.

"Might as well harness some of that energy and put it to good use," Jim said laughing.

"You are the master at dealing with hyper children." Amanda marveled, never even thinking about giving them jobs to help.

"It comes with the territory of being a teacher," Jim said. "I learned that trick a long time ago."

Beverly ran downtown to the store to get the balloons blown up and to buy ice cream. While she was gone, they hung up streamers and a "Happy Birthday" banner, put a table cloth on the dining room table and set up another table to hold the cake and presents. Jim gave Melanie her present from him. She opened it and immediately squealed with excitement. It was probably the most animated that they had seen her, usually so quiet and reserved. Amanda held the dress up and Melanie's eyes lit up full of wonder. "It's so pretty," she whispered.

"It is pretty and perfect for a pretty princess like you," Jim told her. "Dig deeper, there's more."

Under the dress, in the box, was the little tiara, full of little crystals that shined in the light and a pair of pink sequin slippers that matched the dress. "Wow," she said, fingers running against the crystals. "Are these real diamonds?"

"No, but it's beautiful," Amanda told her. "Why don't we go get you in the bath. I want to do your hair and get you ready before your guests come."

Amanda ran a bath, washed Melanie's hair and then dressed her in her new dress. The bottom half of the dress flared out and was styled like a tutu. Melanie twirled around and around and obviously loved her dress. Amanda brushed her hair out and French braided the top, leaving the back down. She placed the tiara on her head and bobby pinned it in place. Last she put the pink slippers on her. Melanie ran into the bathroom to look at herself in the full-length mirror that was on the back of the bathroom door.

"You look beautiful, Mel. Do you like it?" Amanda asked, smiling down at her daughter.

"I love it," Melanie answered, smiling big. Amanda took several pictures on her phone and then they walked out into the living room. Beverly was back and they were hanging up balloons and had placed a balloon bouquet by the table that held the presents and cake.

"Oh my gosh, baby, you look like a real princess," Beverly exclaimed. And it was true. Her little granddaughter looked nothing less than a princess.

She ran over and gave Jim a hug. "You look perfect," Jim told her, swooping her up and hugging her back. "I've got to go out to my truck and get my camera."

While he walked out to his truck to get his camera and take pictures, Amanda preheated the oven and started the process of cooking pizzas. She could only cook one pizza at a time and needed enough time to get them all done before guests arrived.

At one thirty Jim drove down the hill to pick up Ben. Ben was ready but had mixed feelings about going. On the one hand there was no way he would ever miss Melanie's birthday party but knowing that this would be the last birthday party of hers that he would be attending, filled him with sadness. He also knew that the whole family would make a big fuss over him and he hated that. He didn't want to talk about his terminal state but didn't want anyone tiptoeing around the subject either. He just wanted to go to the party and have everyone act normal towards him.

After Jim drove Ben to Beverly's house and helped him inside, he drove down to Aunty Dee's to pick her up for the party. He marveled at how spry she was. Before he was all the way parked, she was walking out carrying a present and a big bowl covered with tin foil. "I'm ready," she called out as he got out of the car to help her with her load and open the car door for her. He helped her with the seat belt that she was having problems with, mostly because she couldn't see well enough to click it.

"How are you today, Dee?" Jim asked.

"I'm good. Thank you so much for coming to get me," Dee answered. What she hated the most about aging was losing her independence and not being able to drive. She was always independent and had really liked being able to go where she wanted, when she wanted, without depending on other people to pick her up and take her places.

"No problem. Amanda said we couldn't have a birthday party without you. What did you make?" Jim asked, eyeing her covered bowl.

"Oh, I just threw a green salad together. I heard that Amanda was going to serve Take n Bake pizzas so I thought I would make something to go along with it," Dee answered.

"How thoughtful," Jim said. He could certainly see why Aunty Dee was the matriarch of the family.

When they got back to the house, several cars had pulled in and people were unloading, carrying in presents and balloons. Jim helped Aunty Dee inside and within ten minutes the house was full of guests. He had never been to a child's birthday party with so many people attending. Much to everyone's surprise, Ashley and her boyfriend drove up for the party. Ashley made the rounds introducing her "boyfriend" to all of her family and they all noticed the turnaround in her. She was more outgoing now with a sunnier disposition. After she had made the rounds, introducing "Steve" to all of her family, she left him with Jim and went into the kitchen to help Ashley and her Mom. They decided to cut the pizza and put slices singly on plates and then anyone wanting salad could dish that up. The process worked well and with amazing efficiency everyone was eating pizza and salad. They had set up several card tables in the living room where they fed the kids.

Troy, his parents, his sister and her two children came to the party also. Although Jim had thought that it might be awkward with Melanie's other side of the family there, it was actually very comfortable and civil. Everyone at the party with the exception of him and Steve had known each other forever and all seemed to get along quite well. Troy spent quite a bit of time visiting Ben, and his parents were obviously very devoted to Michael and Melanie, showering them with attention and doting on them.

Harold arrived while they were eating, and much to everyone's relief, this time was in much better shape than at Thanksgiving. And although he wasn't drunk, he was still somewhat loud and if Jim had to guess, probably high on something. He seemed over animated and was sweating bullets. Harold made his rounds, saying his hellos and then went into the kitchen to talk to Amanda and Beverly. Jim watched him closely from across the room. He didn't want to be suspicious but he just didn't trust Harold.

220

Ben sat in his favorite chair by the fire and Ashley brought him a plate of pizza and salad. He had been right and even though everyone was doing their best to act nonchalant towards him, he could feel the weird vibes mixed with pity and it was making him uncomfortable. What he enjoyed the most, was watching the kids. They were so innocent and treated him the same as always unlike the adults who wouldn't look him in the eye and seemed uncomfortable, not knowing what to say.

After everyone was done eating, Jim hung up the piñata and Amanda blindfolded all of the children, one by one, and let them each take a turn hitting it with the stick. Jim took pictures of each child as they took a turn.

When the piñata was finally busted open all of the kid's scampered around, grabbing as much candy as they could hold. Next, everyone gathered around the table and sang "Happy Birthday" to Melanie who suddenly got shy, not really appreciating all of the attention focused on her. Ben had moved over to a chair close to the table and Melanie quickly jumped on his lap and kept hiding her face in his shoulder. When they were done singing, with much coaxing, Melanie blew out her candles. Jim was able to take some great pictures of her and Ben and he knew that someday these pictures would mean a lot to Amanda and to Melanie, when she was older.

Amanda carried the cake into the kitchen and started cutting it into pieces, making sure that she had enough for everyone there. She was glad that she had got a half sheet cake, instead of a quarter sheet cake. Harold followed her into the kitchen. "Hey Cuz, do you need some help?" A little surprised, since Harold wasn't normally the "helpful" type, Amanda wondered what ulterior motive he had.

"Sure. If you could scoop the ice cream that would be great," Amanda told him. It was obvious that Harold was jacked up and if she had to guess, he was speed balling.

"So, how are you doing?" Harold asked. "You still staying clean?"

"Yeah, I am. I don't plan on messing up again Harold," Amanda said, with conviction in her voice.

"Good for you. I was just wondering because I found a connection for some white and it's good shit," he said, hoping to sway her. If by chance she caved and he could hook up for her then it would help him out. He was out of resources to score and was trying hard to figure something out.

Turning around to grab more paper plates she almost bumped into Jim. "Hey, do you need any help?" he asked, looking at Harold and back at her.

"Sure. Why don't you start handing out the cake," she said, faking enthusiasm that she didn't really feel, while handing Jim a box of plastic forks. She turned away from him and started cutting more cake but her face felt hot and her hands were shaking. It was fairly obvious that he didn't trust her around Harold and although she knew it was her own fault, her feelings were hurt.

The rest of the party went well. Melanie took a long time opening each present, wanting to play with each new thing before opening the next. As expected, her favorite gift was the big Princess doll, from Uncle Ben, but she got so many nice things that it was almost overwhelming for her. Aunty Dee had made a small baby basket for her and had wrapped a little doll up in a blanket and tied it in the basket. She had even made a lifeline for it and hung abalone and beads on the sides, like a real baby basket. Amanda immediately wanted to put it up and save it for her, scared that her daughter would be too rough with it. But Aunty Dee protested. "No. I made it for Melanie to play with and carry around. It's sturdy enough and you don't have to worry if something did happen."

By five o'clock everyone started leaving. Jim took Ben home first and then Aunty Dee. Ashley stayed and helped Amanda clean up while Steve took a walk down to the river.

"I'm really glad you came to the party Ashley. And Steve seems really nice. He's crazy about you, it's obvious," Amanda told her sister.

"Well, I wanted to bring him up and start getting him used to the family and I also wanted to come and see Uncle Ben. As a matter of fact, I think I'm going to go find Steve and walk down and visit him for a while before we head back to the coast. Do you need me to do anything else?" Ashley asked.

Looking around the house, they had pretty much cleaned everything up.

"I think it's all done. Go visit Uncle Ben. I'm going to move some of Melanie's new things into her room and put her new clothes in the dresser," Amanda answered. Both kids were lying on the couch, watching a movie, worn out from the exciting day.

"Okay. I'll be back to say good-bye before we head out. Will mom be back soon?" Ashley asked, not wanting to leave without telling her mom good-bye.

"She should be. She ran to the store with Aunt Sally but, knowing them, they will probably stop at the casino for a few minutes. I'll be here with the kids until she gets back." Amanda started gathering up the clothes that Melanie had received as presents and carried them to the bedroom to put away. As she walked back down the hall to start gathering up presents, she heard a car pull up and assumed it was Jim coming back. She was surprised when Harold came walking through the door and wondered if he had forgotten something.

"Hey Harold. What's up? Did you forget something?" Amanda asked.

"I didn't forget anything. I was just wondering if you could loan me a little money. Like twenty bucks. I'm hurting and pretty desperate right now," Harold explained. There was no point in lying to Amanda. After all, she had been there plenty of times herself.

"I guess. Let me go get my billfold." She didn't really have a lot of money but she knew that he would keep coming back and pestering her until she loaned him. He followed her down the hallway into her room and as she handed him a twenty, they heard someone open the front door.

"Thanks, Amanda. I'll get it back to you," Harold said, anxious to get out of there and go find something. Harold met Jim in the hallway and it was apparent that he was upset, although Harold wasn't sure why. He didn't dwell on it much. He had his fix covered and that was all that was important.

"Seriously," Jim said, not really yelling but definitely angry. "I leave for fifteen minutes and Harold comes back while I'm gone. How convenient. What did he bring you?" Looking around the room, his eyes focused on her open purse.

"What are you talking about, Jim? You think I can only be around my cousin is if we are using together." Although she didn't raise her voice, her tone matched his and inside she was boiling mad. She hated confrontation more than anything and wasn't very good at it. Usually she would think of all the things that she had wished she had said, well after the fact. But she was frustrated at this point after days of feeling that she constantly had to prove herself.

"Well, what am I supposed to think? You did relapse with him. Which I still don't quite understand. After all you have been through I don't know how you could even go back to that." He knew he was saying things out of anger but this whole relapse had been eating away at him for days and he couldn't hold it in any longer.

Turning away from him so that he couldn't see the tears that were threatening to fall, she took a deep breath and spoke, in a low, shaky voice. "I know you don't understand. Maybe only another addict can understand. But I know that I have lost all trust with you. I see it every time I look in your eyes." And it hurts, she wanted to add, but the words wouldn't come out.

"It's not like I want to be so suspicious but it scared me. How fast it could all change; one bad decision and everything you have worked so hard for could be gone. What was Harold doing back here, if you don't mind me asking?" He wasn't sure why it was so important to him, but it was.

"He wanted to borrow twenty bucks. Said he was hurting bad. But I never planned on using with him. As a matter of fact, he tried to talk me into it earlier and I told him that I didn't plan on making that mistake again." Her voice was still shaky but sad more than mad now. "Do you believe me?"

"I want to believe you but there is still a small part of me that has doubts. I'm sorry but I'm being honest." Jim answered sadly.

"I appreciate that. I would rather you be honest than feed me a line of shit. I know I blew it but I don't know what to do now to earn your trust again. It happened and I can't change that." She didn't know what he wanted from her because if she knew she would do whatever it was.

"I wish I knew," he muttered to himself, more than to her. "Look, I think I'm going to go ahead and head home. I need to clear my head and think about things. I don't want to say anything that I will regret later."

"You're leaving?" Amanda asked, somewhat confused. Was this a break-up, a temporary separation or what? It wasn't clear.

"I'm sorry. I just need some time," was all he answered. She heard him stop in the living room and tell both the kids "bye" and then the truck pulled out. She listened as it went down the hill and in five minutes she heard it pulling back out to the highway. Amanda prayed that she would hear the truck pull back in, that maybe he had reconsidered and would rush back in and say that he didn't mean it. Maybe then she could tell him how sorry she was and that it would never happen again, but the truck went on down the highway and he was gone.

The next hour was a blur. Amanda knew that she couldn't break down in front of Michael and Melanie so she just went through the motions, almost robotically. She finished putting everything away and when Beverly came home she left as quickly as possible, saying that she needed to go check on Uncle Ben. Much to her relief, he was asleep in his chair. She just wanted to be alone right now and decided to take a hot bath. She was worn out from the busy day and then the emotional turmoil that she was now experiencing. Stepping into the bath, the tears started flowing and she cried until she couldn't cry anymore. Checking her phone, every five minutes, she was disappointed each time when there was no text from Jim.

She climbed into bed, buried her head in the pillow and the tears started again. Her stomach felt sick and she considered calling Harold and getting high. The pain she was feeling was more than she could handle and a bag of heroin was the only thing she could think of that would make her heart feel better. As tempting as it was she decided that she would just try to get through the night and see how she felt in the morning. Sleep finally came and she slept hard until six the next morning. It only took a second, upon waking, for all of the memories of the previous night to come crashing down on her head. Grabbing her phone, she once again felt a sharp pain of disappointment when the message box was empty.

Amanda walked into the living room and as she already guessed, Ben was awake. He had always been an early riser, probably from the years of working in the woods.

"Good morning, Uncle" she said, trying to sound upbeat.

"Good morning, honey," Ben answered. It only took him a minute to notice how swollen her eyes were and how red her nose was and he could pretty much guess what had happened. He thought that Jim had left rather quickly last night but had assumed that it was only because he had work the next day and was anxious to get home.

Amanda walked into the kitchen and started making coffee. Ben made it up from his chair and followed her in. Putting his arms out, she quickly fell into them, much like when she was a little girl and quietly cried while he held her. There was no need for words; he knew what had happened and she knew that he knew.

"It will be okay. In the end, whatever is meant to be, will be," Ben told her. "Just give this to the Creator and you'll be fine in the end. Jim loves you, I can tell and if he gives up on you, then he isn't the man that I thought he was and doesn't deserve you."

"Thanks, Uncle." Amanda smiled through her tears. That meant a lot to her because she knew how much her uncle liked Jim. He had always had her back and this time was no different.

Chapter Twenty-One

The ride home had been one of the longest that Jim could remember. Although it was a two-hour drive, it felt like it took ten hours to get home. His mind was in overdrive and his emotions waived between anger and sadness all of the way home. He turned up the music in his truck, trying to distract himself but every other song reminded him of Amanda. Cussing under his breath, he turned it off and drove the rest of the way in silence.

Once home, we poured himself a glass of wine and went to bed. Waking up, much like Amanda, he grabbed his phone the minute he woke up and he too was disappointed that his message box was empty. He hadn't really expected her to text first, after all he was the one who had left mad, but somewhere deep inside he had hoped she would.

It was a long day and he couldn't wait for it to end. He snapped at his students and was crabbier than any of them had ever seen him. Getting home he popped a frozen pizza in the oven and watched Monday night football. He was restless and frustrated beyond belief. Part of him wanted to call Amanda but he was feeling stubborn. After all, he was the injured party. He didn't ask her to use and mess everything up but now that it happened he didn't know how to resolve it in his mind. Much to his relief, he fell asleep before midnight on the couch downstairs. His brain felt frazzled and he just wanted to sleep and not think about anything.

Amanda had a long day too. Luckily she didn't have to face anyone, didn't have to explain anything. Her mom went to work and Michael and Melanie went to school. They all knew that Jim had to leave and head back to the coast for work so they were none the wiser that anything had happened before he left.

Amanda stayed with Ben all day, not wanting to see anyone. She cleaned the house, washed clothes and cooked for him, although as usual he ate very little. Her appetite was gone too and although she tried to eat once, the food felt like it stuck in her throat. While Ben took an afternoon nap, Amanda sat on her bed and made a list. She needed to feel some sense of control of what was happening in her life.

Contemplating and taking a lot of time, she wrote a list of all of the things that she wanted to accomplish. Letting her mind go, she just wrote them down as they came to her, in no particular order of importance. First, was to get her driver's license. It was something that Jim was going to help her do but since the holidays, with everything that had happened, they had never made it to the DMV. Second, was to hopefully enroll in school, depending on the outcome of her GED test. Third, was to start some kind of exercise program. Fourth, was to find some kind of outlet, some type of hobby to distract her when she was feigning. She didn't know what kind of hobby and had never really explored what her interests might be. When she was using, it had taken all of her time and energy to "hustle." Now that she wasn't using she felt bored and had never had so much time on her hands.

That was all she could think of for now so she sat her notebook aside and sadly looked out the window. She felt lost and hopeless but today she wasn't feigning like she expected. In some ways that was a relief and offered her a small glimmer of hope. The worst though was the loneliness. There was no one she could confide in. There was her sister but they had never really had that kind of relationship and all of her girlfriends were still using, so that wasn't an option either.

Around six, her Mom and kids came down, carrying in a pot of spaghetti and a loaf of garlic bread.

"Hi, honey. How are you today? I hadn't heard from you but figured you were worn out from yesterday." Beverly said, while turning on the oven to heat the garlic bread up.

"I'm okay. How was your day?" Amanda answered. Beverly could tell immediately, by the tone of her daughter's voice, that something was wrong. Unlike her oldest daughter Ashley, who was so guarded that she often seemed emotionless, Beverly could always tell when something was up with Amanda. She turned around and touched her daughter's arm.

"What happened? I can tell something's wrong," Beverly told her, eyes searching her daughter's eyes.

"I don't really want to talk about it yet, but Jim left upset with me last night and I think it was a break up," Amanda said in hushed tones, not wanting her kid's to hear.

"You're kidding. What happened?" Beverly asked, in disbelief.

"I can't talk about it right now Mom. It's a long story and I don't want to start crying again. I'll tell you soon, when we can talk without Michael and Melanie around." Amanda had never told her mom that she had relapsed and had hoped that she would never have to, which seemed unlikely now.

"Mom, do you think when we take Uncle Ben to his appointment later this week that I could go in and take the written test at DMV. I want to get my driver's license." Amanda asked, over dinner, anxious to get started on her list.

"Of course. That would be helpful. Uncle is going to have quite a few appointments and I don't have enough leave to go to all of them," Beverly said, still shocked to hear that Amanda and Jim had possibly broken up.

Dinner was somber with the kids tired, probably from the day before, and Amanda, Beverly and Ben, each lost in their own thoughts with their own issues that they were facing. Beverly hoped to have a minute to talk to her daughter alone but that night there never seemed to be an opportunity and in some ways it seemed that Amanda was avoiding her.

The next few days passed painfully slow for Amanda. She studied the DMV handbook and did her usual routine of chores and cooking but she was getting bored to death and needed to find something to keep her occupied, soon. And her disappointment was growing by the day, the longer she went without hearing from Jim. As each day passed without hearing from him, the more convinced she was that he wasn't going to call ever. At times the sadness enveloped her whole body and soul and the pain was almost unbearable but she was making it somehow, day by day, hour by hour, minute by minute.

On Thursday, they went to the coast and after Ben's appointment they went to the DMV and she passed the written test, only missing 2 questions. The lady behind the counter handed her a temporary permit and scheduled a driving test for her to take the following week. The permit was good as long as she had a licensed driver, over the age of 25 with her. "Wow, this is the first time ever that I've been legit," Amanda said, shaking her head.

"Congratulations," Ben told her. "You are so smart Amanda. I don't know why you always doubt yourself." His appointment had been short and mostly involved checking his vitals, blood work and whether he was in pain, breathing okay and able to eat and sleep. It was a waste of time, as far as he was concerned. If they couldn't fix him, he didn't see the point in spending time going to the doctor.

"I wish I would get the results of my GED test. There's another week and a half to sign up for college classes. I don't want to sign up until I know if I have passed or not." By now she should have received her results. Her mail was being forwarded from the rehab so there was a few days lapse in receiving her mail. The trip back over the hill was a good one. Uncle Ben was in high spirits and told them funny stories all the way home.

The next day her mom brought the mail home at lunch and in the bunch was a large envelope from the GED testing center. Hands shaking, Amanda ripped the envelope open and pulled out a GED certificate with her name on it. "Oh my God. I can't believe it. I actually passed on my first try." Scanning her scores, she had passed everything with an 87 or higher score. There was one person that she wanted to share this with more than anyone in the world and on impulse she almost called him but stopped herself with much restraint. That night lying in bed she cried herself to sleep. The reality of their break up was sinking in a little more every day. After a restless night, she woke up at six, emotions running high. On the one hand she was happy and excited to have passed her GED and to have a driving permit. On the other hand, not being able to share the excitement with Jim put a damper on it all.

Grabbing her notebook she wrote a letter to Jim, agonizing over every word. She had made up her mind the sleepless night before, that it was really over and had decided to send her phone back and write him a letter. After all, she wanted to thank him. She would have never passed the GED if it hadn't been for his tutoring and faith in her. And as much as she loved her phone, it didn't seem right that he was paying for it, if they were no longer a couple. Although she knew that she should also give him back the necklace and bracelet, she just couldn't bring herself to do that, yet.

The letter was short and sweet, informing him that she had passed her GED and thanking him for all of his help. She told him that while she appreciated him buying her the phone, she didn't feel right keeping it now under the circumstances and hoped that he would not be stuck paying for it on his contract. There was so much more that she wanted to say; that she loved him, missed him and to beg for his forgiveness but she didn't. It had been almost a week now with no contact so it was time to face the reality that Jim wasn't coming back.

She found a little box in the closet, turned off the phone, packaged it and decided that she would drop it in the mail later when she went downtown. Getting up out of bed, the cold air hit her and she rushed out to stoke the fire up. "Good morning, Uncle. It's cold this morning," she said while walking outside to bring wood in.

"It is cold this morning. The news said that we have a cold front coming down from Alaska and we'll probably get snow by morning," Ben answered.

After making coffee and joining her uncle in the living room to watch the news, the nausea hit. Running to the bathroom, she made it just in time before puking and then dry heaving.

"Boy, that hit fast. I must have got a bug from one of the kid's. Do you feel okay?" She asked Ben, worried that he might catch something too. She didn't want him to get sick, knowing that his immunity was probably low.

"I feel fine. Maybe you're pregnant?" he said, half joking and half serious.

"Bite your tongue. I just have a light case of the flu, I think," although she didn't have any other symptoms. She felt fine the rest of the day and every so often his words echoed in her head. A week ago she would have been ecstatic but now everything had changed and while she wouldn't mind having another baby, especially Jim's baby, she would have preferred to be with the father; not alone. Deciding that it was probably just something that she ate, she didn't dwell on it any longer.

That afternoon she ran to the post office and store. She also had the bowl that her Aunty Dee had brought to the party with salad and was going to drop that off before she headed home.

Although she had only planned a short stop, to drop the bowl off, Aunty Dee invited her in and wanted to visit. She seemed so lonely and anxious to have company that Amanda couldn't say no. Looking at her aunt's latest projects, Amanda picked up an unfinished basket and ran her fingers along the design. Even though her Aunt had poor vision now, her basketry work was so fine and delicate. "You do such fine work Aunty. It's amazing," Amanda said, in sincere awe.

"Thank you dear. Honestly, it just takes years of practice. I could teach you. You might have a knack for it, you know." Aunty Dee had a feeling that Amanda would be a natural.

"Maybe. I am bored to death and looking for a hobby," Amanda told her. "I'm not sure that I would be a natural though. I've never been as craftsy as you."

"Well you won't know unless you try. Why don't you come over tomorrow morning and I'll soak materials and get you started on something." She was excited to have someone to work with. She wasn't getting any younger and it would be nice to pass on the tradition to someone in the family.

"Okay. How about eleven, tomorrow morning? I usually get up and get a fire going and take care of stuff for Uncle Ben," Amanda explained.

"Of course. Eleven sounds good." Aunty Dee told her, her mind already thinking about what she would start her on first.

That evening, over dinner she told her mom and uncle about her plans to go over and work with Aunty Dee.

"That sounds great." Her mother exclaimed. "You always were good with your hands. I bet you will be good at it. I wanted to start working with her too, but it just hasn't worked out yet."

"I know you'll be good at it," Ben told her. "It's in the blood," to which they all laughed.

Again, this evening after dinner, Ben, Beverly, Amanda and the kids all relaxed in the living room, visiting and talking. They enjoyed these quiet evenings and although no one would say it, it was even more important now, considering Ben's prognosis and they wanted to spend every minute enjoying his company. Although the changes were subtle, they were definitely there. Ben was easily fatigued, was starting to get frequent, severe headaches and was shrinking away a little more every day.

The next morning Amanda got up early, stoked up the fire, made coffee and went through her usual routine of making breakfast and giving Ben his medicine. Although still sad and depressed, this morning she was looking forward to going to her aunt's house and working on basketry.

Although yesterday she had felt fine, this morning, shortly after drinking coffee, she was once again running to the bathroom to puke. As much as she wanted to delude herself into denial, she knew that she was more than likely pregnant. The next time she went to the coast, she was going to have to buy a pregnancy test. For privacy reasons she did not want to go to the clinic and take a test. She quickly calculated her last birth control shot and last period and if she was pregnant, she decided that it had to be the weekend that they had gone to Jim's employee Christmas dinner.

Aunty Dee had all the basket materials soaking in basins of water when Amanda arrived. "Before we start, I've made a pot of tea for us. Come sit and let's visit a few minutes, first," Aunty Dee urged, glad to have company today.

Although Amanda was not really a tea drinker and was anxious to get started she knew that she had to be respectful and follow her aunt's wishes. She was appreciative that her aunt was willing to work with her and teach her basketry and although she hadn't even started anything yet, she was glad to have a distraction and something else to think about, besides Jim.

"So my dear, I thought that we would work on a baby rattle first. That's something that you can finish after a few days and once you practice and get your designing down, it's something that is easy to sell at the different bazaars and craft shows." Aunty Dee loved the art of basketry but was also practical and many times in her life had supported herself or her family by selling baskets or basket hairpieces, medallions and baby rattles. Baby baskets were harder and took longer to master but she hoped she had time to work with Amanda on that, after she had a little more practice.

Sipping their tea, she showed Amanda some of the baskets that she was working on. One was a medium size baby basket that was about half way done. Aunty Dee picked it up and looking towards Amanda she asked, "So when is your due date? I'm making this one for you."

"What do you mean?" Amanda stammered.

"I looked at you the other day and could tell immediately that you were expecting," Aunty Dee told her.

"Well, I'm not really sure if I am even pregnant yet, Aunty," Amanda said, laughing and shaking her head in disbelief that her aunt might know something before she even knew for sure herself.

"You are. No doubt about it. This baby will bring you and Jim back together. Mark my word," Aunty Dee told her.

Laughing, Amanda momentarily was at a loss of words. "How do you know this Aunty?" she asked.

"I'm not sure. Sometimes I just know things, that's all," Aunty Dee answered, nonchalantly.

"I don't want him to come back because of the baby. He's such an honorable man and I know that he would do that, out of a sense of obligation. I want him to come back because he loves me, misses me, can't live without me. Seriously Aunty, I can't believe that it's been this long and he hasn't tried to contact me." Tears rolled down her cheeks as she finally admitted out loud what bothered her the most.

"Well, sometimes men get stubborn and dig their heels in. I would bet my life that he is just as miserable as you are. He'll be back," Aunty Dee told her while reaching out and hugging her. "Someday when you're old you will both look back and laugh about how silly this whole thing was."

"I hope so Aunty. I really do." Amanda felt better and as she started working on her baby rattle, she thought about the baby that she was carrying. Even though she hadn't taken a test and had tried to deny it, in her heart she knew that she was carrying Jim's baby.

Before she knew it, it was two o'clock and she marveled how much she enjoyed making her basket. The time had flown by and although she was only a quarter of the way done she was happy with her progress. She had to start it at least ten times before it passed her Aunt's inspection but instead of feeling frustrated, she felt proud that she had finally got a good start.

"Thank you so much, Aunty. I really enjoyed this. When should I come back?" She asked.

"Friday would be good. Tomorrow I have to go to the clinic and go get my hair done." Aunty Dee had a standing appointment twice a month to get her hair done and hadn't changed her hairstyle in fifty or more years.

Giving her a hug bye, Amanda walked out to her uncle's truck and headed home. She had told her mom that she would cook tonight and wanted to make lasagna, something that she had been hungry for, for several days. She really missed her phone and at first felt panicked not having it anymore but today she was getting a little more used to not having it and had quit reaching for it, like she had the day before. Maybe tomorrow she would call the clinic and schedule an appointment. She wanted to know sooner rather than later and it might be another week before she got to the coast to buy a test.

Getting home from work, Jim stopped at his driveway and got his mail. He was surprised to see a small package from Amanda and ripped it open before he had even parked his car. Pulling the phone out of the box he felt immediately disappointed. He didn't know what he had expected but it certainly wasn't the cell phone back. Looking in the box he saw the carefully folded letter and hands shaking opened it up and started reading it. Smiling big, he felt so proud that she had passed her GED test. The letter was short and sweet and it suddenly struck him how much he missed her. He had been a jerk and he knew it and now the whole thing seemed so unimportant and stupid. He would have called her that minute, but now with her phone in his hand, he knew that wasn't possible. Although her uncle had a home phone, he didn't have the number, never thinking to get it in case of an emergency.

After he got inside his house he used his cell phone to see if there was a listed phone number for Ben or Beverly but neither was listed. Contemplating whether he should write a letter back or drive over this weekend, he decided on driving over on the weekend. After all, he really wanted to see how Ben was doing too. Although he hadn't known Ben very long, he felt especially close to him, like a lifelong family friend.

After deciding to go over on the weekend, he slept better than he had in almost two weeks and now looked forward to Friday.

On Wednesday, Jim stopped by the Rehab for his tutoring session. There were three new residents that he was working with and now after the holidays the rehab was fuller than it had been prior to the holidays. Afterwards he stopped in to talk to Rayna and although he hadn't planned on discussing his personal situation, before he knew it he was spilling it all out.

"Jim, you do know that relapse happens, right? I relapsed myself once too, in the beginning. It's almost a given that it is going to happen. More importantly is what happens after the relapse. Was it a one-time incident or did it continue? Did the person learn from the relapse? Was their remorse? Honestly, here at the program, we look at all of those factors because a relapse sometimes happens."

"I guess I really didn't take all of that into consideration. As far as I know it was a one-time occurrence and yes she was really remorseful. She was under a lot of pressure with her uncle and got to the hospital and had forgotten her Suboxone." Jim understood what she was conveying to him and it gave him some insight.

"Well, as an addict I can understand how hard that must have been for her, when her coping method has always been to use and get high when things get stressful," Rayna told him.

"And I understood that. I felt bad for her and I get it that she felt bad that it happened. She's been harder on herself than anyone else has. I guess the problem is that now I'm really suspicious. I lost all of my trust in her and my perspective got so distorted." Jim felt even worse now. He knew that there was no way she could change what happened. "I wish I would have been more supportive. I just kind of freaked out and then left."

"Well it's not too late you know. Amanda is an exceptional person. She had a kind soul and a sweet disposition. That's what drew her to you in the first place. Maybe it would help for you to go to Al Anon meetings," Rayna suggested.

"Maybe. I'm sure it wouldn't hurt. I'm going over on Friday when I get off. I just hope that she will forgive me." Jim said, wearily.

"I think it's safe to say that she will. There is an obvious connection between you two and I don't think one little relapse is going to break either of you," Rayna said confidently. Jim and Amanda had something that most people would do anything for, including herself, she thought.

On Friday, Amanda got up early and headed to the Clinic for an eight thirty appointment. Checking in at the front desk, she was grateful to have gotten an early morning appointment. There were quite a few people already arriving at the clinic this morning, but most of them did not have appointments and were trying to be seen on a walk-in basis. After all, it was Friday and if they weren't seen today they would have to wait until Monday when the clinic opened again.

A nurse called her name, almost as soon as she sat down and took her in the back to do vitals and ask what she was being seen for. She was surprised when the scale tipped at 135 lbs. That was around twenty pounds more than when she got clean, three months ago. "So I'm here to take a pregnancy test," she told the nurse, feeling self-conscious although she wasn't sure why.

"Okay. Well when was your last period?" the nurse asked, entering information into the computer while she talked.

"I'm not really sure. I had a Depo shot sometime at the end of the Summer I believe and my periods are pretty light and sporadic," Amanda explained, trying to remember when her last period was.

"Well, let's have you take a pregnancy test first and then you can talk to the Provider," the nurse said, while handing her a urine cup.

Luckily Amanda had drank enough coffee earlier that she had no problem providing a sample. Giving the cup to the nurse she went into the patient room and sat on the exam table waiting. She so strongly believed that she was pregnant that if somehow she were wrong she would have been sorely disappointed.

About five minutes later the nurse walked in, smiling. "Congratulations. The test was positive."

The FNP came in and since they didn't really have a clear picture of how far along she was, decided to do a pelvic and see how big her uterus was. "Well it looks to me like you are about seven weeks, putting your due date around September 7th. Of course the Obstetrician will probably do an ultrasound and will have a more exact date."

Amanda smiled to herself. It had to be the weekend of Jim's Christmas dinner. In retrospect she probably should have gotten a Depo shot around then. With everything going on it had somehow slipped her mind.

"So I'm going to write a referral to the OB doctor on the coast and also send a prescription over for some prenatal vitamins." The FNP quickly scanned her chart and noticed that there was a history of substance abuse. "Are you currently using drugs?"

"No. I am taking Suboxone though. Is that okay?" Amanda hadn't even considered that there might be issues with that.

"I'm not really the expert on that although we have several patients who are pregnant and on Suboxone. That's something you can discuss with the OB." Actually there were quite a few pregnant patients on Suboxone but it was better than the alternative. There had been a spike in the last year of babies being born addicted to opiates and the process of weaning the babies off was a hard and lengthy one.

After her appointment she stopped at the store and bought a package of Danish rolls to take to her Aunt's house. She was excited and anxious to start back on her basket. There was something relaxing about weaving and she was looking forward to working on it again.

"Well, you're right Aunty. My due date is the first part of September," Amanda told her aunt as she walked in the door.

"Of course I'm right dear. And I know Jim will be back. He loves you. Everyone could see that," Aunty Dee told her with conviction in her voice.

"I hope so. I really miss him," Amanda said, her voice trailing off.

By two o'clock her baby rattle was over half done. She was pleased with how it looked, but more importantly her Aunty was happy with her work. "I knew you would be good at it honey. You're such a quick learner and your work is tight and fine. Once you get a little practice designing there will be no stopping you. You do need to start gathering, though. It will be time to get roots as soon as the river drops," Aunty Dee told her. She didn't mind sharing her materials but she could no longer go out and gather herself so it was important that Amanda learn how to do that for herself.

On her way home Amanda stopped at the campus branch office. Feeling nervous she parked Ben's truck and took a deep breath. She had decided to sign up for one class this semester. Originally she had planned on signing up for two classes but now that she was pregnant, along with taking care of her uncle, she had decided she would rather just take one class and had decided to take a computer class. It was offered on Monday and Wednesday nights from seven to nine with a computer lab on Thursday afternoons from one to three.

There were only two more days to sign up for classes and several people were lined up, waiting to fill out papers and sign up for school. The whole process took a little over an hour and because she wasn't taking full-time classes she didn't qualify for financial aid but that was okay. She didn't want to spend too much time away from her uncle anyway.

Driving home, for the first time things seemed brighter. She almost had her driver's license; only needing to do her behind the wheel test now. And she found a hobby that she was enjoying and good at and she had signed up for a class. She was pregnant and even that seemed like a plus because even if she wasn't with Jim, she truly loved him and would have some part of him now. The only thing that couldn't be resolved was Uncle Ben and his declining health. Loss wasn't new to her but it didn't make it any less painful. And then there was her broken heart. It was hard to believe that it was over; it had happened so fast. When Jim had left mad, she had never in a billion years thought that he would leave and not come back but she was obviously wrong. It hurt to know that the best thing that ever happened to her was over.

When she got back to her uncle's house she decided she had better fill up the wood box. It felt like it was going to snow and the sky looked dreary and ominous. Luckily her cousin had come by and cut a big box of kindling and split a lot of wood because that was a skill she had never really mastered.

That night it was just her and her uncle so she warmed up a can of soup and made some grilled cheese sandwiches. Michael and Melanie were staying the night at their Dad's and her Mom was going to the casino for a few hours with her friend from work.

By early evening, the storm that had been threatening all day arrived in full force and looking outside she saw big snowflakes swirling down. She saw headlights coming up the hill, before she heard the truck. Looking out her heart skipped a beat and she stood frozen for a minute, praying that it was him. It was hard to believe that he made it over the mountain passes in this storm.

Once Jim was there for a split second he felt unsure of himself. Maybe this was a mistake and he wished he could have called first. It felt awkward to just come unannounced and with this storm he wasn't sure how he had even made it. Once he had gotten over the first hill, it made more sense to keep going forward. After the second mountain pass he thought he would be in the clear but the snow continued all of the way to Hoopa.

Jumping out and stepping through the snow to the door, she swung it open before he could knock.

"Hi." Amanda said, not sure what else to say. She was surprised, excited, happy and curious all at the same time. He was there and she was happy to see him but she wondered why he had come; especially on a night like tonight. "Is everything okay?" she asked anxiously, not sure why anyone in their right mind would drive through the storm.

"Everything is fine. I'm sorry I couldn't let you know in advance that I was coming. I hope it's okay?" he said, talking fast and nervous. "I missed you and I missed the kids and I wanted to see how Ben was. And I've been an idiot. I'm sorry." Everything just came spilling out fast and he looked at her nervously, waiting for an answer.

"I've missed you too." Reaching out, she hugged him. "I was scared that you would never come back."

"No chance of that. But it's freezing outside. Do you think we could go inside now?" he said laughing as they went inside.

Jim walked in towards the living room, knowing that Ben would be sitting in his chair by the fireplace. Although he hadn't seen him in almost two weeks, he could see a major decline in Ben in that short amount of time. "Hi, Ben. How are you feeling?" Jim asked, concern showing in his eyes.

"Hey Jim. I'm doing alright. What the heck are you doing out in this weather? You crazy fool." Ben was teasing but he was glad to see him back. After the tenth day he had started having doubts too.

"I thought I might hit a little snow but didn't expect a storm like this. Once I was halfway here it was going to be bad whether I kept coming or turned around so I just went for it. It was pretty scary at times though, I must admit," Jim explained.

"It's good to see you," Ben told him. "I hope you plan on staying the weekend."

"Well that was the plan. Of course, only if it's all right with you and Amanda," he answered, hesitantly.

"It's fine. I told you before that you were always welcomed here and I meant it, "Ben said adamantly.

"I'm going to go get my bag while I can still make it to the truck," Jim said, walking out to get his bag and feeling a little disappointed that Michael and Melanie weren't there. Although it had only been 13 days since he left, it felt much longer and even he was surprised by how much he had missed the whole crew.

Going back into the house he carried his bag into the bedroom with Amanda following. Although glad to see him she felt somewhat uneasy, not really sure why he had come and not sure what his reaction would be to her pregnancy, when she told him.

"So, how have you been?" Amanda asked, shyly. She hated this awkward tension between them.

"I've been miserable and unhappy. I missed you so much that I could hardly stand it. And my poor students..." his voice trailed off.

"I've missed you too. I have just felt devastated and had pain like I've never felt." Tears came to her eyes as she spoke. "I was surprised though because as bad as I hurt, I never wanted to use. I wanted to feel every bit of the pain because I love you so much and I just prayed every day that you would come back. But I found out something that made it easier and offered me hope in my darkest hour."

Wrapping both arms around her and pulling her close, he brushed her hair back. "Really, what was that?" he asked.

"I'm pregnant," she said proudly but stiffened a little, waiting for his reaction.

"Are you serious?" He asked, smiling big. "When? I mean how far along?"

"I'm due the first part of September. Are you happy because I'm really happy? But I didn't want you to think I tricked you or was trying to trap you," she said, trying to gauge his reaction.

"Are you kidding? Of course I'm happy. What could be better than having a baby with the woman I love? I mean, I love Michael and Melanie too, but a baby. Oh my god." At that he grabbed her and kissed her, his heart soaring.

"I'm so glad you're happy. "And with that she told him all of her news. That she had a driving permit and would have her license soon. And how she was working with her aunt on basketry and had signed up for a class. "I wanted to sign up for more classes but I want to be here for Uncle Ben and then when I found out I was pregnant, it just seemed to make more sense to start out slow."

"Wow. I'm impressed. You accomplished a lot in such a short time. I love you so much. So I wanted to talk to you about something too, which seems small in comparison to all of your news but I want us to get married. I know that I want to spend the rest of my life with you and I'm hoping that you feel the same." Sitting down on the bed, he pulled her onto his lap.

"Oh my God, of course," she gushed. "I would love nothing more than to marry you. But do you want a big wedding, a small wedding or elope?" She wanted to marry him more than anything but she wasn't sure what he had in mind. Under the circumstances, she really didn't want any grand event and maybe he did.

"I really don't care how we get married, just as long as we get married. It's up to you. We can go to the courthouse or have a small wedding or a huge wedding. It's your day. If you want to be a Bridezilla that's okay too." He said, teasing her.

"Maybe a small wedding. I've always dreamed of Uncle Ben, walking me down the aisle and giving me away, in a church. And I would love for Melanie to be a little flower girl and Michael a ring bearer. But I want to do it before I'm too big and pregnant. That just looks tacky." She could already see it in her mind.

"Well, let's put a rush on it. "He too felt that the sooner the better, not because of the pregnancy but because of Ben.

The rest of the weekend was one of the happiest that she could remember. They planned the wedding, talked about the baby constantly and on Sunday morning, Michael and Melanie came home from their Dad's and they were as excited to see Jim, as he was them.

"I know. Let's go out to breakfast. Is anything open?" Jim asked.

"Well not here but in Willow Creek." Looking out the window, Amanda noticed that it had quit snowing and the sun was shining. The ground was covered in glistening snow and the trees hung heavy with the weight of the snow but everything looked clean and fresh.

"It looks like the snow has stopped. See if Uncle Ben would like to go for a ride and call your Mom and ask her too." Jim hated to leave and go back to the Coast. He loved his little family and knew that he would miss them more than ever. They had decided, the previous evening, that they would wait awhile before telling Michael and Melanie about the baby. He was excited and wanted to tell them but Amanda wanted to wait at least another month, explaining that many times women miscarried in the early stages of pregnancy and she wanted to wait until she was a little further along.

"I know we can't keep it a secret much longer because I have a lot of family members who already know and will slip and say something." Amanda told him and then relayed the story about her Aunty Dee knowing before she had even had a test or had said anything to her about being sick.

"Wow, I guess she's psychic." Ben said.

"She also told me not to worry. That you would come back and we would be together." Amanda shook her head, thinking of her Aunt's prediction.

"I don't know if she's psychic or just a wise woman," Jim said, believing that it was probably a little bit of both.

By ten thirty they loaded everyone up, including Uncle Ben and drove to Willow Creek. Everything looked so clean and pretty with a blanket of white snow brightly reflecting the sunlight. The highway was already clear and except for a few icy patches, was readily passable.

After ordering breakfast Jim and Amanda shared the news about Jim's proposal and their decision to have a small wedding.

"Uncle, I want you to walk me down the aisle. There is no one else in the world that I would rather walk me down that aisle than you." Tears came to Ben's eyes and he felt touched and honored.

"Have you picked a date yet?" Beverly asked and although she didn't say it aloud, they all knew that it had to be soon, if Ben was going to walk her down the aisle.

"We haven't yet but we want to have it as soon as we can get it together. Jim suggested Valentine's Day but that just seems too corny." Amanda said, rolling her eyes.

"I did not suggest that. You did." Jim protested, as everyone at the table laughed at him.

"So we were thinking of the following weekend on February 20th." Amanda had picked the date and although Jim didn't know it, it would have been her brother's birthday. That was not lost on Beverly who dabbed her eyes and took a deep breath trying not to get overly emotional.

They spent the rest of breakfast talking about the wedding and throwing out ideas for it. After a leisurely meal they drove home. Beverly decided to go to her brother's house with them and while Ben and Jim watched a football game, she and Amanda sat at the kitchen table making plans. It felt exciting and gave them something to focus on that was joyous and happy.

At three o'clock Jim reluctantly started gathering his things in his overnight bag. Amanda followed him in the bedroom and locked the door. Pulling him towards the bed, she smiled with a devilish look. "After all I'm not going to see you for another week and these pregnancy hormones are making me want you in the worst way."

"Well, I wouldn't want to leave you wanting me in the worst way." Jim said teasingly, quickly undressing and climbing onto the bed with her. Although they had made love multiple times during the weekend, this time it was with the passion of two people who knew that they were going to miss each other over the next few days.

After Jim said his good-byes to Ben, Beverly and the kids, Amanda walked him out to his truck.

"Oh, before I forget, I brought you something," he said, handing her her cell phone. "This is yours. I hated not having any way to contact you. And be sure to let me know when your appointment is with the OB. I want to take off and go to the appointment with you." The excitement that he felt over her pregnancy, with his baby, showed all over his face. "And be sure to eat healthy and rest. I don't want you overdoing it." It was hard for him to leave her. He would have rather been there, hovering, over her but knew that wasn't practical either.

This trip home was 10 times better than his last trip home. Listening to music, he smiled to himself. He was ready to take on this fatherhood challenge. As soon as he got home he would call his parents. Even though his mother still was a little upset with him and Amanda, he knew that a baby would bring her around. There was one bond that his mother couldn't resist and that was a grandbaby.

Chapter Twenty-Two

The next few weeks were bitter sweet. With not quite a month to plan a wedding, it was a busy time. But every day Ben was growing weaker and it was obvious to all of them that he was struggling a little more every day with the physical effects of his illness. At times, although none of them said it out loud, they each were concerned that he might not make it to the wedding date.

Although they had only wanted a small wedding, with so many family members that was an impossible endeavor. The first week of February, Beverly and Amanda went to Eureka to look for a wedding dress. Amanda wanted something simple but elegant. She was scared she wouldn't find what she was looking for but ended up finding one at the first bridal shop that they stopped at. It was ivory colored with a fitted bodice that fit slightly off the shoulders. The material felt so luxurious and had a small train that trailed down the back. The moment she tried it on, she knew it was the one and Beverly agreed, wiping tears from her eyes. Looking at the price tag, she almost changed her mind but Jim had given her his credit card and told her more than once, to not cut corners and spend whatever necessary for them to have a beautiful wedding. "After all, this will be a once in a lifetime event for us." Wanting to make him proud, she purchased the dress and discussed alterations with the clerk.

That same day Amanda took her driving test and at 24 years old, she was finally a legal driver. Because of her class, that night, they didn't have much time to look at decorations and flowers, but they did get to stop at one store and get some ideas. "I'm not going to stress because Jim is going to bring me out Saturday and I can order flowers and look for decorations then." Amanda said, on their way back over the hill.

"What I'm worried about the most I guess is the reception. We have to have food, champagne and a wedding cake." Beverly had never planned a wedding before but she had helped with some fairly big events and knew firsthand the work that it would entail, especially when food was involved.

"I have been thinking of that too. There are several places to rent, but I haven't narrowed it down yet. I wanted to talk to Jim about it first and also get his opinion on maybe catering out the food." There were several local caterers and although she would have liked to have saved him the money and done it herself, it just didn't seem possible right now. Besides everything else going on, Amanda was fighting nausea the majority of her time. She had never been this sick with her other pregnancies and was feeling tired and a little run down from vomiting several times a day.

In spite of all of the wedding planning, her college class and taking care of her terminally ill Uncle, Amanda was surprised at how calm she felt. She noticed that ever since she had been working with her Aunt on baskets she felt calmer and she loved working with her hands. Since learning of her pregnancy she had quit smoking. It was finally getting a little easier this week and keeping her hands busy seemed to help her beat the nicotine withdrawal. Her Aunt had let her bring her project home to work on and when the cravings got too bad, she would pick it up and start working. The first rattle was a little rough but not bad. The second one was coming out nicely and even her design was a little more intricate than the first one.

The following weekend Jim came over and took her to the Coast. They bought a dress for Melanie, who would be their flower girl.

"She's going to steal the show, you know" Jim said

"I'm sure she will. What about Michael? What are we going to have him wear?" she asked.

"I'm renting him a tuxedo, just like the rest of us," Jim answered.

They decided to only have one attendant each. Amanda had asked her sister to be her Maid of Honor and had told her to pick out any dress that she wanted, knowing that she would pick out something appropriate without any problem. Jim asked a co-worker, who was also a friend, to be his best man. In the spirit of trying to keep the wedding on a smaller scale, her children were the only other ones in the wedding party.

"So I think you are right about hiring a caterer and maybe see if they can take care of the other things too; like renting a champagne fountain, picking up the cake and help with the decorating. I just think you have enough going on and I don't want you overdoing it. I'd rather pay extra for someone to take care of all of it." Jim was worried. Amanda looked pale, tired and was having a hard time holding anything down. As excited as he was about the wedding, he didn't want anything to jeopardize the health of his unborn child or the woman that he loved.

"Okay. There's a local woman who I think would be willing to do all of that and she is really good at it too. Thank you. I just haven't been feeling very good lately. I'm hoping that once I get out of the first trimester, this morning sickness will get better." Amanda appreciated his concern and was grateful that he was trying to lighten her load.

They went to the florist and ordered her bridal bouquet and arrangements for the church. The last thing they had to do was to find a suit for her Uncle. He was so small now and probably hadn't owned one in years, if ever. He was the outdoorsman type who wasn't comfortable in a suit and tie. "I'm leaving this one to you." Amanda told Jim. "I trust you to pick out something appropriate for him."

In the end, Jim bought him a pair of black dress slacks, a long sleeved dark blue shirt and a black leather vest. It seemed to fit her Uncle more than a suit coat and tie and Amanda agreed that it was the perfect choice. They also picked up a pair of black dress shoes in a size 9, triple E. "Uncle has a typical Injun foot, very wide and a high instep." Amanda explained, lovingly thinking of her uncle's fat feet.

During the next two weeks, everything started to fall into place and Amanda started to relax, a little prematurely, she soon found out. Three days before the wedding, Ben started having difficulty breathing and seemed to be struggling for air. With his skin turning gray and his lips turning blue, they had called an ambulance and had him taken out to the hospital. After a long night of waiting, the doctor finally came out, took them into a small consultation room and motioned for Beverly and Amanda to sit down. "So I know how scary this is but it is the natural progression of his disease. There are a few palliative measures that we can take to help Ben. One is to send him home with an oxygen tank and the other is to give him several inhalers to use. I also want to give him some Ativan to help with anxiety. Not getting enough oxygen is making him anxious, which in turn makes it harder for him to breath. Not a good cycle." The doctor explained. "Does he lie down flat when he sleeps?"

"No. He sleeps sitting upright in his recliner." Amanda answered.

"Okay. I was going to suggest that he sleep in an upright position but it sounds like he already does. Ben's disease has progressed pretty fast and these are all signs that he is reaching an end stage. Normally I would send out a Hospice worker to check on him but unfortunately, because of funding cuts, they no longer go up to Hoopa." The doctor felt bad about not having hospice resources available in these rural areas but there was nothing he could do to change it.

Amanda and Beverly both wanted to ask how long Ben had left, in the doctor's opinion, but neither could bring themselves to ask.

As if the doctor was reading their minds he continued, "so it is hard to say how long Ben has. Every patient is different but my guess is that he has maybe 1 to 3 weeks left. He is a strong man so maybe four but again it is hard to pinpoint an exact time. The main thing now is to keep him comfortable and out of pain." He handed them a pamphlet that explained the final stages of terminal illness, along with coping skills for grief.

Ashley came up later that night and had taken time off work to be there for the wedding and to help with Ben's care. At this point he was requiring round the clock care and Amanda had to admit that she was grateful to have her sister there. As a RN, she had the experience to give Ben the proper care that he needed and he seemed to take comfort with her presence.

The morning of the wedding started out a little chaotic. Amanda was having bouts with her usual morning sickness and it felt like there was more to do than time would allow but in the end she knew that they would pull it off.

At five o'clock she arrived at the church with her mother, Melanie, Michael and Ben. Everyone was ready but her and going into a small room that served double as a dressing room, she put her dress on and Ashley came in and helped her with her hair and make-up. Jim, under protest, had moved up to her Mother's house the night before. "It's just a superstition that it's bad luck to see the bride before the wedding," Jim said, but he good-naturedly went along with it.

"Well, I don't know who started it, but there must have been a reason." Amanda reasoned, pushing him out the door. In lieu of a rehearsal dinner, they had a small dinner at her mother's with the wedding party and Jim's parents. Amanda had been nervous about seeing his parents and kept waiting for it to be awkward but both Phil and Helen walked through the door and hugged her as if nothing had ever happened. They were both excited, Helen more so, about the baby and almost hovered over her. They had gotten a room, in nearby Willow Creek, as did Jim's friend Brad, who had come over that evening.

Amanda's aunts Sally and Millie had decorated the church that day and it looked beautiful with flower arrangements and candles and a white runner that led to the alter. Jim had hired a photographer to not only take pictures of the wedding but to video it. It almost seemed unreal and Amanda felt anxious, scared that she would wake up and find that this was all a dream.

At six o'clock sharp, Amanda, Ben, Ashley, Michael and Melanie lined up at the back of the church. Looking towards the front of the church, she saw Jim standing there, smiling and looking handsome and relaxed as usual. Melanie walked down the aisle first, dropping petals out of her basket onto the floor. She took her job seriously and remembered to walk slowly, as she had been told. She looked like a beautiful little princess in her dress. Michael went next carrying the wedding rings on a little white, satin pillow. A few times he speeded up and then as if he remembered, his walk slowed down. Amanda watched Jim's face as he watched her kids walk down the aisle. The love he felt for them was obvious and showed all over his face. It was a look that would be etched in her memory forever.

Ashley was next and she looked beautiful in a long, pale rose-colored dress. At the start of the wedding march, Amanda placed her hand in the nook of Ben's arm and they slowly started walking down the aisle. They had all worried about Ben's ability to walk that far, without oxygen but that day, maybe out of sheer determination, Ben had a little more energy and his color was better than it had been in weeks. There were about 150 guests who rose to their feet when Amanda and Ben started down the aisle. Most were family and there was not a dry eye in the church. Ben was well loved and everyone there was touched, watching him walk his niece down the aisle.

When the preacher asked "who gives this woman away," Ben proudly answered, "I do" while placing her hand into Jim's hand. After saying their vows, the preacher pronounced them "man and wife" and they kissed to the cheers and clapping of the guests. As they walked back down the aisle, Jim swung Melanie up into his arms and holding Amanda's hand they walked out, shaking hands with their guests all of the way out.

The reception was being held at the Community Center but before they went there, the photographer took pictures of the wedding party, Amanda and Jim, his parents and her Mom and Uncle. Jim had instructed the photographer to take lots of pictures, wanting to capture every moment of this day.

Arriving at the reception they stood in the receiving line while everyone went through congratulating them and wishing them well. The lady that they had hired to take care of the reception had done an amazing job, decorating each table with flowers and had hung small, white, Christmas tree type lights that were strategically placed to gleam little rays of lights.

The food was done buffet style and the caterer had rented table clothes, buffet warmers to keep the food warm, plates, silverware and a champagne fountain. The cake was a three-tiered cake that was delicate and almost too pretty to eat. Instead of a live band, they had decided on a deejay. The atmosphere was festive and happy. After everyone had eaten, Amanda threw the bouquet over her shoulder and Ashley had caught it. To that, everyone teased her about getting married next and for once Ashley endured the teasing, good naturedly.

Next, they started opening presents. There was a whole table piled with presents and cards with money. Amanda let Michael and Melanie help open the presents, while Ashley wrote down each gift and who it was from. By far, the best present was from her Aunty Dee, who had made them a basket. It was beautiful, delicate with an intricate design and both Jim and Amanda were completely in awe of her fine work. "Aunty, how did you make this without me seeing it?" Amanda asked.

"It wasn't easy but I just worked on it at night. I wasn't sure if I would have enough lighting, with my bad eyes but somehow it all came out good." Aunty Dee was glad that they liked it. It wasn't easy at her age to do something with that intricate of a design anymore.

Ashley took Ben and Melanie home around ten o'clock. Ben was getting tired and was ready to go home and fall asleep in his recliner. The day had also been long for Melanie, who was yawning and getting whiny. Much to Ashley's disappointment, her boyfriend was scheduled to work at the hospital this weekend so he couldn't join her and she was anxious to get back to her Uncle's house and call him before it got too late.

Around midnight most of the guests had left or were in the process of leaving so Amanda and Jim said their goodbyes and walked out to leave. Jim's truck had been decorated sometime during the reception with "Just Married" written across the back window and tin cans handing down the sides of the truck. They laughed getting in and wondered who had decorated the truck, although she suspected it was some of her young cousins.

When they got home everyone was asleep. Ashley had taken her Uncle's bed, since he didn't sleep in it anymore and Melanie was sleeping with her. Michael had gone home with his grandma around eleven. Jim and Amanda quietly went into the bedroom and he helped her out of her dress, carefully hanging it up.

"This was the best day of my life and I'm so glad that I get to spend the rest of my life with you." Jim told her, while kissing her neck, hands caressing her body.

"It was beautiful, wasn't it? I loved everything about our wedding." She said happily. "Everything was perfect." Tonight she truly felt like the luckiest woman in the world.

"The only thing I feel bad about is that we aren't taking a honeymoon. I really wanted to take you somewhere warm, like Hawaii or the Caribbean islands. I promise you that someday we will have a real honeymoon." Jim knew that it wasn't possible right now but planned on taking her on a trip when it was feasible.

"Thank you. But you do know that it's going to be hard to go on a honeymoon with three kids, right?" Amanda said, laughing at the thought.

"That's okay. I'll hire a babysitter and we will just take them with us. I wouldn't want to leave them anyhow." Jim said, and that was the truth. He had grown so attached to Michael and Melanie that it just wasn't the same when they weren't around.

"I love that about you. You are going to be the best father ever." Amanda said, yawning. Although they had other things in mind, within ten minutes both of them were asleep in each other's arms, happier than they had ever thought possible.

In the next room, Ben woke up around four o'clock and at first thought he was hallucinating. He could see his Mom and his Grandma, looking at him like they did when he was a little boy. His Mom was calling him, holding out her arms and he knew. She was there to get him and take him to the other side. He smelled medicine root and could hear his Dad and Uncles singing their ceremonial songs and the sound of abalone shells clicking together. He closed his eyes and smiled. He was going home.

Early the next morning, Ashley had gotten up first and went out to check on her Uncle. Usually she would wake up and hear him stirring but this morning it was quiet. Quietly walking out, she kneeled down and knew right away that he was gone. Tears rolling down her cheeks, she called her Mom first and then went in and woke Amanda and Jim up. Although they all knew it was coming, it didn't make it any easier. They were comforted that he had gone so peacefully and without struggle.

Ashley called the ambulance, so that they could notify the coroner and then started calling family members. When Melanie woke up, Amanda took her and Michael to their Dad's. While death was the natural process of life, her children were still young and she wanted to protect them as much as she could. Once the Coroner came up and moved him, she would pick them up and bring them back home.

Jim had never experienced death first hand like Amanda and he was impressed by how the tight knit community came together. People stopped by constantly bringing food, drinks and offering their condolences. There were offers to clean the house, chop wood, grocery shop and money to help with the trips to the Coast to make the funeral arrangements. He had never witnessed such an outpouring of love and support and felt that it was a tribute to Ben and the kind of person he was.

As was customary, Ben was laid to rest within four days of his death. The funeral was held in the same church that Jim and Amanda had just been married in and the church was packed with more people than could actually fit. The service itself wasn't long but it took almost 2 hours for everyone to come through the line for viewing and to offer condolences to the family. The pallbearers carried Ben's body to the hearse and the procession of cars made its way to the cemetery.

Although Jim had been to several funeral services, he had never been to one where the family and friends helped bury the deceased. The pall bearers started shoveling dirt over the casket but then all able bodied men would take a turn and in a relatively short time, the hole was filled and flowers were placed on top and around the gravesite. Somehow it made the whole process more personal and he liked the concept.

Afterwards, everyone went to the Community Center and with so many people, Jim was worried that there would not be enough food, but the food was abundant and generously prepared by everyone in the community. Although sad, Jim was impressed by the support that everyone here gave each other during this difficult time and he felt proud to be a part of it.

Jim had made prints of all of the pictures he had taken of Ben during the last few months, which the family used in a slide show that was shown at the funeral service. He had made extra copies for Amanda, Beverly and Ashley and hoped that it would bring them comfort and someday hold happy memories for them. During all of this Amanda stayed strong. Although sad and grief stricken, not once did she think of using drugs to take her pain away. That part of her was gone and she felt stronger than she had ever felt. Her life had purpose now and she had confided in Jim that she wanted to go to school and become a substance abuse counselor. "I want to help people and who knows better what they are going through then someone who has been through it."

"I think that is a great idea. You are so smart and have so much compassion. I know you can do it." Jim was proud of her and had watched her grow into a strong, secure woman. Looking back at the past 6 months, the transformation was nothing short of a miracle. Life was good and full of possibilities and she silently thanked the Creator for giving her this second chance. Too many people she knew either didn't make it or still struggled daily for the very fix that now become their whole existence. No longer worried about going down that path again, she thought of her Uncle and smiled. She knew that he was at peace now and no longer in pain and she knew that he was smiling down at her proudly.

Epilogue

Handing Jim the baby swaddled in a receiving blanket, the nurse smiled. "Congratulations. Your baby is absolutely beautiful and look at all of that hair." Holding his sleeping son, Jim proudly looked down at him, thinking how much he looked like his mother. It had been a long night and he now realized just how intense labor was. All the books and classes didn't prepare him for the harsh reality of childbirth. He was proud of Amanda, who had done great during labor, much better than he had done actually. At seven pounds, four ounces, the baby was healthy, had a good pair of lungs and a full head of hair.

"Have you thought of a name yet?" Amanda asked. Since the day that they had found out that they were having a boy, she had insisted that Jim name the baby, thinking that maybe he would name the baby after himself, which would have been fine with her.

"Yes. I have, as a matter of fact." Handing the baby to Amanda, so that she could nurse him, he hesitated for a brief moment for the dramatic effect. "So I want to name him Benjamin Tis-mil Nicholson." Jim had given it a lot of thought over the past few months and had been leaning towards that name more and more over the last few days.

Tears came to her eyes. "Those are some pretty big shoes to fill but I love it. I'm sure Uncle is smiling down right now, happy to see our newest addition. Where did you get the name Tis-mil from?" Amanda asked, wondering how he knew that Tis-mil was the word for Eagle, in Hoopa.

"Well, early one morning, when I was visiting your uncle, he confided that if he had ever had a son he would have named him Tis-mil and that just kind of stuck in my mind. And I've known all along that I wanted to name him Benjamin. I can't think of a better person to name him after and I mean that," Jim told her, smiling down at his newborn son. In a matter of a few short hours this little bundle had captured his heart in ways that he hadn't even known existed.

"My parents called and said they would be over in about an hour. They are just waking up," Jim told Amanda. It had been a long night and when little Benjamin had finally arrived at five thirty-eight a.m. after briefly seeing him, his parents and Beverly had left to go get some much-needed rest. Phil and Helen had gotten a motel room nearby the hospital and had offered to get Beverly a room but she was anxious to go get Michael and Melanie from their dad's and bring them back out to the hospital to meet their little brother. Ashley had stayed a little while longer, totally in love with her nephew, before leaving for work.

"My mom is on her way back with the kids. She said they are so excited to see their little brother that they can hardly stand it," Amanda said, laughing and anxious for them to get to the hospital.

Jim couldn't take his eyes off of his son. "So, when can we start trying to have another one?" he asked, jokingly.

"Well, not for a couple of weeks but maybe we should wait a little while." Amanda said, laughing. "We don't want to kick him out of the baby spot yet." Looking down at her son she marveled at how perfect he was. A year ago she had never dreamed that she would find so much happiness and contentment. She no longer dwelled on the past, full of regrets. Now her thoughts were of the future and raising her children with the man she loved. Life was good and the possibilities were endless.